# KILLER DEAL

KAREN S. GORDON

THE GOLD AND COURAGE SERIES

*In memory of my beautiful mother.*
*A tea light in the tempest.*

# 1

## MARFIDIO TEXAS

It was to have been the last night for the justice.

*In more ways than one.*

Smiling at the thought, he strolled between the benches separating the long dining tables, exchanging pleasantries with the dinner guests. Buying time, he stopped at the front desk and chatted with the woman working reception while he fish-eyed the dining hall.

The justice threw his head back, belly-laughing at a joke. He clamped his big hand on the heavy-stemmed wine glass and swigged the last drop of cabernet.

*Good to go.*

He slipped out the side door of the lodge, the night stars twinkling like glitter.

Entering the unlocked room, he peered out the window, past the courtyard. The guests, all men, appeared still engaged in a lively discussion. They'd hunted all day and dined on bison and baked potatoes and other manly foods in the great hall decorated with deer antlers and hand-carved wooden furniture.

He closed the drapes, folded one corner of the bed linens to form a small triangle and pressed the percale flat with his fingertips.

Reaching into the canvas bag slung over his shoulder, he removed a gold cardboard box. He set it on the dresser, near the wire-rimmed glasses atop a stack of legal briefs, and selected a handmade chocolate truffle.

Balancing the foil cup on the plump bed pillow, he paused, picked a second chocolate from the box, and placed it next to the first one.

Pulling the latex gloves taut, he gave the one on his right hand a snap, reached into his pocket and held the vial beneath the bedside lamp. Opening the door on the portable refrigerator, he swapped the small glass bottle for the one inside, then wiped the handle clean with a washcloth.

———

ALDO SIMERI LIKED GETTING out of DC and spending time with his hunting buddies. But this trip to Antelope Creek Ranch was a working vacation. He said goodnight to the men and turned in early for the evening.

He hated breaking away so soon after dinner but the big case coming up would be the most important one the Court had heard in decades. The brightest lawyers from coast-to-coast had prepped for over a year.

He removed his shoes, washed his hands and pricked his finger with the glucose monitor. A number flashed on the digital screen. He took the vial out of the fridge, cracked the packaging on a disposable syringe, stuck the needle in the rubber gasket to measure the dose, lifted his shirt, squeezed a fold of fat on his belly and jabbed himself.

Thumbing the plunger until empty, he staggered backward toward the bed and sat. Hand on chest, he swung his legs atop the mattress and leaned against the pillow.

Associate Supreme Court Justice Aldo Simeri coughed, gasped, and slumped over. The pillow rolled upright, then rotated, coming to a rest over his nose and mouth.

Pitter ...

Patter.

The uneaten chocolates rolled onto the Saltillo tile floor.

MIAMI, FLORIDA

"**A**m I on speaker phone?" Vance Courage asked.

"It doesn't matter. I'm alone. Not even a pet goldfish listening in."

"Well, am I?"

Lauren Gold tapped the gray icon and took him off speaker. "No."

"I've been trying to reach you all morning. How about lunch?"

She'd woken up late and had seen missed voicemails and texts she hadn't yet listened to or read. "When?"

"Today." There was a hint of urgency.

"Can't we just talk? Now?" She'd stayed up late binge-watching an HBO series about professional standup comedy. Five episodes later, 2:00 AM rolled around and half the characters were dead.

"I need to see you, face-to-face. Today."

"Dinner would be better."

"It's important, Lauren. Meet me at the Hotel Mutiny at noon." There was a short pause. "Did I just hear you sigh into the phone?"

"Sorry, but it's a pretty lame choice." Convenient for him since he lived on a big sailboat moored at the marina across from the hotel. "What time is it?"

"Ten."

"You're buying," she said.

"Then that's a yes?"

"Uh-huh."

"You could pretend like you're looking forward to seeing me."

"Uh-huh."

"You can order anything you want."

"Lobster sounds good. Since stone crab's not in season."

"Lobster. Filet mignon. Caviar. I don't care. I'll see you there. Noon."

"Uh-huh." She ended the call.

<hr />

AUGUST IN MIAMI was the least touristy time of year and when she arrived, the restaurant at the Hotel Mutiny was only half-full, mostly businessmen meeting for lunch. Vance waited for her at what had become their regular table overlooking Biscayne Bay. He must have gone to some trouble to snag a water view.

He stood when he spotted her. Bonus points for manners. More kudos to him for being on time. She slid into the booth opposite him.

She'd been excited when she'd seen his name on caller ID. But nervous, too. There was the matter of the salvage operation they'd been mired into and the millions of illegal cash secretly recovered. Ever since he called, an uneasy feeling had hung over her. He might have bad news.

Instead, he looked relaxed. Her heart skipped a beat. In person, he affected her like a mind-altering drug. Damn, he was handsome. "You're looking good."

"So are you." He reached down on his side of the booth, produced an overnight envelope, and laid it on the table. "You always look good." He peered inside, removed a four-color booklet and slid it gently toward her.

Lauren picked up the brochure. *Antelope Creek Ranch, A Luxury Oasis Set in Far West Texas.* "Looks nice," she said, turning the crisp pages.

He pushed a folded sheet of paper her way. She opened it. An airline reservation. Destination: Midland, Texas. Two persons traveling. She was one of them. He was the other. "Are you kidding me?"

"Nope," he said, holding back a grin.

She stared at the printout. "The flight leaves tomorrow morning."

"You have plans already?"

"No. I mean, I don't know. This feels more like an ambush than an invitation."

The ranch, on the other hand, looked alluring.

He held the shiny overnight envelope atop the table and riffled inside, feeling for something.

"All right," she said.

"All right what?" He shuffled papers in the overnight.

"I'll go with you."

"Hmmm. Ah, here it is."

He handed her a manila envelope from a law firm, a half-inch thick with documents. Her name was typed on the outside label. It hadn't been opened. It was marked confidential. Her heart pounded. This was the real reason for the meeting. She knew it. The firm's return address was in Houston . . . where Jake Fleming had gone with her friend Davis Frost after Jake had completed his in-patient alcohol rehab. Her hands trembled as she took it from him. "What is it?"

"Go ahead. Open it."

She used the knife at her place setting to cut the seal and removed a stack of documents. Purchase Agreement for Antelope Creek Ranch was typed in bold on the title page. "Oh my God. Did you buy the place?"

"Yep."

"This is a big surprise. So that's what this is all about. Well, I guess it beats buying the farm."

"Very funny. Go to the last page and read it."

The final one was the signature page. She looked at it, then at him blinking, followed by a double take. There were three buyers listed: Vance Courage, Jake Fleming, and *Lauren Gold*. The block next to her name had been signed electronically, but it wasn't her signature.

"Lauren Gold? POA?"

"I used the Power of Attorney you gave me to buy you in."

"You did what?"

"I thought you'd be excited. There're horses there. Listen, I didn't have time."

"You didn't have time to ask me first?"

"I didn't have time to let you say no, think about it for a while, and then change your mind."

She leaned against the booth and folded her arms.

He leaned in closer on his elbows. "I'm sorry. I should have asked first. But it was time-sensitive, and the fire sale price was too good to say no, so I agreed to the deal. Jake has a connection to the place."

"You bought it to launder cash. That's criminal."

"So, what are you going to do? Turn me in?"

"I could. This is a breach, a violation. I gave you Power of Attorney to settle my tax problem. Not this." She was trying to hold her temper. She'd signed the POA long before she knew anything about his personal relationship to a notorious cartel kingpin, or the boatload of hidden drug money he'd salvaged.

"You think I don't know that? It's a little late to have a Girl Scout moment. Did you really think I'd let you leave your thirteen million dollars on the table for Jake to scrap over? I'm betting you knew all along I'd hold it for you."

"Thirteen and a half. Keep your voice down. Please. I need a minute."

She got up from the table and excused herself to the restroom, taking the documents with her.

---

GOOD GOD. The bombshell Vance dropped on her had released an adrenaline rush so strong her skin was still stinging. She sat on the upholstered bench in the ladies' room and began to read. They'd paid nine million dollars for the ranch and the deal was done. She, Jake Fleming, and Vance Courage were listed as one-third equal partners. She googled the law firm that handled the deal from her smartphone. It was one of those big-box outfits in a glass high-rise in downtown Houston. Frank Conn, the lawyer who'd overseen the transaction, was one of the senior partners at Pinch & Elders.

She studied the classy brochure again. She'd never heard of Antelope Creek Ranch. It had a rich heritage dating back to the pre-Civil War era, originally built as an outpost to protect settlers against enemy attacks. It was located close to the US-Mexico border in the Chihuahuan Desert. She weighed her options. Did she really have any?

WHEN LAUREN RETURNED, the waitress was standing over the table. Vance jumped to his feet. Good manners were also a good negotiating tactic.

"Do you need a minute?" the waitress asked her.

Lauren hadn't even looked at the menu.

"Sorry," Vance said, as she sat, "no lobster."

Lauren scanned it and decided right away. "I'll have the ceviche and a side of truffle fries. And a club soda—"

"With lime." Vance pointed to the drink he'd already ordered for her.

After the server was gone, she said, "You abused the Power of Attorney. That's crossing a few lines."

"It's a solid purchase, Lauren. You'd have come to the same conclusion. Eventually. How much video work do you think you'll get this year?"

He struck a nerve. It was hard competing against twenty-five-year-olds living at home with their parents. And templates. *Templates.* "You should have asked me first."

"I'm asking you now. Please say yes and go with me tomorrow. You're an equal partner. It might be fun."

Was he completely out of line or was she letting her ego get in the way? Maybe both. "Fine." She unfolded the linen napkin and placed it on her lap. "I'll go. It's not like I have a choice."

"We always have a choice."

"Then why can't I think of a single good one?"

"There're lots of people who'd donate a kidney to have the options you have in front of you. We'll fly tomorrow. There's a big storm heading for Corpus Christi. We'll make a connection in Houston. Then on to Midland, and from there we'll drive in with the lawyers."

"How long will we be gone?"

He shrugged, one shoulder rising higher than the other. "However long we like. The return portion of the reservation is changeable."

The waitress returned with plates of food. The raw seafood with avocado, garnished with strips of fried plantains, looked fresh and the food on white squares of china, artful. Vance had ordered a hunk of meat served on a cutting board and the waft of garlic emanating from it was magical. He reached across the table and took a few fries from her side dish without asking. She smacked his hand.

"I guess now that you got what you want, you don't have to be polite."

He grinned, sawing at the meat on his little butcher block. Then he started laughing and nodding his head. "You realize what you just happened, don't you?"

"I don't know what you're talking about."

"You thought I was inviting you on a romantic getaway." He batted his eyes.

"So?"

"So, you said yes. You were agreeing to—"

"You should quit while you're ahead. You have this uncanny ability to make me regret knowing you." It was a gotcha moment. She'd agreed to travel with him before she knew it was a business proposition. Not romance. "I would have demanded my own room."

"Yeah, right." He shook his head in disbelief. "Okay. Lie to yourself. What do I care."

"I could have you disbarred on an ethics violation."

"You'd never do that. Plus, do you really think I care if I lose my law license?"

Good points.

"You should thank me," he said.

She popped a plantain chip in her mouth and glared at him.

# 3

DAY THREE, ANTELOPE CREEK RANCH, WEST TEXAS

Lauren Gold awoke with a jolt, eyelids fluttering. It was the first decent night's sleep she'd gotten in weeks, and it took a moment to recall where she was. She'd stayed up late the last night in Miami researching the ranch online. It was the sort of background work she'd do before pitching a client for a video project. She'd printed at least fifty pages of information and reviews about the ranch—newspapers stories, photos and online travel reviews, Wikipedia pages about the nearest town. A lot of customer reviews were complaints that the resort didn't have cell or wireless service. That would have to change.

Now that they were settled in, she'd have more time to comb through the background. She'd tucked the file in her messenger bag before she'd gone to sleep that last night in Miami. The first day was hectic, flying and driving, and yesterday they'd spent most of the day observing the staff and touring the grounds.

She flicked on the bedside lamp and picked up the blue-jacketed legal agreement from the nightstand. There it was, still on the signature page, her forged John Hancock, making her a one-third partner in the multi-million-dollar luxury guest ranch. Tucked inside was a *Wired* magazine story she'd printed off the Net: "A Rugged Oasis for Hackers with Smackers."

She peeked out the drapes. The rising sun cast sharp shadows turning the mountains into rows of crumpled brown paper. She dressed quickly and headed for the dining hall.

Taking a shortcut through the manicured courtyard, past the turquoise pool, she dodged spiked prickly pear pads rooted along the path. The aromas of bacon and maple syrup mixed with the lingering scent of burnt mesquite wood reminded her why guests paid five hundred dollars a night for a room. Rubbing her hands in front of the remnants of last night's fire, now just fading embers in a pile of ash, she spotted Vance nursing a cup of coffee, alone.

He looked up at her. "Tapped on your door to see if you wanted room service. I figured you were still out like a light when you didn't answer."

She wrapped her arms around her torso. "What's up with the weather here?"

"It's called a diurnal temperature variation, the difference between day and night. It's been swinging fifty degrees this week. I love it."

"I don't," she said heading to the fancy silver coffee pot.

The long wooden tables, each seating forty, made Da Vinci's *Last Supper* look modest.

She returned and sat, coffee in hand, a light waft of steam hovering over the mug. Vance was reading the latest edition of the local paper, the *Antelope Weekly Standard*.

PRONGHORN MAKES RETURN TO WEST TEXAS

THAT WAS AN INTRIGUING HEADLINE, below it a large, color picture of the animal. White rump, short white tail, and a dark gray stripe on its snout, its head more greyhound than antelope. It had an odd resemblance to the late Roy Pompadour, the previous owner of Antelope Creek Ranch, who'd commissioned several oil paintings of himself, strategically hung on the walls around the common areas. Like Roy's, the animal's ears were prominent.

"What the—?" Vance was about to bark at her when he looked up and saw it was Jake Fleming who'd yanked the paper from him.

"This'll give the hunters a woody," Jake said. "And the tree-huggers will get a hard-on, too, since we're bringing an animal back from near extinction. A sixty-mile-an-hour target. That's something that'll tickle the most jaded hunters' testicles."

After twenty-eight days of rehab, plus a couple of weeks of sobriety, and a newfound commitment to some sort of spiritual program, Jake Fleming was still a pop-up asshole. But it was Jake who'd had the inside track when Roy Pompadour's prized West Texas ranch went on the auction block.

The attorneys who'd handled the transaction joined them. Frank Conn, the most senior one, sat next to Vance. The two younger associate lawyers wandered off to the breakfast buffet.

"Nine million bucks is a bargain." Frank's way of congratulating himself was to hit Vance on the back hard enough to cause an involuntarily grunt. Vance scowled.

As part of the deal, Frank suggested they bestow twenty of the thirty thousand acres to the Texas Parks and Wildlife Division. Frank's firm, Pinch & Elders, LLP, had donated enough money to the state legislature in Austin to ensure the deal would go through without a hitch. Frank had urged them to make the land donation to keep the environmentalists at bay.

"Greenies from Vermont to California are heralding you as champions for returning most of the land back to the public, where it belongs," Frank said. "The Marfidio County Tax Assessor asked me to personally extend his gratitude."

There was the matter at closing, paying back taxes to the tune of three hundred thousand dollars. She bet the assessor was feeling warm and fuzzy.

"Is it Lib-Tard season or Alt-Right week?" Jake set a plate of food down across from Luther Pernod, who'd joined them, too. The general manager of the ranch, a holdover with a dubious French-sounding last name, took umbrage at the remark, giving Jake a sour look.

Jake kept at it. "Lib-Tards come to suck on Michelin Five-Star prairie grass smoothies and the Alt-Rights think meat tastes better if you kill it yourself. If you say Lib-Tard fast it sounds like Lib-Tard and if you say Alt-Right fast, it sounds like Alright."

Lauren apologized. "He's a dinosaur." Asshole would have been more accurate.

Luther glared at Jake. "The Reservations desk has to be careful not to mix certain groups." His tone was snooty. "The hottest romantic comedy actress in Hollywood was distressed by the sounds of quail being shot from the sky. When she saw a mule deer roasting on the fire pit, she had a full-blown panic attack and had to be Medevacked out. And the CEO of a major oil company did not appreciate being confronted about global climate change by a young tech tycoon wearing aquamarine pedal pushers."

Pernod's job, it seemed, was to keep the peace.

Luther fingered the tip of his black goatee with his thumb and forefinger, pushing his black-framed, blue lenses higher on his nose. "It's the last day of kill-your-own-meat week, to put it your way."

The other two lawyers looked relieved. The pair, a couple of young bucks originally from Oklahoma, had come to hunt. But their boss, Frank Conn, was antsy to get back to the office before the airports closed ahead of a storm now forecast to hit Houston.

"I hear we let the carbon credit traders come whenever they want," Jake chortled. "They're the biggest whores walking the planet. They're too snobby to hunt and too lazy to hike. They just want to do illegal drugs and entertain prostitutes."

"Well, we don't encourage prostitution or illegal drugs." Luther twisted the waxy upturned ends of his mustache. "But their money is the same color as everyone else's." Luther smiled, seeming to enjoy sparring with Jake.

The lawyers couldn't help laughing. Vance just shook his head.

"I assume you don't want to join me and the Oklahomies on the hunt," Jake said, getting up.

"That's affirmative," Vance said. "I'm going to do my impression of a Lib-Tard and go hiking."

"And you?" Jake asked her. "I assume you aren't interested in hunting?"

"You assume correctly." Lauren wanted nothing to do with killing animals.

"What's Frank going to do today? He's not here for the hunting, either," Jake said.

Vance reached across the table and retrieved his newspaper.

"It's not like I'm not here," Frank said

"Reminds me of an old joke." Jake tilted his chin up and blinked, feigning innocence. "Frank's too lazy to hunt so he'll probably hide in his room."

"Tell the truth, Frank," the shorter of the two younger

lawyers said. "You're here so you can tell your friends our firm closed the deal where Supreme Court Justice Aldo Simeri died. There's nothing like a selfie in front of the room to show around the office."

"Oh, don't be such a cynic. He thought there was a golf course here. So did I." Jake looked down at his shirt and blotted a fresh stain of coffee, using the corner of a linen napkin. "Well, we're off like dirty socks." He squeezed Lauren's shoulder, watching for a reaction from Vance, who didn't look up from the paper.

Jake and the boys headed toward the corrugated shed out back where the ATVs and rifles were stored.

"Do you think it's true?" Lauren asked when she and Vance were alone again.

"That what's true?"

"That Frank's here because this is where the justice died?"

He barely shrugged. "It's possible. I don't know. He's been bitching about no golf course since he got here." He changed subjects. "How do you like being a one-third owner of a luxury ranch with a Who's-Who list of regulars."

"It's sort of cool, I guess."

"Come on." He lowered the paper and grinned wider than she'd ever seen him smile before. "Look around. It won't kill you to thank me."

"Okay. It's very cool."

"By the way, did you see the wristwatch?"

"What watch?"

"Luther's."

"No." She'd been distracted by his goatee and glasses. And Jake's Cro-Magnon banter.

"A Patek Philippe."

"Since when did you become a watch expert?"

"They start at fifteen thousand bucks, Lauren."

"Do we pay that well?"

"Hardly."

"Maybe it's a fake."

"No way."

"How can you be so sure?"

"He'd never take the chance, wearing a knock-off. It doesn't fit his personality. He's a wannabe and he knows the guests who come here'll know the difference. He resents not being one of them so he grabs any chance he can to be like them."

"What, you're a shrink now? Maybe he inherited it or something."

Vance raised his eyebrows. "I don't think so."

"Now you're clairvoyant?"

"No. The face is in mint condition."

"Maybe he just had it repaired. I had a new face put on a watch once."

"No. It's brand new. The links are tight, and the metals are in perfect condition. I bet it was in a jeweler's case two weeks ago. Plus, it's the way he wears it low on his wrist, below his sleeve, like he wants to make sure people see it."

"I'm impressed." She hadn't given it a second look. Then again, she wasn't a jewelry freak.

---

A LUXURY CHARTER bus lumbered up the gravel driveway and rolled to a stop.

Checkout was ten in the morning and an odd assortment of people, from the suits in charge of the trip to fashion risks, had been gathering at the front desk. A half dozen people riding mobility scooters raced to line up at the desk.

Lauren got up to watch. She wove her way between duffles and roller bags, to the front desk. Rosa, the receptionist, held her fingers to her forehead like a Marine and raised her thumb up. The guest smiled and returned the gesture.

"Are they veterans?" Lauren asked her.

"Military veterans? Gosh, no."

"Then why the salute?"

"Oh, it's sign language, for the deaf." She signed goodbye to a straggler passing by on a scooter. "They're with NAD, the National Association for the Deaf. Regulars. Out of Silver Spring, Maryland." She smiled as others signaled to her. Covering her mouth, she whispered, "I'm so glad this is their last day."

"Why would a charity spend this kind of money on travel and entertainment?"

"That's not who's paying."

"Who is, then?"

"The usual suspects."

Lauren raised her eyebrows.

"Oh, I thought you knew. Lobbyists. Mr. Pompadour has, or I should say *had*, a lot of contacts in DC and we have special interest groups that bring us regular business. It's how I got the job. My parents are deaf. There was an equally qualified applicant but Mr. Pompadour found my signing ability to be the tiebreaker."

Sign language, that explained a lot, like why Roy would hire someone with blue highlights and a nose ring to run the front desk.

"Paid for by DC lobbyists?"

"You act surprised. This is one is my least favorite groups." Rosa sighed. "They're the most demanding folks *ever*. And they take everything so personally. They're activists, and I'm glad they're leaving today. Be careful. They lipread. One of them free-lances for a professional sports team, football, I think."

"Doing what?"

"He spies on the opposing team's coaching strategy, by lipreading."

One was making a beeline to the desk. He cut the line. The short, bespectacled man was middle-aged, bald with a big paunch, and adult acne. He wore plaid shorts and sandals with white ankle socks. Whatever he was saying to Rosa looked more like a bitch-slapping contest, the way he pounded on his open palm, clapping his hands and whipping his fingers through the air.

Rosa signed back, nodding patiently.

After he stormed off Lauren asked her what that was all about.

"His room had three bath towels in it. He wants me to make a note for next year, that he wants four."

She signed goodbye to a woman with orange hair styled in a pageboy.

A different guest arrived, striding like he was on a mission. He was fiftyish, neatly attired in chinos and a navy polo. Head on, he was borderline handsome but in profile his face looked like it had been smashed with an iron skillet. Lauren had seen him at breakfast, lingering around the coffee bar. He was signing to Rosa and pointing at her.

"He wants to know if you're one of the new owners. I told him you are."

He used his hands to talk to Rosa. His gestures were quick and his body language aggressive. Rosa swiveled her head mouthing, "No."

He got in Lauren's face. "*Innmmmd immmm.*" He held his left hand out with his thumb and forefinger touching, like an okay signal, upside down.

Lauren looked to Rosa.

"He's saying *find him.*"

The man turned away from Rosa and faced her, nodding.

Behind his back Rosa tapped her lips and mimed opening a book.

*The lipreader.*

"Find who?" Lauren asked.

He took the notepad from the desk, scribbled furiously and stuffed the paper in Lauren's hand.

Rosa disappeared into the small cubby office behind the desk.

Lauren followed her into the back room looking at the note. "How long have you worked here?"

"Going on four years. My dream was to be a makeup artist. I love the creepy stuff like zombies and werewolves. I lived in L.A. for two years trying to get work. The best I could do was a gig as an assistant at a Glamour Shots studio where the old toad who owned the place groped me every day. Halloween is coming up in a few of months. I should warn you, I go all out."

Rosa tapped the keyboard, looking at the computer monitor set atop a rustic, hand-carved desk. The printer behind her spat out documents. Rosa reached over and held them up. "The next group. We have to have the rooms ready by three o'clock. We'll have a nearly-full house by dinner."

She remembered why she'd stopped at the desk. "Who does the marketing?"

"They didn't tell you before you bought the place?" Rosa slid past her.

"It was a bit of a rush. They wanted to close the deal quickly."

"Well, I'm glad I still have my job." Rosa thumbed through the guest manifest. "We use a company out of Houston that looks at data, sends out email blasts. They try to get former guests to come back. Luther handles the celebrities and billionaires directly. Roy had his pet accounts. I'm responsible for the groups like the one that just checked out. Unfortunately."

The fancy coach rolled past the front door and headed down the driveway, leaving a trail of dust and a streamer of black diesel.

"You'd be surprised how we live and die by online reviews."

"But the ranch doesn't even have Internet or cell service." If the previous owner cared so much about peer reviews, why wasn't there cell or wireless. Lauren asked her about it.

"We used to have it. When I first starting working here, Mr. Pompadour checked the reviews hourly. Last year he decided the Internet had become toxic and cut service. He'd drive into town and use the computer at the library, like he couldn't help himself. He answered a lot of complaints personally, most of them about no wireless or cell service. Kind of funny." She looked at Lauren, amused. "He also thanked people for the positive comments."

"Is that what you do now, go to the library?"

She grimaced, showing all her teeth. "I cheat."

"How so?"

"I call the marketing agency, on the landline. If there're bad reviews, they handle them." She raised her shoulders and shrugged an apology. "It's forty miles round trip to town."

Lauren pushed her hair behind her ear. "I don't blame you. I'd do the same thing."

A color monitor was mounted on the wall above Rosa's desk. The four-camera quad-split color picture showed as many different angles on the gate. "I thought the place didn't have wireless."

"It doesn't."

She scanned the room. Her eyes followed the cable leading from the DVR to a wall plate.

"Mr. Pompadour had the cameras hard-wired. They dug a trench a couple of years back and laid cable, a thousand feet of it from the front gate to the office."

"Would you mind showing me how it works."

"I guess not, but I only have a minute." Rosa riffled through the desk drawer for the remote control and clicked the buttons, isolating each camera to a full screen image. She pressed another button and video of the bus that had just departed played full screen, turning right onto the four-lane highway. She pressed another button and the live shot of one camera came up. An exotic sports car with tinted windows, a fire-engine-red Audi R-8, slowed as it approached the entrance, then sped away, heading east.

Rosa saw it, too. "You don't see those every day." She clicked the remote bringing up the four angles.

"How long do you store footage?"

"We used to keep it for a month."

"A month?"

"I know. It seems like overkill, but Mr. Pompadour is—was—very anal about a lot of things. Luther changed it to twenty-four hours, now that he's in charge." She corrected herself again. "Was in charge. I can change it back if you'd like."

"No, no. It's fine."

Lauren showed her the note the deaf man had stuffed in her hand.

Rosa laughed and rolled her eyes. "That guy thinks George W. Bush planned Nine-Eleven. We were swarmed with reporters for a week after the justice died. That crazy man tried to corner me last year and get me to interpret sign language for him so he could rant to Roy about some cockamamie story about people who were out to get the judge. Roy made me tell him I'd get fired if I did any more translating. He stopped bugging me after that."

Lauren followed her back to the front desk. "Why do you think he gave me this?"

"I don't know." Rosa narrowed her eyes. "If he's implying that

Justice Simeri was murdered here, that's ridiculous. Don't you think we would have known? Especially Roy?"

"I don't know. I suppose so."

The landline at the desk rang. Rosa picked it up and cradled the handset on her shoulder. "Sure, I can hold." She placed her hand over the mouthpiece, and whispered, "Um, I don't want to be rude but I have to take this call and get started on the new group."

"I hope they're not as demanding."

"They're all demanding," she said before the caller came back on the line.

Lauren folded the note and put it in the back pocket of her skinny jeans.

---

SCOUTING locations always got Lauren's creative juices flowing. They might need new ways to market the ranch, especially if some of the groups stopped coming. The place was a video production dream. She'd read online that *Giant* starring Liz Taylor and Rock Hudson and *No Country for Old Men* had been shot in Marfidio.

Videos. That's what most people wanted to see these days.

She walked a dogleg toward the southwestern edge of the property where a one-time lookout post, now converted to a tiny guesthouse, was located. She'd backtrack from there. It was just after ten in the morning, the temperature high fifties on track to the upper eighties, without a cloud in the sky.

The pictures she'd seen online were amazing; in real life, it was even more so. Built in the 1800s as a fortress, the original, round, thirty-foot-tall watchtower had been renovated and could accommodate guests, and rumor had it Luther occupied the first floor.

Mr. Pompadour had been so obsessed with keeping the original integrity, he'd found craftsmen who could identify the materials and tools to restore the fortress to the highest level of authenticity. To restore the adobe, he'd even had special mud hauled in.

The L-shaped hacienda where most of the guestrooms were located backed up to an *acequia*, a rock-walled freshwater canal connecting to Antelope Creek. Up close it was magnificent, lined with containers of colorful flowers blooming against the bland landscape. Clear water burbled beneath a quaint wooden walkover bridge.

An employee lived in the house, not much more than a mud hut, on the other side of the canal. The curtains were open and so was the front door. Lauren headed that way. The woman inside appeared to be drying dishes. She stepped up on a wooden chair and hung a pot from a hook overhead.

When she saw Lauren, she stepped down from the chair and walked out onto the weathered porch, built like a shipping pallet, wiping her hands on her apron. Sixtyish and sprightly, she introduced herself as Maria, and extended both hands in a greeting. She obviously knew who Lauren was, inviting her to sit on an aging bentwood rocker. First the woman wiped dust from the seat with the corner of her smock.

A second later, gunshots rang out in the distance.

Lauren's neck twitched involuntarily at the loud pops. "I couldn't do it. Kill the animals."

Maria smoothed the apron on her lap. "It's for the men. You could, if you had to. We all could."

Lauren had gone out without a warm jacket and there was a chill in the shade beneath the overhang.

Maria noticed and went inside, returning with a thin blanket.

Lauren asked how long she'd worked at Antelope Creek Ranch.

"Worked here?" She paused. "Thirty years."

Wow. "So, you were here before Mr. Pompadour bought it?"

She nodded. "Way back then, when he'd first come to hunt, this place was nothing but a few rundown buildings."

"Oh," she said. "Then you knew him well? Roy?"

Maria gazed toward the main lodge. "Not well. More like for a long time."

Didn't knowing someone for a long time qualify as knowing them well? On the other hand, how many stories had she heard about neighbors being surprised that the guy living next door kept body parts in his freezer? Or was a serial rapist? Suddenly, Lauren felt self-conscious, like an interloper invading someone else's sacred space. She searched for something to say.

"What do you do here?" There was no delicate way to pry. She needed to learn the ropes.

"I'm in charge of housekeeping. And I do a little work in the office, a little of this, a little of that. We're like a family, the staff."

"I know it must be hard, with new owners and all."

"If you want to learn about the ranch, don't talk to Luther." Maria's eyes turned sharply toward her. "Talk to Rosa."

"Why not Luther?"

"Because he's stingy with information. He likes to keep things to himself."

"Why?"

"He's always been like that . . . it got worse after Roy died. He thinks he can control the place if he controls the information. If you want to know things, ask Rosa, the young lady who runs the front desk." Maria's salt-and-pepper hair hung loose over her shoulders. She fondled the ends. "There's a rumor that you like horses."

Lauren lit up. "I do."

"You can talk to Josh, too, then. Maybe you've seen him around. He's the hunting guide and he runs the stables." Maria bit her bottom lip for a second. "We have many important people who stay with us. Regulars."

Lauren had noticed Josh several times. She'd asked Luther who he was, and even getting any intel about the striking-looking ranch hand had been like pulling teeth. "Why do you trust Josh so much?"

"I've known him since he was a baby."

Maria didn't elaborate, leaving her in an awkward spot. "A baby? Are you family?"

"Yes." Maria's expression was stony.

Lauren wanted to push for more details but she'd have to be patient. The family connection question would have to wait. "Did you know the man who died here? The judge?"

Maria cocked her head, and snapped her shoulders back. She folded her arms across her chest. Her eyes turned to slits. "No. I didn't know him," she said getting up. "I have to go. There're lots of things to do, to get the rooms ready. It's the calm before the norm, as we say around here."

Lauren crossed the wooden footbridge leading back to the lodge. The three-story watchtower, with its windows inset like Chiclets, cast a long shadow. There were no guests at the swimming pool or milling about the courtyard. Compared to the hustle of people checking out earlier, the ranch was a ghost town.

How could Maria not have known the justice? She'd just told Lauren that the ranch staff was practically a family. Wouldn't that include regular guests?

She spent the rest of the day touring the grounds, and taking Maria's advice, introduced herself to Josh. He invited her to tour the area on horseback tomorrow. She joined Vance for a light supper and retired to her room early.

Before traveling, she'd scanned dozens of online reports about Justice Simeri's death. Some were written by journalists, others by bloggers. The judge and Roy Pompadour were reportedly close personal friends. When she'd selected the Images tab on her browser, a hit came up of a photograph of Roy posing with the justice in a group picture with two dozen or so other men dressed in black robes.

She propped a pillow behind her back and studied the documents. Each story seemed to have a least one conflicting detail surrounding Simeri's death. It had unexpectedly opened a seat on the Supreme Court six months ahead of the last presidential election. Lauren dismissed a lot of it. It was the Internet, after all.

After arriving at the ranch, she recognized the setting of the group photo. They'd assembled in the courtyard, grown men, many of power, dressed in Halloween get up. Weird. It wasn't as if they were on their way to hear a case in front of the high court, or to meet in the basement of some Ivy League school. They were in the desert.

Lauren thought again about the satellite image she'd seen online. The ranch buildings had been redacted from the aerial view with big, black bars.

Who did you need to know to make that happen? Why would anyone do it? There was so much to learn about the place. Meeting Maria was a stroke of good luck and she'd been a big help already. Tomorrow she'd get the chance to pick Josh's brain.

---

THE LOUD BANGING jolted her from a deep sleep. Lauren had stayed up way too late and awoke with a file folder on her chest. Clambering to her feet, she wrapped the blanket over her shoulders and cracked the door an inch. The morning sun stung her eyes.

Vance was pacing. "Emergency meeting at the lodge, with Jake, Luther and the lawyers. You need to hurry."

Lauren opened the door wider. "Why?"

"The ranch hand, he found a body."

"Josh? He found a body?"

"I guess. Yes, a dead body."

"Here? At the ranch?"

He nodded.

Her hands trembled. "Like a migrant?"

"I don't think so. It was in one of the buildings."

"Who died?"

"I told you. I don't know yet. Hurry up. I'll meet you in the dining hall."

Lauren wiped her face with a Towelette, fumbled her hair into a ponytail with fingers shaking, and hurried to meet them. The men appeared to be arguing, lowering their voices when she arrived. She sat next to Vance.

"If we're not careful, we'll start a dispute between the state, federal and local law enforcement agencies," Luther continued with what he'd been saying. "Every time something happens here, a jurisdictional tug of war begins. I think we should let the sheriff handle it, you know, on his own."

"Did something happen to one of our guests?" Lauren asked.

"No. One of our employees," Luther said.

"Which one?" Lauren looked around the table, waiting for an answer.

"The head housekeeper, Maria," Luther said.

She gasped. "Oh my God. What happened?"

"A suicide." Luther tugged at his goatee. "You need to stay calm. There's no sense in upsetting the guests or the staff."

*Upsetting the guests or the staff?* Lauren looked at Vance. "That's horrible. What happened?"

"She hung herself." Vance drummed his fingers on the wooden table.

"That's impossible," Lauren said.

"How would you know?" Luther's tone was condescending. "You've never even met her."

"That's not true. I talked to her yesterday."

"What possessed you to talk to her?" Luther glared at her.

Vance came to her defense. "She's an owner and can talk to whoever she pleases. So can I."

"Look," Luther said. "We're heading into the high season and we're fully booked through the fall. We don't need bad news circulating." He leaned closer and whispered, "The staff hasn't heard yet. Josh and I think we should keep it that way. For now. You don't need trouble."

"Seriously?" Jake was hunched over on his elbows, chin in hands, jowls in their usual sag, staring at the manager. "Like we're covering it up? I don't know if I like that idea. That's what gets people into trouble, the cover-ups."

"I'd like to see it, the scene." Vance stood.

"Why?" Luther snickered.

"I was with Miami homicide. Lauren can show me the way."

"Fine. But there's something you need to understand. We're not just in the luxury travel and entertainment business. We're also in the security business."

"Is that right," Vance said. There was something new in his voice, a slight drawl.

---

LAUREN WALKED QUICKLY, leading Vance to Maria's hut. The morning sun cast backlight on the porch. A silhouette paced back and forth near the front door, neck craned slightly forward to keep from brushing his head on the top of the wooden overhang.

It was Josh, *family to Maria.* He'd been impossible not to notice. He looked like he'd been dispatched from Central Casting to make the place more authentically Western. When Josh spotted them, he stopped pacing and stood in the open doorway, filling it with his fit body.

Vance leaned around trying to look inside but Josh blocked his view.

"May I take a look?" Vance asked him.

"You own the place so I don't think I'd have grounds to stop you. But you," Josh said to Lauren, "you should wait outside. For your own sake."

Lauren had no desire to go in and see it. During the moment it took Vance and Josh to enter, she saw the outline of a petite body hanging from the rafter, like a macabre Halloween decoration. A straw ladder-back chair had been kicked over; it rested on its side.

Curiosity was getting the better of her. She moved to the small window and by standing on her toes, peered into the milky pane where a three-inch gap in the drapes gave her a narrow view inside. Maria's head was covered with a black hood. The body was draped in an oversized gown held with a loopy bow tied around her neck. The available light inside was dim and the windowpane dull, still she could make out the gown's bright green cuffs and gold piping.

The body swiveled gently from the cottonwood beam. A strange smell wafted from the house, as though something had burned. Lauren's stomach did a cartwheel.

Josh had barely let Vance cross the threshold before he ushered him back out, following him, and pulling the door shut.

"Okay, this is a weird," Vance said. "Why would she dress up like that?"

Josh didn't answer. "I'm gonna cut her down."

Vance grabbed his forearm to stop him. "You do that and you'll contaminate the scene."

"It's not a crime scene. It's a suicide." Josh shoved Vance hard enough to unbalance him. He fell to one knee on the porch and by the time Vance recovered from the fall, Josh was already inside, sawing at the rope with a buck knife. He was tall enough to reach up and cut it with his boots flat on the floor.

Vance rushed toward the doorway but Josh had already carried the body to the cot near the window where Lauren was spying on them. Josh looked up at the dangling rope, picked up the chair and threw it against the wall. His chest heaved. He strode past Vance, giving him a solid shoulder bump on the way out the door.

"I couldn't leave her like that." His tone was menacing.

Vance walked over to Lauren and whispered, "Can you believe this shit?"

She shook her head. She could understand the part about why he cut her down, why he couldn't leave someone he knew like that. *Family.* She hadn't had the chance to tell Vance that detail yet.

"Come on," Vance said, turning away from the morbid scene.

Luther arrived. "You two should go back to the main house and go about your business. Let Josh and I take care of this. The Justice of the Peace in Marfidio County is a friend. We have a good relationship with local law enforcement."

Vance downloaded on Lauren on the walk back to the lodge. "We own this place. And Luther and that cowboy think they can do whatever they want."

"I know. But you have to remember this is their home. And

we're outsiders, even if we own it now. They're processing a suicide. We don't know what they're feeling."

They were quiet for a minute walking along the path back to the lodge. She needed to tell him what Maria said, that she'd known Josh since he was a baby. She needed him to cool down first. "Where's Jake?"

He'd been with them earlier, during the emergency meeting.

"Who knows. When the going gets tough, Jake disappears." Vance kicked a rock out of the way.

"There he is," she said.

Frank Conn, the senior lawyer, was waiting by the courtyard pool. Jake was with him.

Vance briefed them on what he'd just seen.

"The boys and I have decided it's time to return to civilization," Frank said.

Jake chimed in, "And I'm going with them."

"How convenient." Vance clenched his jaw. "Getting out of Dodge before shit blows up."

"After shit blows up, you mean." Jake shrugged. His shoulders rose up, practically covering his ears, like a turtle's. "We were leaving anyway."

"You're supposed to leave tomorrow night. Might as well save the money and stay here for one more." Vance looked to Frank, checking for a change of heart.

But Frank was just as spineless. "No, thanks. If we can't get a flight tonight, we'll stay in a hotel by the airport."

Vance shook his head.

One thing Lauren was certain of was that Vance Courage didn't like cowards.

## 4

"What happens if you can't get a flight out?" Lauren asked Jake.

Jake sat at the long table with a roller bag next to him. His back was pressed against the tabletop, the heel of one loafer bouncing like a sewing machine needle. "If it were up to me, I'd be sitting in the President's Club at Midland eating free peanuts and pretzels by now. I'm waiting on the lawyers. They take longer to pack than both my ex-wives. Combined."

Jake had gotten to the ranch first. He'd escaped Freeport after Harvey had come ashore in Rockport, Texas as a Category 4 hurricane forecast to stall over Houston and dump 50 inches of rain. He'd driven daily to Marfidio where there was cell service, to get updates on his phone.

"Yeah, I've talked to Davis every day. He's riding it out."

Jake's sixty-foot live-aboard yacht, the *Arm & A Leg*, was docked at a rundown marina in Freeport, Texas, an hour south of Houston. Though it was waterfront, it was hardly a garden spot, surrounded by refineries and chemical plants.

"Davis is going nuts. He has a bad case of cabin fever and wants to get back to Florida. There's another hurricane brewing and every meteorological model has it making a beeline to the Florida Keys. He wanted to go home before it strengthened. But the airports from Daytona to Key West are already closed. He's threatening to rent a car and drive. He hates Freeport that much."

The idea of using Davis as an excuse to leave the ranch was embarrassing.

Vance joined them and called him out on it. "You want to leave so you don't have to deal with a problem." Vance looked at her, then back at Jake. "It's so annoying when you think you can bullshit us."

She wished she'd said it herself.

---

LAUREN DECIDED to sneak back to Maria's house.

On the walk over, she considered Luther's adamancy about keeping Maria's suicide under wraps. He couldn't keep it secret forever. As soon as the employees found out, they'd start talking. What about grieving? Maria said it herself, that she'd been there since before Roy bought the ranch. And the staff was practically a family.

Something was definitely off. Maybe there was a note, or some other clue that Vance missed. People didn't just up and kill themselves out of the blue. On the other hand, she and Vance had only been there a couple of days. She was hardly an authority when it came to judging the employees. She wasn't sure if she had the stomach for it as she jiggled the doorknob, with the body still in the room, but she didn't get the chance to find out.

"Can I help you, Miss Gold?"

Josh startled her. He stood behind her with a pick ax over his shoulder.

"I'm sorry." She felt her face flush. "I just thought maybe you, um, or my partner missed something."

"Like what?"

Her heart rate ticked up. "I don't know. Uh, she just didn't seem depressed to me. Usually people leave a note, or they're despondent."

"You talked to her?"

"Yes." Her heart fluttered. This time not because she'd come so close to being caught, but because she saw how handsome he was with his chiseled features and eager eyes. "I saw a tablet in her room. When I stopped by to introduce myself earlier, her door was open."

Josh stood silently under the overhang, his cartoonish biceps rippling each time he moved his arms, casting shadows on the bulges and curves.

"I thought I might find some sort of clue. Maybe there's something on her tablet."

"Like what?"

"I don't know. People who are thinking about killing themselves leave clues, like cancelling appointments."

Lauren knew first hand. One of her best friends spent an entire year planning his death, down to the smallest detail. He called the suicide prevention hotline, told them not to hurry, left the house keys in the front door, and requested they dispatch the police to pick up the handgun. She'd been in shock. He'd left a Bankers Box full of instructions about what to do with every possession and dollar left behind in his estate. His brother gave her a note he'd written. He'd apologized for what he was going to do. The note had been written six months earlier.

Josh didn't answer. He just stood there with his big arms folded across his chest. Lauren's hands trembled. He'd caught her sneaking around. Staring at her without answering was making it worse. "She told me she'd worked here for thirty years." *Why won't he say anything?* "That robe she was wearing—"

"So, you think if you can snoop around in her tablet, you'll be able to prove something?"

"It's possible. That maybe I can prove she wasn't planning to kill herself. At least that's what I hope to prove."

"Why would you hope to prove anything? You just bought the place. You don't need trouble."

"Because I don't believe it," Lauren said.

"It doesn't make any difference to me, but if you want to, I don't see why not. Wait here."

*What the hell?* It didn't make any difference to him? When Lauren's dog was killed by a car, she'd gone into an emotional meltdown. Vance had reminded her that people handled tragedy in different ways. Didn't Maria tell her she'd known Josh since he was a baby? That he was somehow family? If that were true, it would explain why he cut down the body. But right after he threw the chair against the wall, he'd composed himself. Now, just an hour after she'd seen him cut the rope with his bowie knife, he seemed so indifferent, beyond stoic, more like a zombie.

He strode away, his square-toed farmer boots leaving wisps of dust, and stepped over the three-foot adobe wall where the official ranch Humvee was parked behind the dining hall. He opened the passenger door and leaned over the driver's seat. A minute later, he headed back, hopping the wall using one hand. He handed her the tablet he'd tucked under his arm.

"I took her valuables for safekeeping. Let me know if you find anything. Any clues, or whatever you're looking for. Don't go inside the house. Let the sheriff handle it."

He'd left the ax leaning against the closed door. He picked it up and slung it over his shoulder as he walked back to his truck.

BACK AT HER ROOM, she opened the cover of the tablet. An app designed to teach English to Spanish-speakers opened without a password. She peeked out the window. In the distance, Josh was cutting down a cottonwood tree and the sun glistened off his bare-skinned back. The sun, an orb of gold, was directly overhead. Soon it would begin to move to the west.

---

"I'LL MAKE THE CALL," Vance said to Luther. He was infinitely more qualified. "Just give me the sheriff's phone number."

"You might be the new owner," Luther said, "but that's not how things roll around here."

"What are you implying?"

"You don't know the people who run this town, and I do," Luther said. "There's no rush to report it. Let's think it through first. That's what Roy would have done."

Under normal circumstances Vance would have set Luther straight. But these were hardly normal. He worked at maintaining his composure. "There's a dead body on the premises. What if it wasn't a suicide?"

"Are you serious?" Luther looked at him like he'd lost his mind.

Vance weighed the options and concluded Luther had the upper hand. "Fine." They'd do it Luther's way. For now.

Vance listened while Luther made the call to the sheriff and when he was done, watched as he set the handset in the cradle, the curlicue cord draping over the edge of his tidy desk.

Vance was mystified. "Why did you tell him that Jake and the lawyers left?"

Luther hesitated, fondling the triangle on his chin. "He

wanted to know who else knows. Discretion is of the utmost importance." One shoulder blade twitched. "The sheriff is coming out when he gets a free moment."

*A free moment?* Vance regretted agreeing to let Luther take the lead, already doing a slow burn inside. "You told him it could wait." Now he was kicking himself for not going with his gut feeling and not ripping the phone from Luther's face when he'd told the sheriff it could wait.

"I know *all* about you," Luther said.

"What's that supposed to mean?"

"You were suspended from Miami PD. That you have family ties to a big drug cartel. We like to know who's here."

"Defunct cartel. That was a long time ago. I'm not responsible for what my relatives did. Or do."

"Maybe not," Luther sniped, "but I don't think your background would be good for business. If our guests found out—"

"That sounds like a threat, Luther. And if it is, there's something you should know about me. I don't cave easily." Vance stood to leave.

"Of course I'm not threatening you. I'm just doing my job, looking out for your investment. Now if you'll excuse me, I have work to do."

## 5

J ake Fleming was behind the wheel of the rented Chevy Suburban, heading east on a bleak stretch of highway toward the Midland/Odessa airport. The three lawyers with him wanted to get out before law enforcement arrived to investigate the death.

Frank Conn hadn't wanted to go on the trip in the first place. He'd tried to back out at the last minute.

"Ten thousand acres and no golf course? Are you shitting me?" Frank had said when he'd heard the bad news. "Plus, I hate guns. As far as I'm concerned, they can cancel the Second Amendment."

It wasn't all that strange of an opinion for a big city Texas lawyer, but it wasn't based on morality, social pressure or crime stats. Frank was afraid of guns, having had a bad experience mishandling a BB gun as a kid.

Jake had tried not to laugh when Frank's wife over-shared that tidbit after one too many at the annual Christmas party. It was back in the days when Jake's investment bank was a client of the firm. Frank "almost shot his eye out" when he was twelve.

It was going to be a long three-hour drive. Frank was

bitching and complaining *again* that they hadn't flown privately, reiterating his love of golf and dislike of hunting and fishing. It was grating on Jake. Why, Frank wanted to know, was he not told the ranch had a private airstrip? Jake hadn't been holding out on him. Maybe if Frank had read page two of the sales documents his firm had prepared, he'd have known.

But Frank was a schmoozer who didn't do actual work. That was left to the associates. Sure, Frank had a nice set of clubs and was a scratch golfer. But he didn't have an airplane, or a pilot's license. Frank should have been thanking him. The sale produced a nice chunk of change for the firm.

It didn't take much for Frank's asshole to grow in circumference or diameter. Every missed first-class upgrade, overlooked dinner invitation, nosebleed stadium seat, or perk Frank didn't get, he took personally. Now he was harping about the airstrip.

Jake was almost glad to see the emergency lights in the rearview. He slowed to let the vehicle pass, a dark-brown pickup. Instead of going by, the truck got on Jake's rear bumper and whooped the siren. They couldn't have been more than twenty miles from the ranch. Jake pulled over on the shoulder. The pickup slid in behind him.

Jake watched from the side mirror as the cop got out. He approached the Suburban with his wrist on the butt of the gun holstered to his tooled leather belt. A buff Hispanic fellow Jake guessed to be a borderline Gen X/millennial, dressed ranch casual wearing a fancy felt Stetson hat, tapped on the driver's-side glass. He could have been heading to a line-dancing competition or maybe the local rodeo, except for the gun, and the Marfidio County Sheriff's badge pinned to the breast pocket of his cowboy shirt.

He ordered Jake to step out.

He seemed agitated, almost disgusted, casting his eyes up and down, surveying Jake's pastel pink shorts and sockless

Italian loafers. He lowered his mirrored aviators and walked around him like he was some sort of newly discovered species.

"Was I speeding, Officer?"

"Not *Officer*. Deputy. *Deputy* Torres. License and registration please." He stuck his head in the cockpit of the SUV.

"It's a rental. I'm not sure where the registration is." Jake fumbled for his wallet and handed him his driver's license.

"Florida, huh. You boy's been drinking?" Torres pushed his glasses back up with his middle finger.

His eyes were hidden but he seemed to be looking at the center console, at a bottle of eighteen-year-old limited reserve scotch. At two hundred bucks a bottle, Frank had insisted they bring it with them. Worse, he'd put it in the jumbo cup holder between the front seats. It was hardly secret Jake was in alcohol recovery, but Frank put it there anyway. The lawyer said he planned to repack it in his checked bag when they got to Midland.

"Everyone step out of the vehicle."

Deputy Torres leaned through the open door on the driver's side and sniffed. He opened the scotch and put his thumb over the top of the bottle, shaking half of it out, spewing it around like an arsonist splashing gasoline to prep a fire. He handed the bottle to Jake who put his hand up to stop him. Torres shoved the bottle into Jake's chest. Jake pushed it away firmly, like poison, yet trying not to anger the deputy.

"Gimme your cell phones." Torres set the bottle down on a patch of dirt and held out one open hand.

"Why?" one of the associates asked.

"Don't make me say it again." Torres' tone was flat and ominous. "And turn 'em off first."

Torres picked the bottle up and thrust it into Jake's ribcage. "Drink."

Jake's eyes widened. He pushed the bottle back toward Torres, harder this time. The deputy shoved it back at him.

Jake had been sober for almost seven weeks, the toughest forty-five days of his life. If he was going to slip, it wasn't going to be on a dusty highway in the middle of Bumfuck, Texas, in front of some crazy Stephen King character.

"Is this a joke?" Jake forced a grin, his upper lip quivering.

The lawyers said nothing.

"Drink up, asshole."

"I'm in recovery. Seriously, I'm an alcoholic and I can't drink. Not even a drop. I have a disease."

"A disease, ha." Torres chortled. "Yeah, right. You think people around here believe that disease shit? What you have is a moral constitution problem."

Frank spoke up. "He's telling the truth."

"Did I ask you for your opinion? If you're so concerned about your buddy here why'd ya let him drive with an open bottle of high-dollar hooch riding in the console? Drink." The deputy grabbed Jake's hand and wrapped his fingers around the neck of the bottle.

"Drink it, Jake," Frank said.

"*No way*. This is nuts."

The deputy came closer until he was nose-to-nose with Jake. "I'm not saying it a third time. *Drink*." He took his gun from the holster.

"Okay, okay." Jake blinked. He put the bottle to his lips, tipped it back, swished a teaspoon in his mouth, and spit it on the asphalt. He winced and coughed. The taste activated the limbic part of his brain and it screamed for more. His addiction therapist told him to envision a skull with crossbones whenever the temptation got too strong. He was doing just that and it wasn't doing squat to help him.

"That's not drinking," Torres said. "I want to see you drink up, like a man."

Frank and the associates, Wimpy and Shorty, had taken several steps away from the road. They backed farther from the horror show.

Torres pointed his gun at Jake's forehead.

*Shit.*

The wimpier associate jogged closer and spoke up. "Come on, Officer, uh, I mean, Deputy. This isn't right. He's an alcoholic."

His boss, Frank, turned ugly. "Come on, Jake, do as the man says so we can be on our way."

Jake chugged what was left, about a third of the bottle. The scotch burned his esophagus on the way to his stomach. Euphoria practically lifted him out of his loafers. It was short lived when the shock to his system kicked in. He heaved uncontrollably, holding his lips tight, fighting what felt like the verge of a volcanic eruption. He tottered, losing his balance and staggered a few steps before falling into the nearby barbed wire fencing. It tore the skin on his knee and blood dripped down his calf, welling on the top of his foot.

Kneeling on the roadside, he gripped his heaving stomach with his two arms, rocking his body, trying to keep the contents down while the full effects of the whiskey bloomed. When he saw streamers of blood running down his ankle, he vomited.

Deputy Torres reached into his pocket and attached a device to his smartphone. He knelt next to Jake, holding it under Jake's upper lip. "Blow."

"Huhhhh?" His word was sloppy.

"Blow in it."

"We're lawyers," Frank said. "This charade has gone too far."

Torres spun and pointed the gun at Frank who cowered and backed away.

"I said blow." Torres put his mouth on the straw attached to the device. "Like this." He handed it to Jake.

He rolled over from his knees onto his butt and took the phone from Torres. He closed one eye and lined up the straw with his mouth and blew into it, both eyes closed.

Torres looked at the screen. "Again. Harder."

Jake took a deep breath and blew harder into the Breathalyzer, his mouth gurgling.

Torres took it from him and shaded the screen with his hand. "Thing smells like puke now, asshole." He took a hanky from his jeans pocket and wiped the mouthpiece. "Huh. A zero-one-six. That's two times the legal limit. Get up," he said, "and close your eyes. I wanna see you walk a straight line with your finger on your nose." He clicked the red button on his phone to record video.

A semi tractor-trailer coming from the opposite direction was racing toward them.

Jake stumbled again, and using his hands to balance himself, moved into a cross-legged sitting position. He tried to stand but he was too wasted to get higher than all fours. He dropped back to his bare knees.

"You're going to get him killed," Frank said as the truck barreled toward them. "This is ridiculous."

"I'm making my case." Torres' tone was measured. "He can't walk a line because he's drunk as a skunk and can't get up off his ass."

"You—"

Torres cut Frank off. "Recite the alphabet backward."

"Huhhh?" Jake's mind was barely recording the events.

"Recite . . . the . . . alphabet—"

"Zeeeeeee," Jake said. He couldn't find the letter before Z. He heard the truck rumbling by, kicking up tire marbles and dirt.

He spat a piece of gravel from his mouth. Another small rock stung his cheek.

The deputy wiped his phone again and put it in his pant pocket. "I'm taking you boys in for drunk driving."

"You can't do that," Frank said. "We're high-powered lawyers from Houston. This is an illegal search and seizure. This is entrapment. You're framing us. I've heard clients tell stories like this, about dirty cops, but I never thought they were telling the truth." He glared at the deputy. "You *can't* do this. We have a flight to catch."

"You'll make some standby passengers happy. Storm's been messing up the airports. Locals are always getting bumped for big shots like you boys. Anything you fellas want now will have to go through a local judge. You gentlemen are not in Houston. Lawmen around here squabble about whose jurisdiction it is sometimes. But they never fight on the side of city slickers. Right now, you're all mine."

Jake was on his hands and knees, staring up at a funhouse mirror version of himself reflecting off the deputy's aviators, and trying like hell to follow the conversation happening above him.

"Even the Feds and Border Patrol aren't sure where Marfidio County ends and Big Bend National Park begins. State Troopers, FBI, Texas Parks and Wildlife, US Marshals, a whole lot a law's gotten tripped up out here. Like I just said, right now you're in my custody. Turn around and put your hands up against the vehicle."

Torres' slow drawl spitting out a medley of jurisdictions made Jake sick again. He looked up. The late afternoon sun overhead blinded him.

"You can't do this," Frank protested as Torres patted Jake down and zipped a plastic tie around his wrists.

"Get in." He opened the back door of the crew cab. The attorneys crawled into the back seat. He opened the passenger door and helped Jake onto the running board. Torres walked to the rented SUV and pressed the key fob, locking it. Their suitcases and hunting rifles were in plain sight through the vehicle glass. He stuffed the key to the rental in his pant pocket.

Torres got in. "You boys ain't got judge-friends in these parts. Bet you wish now you'd come to our annual fundraising barbeque last year. Judges are elected here just like they are in the big city. Makes for a legal sewer system but I don't suppose I need to explain that to you boys. You can take it up with the bail bondsman."

A tractor-tire-sized tumbleweed rolled across the highway. The driver of a semi tractor-trailer hauling cattle waved and pulled his air horn as he passed by. Torres waved back, friendly. The smell of livestock coming in through the open window made Jake's stomach quake.

Torres said, "Do not puke in the cab of this truck." He pressed the talk button on his police radio. "Got me a DUI. Need a wrecker." He read the rental's plate to whoever was on the other end of the call and did a three-point turn heading back toward town.

"You gotss to be shitting ussss," Jake said. He was blotto and talking gibberish, making all sorts of threats against Deputy Torres. "You're probably a homo who likessss old guyssss."

Frank told him to shut up but the booze was talking. He mumbled jumbled phrases about building a border wall, police brutality, and illegals.

Deputy Torres kept his eyes on the road.

When they arrived at the cinderblock courthouse, Torres snipped the zip tie on Jake's wrists and all of them were printed the old-fashioned way with their fingertips pressed onto an inkpad and rolled one by one on white index cards. The alcohol in Jake's brain was beginning to recede.

A woman with lacquered hair and hand-drawn cartoon

eyebrows handed them placards to hold in front of their faces. She doubled as the jailhouse photographer, shooting face and profile shots of the four men. Though he'd been sobering up, Jake's mug shot was so ghastly the woman held it under Jake's nose for her own amusement.

When Frank asked about making a phone call, Deputy Torres and the rest of the folks on duty in the rundown one-stop-shop courthouse roared with laughter.

They were locked up in a filthy little cell. Rust seeped along the lattice bars covering the small window, through the layers of white paint, down to the cement floor. Frank jumped when he stepped on something that crackled under his deck shoe: molted snakeskin, from a six-footer.

The metal toilet-sink combo in the middle of the floor served as the facilities and Jake hoped he wouldn't have to stick his head in it. He lay on the concrete floor in the fetal position, praying for his brain to clear.

The man in charge stopped by for a visit. He looked at the four of them and shook his head. "Tsk-tsk-tsk. You boys need to behave yourselves outside those fancy fences and gates. Wouldn't be good for business, a nice big front page photo in the *Antelope Weekly Standard*, four of ya'll sitting here in my jail. Hard to explain how a bunch of big-shot lawyers representing the sale of Pomps' fancy ranch got themselves tossed in the pokey." He looked at Jake, "Along with one of the new owners."

Sheriff Manny Rodriguez took Deputy Torres' phone. "Uh-oh. Looks like one of you blew an oh-one-six." He raised his eyebrows. "Dang, look at this video. This would go viral in the first minute. And you know what? Once the video and mug shots are out there, they're out there for all eternity. Don't tell me, this drunkard was the one behind the wheel?" He glanced at Jake curled up on the floor.

Torres nodded.

"You boys oughta know that some folks call this thing a smart phone. I call it the WWW, not for the World Wide Web, but for the Wild Wild West. Now there was a time not so long ago when we could stake that claim. Who knew a bunch of girly boys with fancy college degrees would turn this thing into the new frontier starting all kinds of shit storms no lawman on earth has the power to stop."

The words jackhammered in Jake's head.

"Hell, our country's on the brink of war with bad *hombres* 'cause they got technology to shoot a damn nuke at Guam, or maybe San Francisco. I can tell you this, them Commie terrorists ain't got much interest in hitting a fancy ranch with half its ass in Mexico." Manny shook his head some more. "Tsk-tsk-tsk. Your friend is going to need some extra-strength aspirin in the morning. An oh-one-six blood alcohol level. Woowee. That man's head's gonna be hurting."

The sounds of their boots dragging on the cement floor echoed in Jake's ears.

"What the fuck is going on?" Frank asked when they were gone.

Jake was in no condition to weigh in.

"That fucker said your head is going to hurt in the morning. You know what that means?" Frank asked.

"Shut up," one of the associates said.

The young guns were doing a better job of accepting their fate, something Frank had not yet grasped. It meant they were going to be there overnight.

Jake passed out.

## 6

V ance was exhausted by the time he headed back to the main house. He'd been bunking with Jake and at least now he'd have some privacy with him gone. Earlier, he'd mingled with some of the travelers and hung around watching the visitors and staff, taking the pulse of the place. The employees were impressive, the way they handled the demands of the guests, most of whom were rude and tiresome.

It was around 10:00 PM when he took the long route to the house, circling the pool, heading toward Lauren's room where he assumed she'd taken refuge. She'd picked at her meal at dinner, not making much of an effort to hide how pissed she was that he'd agreed to Luther's demands, leaving the housekeeper's body in the house for the night.

Gravel crunched under his boots as he strode along the lighted pathway, past small groups of men gathered around the pool and patio. Orange and yellow streaks shot from the from the outdoor fire pit. The scent of burning wood mixed with Cuban cigars wafted, and the sounds of guests enjoying themselves was a respite from the dread that had been hanging over him since the body had been discovered.

He slowed as he passed beneath the veranda outside Lauren's corner room; the drapes were drawn and the lights were out. Asleep, he assumed.

The temperature had dropped at least forty degrees since the day's high of eighty-five and he jogged the rest of the way to ward off the chill. In the distance beyond the L-shaped hacienda, a yellow porch light burned beneath the rickety awning over Maria's porch, casting a sickly tone. At least the cold would help preserve the body until morning. Rigor mortis had probably set in, but the colder temperatures would slow *algor mortis*, coroner lingo for decomposition.

———

LAUREN HAD FOUND the antiquated nightly turndown a nice touch, an old-fashioned amenity instituted by Mr. Pompadour, a service she'd insisted they continue. The ranch was all about getting away from the stresses of everyday life. Each evening while the guests dined, the housekeeping staff folded the mono-grammed bed linens back into tidy triangles and placed a hand-crafted chocolate atop each guest pillow.

She'd been so tired that she'd come straight to the room right after supper. After a long hot shower, she sat on the edge of the bed wrapped in a robe with her hair wound in a towel. She'd stretched out for a moment and when she awoke, the old-fash-ioned digital clock said it was a few minutes after 10:30 at night.

She'd been asleep for more than two hours. Turning on the bedside lamp, she saw the chocolate treat she'd set on the night-stand. She bit into the truffle, letting the flavors blossom in her mouth.

Maria's tablet was on the dresser where she'd put it earlier. The towel atop her head dropped when she stood, revealing a maze of damp tangles. She ran her fingers through her hair, trying to smooth the cowlicks. Picking the tablet up, she rolled back the leather cover and saw something out of the corner of her eye on the dresser, in the background, something she'd surely have noticed before. It rested on its side like an old-fashioned ship in a bottle, except whatever was inside, was moving.

She flipped on the overhead light and approached slowly, and staying a couple of feet back from the dresser, leaned at the waist to get a better look. She lurched back when it came into focus.

*Holy crap.*

It was a big scorpion, and it was pissed off, stabbing at the glass with its hooked stinger. She dressed quickly, ran to the main guesthouse and pounded on Vance's door.

A moment later he opened it. "What's wrong with you?"

"Someone put an insect in my room."

"I thought you were asleep. Jeez, you're a mess."

"Um, I dozed off." She smoothed her hair with her hands.

He looked like she'd awakened him.

"We're in the desert. Stuff lives here, weird stuff." He shrugged. "Do want to come in?"

"No. You're not listening to me. Someone put a bug in my room."

He leaned on the doorframe rubbing his eyes with both fists. "It probably came in under the door . . . or through the wall. Or something. I don't know." He yawned.

"It's inside a glass bottle, with air holes cut in the cap."

"What are you talking about?"

"A scorpion. It's in a glass bottle on top of the dresser in my room. It may as well have come with a freaking note from the sender."

He repeated what she'd just told him, and then said, "It's alive, in a bottle? How long's it been there?"

She had to think. She wasn't sure if or when she would have

noticed it. Then she remembered. The tablet, the bottle wasn't there when she put it on the dresser. "It had to be while I was at dinner. Or maybe a little before?"

"Jesus." He pulled his cowboy boots on and followed her to her room. "If it's a scorpion, technically it's not a bug."

"Whatever." She wasn't up for a biology lesson.

The horrible thing was motionless inside a thick glass milk bottle. When he picked it up, it ran along the bottom, wagging its tail.

"Ewwe." She backed away.

He rolled the bottle in his hand slowly, watching the scorpion slide. "This is strange." He still sounded half asleep. "Maybe someone left it here, by accident."

"I don't think someone *left* it here. I think someone *put* it here."

Vance was mesmerized, watching its arced tail striking the glass. It was big, around three inches long and its body glossy black. It tried to run up the sides but the smooth glass acted like a greasy treadmill. The faster he rotated the glass in his hands, the quicker the awful creature ran and the madder it got.

"Stop playing with it and focus on who would do this."

"I have no idea."

"You're the detective. It had to be someone with access to my room."

"That could be any number of people."

True. "This place is seriously creeping me out."

He put it down on the dresser. "Maybe you need a big strong man to watch over you tonight."

"Don't make me regret asking you for help." There was no point avoiding it any longer. He'd been making innuendos about it since she'd admitted it. She'd tried to explain that it was a bad choice. "I already told you, sleeping with Jake was a mistake. I was an emotional wreck." Her dog Sinbad had been hit and run over by a car, and died in her arms.

"You're an emotional wreck right now."

"Nice try." She wrapped her arms across her chest and tightened her grip. On the one hand, she would have liked him to stay. Or, better yet, she could stay with him at the main house and sleep in Jake's empty bed. Both were bad choices. "I'll be fine, but do me a favor. Please take that thing with you."

"All right. Sure you're okay?"

"I'll be fine, as soon as that thing is gone."

He left carrying the milk bottle. She closed the door and set the deadbolt and chain. Antelope Creek Ranch was supposed to be an oasis of serenity, relaxation, and, above all, safety. That's what Luther told Vance earlier at the emergency meeting, that they were in the "security business." She climbed under the soft linens and shut off the bedside lamp. A sense of doom fell over her. She focused on her breathing, in and out, in and out.

Her heart still pumped hard in her chest.

She stared at the ceiling, trying not to think of the image of Maria's body hanging from the rafter. The harder she tried to put it out of her mind, the clearer it became. The picture changed to the scorpion that had mysteriously appeared on the dresser. Someone had been in her room. Now she regretted not taking Vance up on his offer to stay in the big house.

She was starting to unwind when the landline in her room rang. She answered it. Rosa wanted to know how to handle the calls coming in from Frank Conn's wife, who was looking for him. How the hell was she supposed to know where Mrs. Conn's wayward husband was?

She curled into the fetal position and pulled the covers over her head. She was afraid of the dark as a little girl and had learned to rock herself to sleep. Hugging her torso, she rolled gently side-to-side until she slept.

## 7

Lauren awoke shivering under the sheets. Compared to the tropics of south Florida, forty degrees was practically the deep freeze. She wrapped herself in the blanket from the bed and peeked through the striped drapes, toward the small house where the body had been left overnight. The view looked peaceful with the faint glow of a blood red sun rising over the Chinati Mountains, casting a pink veil over the ranch.

She ran her hands through her hair and shook her head, trying to clear it. Recalling the events of yesterday, the ranch was turning out to be anything but *Walden Pond*. More throw-up, than Thoreau. She'd have to use that line on Jake. He'd appreciate it.

She'd barely picked at her food at dinner and was so hungry her hands quivered. Someone pounded on her door. She unchained it and peeked out: Vance again.

"Get dressed. We have to bail Jake out of jail."

"Very funny." Lauren tried pulling the door shut but he'd stuck the toe of his boot on the threshold.

"I'm serious. And the sheriff's on his way."

She let him in. He sat on the bed while she riffled through the dresser drawers for clean underwear.

"Jake got a DUI on the way to the airport. What a dumb ass."

Carrying a change of clothes over her forearm, she turned and scowled. Shaking her head, she went into the bathroom and shut the door.

He stood on the other side. "The lawyers are there, too. The jail doesn't officially open until nine."

She cracked the door open. "Then what the hell are you hurrying me for? It's barely seven-thirty."

"I'm not hurrying you. You're hurrying you. The sheriff is on the way, so being dressed would be good."

She pulled the bathroom door closed so hard it shut with a bang.

He spoke louder from the other side. "I called Davis Frost from the landline this morning. He was expecting Jake last night. Rosa said that Frank's wife started calling late last night."

She cracked the door open. "I know, Rosa called me, after you walked me back. She said Frank's wife was driving her crazy looking for her husband. Rosa said wives call all the time with the same question. I figured they took some sort of boys-night-out detour."

"So you knew they were missing?"

She came out dressed. "Not exactly missing. Just that Frank's wife called Rosa. They're guys, men of power. I thought maybe they went to Laredo or something. Maybe there was a weather stop at the airport. Or they couldn't get out. Or whatever. This really is disappointing that Jake got a DUI. I was hopeful. I didn't see him drink while he was here."

"That's what good alcoholics do, Lauren. They hide it. Or they try to hide it."

"It doesn't make sense that the other guys let him drive drunk. Unless they were all drunk."

"They shared a cell last night in the county jail. Luther says there's video of a field sobriety and a blood alcohol test. After we're done with the sheriff here, I'm going to into town and I want you to go with me."

"I don't want to go to the jail."

"Then I'll go alone."

"Do you think that's a good idea?" Too many weird things were happening. "I think you should take Josh with you, for insurance. He seems to know his way around, better than you do."

"Seriously? He cut a dead body down yesterday with a knife, busted a chair, and spent the afternoon fixing fences."

"That's my point. He's my pick to go with you."

"Maybe he's a sociopath. Did you consider that?"

She had. "If you want to go alone, go right ahead. I'm staying here."

"Let's meet in the middle. What if I ask Luther to go with us?"

"Then I'm definitely not going. You're better off going by yourself than asking him. I need coffee in the worst way."

He offered to get it. "Fine. I'll talk to Josh."

"Room service?"

"Uh-huh."

"Thanks. How much is their bail?"

"Five thousand. Each."

"Geez, that's twenty grand. We have to pay it?"

"You have to pay it. I didn't bring enough cash."

"I changed my mind."

"About what?"

"I'm going with you. Only if Josh agrees to go with us and that creep, Luther, stays here."

"You know what they say about women changing their minds?"

She glared at him. "Hurry with my coffee."

## 8

The gates protecting Antelope Creek Ranch made an unforgettable landmark. Luther remembered the day the workmen finished erecting the twenty-foot-high cedar posts, set thirty feet apart. It was a sight to behold, the front-end loader stacking giant boulders into pyramids next to the enormous, vertical logs. The arched, wrought-iron sign mounted by men on a cherry-picker could be seen from a quarter mile away.

Luther stood in the small office behind Rosa's desk, staring at the cameras monitoring the gates. A marked sheriff's pickup appeared on the screen and Luther pressed a series of numbers into a wall-mounted keypad. The gate opened and the vehicle crawled up the gravel incline. The driver parked his dusty brown truck under the Spanish tile overhang.

Sheriff Manny Rodriguez strolled in sporting snakeskin boots and wraparound sunglasses. He removed his shades and scanned the lobby. His button-down, long-sleeved shirt with pearly buttons was tucked into starched jeans with a permanent vertical whitish stripe down the centerline. A small, jeweled map of Texas held the string tie around his neck. Snake rattles attached to the bottom of the bolo shook in stereo, hissing like the real thing.

Instead of a police-issue patent leather utility belt, he holstered his Glock in a garish leather belt with floral carvings, held together with a two-inch silver rodeo buckle. The badge pinned to his shirt clashed with the Montblanc pen poking from his shirt pocket. His hat was smallish, a five-gallon instead of ten. He could have dismounted from the page of a Larry McMurtry novel and strolled into the lobby of Antelope Creek Ranch.

"Thanks for not getting me outta bed before sunup. You know what they say. Patience is a virtue. Got any coffee?" The sheriff headed to a long dining table where Vance sat.

He removed his hat, revealing a permanent circular dent in his short black hair, peppered gray. His elbows were set slightly away from his body, like he was carrying oranges under his armpits. He put his metal clipboard on the table, took the fancy pen from his shirt pocket and straddled the bench.

Luther returned with coffee. Vance was finishing telling Manny what they'd seen. The sheriff asked to look at the house for himself. The trio crossed the courtyard, and passed the pool to the rustic little archway bridge over the creek leading to the outer edge of the compound.

Manny twisted the front door knob. It was locked. He funneled his eyes with his hands and peered into the window, through the gap in the curtains.

"I thought you said she was wrapped in some kind of a robe." The sheriff looked sideways at Luther, his eyes narrowing. "Who's got the key?" The leather soles of Manny's boots made a two-beat on the wood-planked porch deck as he walked back to the front door and jiggled the handle, this time, audibly harder.

Luther peered in the window. "I have a master key," he said. "And that's not what she was wearing when I saw her. Hanging."

VANCE CUPPED his hands over his eyes and peered inside, too. Luther was right. The body on the cot was dressed in a brightly colored Mexican skirt and a plain white blouse. The bottoms of her feet were covered with sandals, arms folded peacefully across her chest, her face concealed with a lacy cloth, like one worn to church on Sundays. Maybe that's what she'd been wearing under the robe?

This was exactly what Vance was worried about when he'd agreed to let Luther handle the call to the sheriff. Someone had to have been in the room. The scene had been tampered with. Suicides were easy cases. Usually the investigating officers consoled the family, dispatched the coroner, and that was that. So why dress her up, or undress her, or alter the site at all?

Josh startled them, coming up from behind.

"You wait outside," the sheriff said to Vance and Luther. Josh followed Manny in.

This wasn't police work. It was a freak show. Vance went back to the window and strained to see what they were doing. Manny had moved to the foot of the cot, blocking his view. From the little he could see through the milky window, it looked like Josh lifted Maria's blouse but Vance couldn't be sure. He crept to the doorway. It was cracked a couple of inches. Manny was taking pictures with his phone, bending over to get close-ups of the woman's neck and stomach.

Luther leaned against one of the beams holding the tired overhang.

"This is bullshit," Vance said as Josh and the sheriff exited the little house, Josh careful not to bump his head while Luther turned the master key locking the deadbolt.

Josh left before Vance confronted Manny. "I don't care what size town this is, or how many law enforcement agencies have jurisdiction, this isn't how it works. The scene's been messed with. No prosecutor in the State of Texas would admit any evidence." He scraped his fingernails through his hair. "If any had been collected." He'd been played. Sidelined. And he had every right to be hot.

"Now, hold your horses and don't go gettin' your bowels in an uproar," Manny said. "I know this probably isn't how y'all do it in the big city, but it's a damned suicide."

"This isn't how they do it *anywhere*. And you don't know if it's a homicide or a suicide. Getting your beauty sleep was apparently more important." They'd never know for sure now.

"Let's have a chat. Privately, just you and me," Manny said to Vance. "Luther, would you please excuse us."

Luther threw dagger eyes at both of them before heading toward the walkover bridge.

Manny leaned against the side of Maria's house with one heel on the adobe. He was apparently going to play the we're-both-cops, or, in Vance's case, current-sheriff-to-ex-cop card. Thumbing through the pictures on his phone, he showed Vance a close up on Maria's neck. The purplish strangulation marks were consistent with a hanging.

"Jesus," Vance said.

Manny tipped his hat back on his head a few inches. "Take a look at this one."

Vance raised one eyebrow. "What is that?"

"Burnt skin. On her belly."

It looked like a brand, the kind used on cattle, yet fresh enough that the blood still glistened. Was that what he'd smelled yesterday? *Burnt flesh?* Bile percolated in his throat.

The sheriff showed him another picture and enlarged it with his thumb and forefinger. "It's an emblem, a cross of some kind. Been thinking of ways she coulda done it to herself."

"You can't possibly still think this is a suicide." Vance shook his head and rubbed his throat with an open hand.

"Didn't say I did."

Vance pressed harder. "The crime scene's been contaminated. I have liability. So do my partners."

Manny held his free hand up defensively. "Whoa. Wait a minute, buckaroo. Don't put that on me. That was your people. Luther reported it a suicide and y'all agreed it was best to keep it low key." He put his phone back in his shirt pocket. "I've seen a lot of things around here, but nuthin' like this." Manny started toward the gravel path leading to the creek.

Vance blew his cheeks up like a puffer fish and let the air out slowly. "We didn't *all* agree."

Manny unclipped the mouthpiece from the radio attached to his tooled belt and pressed the talk button. "Have 'em send the ME over to the Ant-tee-lope Ranch. We got a body." He snapped the talk piece back on the radio without looking. "The coroner's gotta come all the way from El Paso, so do me a solid, no one else goes in the house. Now that I've seen what I seen, more folks in there will just cause trouble. Neither one of us wants that, do we?"

Vance calmly shook his head no. He'd have liked to put his fist through the window. Or bust the door down with his shoulder. Maybe smashing his knuckles in Manny's cowboy face might feel good. He kept his hands in his pockets, his jaw set tight.

"Guess I'll be seeing ya down at the jail shortly." Manny tipped his hat gentlemanly-like and strolled across the walking bridge over the *acequia*. Vance perched on the edge of the planked wooden porch, rocking on his heels. He shielded his eyes from the morning sun still making its way over the Chinati Mountains, casting dark shadows on rugged peaks jutting from the desert flatlands.

It took the delivery driver four trips with a fully loaded dolly to bring the day's shipments into the lobby. Rosa was going through the stacks of packages and boxes, organizing them so housekeeping could deliver them to the appropriate guestrooms to await the arrivals.

"Jeez," Rosa said when she looked up and saw Lauren. "How did they survive before online shopping? They ship all this stuff in and leave most of it behind. Sometimes we fight over the leftovers." She laughed.

"I guess that's what people do when they have more money than good sense. Can I give you a hand with those?"

Rosa waved her hand no.

Lauren leaned on her elbows on the guest side of the desk, watching Rosa work. "Did you ever meet Justice Simeri?"

"I did, and he was nice. Polite, too. I've met a lot of high-profile people working here. Aldo was very down to earth. Roy had so many connections in DC. He liked to host groups with political causes, even though he didn't agree with of a lot of them. He said he liked to listen to all sorts of points of view."

"I guess it's good for business, if they keep coming."

Rosa's expression was sheepish. "That's why it's best to keep our problems to ourselves. I know it sounds heartless, but Josh and Luther are right. This was Maria's home, too, and she appreciated how much care Roy put into making the place extraordinary. What good would it do to make the news public?"

That was surprising. Rosa seemed to know a lot. "What about when the justice died here? That was front page news. Didn't that hurt business?"

Rosa, who was kneeling again, glanced up at her. "Oh, no. On the contrary, we had a spike in reservations, curiosity-seekers mostly, from everywhere. You know how people are," Rosa said, standing to sort through the towers of boxes. "Aldo's death turned into a drama. If we'd tried to keep it quiet, Roy said the conspiracy theorists would be out in force. Maria's death is different. She's not famous. There's no reason to broadcast it."

"Who's that?"

Rosa rolled her eyes and whispered. "Oh gosh, I call him Deputy Dumbass. Others call him Deputy Torres."

"Hello, Rosa." He turned toward Lauren. "You must be one of the new owners. I'm Deputy John Torres."

"Lauren Gold, nice to meet you." She extended her hand but Torres turned toward the boxes.

Rosa glared at him. "Are you expecting a delivery?"

"Luther said it would be okay." He rested his wrist on the butt of his service weapon. "Ah, there is it."

CAUTION: LIVE ANIMALS.

*PRECAUCION: ANIMALES VIVOS*

The red label was in English and Spanish.

"It's for my son. School project," Torres said, tucking the box under his arm. "Thanks," he said, going out the front door. He'd left the front door of his patrol truck open.

"That was weird," Lauren said. "A little too cozy for my taste."

"He was here yesterday picking up something, too."

"A way to outsmart the porch pirates."

"Maybe. Or he's using Luther's online account to save the shipping costs."

Maybe. "What were you saying?"

"That we shouldn't broadcast Maria's death."

"Hmm. Maybe it's the right decision. I'm not sure." Lauren needed more time to process it. "Do you by any chance have the records for the hunting group, the ones who were regulars? The group the justice belonged to?" Lauren tilted her head toward the office behind the desk.

Rosa wrinkled her nose. She squinted and her forehead followed suit. "No. Those were Mr. Pompadour's private clients. Luther handles them now. Mr. P. kept a lot of information about certain guests and groups in his own personal files."

Lauren strolled behind the desk and went into the office.

The bell on the counter dinged and Rosa dropped what she was doing.

Vance leaned against the desk.

"Oh, Mr. Courage. How can I help you?" Rosa was practically fawning over him.

"I'm looking for Ms. Gold." Vance winked at Lauren, who stood in the doorway of the office behind the desk, rolling her eyes.

---

"Crime scene?" Lauren had followed Vance to the dining hall and was sitting across from him, incredulous, listening to the turn of events. "Did you talk to Josh?"

"I did. But not about that. He's agreed to go with us to bail the guys out. Oh, no"—Vance flicked his eyes—"look who's coming."

Luther sat next to Vance. He put his elbows on the tabletop and placed his palms together in a steeple. "Can you imagine what a murder would do for business? We're heading into high season. It could kill our revenues."

"So now you agree it wasn't a suicide," Vance said.

"Is that *all* you care about?" Lauren asked. "That her death will be bad for business?" She got up from the table, disgusted, and headed toward the lobby door.

From his seat facing the entrance, Vance saw Manny sitting alone in the alcove in a comfy leather chair near the front desk, making notes on his clipboard. As Lauren approached, Manny stood in front of her and nodded respectfully, tipping the brim of his hat with his thumb and forefinger. Then he held his hand out. She offered hers submissively, fingers together dipping downward in a soft arc. *Ladylike. What the fuck?* With Vance she'd been assertive from the get-go, giving him a bone-crushing handshake on their first date in Miami.

The sheriff bent slightly at the waist. "Ma'am," he said loud enough for Vance to hear.

*Give me a break.*

"Have you been listening to me?" Luther was annoyed.

Vance narrowed one eye and shook his head. "Sorry."

"Like I said, rumors about a suspicious death would hurt business." Luther was droning on and on about what bad news would do for bookings. Vance watched Lauren, who'd moved to the courtyard, now pacing around the swimming pool.

She stopped and stared into the distance. He craned his neck to see what she was looking at. The dry West Texas soil puffed up and plumed, creating a dust cloud. When the air cleared, he saw what had caught her attention: Josh was checking the fence posts the ranch hands had been working on. He looked like he'd dressed up for the trip.

"She your wife?" Manny surprised Vance, looming over him.

The sheriff snapped his head toward the pool.

Luther licked the corner of his mustache. "The way he stares at her, I wouldn't think so."

"No. She's a business partner," Vance said.

"A high-strung one," Manny said, making a note on his clipboard. "Never thought I'd see the day we'd have a gal owner of this ol' ranch. This is a tough place with an even harder history."

Luther spoke up. "We're a Four Star Michelin resort, for chrissake. Silicon Valley entrepreneurs jet in for our famous nouveau Mexican-French cuisine, and to relax."

"Human traffickers and drug smugglers are what I deal with

most," Manny said. "Burned-up bodies. Beheadings. Rapes. This place ain't really changed over time. Oh, sure, y'all have a fancy city-slicker website and them color ads in all them nice travel magazines. The folks paying five hundred dollars a night are paying mostly for security. They might not know it, but they ain't paying that much for the food and bedding. A murder? That's the kind a news that'll bring back tumbleweeds and spare tires."

Luther, that smug prick, smiled. *Mister "It's-A-Suicide."* He'd been the one who'd gone on ad nauseam about the importance of security, something never brought up during the purchase.

"While I appreciate the history lesson, Sheriff, when will the coroner get here?" Vance asked.

"Can't say for sure." Manny adjusted the brim of his hat side-to-side. "Like I said, he's coming from El Paso. Just about two hundred miles, give or take."

"Can I at least get an ETA?" Vance was about to lose his shit.

"I'll see what I can do." Manny looked at his watch. "I'll see you shortly. Don't forget. We only take cash. Jail opens any minute now. Banker's hours."

Vance walked him out. The sheriff ambled through the foyer, the leather soles of his boots brushing the orange Saltillo tiles. Outside, cotton balls of dust floated from his heels as he strode toward the truck. He did a slow three-point turn, heading toward the electronic gate and turned east on the four-way.

The ranch drew a class of people he'd never seen before. The tech moguls, mostly from Silicon Valley and the Pacific Northwest, were arriving en masse for breakfast. They looked foreign. He was mesmerized watching them while he waited for Josh and Lauren to meet up with him so they could head out to the jail and post bail.

LAUREN GOT THERE first and when Josh showed up, instead of joining them, said he needed to make a pit stop in the restroom before they left.

That gave Lauren the opportunity she'd been waiting for. "There's something I need to show you." She took the hand-written note the deaf man had given her from her purse and handed it to Vance.

Find out who killed the Justice

"When did you plan on sharing this? This is rich, Lauren."

"I thought the guy was crazy, until now." She told him Rosa's story, about Roy's dismissals of the lipreader as a nut job. She filled him in on what she knew about the group of hunters that met at the ranch. "They're a global organization, conservationists is the best way I can describe them. But here's the thing. They wear robes, like the one the housekeeper was wearing when—"

"What are you saying?"

"I'm not sure. It's just that the robes in the pictures I saw on the Internet look like the one she was wearing. While she was, ah, hanging."

Vance told her about the photos Manny had shown him.

"A brand? Burned into her stomach?" She chewed her bottom lip.

"You're taking this better than I thought you would."

"Not really." Her delicate jaw twitched.

"Damn it." He punched the air. "Without securing the crime scene, it's impossible to do proper forensics now."

"Someone went to a lot of trouble to make it look like a suicide. And now it looks like a murder." She glanced around, making sure no one was listening.

"I look like an idiot. And this fucks up my theory."

"Which is?"

"An ex. The brand burned on her belly, that suggests something personal."

"Oh, God." Lauren placed her hand on her stomach and swallowed hard. "That must be what I smelled."

His eyes followed hers around the room. "We don't know any of these people, Lauren. Not really. It's possible that Maria had an ex with a grudge. Every cop worth his salt knows the number one suspect in crimes against women is always their lovers and husbands. I have an idea."

"What?"

"Let's check the surveillance video."

Lauren glanced up at the clock on the wall in the dining hall. "That won't do us any good."

"How do you know?"

"The system only stores footage for twenty-four hours."

The lines in his forehead deepened. "How do you know that?"

She told him about her chat with Rosa.

"Hotels and buildings usually keep videos for thirty days." Vance thumped his fist on the table. "ATMs store footage for six months. It doesn't make sense. It's so easy to store the stuff on hard drives. How is it that Luther lectures us about security and the video surveillance system only keeps twenty-four hours at a time? That doesn't add up."

"Rosa said Roy used to keep recordings for thirty days, but that the plan was changed recently, to the twenty-four-hour cycle. Rosa said Luther changed it."

He calmed down a little. "The first piece of my puzzle fits even it if flies directly in the face of all Luther's bluster about security. If an ex had access, he could have entered undetected. A territorial man is a dangerous one. I bet we could solve this in ten minutes if we had the video files."

"You still think Maria had a male friend with an agenda? It

would be hard to keep a domestic grudge a secret around here. The place is about as private as a cubicle farm. Plus, I don't think she had a boyfriend. Or a husband."

"Really?" Vance said, irritation rising in his voice. "We've been here a few days and you talked to her for like what, ten minutes?"

"I know. It sounds crazy. Call it a woman's intuition."

"Speaking of women's intuition, what was up with you and the sheriff?" He imitated her limp wrist.

"Am I interrupting something?" Josh loomed over them.

She smiled at Vance. "No, we were just waiting for you."

"Is Manny still here?" Josh swept his forehead with the back of his hand and rubbed his palms together.

"You just missed him," Lauren said.

"Are you two ready to go?"

"I'll be right back." Lauren needed to get the twenty thousand cash from the safe in her room. She'd almost forgotten.

## 9

Vance opened the back passenger's-side door for her and she climbed inside with the envelopes of money she'd stuffed inside her messenger bag. The H-1 interior was loaded: a second row entertainment center, leather seats, premium sound system, front and back cameras. Josh swung the big SUV around the horseshoe driveway and headed slowly toward the automatic gates.

They'd been riding in silence for at least ten minutes when Josh tapped the brakes. A mule deer darted across the highway. Josh made eye contact with her in the rearview. "Do you always travel with that much cash?"

She didn't answer.

Josh laughed. "I've had to bail folks out before, lots of times. We tell guests not to leave the ranch unless they have to fly commercial. The airstrip is private property. When you bought the place, you kept the runway. That was smart."

She would have liked to take credit for being smart. But worrying about local dust-ups with the law had nothing to do with it. The airstrip had never come up during negotiations other than a quick review of the expenses associated with maintaining it. The law firm's accountant showed them how many regulars flew privately. Antelope Creek Ranch could stand to lose half its clientele without it.

Josh stood on the brakes, bringing the Humvee to a sliding stop. Her heart thumped. There was no reason for the sudden maneuver.

Josh pointed north, across the highway. "It's a fawn. I'll be damned." He looked like a kid on Christmas morning. "A Prong-horn. They breed in the fall and carry for about seven or eight months." He leaned across Vance and took a pair of binoculars from the glove box.

He peered through them. "It's maybe four or five months old. This was Roy's dream, bringing them back."

"We should keep moving," Vance said. "I think the guys would probably like to get out ASAP. Maybe we can take in the wildlife on the way back."

"If Roy was here, he'd tell you to get out and walk. They can wait another five minutes. We've been waiting for this for almost a decade." When he was done looking, he handed the field glasses to Lauren in the back seat.

The animals were even more impressive than the pictures she'd seen in the local paper.

Josh pulled out onto the main highway.

The closer they got to Marfidio, Texas, the weirder the trip got. Roadside stops were dotted with tourists gawking at huge pieces of modern artwork clashing with the barren landscape. They were on a different route from the one they'd taken when they'd first arrived.

"Most people figured the locals would want those things removed by now," Josh said. "But in a strange twist, they've developed an odd affinity for the shit."

They passed a huge watch sticking up from the desert land-scape. It was at least ten feet tall and three feet wide.

Josh made eye contact with her again in the mirror. "Not a favorite of Mr. Pompadour's. But the locals liked it so much they started attending every City Council meeting. The same folks that used to go to meetings to stop outlet malls started rooting for the Rolex."

Josh slowed the Hummer as they drove past a huge smartphone lying sideways on the desert like a fallen tombstone. "The artist made it from car mirrors he got from the junkyard. He named it *The Selfie*. Last year City Council used tax dollars to fix it up. The volunteer fire department got caught trying to remove it after it sparked a number of brush fires."

Vance stared out the windshield. A bright red Audi R-8 roared past them crossing the double yellow line. The driver, hidden behind tinted windows, tooted the high-pitched horn.

"You know him?" Vance asked.

"It's a small town," Josh said, pivoting back to the artwork. "The council members are impressionable local yokels." He went on to explain it was marketing propaganda courtesy of a Brooklyn-based real estate developer who'd made campaign donations to local politicians. "When we get to the courthouse you'll see why siphoning those funds wasn't a good idea. Don't say I didn't warn you."

---

JOSH TOOK UP TWO SPOTS, parking the Humvee between a pair of listing visitor signs planted in the crumbling asphalt. The cinderblock building was by far the biggest on Main Street housing the Sheriff's Department, Justice of the Peace, Social Security, DMV, and county jail. It was the busiest place, too, but that wasn't saying much. Half the other buildings were boarded up, or were hanging on by a thread. The reflective film covering the plate-glass windows facing the parking lot peeled at the seams. A cheap trick to cover the blight.

Inside, the linoleum was yellowed and the brittle window blinds listed. An elderly couple sat apart in school desks separated by an unoccupied one. Distorted silhouettes moved on the other side of the frosted glass partitioning the waiting room from the back office.

"You'd have to murder all your hopes and dreams to work here," Lauren said.

"You should keep your voice down." Josh smiled when he said it.

The glass window screeched open. The woman sitting on the other side had eyebrows drawn like arrowheads.

"Hello, Josh. Them boys back there is ornery," Sue said. "Guess you're here to pick 'em up. Could still smell the whiskey on 'em when I come into work this morning."

Sue held her hand out. Josh cocked his head at Lauren. Sue raised her cartoon eyebrows, surprised when Lauren handed her the envelopes stuffed with hundreds.

She heard it first, then turned to look through the tinted picture window. The exotic sports car that had passed them on the way to town roared past the courthouse, heading the opposite direction, back toward the highway, going at least three times the speed limit. No one seemed to care.

"Sheriff makes me count it first. I'll be right back." Sue closed the creaky window and disappeared.

A minute later the door separating the back office opened. The four men walked through, single file. She was shocked at the sight of Jake, who looked the worst for wear. He stared at his loafers: Blood the color of coffee had caked on one leg from a gash on his kneecap. The whites of his eyes were mottled with red spider webs and Sue was right, he smelled like booze.

Jake held up a dollhouse-sized toothbrush by the handle,

with bristles that looked like tiny blades of plastic grass. He tossed it in the trash near the door. Drama King to the end.

Sue called out the names of the two folks who'd been waiting. The chair legs screeched as the man and woman struggled to get out from the antique school desks.

Josh unlocked the Hummer doors. Lauren sat up front with Josh. The guys spread out into the second and third row seats.

The mid-morning sun beat down on the windshield. Vance cracked the window to let fresh air in. Josh turned down a side street and crossed over a set of railroad tracks, stopping just outside a junkyard. Behind the chain-link fence topped with rolls of barbed wire sat the rented Suburban with a thin coating of dust.

"Wait here," Josh said. He jogged to the mobile trailer set on blocks and knocked on the window.

A toothless wonder answered. Lauren rolled the window down to listen.

"You know the drill, sonny. Cash only. Four hundred." He leaned out the trailer with his forearms on a plywood counter attached with rusted C-clamps, and spat.

Jake got out. "This is bullshit," he said, peeling four one hundreds from his money clip.

"I'll give you a tip," the old codger growled, snatching the money from Jake.

Jake took the bait. "What's that?"

"Don't bet on the horses."

"Fuck off." Jake grabbed the key fob from the man's bony hand and stalked back to the Hummer.

"This fucking town is corrupt," Frank said from the back seat.

"A DUI is a DUI," Vance said. "And all towns are corrupt. You're just not used to not knowing who to call to get your Get Out of Jail Free card."

"I wasn't driving drunk." Jake's tone was one of defeat. He was sitting behind her and the secondhand whiskey was strong. "It was a set up."

Jake told them what happened. They listened quietly while the ones who'd been with him overnight in the cell did not rebut one bit of Jake's account of events.

---

OTHER THAN A LAYER of dust on the bodywork and the stench of booze fermenting where Torres doused the interior, Jake was relieved the rental car was in good order. His overnight bag hadn't been opened and the other bags and hunting gear appeared untouched. Josh told Jake to get his belongings and load them into the back of the Hummer, saying he'd have to stop for gas to make it to Midland.

"Midland? Why?" Jake asked, lugging his stuff between vehicles.

"I'm going to drive you to the airport. The guys can follow us in the rental. Go back and tell them."

Jake went to the driver's-side window and told Frank about the plan.

When he got back to the car, Vance and Josh were in a heated discussion.

"That's six, maybe seven hours round trip," Vance said. "Bailing them out is enough, in my humble opinion. If we leave now we won't get back until afternoon."

Jake was pissed. "You try spending a night in that hell hole, you selfish prick." Then he looked at Josh. "Thank you. I appreciate your generous offer. And so do the other guys. We just want to get back to Houston."

"We take care of our own," Josh said, pulling out of the service station with a full tank of fuel.

"I'm never coming back to this shithole town, ever." Jake paused to consider it. "Unless I fly private. These people are crazy."

About five miles east of town he noticed Josh staring at the rear view. Jake craned his head around from the back seat. In the distance he saw a cloud of steam spewing from the hood of the rented SUV. It had dropped back behind them and was now pulling onto the shoulder of the road. Frank flashed the headlights through the haze.

Jake felt a rush of adrenaline as a dark-brown pickup with a yellow flashing bar dove in behind the Chevy. Josh's gaze moved back to the windshield. The big green and white Interstate sign read: Midland/Odessa 151 Miles. Jake felt the Hummer lurch forward. He looked at the speedometer. Josh was driving 95 mph.

"WHERE ARE THE LAWYERS?" Vance asked when he looked out the back window a few minutes later. He'd been busy trying to change Jake's ticket using the app on Jake's phone.

Josh was cavalier. "I don't know. Maybe they had to stop to use the restroom."

Jake kept quiet. Any allegiance he might have felt toward Frank was eclipsed by the notion of getting entangled in anything that had to do with the Marfidio County Sheriff's Office. Besides, what did Frank do when that dirty deputy forced him to drink at gunpoint?

"The airline wants to hit you with a two-thousand-dollar fee for a new ticket." Vance held up a banner message on the app warning passengers that new tickets would have to be booked if missed and/or delayed flights hadn't been cancelled in advance.

Jake would pay double that to get out of town. "Go ahead and buy it." Adding, "It's probably a bonanza for them. Think of all the people who forgot to cancel when the storm hit. You know what they say, never let a good crisis go to waste. We loved them on Wall Street."

He took his phone back from Vance. The boarding pass was on the screen. He tried calling the lawyers. Their phones went directly to voicemail, one by one.

"That's weird," Jake said. "They're not answering their cells."

"It looked like they might have had car trouble," Lauren said.

Vance leaned forward in the space in between the center console. "Why didn't you say something?" He sounded mad.

She shrugged. Jake was secretly thanking the Lord Almighty that she'd kept her mouth shut.

Lauren checked the time. It was a little before 3:00 in the afternoon. Thanks to Josh's disregard for the speed limit, they'd made the airport run in record time. A white van idled at the ranch gate and when the driver saw them, he backed onto the shoulder, letting Josh through. The man at the wheel of the panel van tailed the Hummer up the gravel drive. Josh turned left toward the lobby and the van driver hung a right, heading toward the dirt access road behind the guestrooms.

"Let's go see where he's going," Vance said to her as she stepped out of the Hummer.

By the time she and Vance got to the courtyard, the van had disappeared from sight. They could see it again from the end of the row of guestrooms. Luther was directing the driver with hand signals. The van stopped parallel to the *acequia*, blocking the footbridge, and the driver and his passenger got out.

She and Vance found a shady spot beneath a juniper, and watched. The guy in charge and his helper carried a canvas laundry cart over the bridge. Luther berated them for being late.

"What are they doing?" Lauren whispered.

"I don't think they're picking up laundry."

"Oh my God. Are you thinking what I'm thinking?"

"Yep."

Lauren covered her mouth with her hand.

"Pretty creative, I have to admit," Vance said. "Loading the body into a laundry cart to get it out. This is definitely not on the up-and-up."

They watched the two men carry the canvas cart, big enough to fill a service elevator, and place it on the porch blocking the doorway to Maria's little abode.

Vance jumped up.

"Where are you going?"

"To see what they're doing." Vance broke into a trot.

She followed, walking briskly. When she got to the house, Vance and Luther were having words. The cart was clearly too wide to make it through the narrow front door. While they argued, the two men loaded a big bundle of laundry into the cart. The taller of the two pulled the brim of his blue ball cap down, hiding his face.

"This is how the coroner collects bodies around here?" Vance sounded agitated.

Luther pushed back. "Do you have a better idea, detective? Maybe a hearse blaring *You Raise Me Up*? Or an SUV with ME decals on the doors? Is that what you had in mind? I thought we agreed to keep it low key. Do you want me to call the local florist and have some wreaths delivered?"

While Vance and Luther bickered, the two men carried the cart like a hovercraft, the small black wheels turning randomly. They walked it over the bridge and loaded it into the back of the van.

Vance turned and jogged toward them but by the time he got there, the driver was backing to turn around. Vance held his hand up to stop the driver. The fellow behind the wheel rolled the window halfway down and slowed, but he didn't stop. He wore a navy-blue ball cap with a needlepoint American flag stitched onto the crown. Vance looked through the driver's-side window. A mesh metal grate partitioned the cab from the cargo area. Vance jogged next to the window, trying to have a drive-by conversation with the driver.

"It's a laundry pick up."

"Yeah, right. You loaded a body into that basket," Vance said, flipping his head toward the area behind the driver. "Are you the medical examiner?"

"I'm not at liberty to give out information."

Vance was still trying to keep up on foot as the driver drove slowly toward the sloped driveway.

She was trying to catch up, running a few steps behind him so she could listen.

He panted. "I'm one of the owners."

"Oh. So you're new around here. You need to talk to the Justice of the Peace. The sheriff can help you with that."

"Hey, wait a minute—"

The driver cut him off, rolling the window up and gunning the accelerator, creating a bloom of dust and a spray of pebbles. She and Vance stopped and turned away, covering their faces, coughing.

"What were you going to ask him?"

"Who he's working for. He's not with the coroner."

She looked at him pensively. "Agreed. This thing is getting fishier by the minute."

The little house was buttoned down, curtains drawn, front door locked. And there was no sign of Luther.

## 11

Sheriff Rodriguez walked to the car window and tipped his hat. Frank rolled the window down on the dead Tahoe. A hissing came from under the hood and a chemical smell wafted from the cloud of steam.

"Step out of the car," Manny said.

Frank opened the door. "I don't know what happened. All of a sudden a warning light came on the dash and the engine shut down."

A milky haze spewed from seams in the hood.

"I don't smell whiskey, do I?"

*Of course you smell whiskey. Your fuckwad rogue deputy doused the interior with eau de 18-year-old Scotch less than twenty-four hours ago.* "You have to be joking," he said.

Manny's head bobbled. "Looks like you fellas are slow learners on a number of fronts. You city boys should have checked the fluids before heading out."

The associate riding in the back tapped the screen on his cell.

Manny stuck his head in the SUV. "You two, out. And gimme your phones."

When the engine seized up, Frank had flashed the head-lights and blared the horn but the Humvee kept on going: *How had Josh missed that?* Now it was barely a dot on the horizon.

The sheriff instructed him to step in front of the rental. Through the dissipating vapor he saw the fresh handprints on the dusty hood. If it were possible, Frank would have kicked his own ass. He'd been distracted at the tow lot, checking the luggage, hurrying. He'd wanted to get out of that godforsaken town, back to civilization.

Manny ordered them into his patrol truck. The junior lawyers climbed in back, trying to make eye contact with Frank, their expressions imploring.

He avoided them. Playing it back in his head, there was no scenario that would have caused him to check the hood for handprints. The rented SUV had been towed, and even if he'd seen the marks, it wouldn't have sent a red flag. Frank snapped out of it when Manny rolled down the windows, letting desert dust and dry heat fill the cabin.

The sheriff pulled in around back at the courthouse. He commanded them out of the vehicle and walked them in through the back door. The only delay that might have been afforded them before being locked back up in the filthy box— prints and mug shots—had already been done.

"What are we here for?" Frank froze when he saw three scary dudes in the cell, blue tears tattooed beneath their eyes.

Manny said nothing.

"You're not putting us in there, with them," Frank said.

"Only got one jail cell," the sheriff said.

Deputy Torres joined his boss. "We meet again. Immigration is coming to get 'em. We hold felons for Border Patrol 'til ICE picks 'em up. Sue's got a pool up front taking bets on which one a-ya gets out first."

Manny unlocked the cell door and motioned the three attorneys in. They hesitated, trying to talk their way out of going back into the cage.

Torres drew his weapon.

The lawyers inched toward the rusted bars. Surely the sheriff would come to his senses. They could be killed. The younger attorneys ventured in first, cowering.

Torres said something in Spanish to the prisoners already being held, flipping his head up in a gesture of daring.

Frank hoped it was warning not to slaughter them. He joined the Oklahomies where they huddled in one corner. Frank squatted on the concrete and put his head between his knees. He'd been worrying he'd be pulled over for speeding when he'd clocked Josh doing 95 mph. He'd decided to drop back and abide by the speed limit until they were out of the county limits. Either way, it turned out, he was destined for hell.

"Don't we get to make a phone call?" one of the associates asked.

"I don't think so," Frank said.

"That's right, honey buns."

He hadn't noticed Surly Sue there.

"Play nice," she said, closing the door between the office and the cell.

The shirtless gangbangers circled the lawyers like prey. Frank's flight instinct kicked in and adrenaline flooded his system but he had no options other than to swell with fear.

Deputy Torres returned and barked again at them in Spanish. The men glared, then took a couple of steps back. The one who seemed to be their leader knelt and drew a line across the cement floor with his finger. He looked up at Frank with dead eyes.

Frank nodded, trying to not look scared shitless. He'd honor the imaginary demarcation. He didn't want trouble. More than that, he wanted to get out alive.

JAKE LANDED IN HOUSTON, not sure what to expect. Neither did the flight attendants or pilots who, during final descent, delivered various warnings about ground travel. The view from the window was surreal. Much of the metro area was submerged in a sea of brown water. He'd left his Porsche in long-term parking.

He'd checked with Davis several times either using the landline or making cell calls from town. Most hurricanes pummeled the coastal areas before racing inland. Harvey was different. It had stalled atop Houston dropping more than 50 inches of rainfall over several days, flooding more than 300,000 structures.

Davis had ridden out the storm on Jake's sixty-foot yacht. The most Davis had had to deal with was a step-up tide that barely breached the bulkhead. And a short power outage. The worst of the carnage was near the bayous, made far worse when the Army Corp of Engineers released water from the city reservoirs to avoid dam collapses.

Jake rode the airport shuttle to long-term parking. The Porsche had been spared. He drove south on I-45, toward the Highway 288 spur toward Freeport. Mountains of debris were piled on yards and streets in front of houses and businesses. Viewing the wreckage from the Interstate flyovers, he could see that Harvey had been an equal opportunity scourge. The rotting guts of homes, now piled curbside, revealed nothing about the socio-economic status of the ruins.

On the hour-plus drive south he settled on a local AM radio news station recapping the aftermath. Another named storm, Irma, had formed in the Gulf and forecast to be a beast. His phone buzzed. He looked at the number and let it go to voicemail: Frank's wife calling again. She'd left a near-hysterical voicemail while he was in flight. The partners at Pinch & Elders had left several messages, too, inquiring about the missing men.

The last leg of the drive was just as depressing. The refineries were back up and running, oozing plumes of tarnished silver exhaust. Flares from fifty-foot towers burned like giant candles. Police cars blocked the exits to the city of Lake Jackson. Brazoria County had taken the final brunt from Harvey when the rivers crested their banks, wiping out another 8,000 structures. It got little news coverage, eclipsed by the bigger catastrophe to the north.

Jake craved booze. His heavy drinking had *never* been his fault. Marital arguments, bickering kids, family visits, a crappy day on the golf course, closing a big deal, a hole-in-one, boredom, fatigue: These were just a few of the reasons he drank. He'd been sober for the longest stretch since junior high, and this time *it really wasn't his fault*. It was Deputy GO-FUCK-Yourself who made him drink until he puked his guts out on the side of the road.

He gripped the padded leather wheel of the sports car to steady his hands. His shirt felt damp, even with the air conditioning set to LO. He'd freshened up in the airport bathroom and changed clothes, but he needed a hot shower and decent food. He could use the company, even if it was Davis Frost's.

He'd been working hard to put the good pieces of his old life back together. After he'd sobered up, his ex-wife started taking his calls. His kids were speaking to him. He'd gambled his life savings on speculative real estate. That was right before the housing bubble burst. After that he needed more booze to blur the reality he was teetering on bankruptcy. The analysts predicted the housing market would recover in ten years. He didn't have enough to make it that long.

Jake Fleming did not go through the agonizing process of cleaning up so some asshole deputy could make him chug booze on I-FUCKING-10 in West Texas.

If it weren't for the Pinch & Elders lawyers who'd witnessed it, no one would believe he'd been framed for a DUI, least of all his most current ex-wife. He'd run a lot of worst-case scenarios that would lead to a relapse, but something like this had never crossed his mind.

He turned off before a huge, rainbow-shaped bridge over the Intracoastal Waterway and took a left beneath it, heading toward the marina. A couple stood on the elevated deck of their modest canal front home, staring at his Porsche 911 GTR. The car's engine whined notes of constrained horsepower, a magnificent sound that stood out from the cacophony of heavy workboats passing through.

Davis stood on the wooden dock waiting for him, his hulking body a landscape of cleavages formed from fat. Jake parked and boarded the boat.

"You look bad, boss."

If he looked nearly as bad as he felt, a vulture might land on his shoulder. "Tough couple of days. Boat looks great." He walked the bow and surveyed her, brown water lapping at the hull. The wake from a barge rocked the yacht, upsetting his stomach. The marina owners weren't big on maintenance. "Place looks like it did when I left." Which in this case, was positive.

"Weird," Davis said. "A storm that big comes ashore and floods the metro area." He shrugged his flabby shoulders. "Doesn't make sense. We had nonstop rain and a high tide. But that's it."

"They're calling it a thousand-year flood. Except now it's yesterday's flood."

He'd intentionally withheld information from Davis. He and Vance had hidden thirty million in cash in the hull of the *Arm*. The reason Jake didn't tell Davis about it wasn't because he was worried Davis would rip them off. He kept it secret because Davis was no fool. He'd know the types who'd come calling.

Jake had a problem. Frost hated Freeport and wanted to go home to Florida. When he'd hired Davis to captain the yacht from Miami to Texas it was with the understanding that Davis would stay on a month or so. Then shit kept on happening and then Hurricane Harvey came along and Jake got stuck in West Texas. He'd hoped that Davis would change his mind and want to stay longer. The opposite happened. Davis hated Freeport more now than he did the first day they'd arrived.

Jake was prepared to make him an offer he couldn't resist but Davis refused to hear him out. The new named storm, Irma, just might work in Jake's favor, buying the time he needed to sort things out.

Jake showered and napped, and when he awoke, he found Davis sitting in the galley, drinking a cold beer. The faint smell of alcohol activated the obsession. He wanted to go topside to get some fresh air but Davis warned him that the mosquitoes were big as helicopters, and hungry too. He half-listened as Davis rambled on about how Freeport sucked and how much he wanted to get back home to Plantation Key.

Davis showed Jake the news bulletin that flashed on his phone. Irma, now forecast as the most ferocious hurricane *ever* to form over the Gulf of Mexico, was making a beeline for Florida. It wasn't a matter of where she'd make landfall, only which direction she'd turn after crushing the Florida Keys. Jake had seen the ramshackle rental where Davis lived. As far as he was concerned, a Cat Five hurricane would be a gift to the property owner who could 'doz the land and build something worthy of the location.

"Oh, I almost forgot," Davis said. He came back with a box. "This came for you today."

Jake wasn't expecting a delivery. He took it into the galley and used a kitchen knife to cut the packing tape on the box. Rummaging through the Styrofoam peanuts he found a shoebox filled with tissue paper. He opened it and held it up. "Jesus. What the fuck?" At first it looked dead but then the scorpion tried to trot up the sides of the milk bottle.

"What is that?" The fat on Davis' forehead folded in half.

Jake set it down. "A scorpion. In a bottle."

"Cool beans. Let me see it." Davis picked it up and put his eye an inch from the glass. "It's an emperor scorpion. These guys can live six to eight years."

Whoever sent it had poked tiny air holes in the metal cap.

"They don't need water . . . they need heat and humidity," Davis said. "And somewhere to hide."

Jake went back and inspected the box but there was no label on it.

"Who delivered it?"

"A courier."

"Did you sign for it?"

"You mean, like get a receipt?"

"Yeah."

"No. The guy knew your name. I figured you were expecting it." He shrugged. "Did I do something wrong?"

"Did you see a company name on the truck? A logo, maybe?"

"Not that I remember. I think the guy parked by the clubhouse and walked over. I don't know."

It couldn't be a mistake if the delivery guy knew his name. And where to find the *Arm*.

"Can I have it?"

Jake raised his eyebrows.

"The scorpion. Can I have it?"

"It's either that or take it to the dumpster. Or drop it overboard."

Davis studied the scorpion.

Jake said, "Sure. Keep it. Give it a name. Make it your new friend. Just don't let the fucking thing out."

"Okay," Davis said.

"I'm not kidding. Give me your word."

"I promise." Davis held the glass bottle in his open palms and grinned at the creature inside.

Jake ran calculations in his head. Who knew where the *Arm* was docked? It was a short list. And who would send him a scorpion in a bottle? Someone was sending a message but it wasn't making any sense.

## 12

"Oh my God, is that who I think it is?" Lauren was starstruck.

Rosa nodded, not nearly as enamored.

He was simply *the hottest actor* in the Milky Way. She'd read somewhere that he was five-foot-seven, but seeing him in the flesh, she guessed his PR team added a couple of inches.

"My wife says you have a tip sheet for stargazing?"

*Wife?* That ruined it.

Rosa handed him a brochure. A woman arrived. Lauren recognized her from magazine covers, the supermodel who'd quit the runway to raise a family, and who towered over the actor.

Lauren waited until they were gone. "They're together?"

"They're married. And they're here with their kids. And they're regular guests. Gee, Ms. Gold, you're going to have to get over it. We get a lot of famous people here."

"I know." But still.

"A lot of them are businessmen. I wouldn't know most of them from Adam. Did you know Mr. Pompadour made his fortune in technology, that he made an early investment in a computer company before it went public and took over the world? It's so interesting how people make their money."

Yesterday she'd accepted an invitation from Josh to go on a horseback ride. Lauren had been on her way to the stables when seeing the actor at the desk distracted her. Then the bit about how Roy made his money piqued her interest.

"Some of the tech billionaires are practically celebrities," Rosa said.

Lauren watched the actor and his wife join their kids at the pool. While it was true lots of people earned their money in interesting ways, she'd planned on keeping the way she got hers a secret. After meeting Frank Conn she told him she'd inherited the three million she'd invested. Fibbing to Frank was a reconnaissance mission, sort of like testing out the lie. "I guess after you make your first billion, it's hard to remain anonymous," she finally said before heading out to meet Josh.

She got to the barn before Josh and was bent over, cleaning the inside of a hoof with a metal pick when he walked up behind her.

"A gal who knows her way around horses." He grinned and nodded. "I'm impressed."

She'd thrown a heavy Western saddle over the hitching rail and when she was finished grooming the animal, slung it gently atop the horse's back and cinched the girth.

Josh took a rope halter from a hook hanging next to the tack room door and hung it over his left shoulder. "Why did you pick old Smokey?" he asked, referring to the horse.

"I stole an apple from the dining hall and stuck it in my coat pocket. I decided the first one that came to the gate to get it would be the one I'd ride."

He smiled big and shook his head.

She put her left foot in the stirrup, grabbed the saddle horn, and pulled her body up on the horse's back. Josh was tacking up a flashy animal, one she guessed to be his personal horse. His coat gleamed copper everywhere except behind the saddle where it looked like a Dalmatian's coat had been glued on.

Waiting for him to finish up, she tested Smokey, kicking him gently in the flanks and working the reins in her fingers. The horse didn't respond, desensitized like a pack mule. Perfect. A tour bus with hooves.

Vance had acted strange when she'd told him Josh had invited her out to ride. He wouldn't have come with them even if he had been invited. He had an irrational fear of horses.

Josh stuck two fingers in his mouth, let out a sharp whistle, and swung his leg over the Appaloosa's back. A twelve-gauge shotgun hung loosely over his shoulder. He whistled again. "Cheks."

A black-and-white spaniel appeared from out of nowhere. The dog was on high alert, ears pricked, tail pointed.

She grabbed hold of the saddle horn. The kind of sport horses she was used to riding would have reared up or spun, but not Smokey. He could have cared less. He was a dude ranch horse, trained to follow the leader.

"What sort of dog is he?"

"An English Springer Spaniel."

*Cheks?* "Patches might be a better name." His coat was marked like a Paint horse with big splotches of black on white.

"His full name is Chekov's Gun. Cheks for short. He came from a breeder in Dallas. He was Mr. Pompadour's dog."

She was learning more and more about Roy. He liked dogs.

"Mr. Pompadour predicted that within a generation the attention span of the average human would be fifteen seconds and hoped he could stave it off by keeping good books on the shelves at the ranch."

"I think it's already down to about ten seconds." She'd admired the classic Westerns filling the rustic hutches.

"Chekov's Gun. Cute." The dog barked as if to agree. "That's a pretty fancy vest he's wearing."

Josh clucked and his mount, Spot, picked up the pace to a brisk walk, the dog trotting ahead of them. She rode in lockstep as they headed south toward the foothills.

"State-of-the-art. It's made of Kevlar. Roy bought it from an Army buddy who's in the business. You'd be surprised how much the Department of Defense spends on high tech K-9 gear. By the time a bomb sniffer is trained, the Army has fifty thousand dollars invested. He's wearing the same thing the dogs in Iraq and Afghanistan wear. If I take it off now, he acts insecure and whimpers." Josh laughed. "Springer Spaniels are smart. *Yah.*" Josh leaned forward, spurring his horse into a gallop.

Lauren's horse tucked in behind and followed his. When they reached the base of the mountains, she stood in the stirrups leaning over Smokey's neck, making it easier for the horse to climb.

The panorama from the mesa where they stopped to rest was spectacular. Copying Josh, she dismounted and led her horse on foot. He stood beneath a double-decker cliff ledge bigger than the one they were on. He showed her pictographs and fossilized handprints left by the native Indians who'd lived on the land 900 years ago.

"The mesas and canyons were formed by flows of igneous rock. Basically, it's a dead volcano."

The Chinati mountain-scape was nothing like anything she'd ever seen. From a mile away the reservoir water feeding Antelope Creek looked like a thread of liquid turquoise.

"It's more amazing than I expected." The ranch buildings amounted to tiny matchboxes set on the desert floor. The satellite view didn't do it justice.

"Roy bought the ranch out of a personal ambition to restore the land. He spent years studying photographs and talking to the locals so he could return it to its original condition. He fought tooth and nail with the Texas Parks and Wildlife Department. The residents were suspicious, like folks around here have a right to be.

"The town has been plundered more than once. Miners struck silver in the late eighteen-eighties." He covered his eyes with his hand to break the sunlight. "But like most big discoveries, only a few profited. When Roy bought it, it was just ruins. It's the water, of course, that makes the land valuable."

"I saw the front page of the local paper. And from your reaction in the car, I guess it's a big deal that the Pronghorns are making a comeback."

"Look," Josh pointed to a herd of bison grazing on the mesa below. "Roy imported them from a rancher in Montana. He planted all that prairie grass, too. He spent millions. He wanted this part of the earth to be his gift to the people. And the first time he saw a satellite view on the Internet, he went ballistic."

It was the perfect lead in. "When I did a Google Earth search, I saw a black bar over the buildings. I didn't know you could get them to do that."

"Roy hated the invasion of privacy," he said, turning one hand into a telescope and putting it over his eye, smiling. "The way they spy on everyone and everything. Come on. Let's go."

They mounted their horses. She hadn't noticed Cheks was MIA until he dashed out from behind a big boulder, panting and pointing with his right front leg bent at the knee. The stainless-steel accents on his bulletproof jacket glinted in the full sun.

A series of shots rang out. More like explosions.

Smokey leapt sideways. She grabbed the saddle horn to keep from falling.

It boomed like a Civil War cannon. She regained her balance and grabbed a hunk of mane with her palm, winding the hair around her hand. Her body stiffened, putting the horse on high alert. More shots blasted, echoing off the canyon walls, making it impossible to know where they were coming from. Her heart pumped.

Josh's horse pricked his ears but was otherwise oblivious. "Follow me."

Her horse galloped behind his, hooves pounding the hard ground, resonating like a stampede. They took cover behind a wide opening near the covered mesa wall. Josh dropped the reins and pulled the shotgun from over his shoulder. He rested it horizontally across the horse's withers and unfastened the hand-held radio from a leather case attached to his belt. He pushed a bud into his ear and holding the talk button, pressed his lips close to the microphone.

"Are there any hunters in the vicinity?"

He gave their location to whoever was on the other end of the radio. Smokey's back twitched under the saddle pad. His horse nuzzled stems of foliage sprouting from the rock wall.

She swallowed hard, nervously working the mane in her fingers, waiting for a verdict.

"That was Luther. One of the guests wanted to hunt. I'm the guide, but since I was out, they sent someone else." He slung the rifle over his shoulder. A private jet appeared as a dot on the horizon. He took a set of field glasses from his saddlebag and peered through them.

"Race you back," he challenged her, slapping his horse on the neck, using the loose ends of the reins.

"I'm reporting you to PETA."

He laughed. "I dare you."

The horses galloped back to the barn with necks stretched forward, ears laid back and tails flying. She and Smokey beat Josh and Spot by two seconds with Cheks coming in a close third.

Dismounting, he asked, "Are you and Vance . . . a couple?"

"Oh, God, no."

"Are you married?"

"No." Why the sudden barrage of questions?

"Been married?"

"Yes. What about you?"

"No." He pulled the saddle off Spot's back. "I came close, right after I graduated. I bailed out a week before my bachelor party. Didn't seem like the right move."

That was a multi-part surprise answer. "Where did you go to school?"

"High school or college?"

"Both? Either?"

"I went to boarding school in Connecticut. Then I went to Rice."

The last answer threw her for a triple loop-de-loop. That was an expensive school. "Rice University? In Houston?"

"Yeah. I graduated the Jones School of Business with an MBA."

The school was as Ivy League as it got, in Texas.

"You look surprised."

Shock was more like it. Josh put his hand on her shoulder. It was a brotherly gesture; still it was awkward. She took a big step away, reached up, and pulled the bridle over Smokey's ears.

"I could ask you the same thing, you know. Where did you get your money? But I already know you inherited it."

"Who told you that?

"Your lawyers told *my lawyers*."

"Whoa," Lauren stuttered. "*Your* lawyers?"

"You bought the ranch from a blind trust."

She didn't know exactly what that meant. Jake had handled the deal. And Vance.

He put his hand on her shoulder again. "I wasn't planning on staying. Now with what's going on, I'm not leaving. Not yet."

"What are you saying?" Then it dawned on her. "Why didn't I know this, before I agreed to invest?"

"That's the point," Josh said, "of a blind trust."

An old ranch hand with a tanned turkey neck met up with them. Josh spoke to him in Spanish. The man untied the horses and led them to the irrigated grass pasture.

"Let's do it again sometime," he said. "You ride well."

She tried a fake smile but couldn't make it happen. He'd ended conversation before she'd figured out how to keep it going. She had so many questions. Instead of getting information or clarifying anything, she was now more confused. How could Josh be the seller and her not know? Why had the ranch been held in a blind trust for Josh? What was his connection to Roy Pompadour? She needed to tell Vance right away.

## 13

Vance was going over food and beverage costs with Luther when he saw Lauren stalking back to the main lodge. She crossed the courtyard and entered through the back door. He excused himself and met her at the guest refrigerator. Lauren pulled the sliding glass door open and grabbed a bottle of water.

"The deaf apparently eat and drink twice as much as the hearing do, and according to Luther they were on the meal plan. How was your trail ride?"

"Troubling."

Vance cocked his head. "How so?"

She told Vance about nearly falling off, about the gunfire.

"I've been with Luther since you left. He didn't use his radio."

"Maybe you missed it."

"Like I'm blind, and hard of hearing?"

"That's not what I meant. Maybe you went to the men's room, or something."

"I never left his sight."

Luther had stayed at the table, going over the documents.

"Maybe Luther left the table?"

"No. I'm pretty sure he didn't."

Vance took a few seconds to reconsider the possibility and insisted he'd been hunkered down with Luther, going over paperwork the entire time.

Then she told him about the blind trust.

He raised his eyebrows. "He told you that?"

"Uh-huh."

"And you believed him?"

"Why wouldn't I? Why would he lie about it?"

"A fucking blind trust. Blind to keep us in the dark. That's bullshit."

"Josh went to prep school in Connecticut. He has an MBA from Rice University."

"We'll see about that." Vance marched toward the table where Luther sat, the heels of his boots pounding the big tiles. Luther looked up, unfazed by the body language.

"Josh told Lauren that we bought the ranch from him. Is that true?"

Luther didn't seem the least bit surprised. He stroked his goatee.

"You knew?" Vance asked. *Of course he fucking knew.*

Luther's tone turned ugly. "You should talk to Josh about it. I just work here."

He was such a prick. The urge to punch him in the mustache was getting unbearable. "You 'just work here' when it suits you. When it comes to making important decisions, like reporting a suspicious death, you're an authority. You can't have it both ways." Damn him. He wished like hell he could fire him on the spot but they needed him until they got the lay of the land.

"It's a common way to do business, especially when one is concerned about conflicts of interests." Luther said it holier than thou.

"What conflict?" Vance folded his arms tight against his ribs, just in case one arm went its own way, right into Luther's teeth.

"Potential conflicts. You're a lawyer. Josh has a business degree. You should talk to him. You'd have plenty to discuss."

Lauren moved closer to where Luther sat. "Did Vance tell you that someone put a scorpion in my room last night?"

She surprised Vance, but it was well played.

Luther's eyebrows winched upward as if being pulled by some invisible force. "That is strange. Are you sure it didn't come in on its own accord? We are, after all, in the high desert and we do have some unpleasant wildlife that makes its way onto the grounds, and under doors, from time to time."

Vance lowered his voice to a theater whisper. "It was in a bottle, like a ship. I doubt it floated in."

"Oh," Luther said, tapping his forehead with his middle finger, "I almost forgot. The sheriff wants you to call him. He has some news, something to do with your lawyers. Use the landline at the desk. I am sorry about that scorpion." Luther's two-way radio squelched. He put the earpiece in and tapped it. "Luther here," he said, followed by "Be right there," to the person on the other end. "Excuse me, you two. I've got to run. Josh wants to talk. Some sort of problem."

After Luther was out of earshot, Vance said, "A suicide that's looking more and more like a homicide. The body is hauled away in a laundry cart. The hunting guide just happens to be the anonymous seller, who had to have a connection to the previous owner, and guess who's not here."

"I know," Lauren said. "Jake. Don't forget the special delivery scorpions."

"Oh, yeah." He palmed himself on the forehead. "Have you heard from him—Jake? He's the one who got us into this mess."

"Speak for yourself. I'll try calling him after you talk to the sheriff," she said following Vance to the front desk.

He closed the door to Rosa's office and dialed the courthouse. After he hung up, he told Lauren the lawyers had been rearrested.

"Why? Did he say?"

"You mean she. And no, she didn't say." He figured the voice belonged to the squatty woman with helmet hair and cartoon brows who doubled as the jailhouse cashier.

Lauren drilled holes in him with her eyes. One shoulder twitched. "I thought they had car trouble."

"Call Jake, see if he got back okay."

"What should I tell him? About the lawyers?"

He paused. "Don't tell him anything."

"This is starting to feel like a shakedown," she said.

Lauren got Jake's number from her service-less cell and dialed Jake from the ranch landline. Vance stepped out for some fresh air. He spotted Josh and Luther meeting by the pool. He crouched behind the manicured hedge and listened in. They were talking about the scorpion Lauren found in her room.

"There was one in my room, too. I don't care where those evil-as-shit-looking land lobsters came from." Luther was mad. "This is unacceptable, Josh. This is totally and completely unacceptable. You need to find out who's doing this. Oh, and one more thing: Why did you tell her they bought the ranch from you?"

Vance wished he could see the look on Josh's face.

"They were going to find out sooner or later. I figured it was better to get ahead of it before someone else told them. It makes it look like I'm on their side, that we don't have anything to hide. Oh, Rosa wants to move into Maria's place."

"Really? She's not, um, a little disturbed at what happened there?"

"I didn't ask her. I think it's fine, if you agree."

"Sure. Why not. If I didn't have my own quarters in the tower, I'd want to live there. Privacy is a scarcity around here."

Luther and Josh split up and headed in different directions.

Vance saw Lauren crossing the courtyard and after they were gone, rose from behind the hedge and caught up with her.

"Jake got a delivery," she said. "From a courier, dropped off at the marina. Care to guess what was in it?"

"I give up."

"A scorpion in a bottle. He's not happy about it."

"Does he know who sent it?"

She shook her head.

"Wow, someone is definitely fucking with our heads. Go get ready," he said. "We need to bail the guys out again."

"Again?" She sounded angry. They'd just spent twenty grand they'd likely never see again.

He stared at her blankly.

Her nostrils flared. "Fifteen thousand more? Are you really going to let them play us like suckers?"

"Do you have a better idea?"

She stared at him silently, her fists balled in her jacket pockets.

"Do you have enough cash?"

She nodded. "I have to get cleaned up."

"You better hurry. We have just over an hour to get the courthouse or they're going to be spending another night in jail."

"Do they charge by the night?"

"Ha, ha. Hurry up. I don't want to know the answer."

Vance watched her stalk to her room.

He passed the desk and saw Josh huddling with Rosa. They looked a little too cozy.

LAUREN ANSWERED the door to her room about ten minutes later. "What now?"

Vance pushed his way inside and raked his hands though his hair. "Sheriff Manny just stopped by in person, to talk. He says the pathologist found DNA under Maria's fingernails."

"Like there was a struggle or something?"

He shook his head in disbelief. "He says the DNA's a match for Frank Conn's."

Her mouth dropped open and stayed that way for a few seconds. "No way." She felt like a rag doll falling into the over-size chair by the window. "This has to be a mistake. Or part of another shakedown."

"That's what I said. But when I pressed the sheriff, he said the crime lab got a hit. Frank's brother is in the database. He did one of those DNA tests, the kind they advertise on TV." Vance looked drained. "Manny said he had a hunch."

"Do you believe in hunches?"

"Only my own. And my hunch is we're in the middle of something. Something I don't understand." His eyes narrowed to slits.

"Is it even possible to run DNA that fast?"

"I asked that, too. The sheriff says certain crime labs can get a match in hours. It's called 'Rapid DNA.' He said he sent it to a lab in El Paso. It was set up so Border Patrol can access a national database quickly. Look at the bright side."

"What could that possibly be?"

"We only need to come up with ten thousand bucks instead of fifteen. Frank is being held without bond."

"What are the other two charged with?" She knelt on the woven Mexican rug in front of the small safe on the bottom shelf of the ornate armoire, and turned the dial on the door of the metal lockbox where she kept her emergency cash. It clicked open. A clear plastic baggie fell to the floor. "What the—?"

"Don't touch that." Vance sprinted across the room and picked it up by the corner, using his thumb and forefinger. He held it under the overhead light.

"It's a syringe. A used syringe with a needle."

"I have no idea how that got there." Her heart pulsed.

The money looked untouched and her watch and grandmother's diamond ring were still in the same place she'd put them for safekeeping, in front of the stacks of bank envelopes.

"It wasn't there when I opened the safe last time. I'm positive of that. I'd have seen it." A pit formed in her stomach.

He set the baggie on the dresser. "I'm gonna call Sarge. Maybe he can help with a forensic analysis. Under the radar. Someone planted this in your room for a reason."

Vance pulled his 9-mil Glock from the back waistband of his jeans and held it up. She'd laughed in his face when he'd told her he'd shipped the gun overnight ahead of their arrival. The ranch was practically a munitions depot with firearms and ammo. Now it didn't seem so stupid. Or funny.

"I can't come up with a motive. Why would Frank kill the housekeeper?" Vance asked.

"Why am I being targeted?" She licked her lips.

"All three of us are being targeted. I think Jake *was* telling the truth about being framed for a DUI."

"Me, too," she said.

"Hurry up. We need to go get the guys. The clock's ticking."

Lauren handed him ten thousand cash and locked the safe. He took the baggie and told her he'd wait for her in the lobby.

---

VANCE HAD LIED: He intended to leave without her. He'd tracked the mileage from the morning trip. The Marfidio courthouse was a tick over twenty miles from the ranch. He put the baggie in his coat pocket, careful not to prick himself with the needle.

He took the Hummer without permission. Not only was Lauren going to be hacked off, so was Luther. It reminded him of the time he'd driven his father's car without asking, to impress a girl. That was in high school. When Luther told him he needed prior approval from either him or Josh to drive the ranch vehicle, he told Luther to fuck off. When no one was looking, he'd taken the keys from the hook in Luther's office.

En route to the courthouse, Vance dialed his friend, retired Sergeant Daniel Ruiz. The two had history going back to when Vance was still on active duty in Miami. Sarge was key to helping them salvage the millions of hidden cartel cash, from the same stash they'd used to buy the ranch. Unlike the rest of them, Ruiz turned out to be the only one who was incorruptible. He'd refused to accept a dime for his invaluable service.

He needed to get the syringe to him ASAP for a forensic analysis.

## 14

J ake didn't want to drive him to town but Davis had groveled. He'd been stuck on the yacht riding out Hurricane Harvey. The marina's wireless had been down since the storm hit and cell service was spotty. Davis wanted to go somewhere that served hot food and cold beer, where he could watch weather updates on a big screen TV.

He was too tired to drive and could use a hot meal too, but letting Davis get behind the wheel of his Porsche was out of the question. So he'd compromised sharing an Uber to Lake Jackson, about a dozen miles north from the marina. Davis had cracked open the back passenger's-side window. He rolled it up when he whiffed the strange odors coming from the refineries and chemical plants.

"We're here. Civilization." Davis hoisted his whale body out of the car.

The place didn't look at all like Jake's version of civilization. It was a chain restaurant where food was first defrosted, then microwaved. On the other hand, it was better than being cooped up with Davis on the *Arm*. Jake chuckled at a pickup truck with a gun rack and a bumper sticker parked in the handicapped spot:

## TEXAS,
## BIGGER THAN THE WHOLE COUNTRY OF FRANCE

He twirled lumpy fettuccine around a bent fork, trying to ignore Davis' frosty mug of beer when his phone buzzed in his pocket. He squinted at caller ID. Without his glasses he couldn't read the screen. "Hello." He stuck his finger in his free ear to listen through the crowd noise. He expected Lauren but this time it was Vance.

"Lauren said your boat made it through the storm."

"Yeah, lucky me."

"We have new developments."

"Oh yeah?"

"The lawyers, they've been arrested again. I'm on my way to bail out them out. Except they're holding Frank without bond."

"Why?" When the sheriff's truck had pulled in behind the rental, light bar flashing, Jake figured they'd stopped to lend roadside assistance for car trouble. He'd imagined Frank and the boys would miss their flight. But not this.

"The sheriff says they found Frank's DNA under the dead woman's fingernails."

"The housekeeper?" *No way.*

"There's more. Josh is the one behind the blind trust."

Jake lowered the phone and held it a full arm's length away. He planted it back on his ear. "Is this a joke?"

"No. That's what Josh told Lauren. The business about the DNA, that came straight out of the sheriff's mouth. And I overheard Josh and Luther talking privately about the sale." After an awkward silence, Vance asked, "Are you there?"

"Yeah, I'm here. What did you overhear?"

"Luther seemed angry that Josh told her about the blind trust," Vance said.

"Yeah. Keep me informed, I guess." It was too much to process all at once.

"Will do. Lauren said you got a surprise delivery."

*The scorpion.* "Horrible surprise. I've been trying to think of who would send it but I can't think of anyone who'd do that. It had to be someone who knew where my boat's docked."

"Lauren got the first one. Someone left it in her room."

"The *first* one?" He looked at Davis who was in a trance watching the projected path of Hurricane Irma on the TV hanging in the corner.

"Luther got one, too."

A baby began to cry at a nearby table. Jake turned his free ear against the booth.

"When are you coming back?"

"Um, I don't know," Jake lied. He had no plans to return. All he could think was how good a shot of whiskey would be right now. And how he'd rather lose three million bucks than return to the psycho ranch from hell.

"All right," Vance said before ending the call. "I'll keep you posted."


THE INVESTMENT WAS GETTING messier by the hour. Jake sat on his hands to hide the shakes. He needed a drink. The addiction specialist was right. She'd warned him that his alcoholism would pick up where it left off at the first drop. That's how it felt, like he was starting detox all over again. *Fucking Deputy Asshat.* At least Frank's wife had finally stopped calling, and so had his secretary at the law firm.

What did he really know about his old colleague, Roy Pompadour? Frank being held on suspicion of murder was shock enough. Finding out Josh was the seller turned it into a double whammy. Some of Jake's old business associates had told him Roy had turned political, donating more and more money to lobbyists and candidates. Jake had shrugged it off at first. Lots of businessmen, especially wealthy ones, gave to all the political parties. It was smart to be a whore and hedge all bets.

Roy's path to the top of Wall Street was the opposite of his. Roy was a Vietnam War commander who'd gone to college on the GI Bill. That made him an oddity amid the bluebloods and Ivy Leaguers on Wall Street. While there was no doubt the discipline needed on the battlefield was exactly the same skill set that could lead to big victories in deal making, it wasn't the norm. Jake's only encounter with the Vietnam War occurred attending a Listen-In during his freshman year. The organizers served pizza and, more importantly, free beer.

Roy had a Wikipedia page. Jake read he'd been petitioning US presidents for decades to recognize his Vietnam platoon for their extraordinary heroism. Roy had been injured, earning two Purple Hearts. The rest of the men had been ignored. Finally, three years ago they were honored with the Presidential Unit Citation. Roy's picture shaking the Democratic president's hand went viral. The partisans went wild.

Jake was a hard man to scare. After the call, he'd lost his appetite. The waitress dropped the check. Jake put his credit card inside the folder while Davis remained hypnotized by the Weather Channel.

---

SUE WAS the highest-ranking member on duty when Vance arrived at the County Courthouse. Probably because it was nearing closing time.

She recognized him. "Got the cash?"

He nodded, handing her the envelope.

"Ten thousand?"

"No."

"What do you mean, no?" she snarled, snatching the envelope from his hand and looking inside.

"Ten more, plus the twenty grand we gave you earlier. That's thirty thousand."

She tapped her cartoon eyebrow with the eraser head of a pencil. "Clever," she said pulling the squeaky frosted window shut, the outline of her body morphing into an alien-looking silhouette.

A couple of minutes later the two junior attorneys walked through the door, looking beat to hell. They were wearing the same clothes from yesterday. When they saw him, they got the wrong idea, thinking he was going to drive them to the airport. Sue opened the window and held out a plastic dog bowl. It had their personal effects in it. They approached cautiously and grabbed their wallets, phones, and keys.

He told them he wasn't driving them to Midland.

"*Please,*" the wimpy one pleaded.

"Drive the rental," Vance said. "You're lucky I got here before visiting hours were over."

"The engine is kaput. There was no oil or water in it," the other one said.

"Call a cab. Put it on your expense report. Make some taxi driver's day."

"Don't forget your suitcases," Sue hollered from the opening. She funneled her mouth with her hands. "They're 'round back. I'll meet ya there."

The associate lawyers didn't mention anything about leaving Frank behind.

"Look, I can give you a lift as far as the Waffle House," Vance said as they climbed in the Hummer, "but I can't go to Midland. It's getting late." He drove them around back to get their bags.

"Where're our rifles?" the shorter lawyer asked, looking at two small roller bags leaning against the exit door.

"What rifles?" Sue furrowed her forehead, her brows meeting in the middle, like a single stroke of brown crayon.

"What's going to happen to Frank?" Vance asked Sue.

She made a frowny-face and shrugged. "Ain't up to me, darlin'."

"Come on," Vance said to the men, "let's get out of here. I can drop you at the train station, if you'd like." He'd seen the Amtrak running the first day when he and Lauren drove in from Midland.

They looked at each other and nodded. "All right," the nerdy one with glasses said.

He loaded their bags into the back of the Hummer. From what Vance had learned about Roy, the associates weren't the kind of guys he would have liked. They were leaving their man, Frank, on the battlefield.

---

ON THE WAY back from the train station, Vance passed the tow yard. It was closed for the day. The rented Tahoe hung from the hook of an old wrecker, hood open, listing to one side, as if sent to the gallows for heavy metal. On the final stretch back to the ranch his phone went dark.

When Vance first pressed Luther about why there was no wireless or cell service, he'd confided that some of the tech execs had sophisticated satellite systems on their private jets that doubled as cell towers. What was the point of keeping the ranch off the grid if it could be circumvented?

He said Roy was old school and didn't want online discount resellers booking rooms. Okay, that was reasonable. Presently, guests had to make reservations on the landline or over fax.

Even credit card charges were done the old-fashioned way, over the telephone. Some clients were billed like it was 1999: snail mail, and paying by check. Weird for a guy who'd made his fortune in an early investment in technology.

Celebrity Chef Gordy assured Vance he'd get used to being off the grid and that it would be harder to go back to the connected world. He had his doubts. In fact, he hoped one of those tech execs with a portable cell tower landed soon. He'd grovel if need be in order to gain access.

Vance got to the only overnight drop off at 5:00 PM, missing the cutoff time by a half hour. He pulled a quarter from his pant pocket and dropped it in the bin. It thudded instead of clattering. Gambling the driver was running late, he filled out a form, stuck the baggie in an overnight envelope, checked the earliest delivery option, and dropped the package in the box. He backed into a spot in front of a Laundromat, watching for the delivery truck to show.

## 15

L auren slipped into the red bikini she'd packed but hadn't expected to wear. Unlike Florida when it was hot out, people in West Texas covered up. They preferred Wranglers to shorts, cowboy boots over flip-flops, and shade trees to chaise lounges. She'd unfurled the striped beach towel, stuck a floppy hat on her head and sprawled out on the chaise at the pool outside her room.

She'd seen Josh outside, driving stakes into the ground. Her favorite A-List actor paid notice. She hoped he'd go away. His supermodel wife appeared in a black one-piece and scowled when she saw him checking her out. Josh did a double take from a hundred yards away. *Good.* She waved to him, smiling. He said something to the workers and ambled toward the pool, Cheks tagging behind him.

Maybe Vance was back from his trip. If he was, she hoped he was spying on her from a window somewhere. It would be payback. She'd gone looking for him after breakfast. Luther told her that the Hummer was gone and so was Vance, even though he'd promised her he wouldn't go alone.

"The stargazer lilies at the front desk are a nice touch," Lauren said when Josh pulled up a chair and sat.

"Roy thought so. You're quicker than the others. For all the geniuses who've stayed here, not one of them ever made the connection."

"Oh, I'm hardly a genius. I've seen more stars here than I've seen in my life. It's so amazing."

Chekov's Gun sprawled out next to Josh's feet, wearing his fancy flak jacket. "Then again, there's no blue ocean. I suppose it depends on what speaks to you."

"True." She changed the subject to what was gnawing in her head. "Do think Justice Simeri's death was, um, natural?" She watched for a reaction; there wasn't one.

"You don't?"

A question answered with a question. She dropped her sunglasses to the tip of her nose.

"Seriously?" He took off the light jacket he was wearing and covered her torso. "The swimsuit? Bait to probe me for information?"

Her face felt as if on fire.

"You could have just asked me."

"Well, do you?" she asked, folding her knees to her chest and pulling his jacket close to her neck.

"I'm not going to lie. He was unpopular with people with certain political leanings. The oil and gas clients, they liked them, and he liked to hunt with them. He didn't hide his feelings about it."

"Which was?"

"That electricity and the combustion engine were the single greatest contributions to the advancement of humankind."

She reached over for her towel, holding his jacket over her bikini top. "What did he think about the Silicon Valley crowd?"

"He thought the first wave of tech was good, computers and

mobile phones. But the next wave, especially social media, not so much. Privately he called it Big Shit. He worried what it was doing to our children."

"What did he think it was doing?"

"Look, if you want to do your own investigation, get the guest list from February thirteenth of last year."

Her eyes narrowed behind her shades.

"Luther should have a copy."

"All Luther cares about is the online reviews."

"Don't ask him for it. Tell him to give it to you."

"And you think he'll hand it over?"

"Look, Roy believed the only way to keep information private was the old-fashioned way, on paper, in files that he kept in the office. Never on a computer connected to the Internet. He was very disciplined about that."

She pushed her sunglasses on top of her head. "Why was he so obsessed with privacy?"

"Roy knew information on the Web wasn't secure. The Internet was never intended for commerce, or banking, or privacy. Do you have any idea how much electricity it takes to keep Big Data's servers running?" He stood to leave. "If you wear hiking gear from LL Bean instead of an Armani suit, then you don't look like the rich guy on the Monopoly board with the mustache and the top hat." He paused. "Or if you wear a tiny red bikini, it won't look like you're trying to manipulate me because I will be become temporarily stupid. Because I'm a man."

"You're right, it was a bad choice." She felt like an idiot. She looked even more ridiculous double-wrapped in a towel over his coat.

"This place is yours now. Ask Luther for the list."

"Why are you telling me this?"

"Because I know you'll follow the lead." The dog got up

slowly. "I'll see you later. Just leave my jacket in the tack room. No rush."

How foolish she'd been. She jogged to her room, hoping no one would see her.

———————

WHEN VANCE HAD PARKED near the overnight drop box, he'd planned to wait for the driver to show up. Instead, he'd fallen asleep. The panel truck awoke him around seven PM. The hurried driver carried an armload of packages to his truck, scanned them, and tossed them in the back.

Vance did a three-point turn and headed back to the lodge, hoping it wasn't too late to get a hot plate of food, and that Lauren wouldn't see him and scold him like a schoolboy for taking the Hummer out all by his lonesome. None of those things happened.

THIS MORNING he'd snuck out again after Lauren went back to her room after breakfast. He was behind the wheel, on hold on his cell, waiting for the technician at the forensics lab in El Paso to pick up.

He stopped on the roadside, pulled the hot lighter from the dash, got out and lit a cigarette from a pack he'd found hidden in the center console. Staring at the red rings of metal on the tip of the car lighter, he drew on the filter.

It was probably a waste of time and energy sending the syringe out. He released the smoke slowly from the corner of his mouth, making a contrail that swirled upward and disappeared. He crushed the cigarette under the heel of his boot. The note he'd sent overnight with the syringe made it clear he needed that report ASAP.

"Mr. Courage?"

"Yes," he said, leaning against the vehicle.

"It tested positive for chloral hydrate."

"What's that?"

"It's a sedative. If mixed with alcohol it can cause a marked increase in CNS anomalies."

"In what?"

"Oh, sorry," Sarge's referral said. "Central nervous system. Choral hydrate can mimic a heart attack."

When Vance pressed him on his quick analysis, he told him it was so commonly used in homicides it was practically routine to test for it. He went into detail about the forensics, mixing minute traces of liquid in the syringe with potassium hydroxide and another chemical.

"When we heated it up, it turned red," the tech said.

"Did you test for prints?"

"Yup. There's a partial. Actually two partials."

"Any matches?"

"You know I can't tell you that. I'd need a court order. Sarge told me you're a lawyer. I'm already pushing the limits, telling you what I'm telling you." His voice dropped to a whisper. "This shit usually takes weeks. Sarge asked me to help you out. I cut a few corners, you know, to get you headed in the right direction. I'm not losing my job over a personal favor."

"I appreciate what you've done so far. What if I get a court order?"

"Get that and I'll give you everything I got."

"Where would one get choral hydrate?"

"It's a controlled substance. Someone in the medical business would have access. The *farmacias* across the border are like convenience stores. There's one on every corner. I'm from Del Rio. You couldn't get me to move back there for anything. I looked your ranch up, from the address on the shipping label. I'd make an exception, to go there."

"Maybe one day I'll invite you." He paused for a second. "How long does it take to do a DNA test?"

"Depends. A rape kit, saliva—"

"Saliva."

"We can turn it around in twenty-four hours. We charge a premium. Mostly we do paternity tests. The family lawyers, they can be demanding."

"What about for a criminal case?"

There was a long silence. "Depends on the lab." He was reluctant. "Let's just say faster than you'd think, hours if they have the resources. The capabilities of some of the crime labs near the big border towns are cutting edge, with the immigration issues, and family stuff. You know. You see the news."

He used to see the news. And even get blasts on his phone. But recently, he'd been living in the dark ages. Vance thanked him for his time and promised to work on getting a court order. He headed back to Antelope Creek Ranch.

The medical examiner who'd issued Simeri's death certificate listed the cause of death as natural. Simeri was overweight and almost eighty years old. It was believable. His family had declined an autopsy. On the other hand, hours after news of his death spread, the Senate Majority Leader released a statement that there would be no vote on his replacement until after the upcoming presidential cycle. That was last year. He made another mental note: Find out if Justice Simeri was drinking that night.

He still had cell service but the bars on his phone were fading. Rosa answered the landline. "Can you get Lauren on the phone?"

"You'll have to hold."

"Sure." He braced himself. She'd be angry. Lauren hadn't

noticed he'd sneaked away yesterday afternoon. At least she hadn't mentioned it over breakfast. But now she'd know. He calculated she'd forgive him since he had what might be useful information.

The broken yellow lines on the four-lane clicked by, hypnotizing him. The dull landscape was as different from Miami as it got. Where the blue water and warm climate of south Florida attracted transients and tourists, Marfidio was the opposite, more of a diapers-to-diapers place, the kind people never left.

"Hello."

Lauren's voice brought him back to the present. "Hey, it's me."

"Where are you?" She sounded snippy.

"On my way back from the land of cell service." He grimaced, admitting to her he'd slipped away yesterday and he'd shipped the syringe overnight. "I didn't tell you because I didn't want to get your hopes up." Avoiding a lecture was closer to the truth. "I got a preliminary report."

"Already?" Her tone switched to one of curiosity. "And?"

"It tested positive for chloral hydrate."

"What's that?"

He told her what the lab technician told him, adding, "It's rarely prescribed. It's mostly used for pre-op, for surgery." He'd looked it up on the Internet, on his phone, after the call with the tech who didn't want to get fired.

"That's weird," Lauren said.

"Do me a favor. Find a way to casually ask whether or not Justice Simeri was drinking that night."

"Hmm. I can ask Rosa. She might remember. Are you thinking what I think you're thinking?"

"Uh-huh. We might get lucky. There's fingerprint evidence on the syringe, too." He heard her take a short breath, a gasp.

"Oh my gosh. Do you know whose?"

"We can't get it without a court order."

"That's falls under your department. By the way, I'm still mad at you. You think I didn't know you left the ranch last night."

Wow. She knew. And kept quiet. "Sorry. I'm on my way back. I'll see you soon." He tapped the red dot on his phone. A six-foot rattlesnake slithered across the roadway, crossing the yellow line. By the time he saw it was too late. It felt like he'd run over a garden hose. Twice.

## 16

L auren sat at Rosa's desk behind the reception counter watching the cameras monitoring the gates. When she saw the Hummer, she slung her messenger bag over her shoulder, walked outside and waited at the top of the gravel driveway. Vance stopped, leaned down and unlocked the passenger's-side. She climbed in and rode to the main guesthouse, where Roy had lived when he was still alive.

He invited her inside. Roy's house was styled similar to the rest of the ranch. The furnishings were rustic and intricate, with hand-forged handles, shelves filled with brightly painted ceramics of many shapes and sizes. Streaks of sunlight poured through the tall archways dividing the rooms.

"So Josh just came out and told you we bought the ranch from him?" Vance asked, taking his boots off.

"Is that you that smells like a cigarette?" Riding in the vehicle she guessed it was secondhand smoke from a guest. But the smell was just as strong in the house.

"Geez. You're turning into Nancy Drew. Okay, guilty as charged. I smoked a cigarette." He was looking at the navy-blue binder she'd removed from her bag. "What is that?"

"I didn't know you smoked."

"I don't. What's in the binder?"

"Files on the ranch."

His eyebrows arched. "Where did you get them? And what kind of files?"

Lauren sat in a plump leather club chair and popped the three-ringed binder open. "I did some research. After you bought me in. Behind my back."

"You retaliated by printing out a ream of paper, punching holes, and organizing it like that?" Vance looked amazed.

"Uh-huh."

"Looks like the handiwork of someone who's pretty enthusiastic about their new investment."

"What's that supposed to mean?"

"That maybe you were a little bit excited to be a part owner of one of the most historic resorts in Texas?"

"It's possible."

"When did you put that together?"

"The night before we flew out. I stayed up most of the night and after I started reading, I thought I better print out as much as I could."

The reason she hadn't confronted Vance about disappearing last night and this morning is because she'd converted the comforter on her bed into something akin to an FBI profiler's corkboard. She'd put the sales agreement in the middle like a hub and spread documents like spokes on a wheel, wondering if she'd missed anything.

Despite the effort, she hadn't discovered anything new. She popped open the rings, removed half the pages and gave them to Vance.

"What am I supposed to do with this?"

"Read. See if you see anything I might have missed."

"Like what?"

"If I knew, I wouldn't be asking you. Aldo Simeri's death was big news in DC. Supposedly, the local Justice of the Peace told reporters that Simeri 'had stopped breathing.' " It didn't seem strange when she'd first read it, but now it sounded ridiculous.

"That's brilliant." Vance was sitting on a worn leather sofa across from her with his feet up on the matching ottoman.

She'd chosen the seat near the window because it had good natural light. "In Roy's statement to the media he said that Justice Simeri seemed to be in 'good spirits' and he told everyone that he was feeling a 'little tired' before he excused himself from the table and retired to his room early." She turned the page. "Oh, wait, listen to this: *'That night they were dining on bison steaks and drinking red wine.'* Hang on," she said, scanning the paper, "Roy said *'he had one glass of wine and didn't finish his meal.'* "

Vance found his own nugget. "This is unbelievable. Did you know Simeri flew in privately, the guest of a guy named Robert Sullivan?" He paused, and read from the page. "And that Sullivan is the managing partner of a K Street law firm? And the trip was *comped*?" He looked at her. "Simeri was here with a *lobbyist*."

"Can members of the Supreme Court do that? Accept gifts?"

"I don't know. It certainly raises questions for me. Is this the picture you told me about?" He held it up.

It was the group photo with Roy Pompadour. The men wore black robes. "Yes."

"The International Order of Saint Eustachius?"

"I know. It sounds weird and it's weirder looking. They say they're some sort of hunting group."

"Why didn't you mention this before?"

"I don't know."

"The stakes were high." Vance thumbed through the pages.

"When Simeri died, the president nominated a replacement. But the Majority Leader in the Senate—"

"One nation, under God." Lauren rolled her eyes.

"Don't be so cynical."

"I hate politics." She was being truthful. "I vote for the lesser of the evils." That wasn't true. She didn't vote.

"Power might be the most intoxicating drug of all. Speaking of drugs, since Simeri might have been drinking that night, what if he was poisoned to make it look like a heart attack?" Vance's eyes were glued to the documents.

"What are you suggesting?"

Vance looked up from his reading. "I'm not sure."

"Hang on. Shit." She ran her finger below the line of text like a typewriter return, re-reading it three times. "There's a statement from the Marfidio County Justice of the Peace. 'The Supreme Court Justice had several medical conditions. He had high blood pressure, was overweight and diabetic . . . ' If he did his own injections, someone could have tampered with his insulin."

"It's possible."

"If he used insulin, he would've needed a refrigerator in his room. Someone put a scorpion in mine. And got into the safe."

Vance tapped the stack of papers on his knees into a neat rectangle and handed them to her. "Rosa would know if he needed a refrigerator. Check it out, and ask her about his drinking habits."

She took the documents from him, placed them back in the binder, and snapped the rings.

WASN'T THERE a theory that the simplest explanation was usually the right one? Occam's Razor, that was it, she remembered it from school. At the moment they had two working theories. One was that he died in his sleep of natural causes. The other was that he'd been murdered. Wasn't the simplest explanation the first one? If he'd been murdered, it would have to have been a conspiracy. And that would not follow Occam's law.

———————

LAUREN WATCHED the new crop of guests checking in. They hovered over rolling carts loaded with designer luggage, bossing their private pilots who doubled as baggage handlers. Some had kids who thumbed their phone screens. The ones whose daddies didn't travel on a private jet with a portable cell tower were shocked to discover the ranch had no cell service. One pre-teen smashed her smartphone on the tile repeatedly until it splintered like shards of glass.

Manny strolled over, removed his five-gallon hat and set it on the counter. "You know how many acres Jack Willis owns around here?"

She didn't recall Vance mentioning anything about an upcoming visit from him.

"What can we do you for, Sheriff?" Vance asked.

"Ole Willis, he's one of the last living wildcatters. Oil speculator. A legend, the sort that picks a place to drill blindfolded and hits black gold. Can't go anywhere around these parts without hearing a Jack Willis story. Long time ago he ran for governor and lost to a woman after telling an off color joke. He owns an eighty-thousand-acre ranch near here. Know how long it takes to get from the front gates to the ranch house?"

Vance shrugged. "I give up."

"What's this got to do with us?" Lauren asked.

"Forty-five minutes at thirty-five miles an hour. Has a shindig so big every year it books up every hotel in a two-hundred-mile radius. Sammy Hagar was the entertainment last year." Manny tugged at the string bolo around his neck. The snake tails rattled. "You know how many arrests have been made at his place over the last twenty-two years?"

She looked blankly at the sheriff. Vance said nothing.

"None, zero, *nada*, zippo. That's how many."

"What's your point?" Vance asked.

"That people around these parts ain't too keen on these rich fellas that come here and think this is some kinda playground with no rules. Folks from around here don't respect that. They respect a woman who can sew a button on a shirt or a man who can change the oil in his truck. And you know what they think about visitors flying in on private jets and spending five hundred smackers a night on a room?"

*Envy?* She didn't say it.

"Enlighten me," Vance said

"We got families that go a whole month on what they spend here on a two-night stay." He tossed his head toward the couple checking in with Rosa. "Folks around here got kids and wives to feed. My wife's sister died last year. She was a damn pauper after working her whole life. I had to take out a loan to pay for the funeral and it wasn't no kind a fancy affair. Sanjay Gupta over there? He comes from halfway around the world and engineers some computer shit we don't need. Makes a better life for himself, not for us. I know. Go ahead and say it." He glared at her.

"Say what?" Lauren asked.

"That I'm a bigot."

She wasn't even thinking that. She was trying to piece this strange puzzle together, trying to figure out where the conversation was going.

"Just 'cause they got a lot of money, it don't mean they're above the law. Not around here anyway."

"Good to know," Vance said.

"Even old Jack Willis had to find out the hard way." The sheriff laughed at the thought. "My predecessor gave him a warning for poaching. That old codger has all that land and he still likes to poach on his neighbor's property. Says it's too tempting. Gets some kind of thrill outta it. One warning is all it took. Never heard another complaint about him trespassing on another man's property. We uphold the law around here. Don't give a rat's behind who you know or how much money you got."

"I don't doubt that," Vance said. "Did you stop by to be friendly or do you have a reason?"

"That big-shot lawyer friend a yours. Ol' Frank. Now there's an example of a fella who thinks he's north of the law. Like I said, around here we do things the old-fashioned way."

"He never wanted to come here to begin with," Vance argued in Frank's defense. "When he found out the place didn't have a golf course, he tried to back out. He has no motive to kill that woman."

"Forensics don't lie," the sheriff said.

"You're right, Sheriff. People do."

Manny twisted his hat back and forth across the wooden countertop.

"I've met and worked with dirty cops," Vance said.

"I hope you're not sayin' what I think you're implying. Either way, I'd best be going." Manny planted his hat on his head.

Lauren was surprised that the sheriff hadn't taken more offense to the dirty cop remark. On the contrary, he was gentlemanly. He tipped his hat with his thumb and forefinger. He sauntered toward the door where his truck was parked under the portico.

Vance jogged behind him. Lauren followed.

"Wait," Vance said.

Manny turned. "What?"

"I need a favor."

"What kinda favor?"

"I need a court order," Vance said.

"What for?"

"I had something tested at a lab, over in El Paso. They can't give me the results without an order from a judge."

"What didja have tested?"

"I found a used syringe in my room," Lauren said. "My sister was here visiting and she's, well, been in and out of drug rehab. I know I should trust her, and she swears it wasn't hers, but addicts, they don't always tell the truth."

"I understand." Manny sighed. "Have a brother with a drinking problem. Used to have a sister-in-law, too, who claimed she couldn't give it up. Don't know if I believe they couldn't quit the booze, but they both sure couldn't quit lyin'. The Justice of the Peace can help you out." Manny took a notebook from his pocket and wrote the number with his fancy pen.

Vance looked at the paper. "Is this a joke? Judge *Pandora*?"

"Keep the jokes you're conjuring up in your head to yourself," Manny said. "Already heard 'em all. Give ol' Jane a call." The sheriff looked at Lauren sympathetically. "Hope she's not lying to you, your sister. It's no good when that happens."

"I hope so, too. Thanks," she said.

Manny walked out the front door.

"Nice work," Vance said when the sheriff was gone. "A sister with a drug problem? Do you even have a sister?"

"No. But Judge Pandora is real. She's the JP who got a little fame for declaring Aldo Simeri dead. She told reporters Justice Simeri 'stopped breathing.' "

"That's one of the things that happens when you die."

Manny surprised them when he strolled back in. "That's what I like to see."

A young couple was checking in. The man pushed a luggage

cart with a wedding dress hanging from the rack, covered in dry-cleaner plastic.

"That's what Mr. Pompadour had in mind when he bought the ranch. Wanted it to be a place where everyday folks could come connect with the land."

"At five hundred a night, it's not exactly accessible to everyday people," Vance said.

"I think it's sweet," Lauren said.

"Folks save up and go off to Paris and Rome," Manny said. "Roy wanted this place to be special, like that. When I saw the wedding dress it made me think. I radioed the station. Sue says the JP's coming over here tonight. Presiding over the wedding. Wed and dead, it's what she does mostly. I'll ask ol' Sue to get the paperwork going for your court order. If you call ahead, you can save yourself a trip into town." The sheriff helped himself to a handful of mints on the way out.

Luther showed up. "What did he want?"

"He was just being friendly," Vance said.

Lauren asked Luther for the February 13th files.

"With all due respect, we have a longstanding policy of not copying or sharing guest files. If you'd like to review them, you can look at them in my office." He reminded her Roy Pompadour had pledged to keep information private, especially for VIP guests.

The idea of changing policy never crossed her mind. She just wanted to see the guest list, like Josh suggested. Private jets were landing now and then and the new crop of guests arriving was young. And wealthy.

"It's Lib-Tard week, as your MIA partner, Jake, would say," Luther said. "They're so high-maintenance."

"Is there some kind of special event happening?" Vance asked.

"No. I told you before," Luther said. "We try to keep some

groups separate. At least we try to book the oil and gas executives on different weeks than the techies. But they all fly privately."

The atmosphere was morphing from one of mild irritation to chaos.

## 17

Vance drove back to town. It seemed like a week had passed since he'd bailed the associates out for the second time, but that was just this morning. He'd telephoned Sue and she'd agreed to go ahead and draft a court order but delivered the bad news that he'd have to sign the request in person. Since he was living in the Stone Age, and an online document signature was too futuristic, he took the Hummer to town again. Without asking.

The desolate highway was becoming familiar. He recognized discarded tires as landmarks, different styles of barbed wire fencing, and the odd art installations.

He turned on Main Street and parked the ranch Humvee out front of the cinderblock courthouse. A red warning sign was duct-taped to the inside of the front door.

PURSUANT TO SECTION 30.06, PENAL CODE (TRESPASS BY LICENSE HOLDER WITH A CONCEALED HANDGUN), A PERSON LICENSED UNDER SUBCHAPTER H. CHAPTER 411, GOVERNMENT CODE (HANDGUN LICENSING LAW),

MAY NOT ENTER THIS PROPERTY WITH A CONCEALED
HANDGUN.

HE LIFTED HIS RIGHT THIGH, grabbed the 9-millimeter, leaned
over the passenger seat, and stowed it in the glove box.

He tapped the frosted glass and leaned against the old pipe
railing, resisting the urge to pick at the layers of peeling paint.
Shadowy figures moved on the other side. He knocked louder.
Nothing. It was quiet except for the faint sounds of muffled
voices coming from slow-moving silhouettes on the other side of
the opaque glass. He pulled his phone from his pocket and
turned it on. Four bars.

Setting his phone down on one of the old school desks, he
slid into the seat. He looked at the green text bubbles popping
up. One was from the harbormaster where he'd docked his live-
aboard sailing yacht, *The Second Wind*. The man had sent him a
YouTube link to aftermath footage from Hurricane Irma that
came ashore. The marina and the *Wind* made the 24-hour news
cycle.

He watched a few seconds of the video, then tapped on the
search browser icon. He typed "Saint Eustachius" and scrolled
through the top hits. Clicking on the website, he enlarged the type
and swiped through the list until he found what he was looking
for. He took a small spiral notebook from his pant pocket and was
making notes when the window screeched open. Surly Sue stuck
her head out. Secondhand smoke wafted from the opening.

"You adding up what you owe me?" she asked, cackling.

Her tone made him want to stuff a bandana in her mouth.
Instead, he smiled and politely asked, "I owe you something? I
thought I was coming in to sign some papers."

She rubbed her thumb and middle finger together.

"You're going to charge me? For the court order?" The space between his eyes tightened.

"Uh-huh. Pay now or pay later. Just like the big city. Five hundred."

He shook his head at the absurdity. The cash handouts had gotten comical.

"You want it or not?"

"I do." He pulled his billfold and slapped the money on the metal threshold.

She handed him a manila envelope. "Sheriff says you're an ex-lawman and a lawyer."

He unfastened the metal clip and looked inside. He removed the document and studied it. "It needs to be notarized by the JP."

"That'll cost you another hundred."

He was just about to blow his stack.

"Just kidding."

She returned with a metal embosser, stamped the paper, signed it, blew the ink dry with her smokey breath and handed it back to him. "I'm bendin' the rules a little. You gotta have the judge sign it. Shoulda had her sign first but you look like the type a fella that can keep a little secret."

"Thanks." He paused. "What about Frank Conn?"

"He's still here, if that's what you mean." She patted her lacquered '50s do.

"Has he talked to a lawyer?"

"Says he's not interested in anyone local and he don't even want to talk to the Public Defender."

"You have one?"

"Yeah. He ain't worth a lizard's nose and never won a case. But it's that or nothing for most folks."

"May I speak to him?"

"The Public Defender?"

"No, to Frank."

"You licensed in Texas?"

"You got me there." She was cagey. He'd give her that.

"We see it all here, Mr. Courage. Fancy-schmancy lawyers from California, mostly. The ones from San Francisco, they think they walk on water. People come here and figure they can push us around and buy their way out of trouble. We're old-fashioned."

He was thinking more along the lines of *corrupt*. "Well, thanks," he said, holding the envelope up and turning to leave. Sue pulled the squealing window shut.

———————

A SPOTLESS, dark-brown SUV with Marfidio Sheriff's Office decals on the doors pulled up next to him. A pair of pumps attached to shapely calves swung out from the driver's side. A buxom woman wearing a tan skirt and sheriff-issue shirt with epaulets and a badge stepped out of the vehicle. Her bleached-blond hair was wound into a tall beehive. Beams of sunlight bounced off the buttons on her shirt that was about to burst.

She removed her sunglasses and inspected him, her long eyelashes sweeping over him, her head moving side-to-side. "You one of them new fellas that bought Pomps' place?" She offered her hand as she pushed the car door closed with her derriere.

"Vance Courage," he said. "Nice to meet you. And you are?"

"Jane Pandora."

Justice of the Peace, Jane Pandora. That explained the uniform and vehicle.

"Oh, stick your tongue back in your mouth. It's important, looking good for God."

She wasn't his type, but still what red-blooded man wouldn't be awestruck? "So I've heard," he lied. He'd never heard about looking good for God, but if he had, this might be it. "I was going to phone you," he said.

"Honey, if I'd have seen you first, I'd have called you and invited you out for a cocktail." Leaning against the SUV, widening her shoulders, she gave him another good going over. "So happens I stopped to get that court order for you. Was gonna bring it with me tonight."

Vance told her Sue said he needed to come in person.

"Oooh," Jane said, shifting her weight, raising the other hip. "How much did that cost ya?" She shook her head gently, balancing the swirling blond steeple atop it.

Vance narrowed his eyes and ran his fingers through his hair.

"That woman oughta be selling used cars in Odessa, I swear it. I'll see y'all later."

"You could sign it now." It was worth a try, it would give him a running start. He could fax the report to the lab before it closed for the weekend. He pled his case.

"Gimme that." Jane took the manila envelope from him, looked inside, and crinkled her nose. "It's just about closin' time on a Friday, hon. Sue's usually cranky by now—if you saw her husband, you'd see why. Not a good idea to ask her to do more than she's done already."

He wasn't sure what else there was for Sue to do but he was in no position to push the issue. He'd planned on having her sign it later at the ranch anyway. "It was nice meeting you." He turned to leave.

She grabbed his arm, her red doll lips barely moving. "By the way, welcome to West Texas, stranger." Holding his hand, she peeled his fingers open slowly, one at a time, and pushed her business card in his palm. "We're a friendly place. Call me. If you need anything at all."

He looked at the card. He'd just been turned down for the one thing he wanted: The signed court order. He held his breath and chewed the inside of his lower lip until he tasted blood. "You've been a big help, already."

"I'll see you soon." Jane sashayed toward the front door of the courthouse. She turned her head slightly to steal a glance. Jane Pandora was no doubt used to men fawning over her. He looked away. He wasn't giving her the satisfaction.

---

BACK ON THE road a pit formed in his belly. It lasted a full thirty seconds. Twice in one day he'd left Frank Conn in the same godforsaken building. He hadn't even bothered to ask Sue if he could go and say hello, see how he was holding up. That might have meant a lot to Frank, a personal visit. Vance had already seen what one night in the Marfidio jail had done to Jake and had a good idea what shape Frank would be in. Screw it. Frank would have done the same to him. In fact, Frank had already screwed him over.

If Frank had been on the level and told him Josh was the one selling the ranch, a character who didn't fit into the picture Jake had painted, it would have been a big red flag. It explained the uneasiness that plagued him during negotiations. He wouldn't have dragged Lauren into whatever it was they were involved in. He wasn't sure how much Jake knew about Antelope Creek Ranch. And Vance didn't know Frank Conn from Adam. Maybe he had killed the maid. Maybe he had a motive. Or maybe he was being framed like Jake had been for the DUI that put them behind bars in the first place.

---

LAUREN SAT in his windowless office, leafing through the paper-work. Luther had pulled the file for her, the one she'd asked for. He'd taken his glasses off and set them on the metal desk, and stared at her. Without them, his eyes were beady and boring into her. If he was trying to intimidate her, it wasn't working. Instead it was making it hard to concentrate.

The new crop of guests still checking in had Luther and the rest of the staff jumping. The celebrity chef, Gordy, barged in without knocking. There was an emergency going on in the dining room, something to do with a gluten-free muffin. Luther rushed out. She riffled through his desk drawers and pulled the rest of the VIP guest files. She ducked out with the paperwork tucked under her shirt.

It was another glorious afternoon. The endless blue sky had finally warmed things up. She cranked open the window and sat on edge of the bed, fanning out the files. One caught her eye: 'ISP PLAN' had been handwritten on the tab. She flipped it open and scanned the top page listing dozens names, typewrit-ten, in alphabetical order. Aldo Simeri was near the bottom of page two. What did ISP stand for? Internet service provider, maybe? That didn't make sense. The ranch didn't even have Internet.

Next to the names were addresses and affiliations. She'd only heard of two. The pair had swapped the number one slot on *Forbes* 400 Richest Americans list for decades. One was in computers and the other, a Midwest investment icon. The investor was so cheap he went to the same fast food drive-thru every morning with exact change. All the others were from the European Union, Canada, Greenland, Iceland, Australia, Israel, New Zealand, Japan, Taiwan, South Korea, and then something dawned on her. She studied the notes in the margins next to each name. All were businessmen in banking, energy, telecom, medical, legal, automotive, insurance, manufacturing and pharmaceutical industries.

Aldo Simeri didn't fit in.

There were attachments with copious notes, mostly handwritten, detailing personal information with emergency contacts, mailing addresses, and telephone, mobile, and fax numbers. Colorful arrow-shaped sticky markers cluttered the pages with dietary and medical information. Two ate a kosher diet, a dozen were allergic to peanuts, and one even traveled with a portable kidney dialysis machine. Three were lactose intolerant.

Simeri's profile said SCOTUS. That's all.

Lauren heard the V-8 diesel and pulled back the drapes. She quickly assembled the papers back in the file folders, stuffed them in her bag, and ran out to flag Vance down. She rode with him as he took the dirt road behind the kitchen, parking in front of the main ranch house where he lived.

"Look what I got," she said, patting Luther's files resting on her lap.

Vance looked at them. "What are those?"

"Luther's private guest files."

"He gave them to you?"

"Um. Not, exactly. I borrowed them. From his office. When he wasn't looking."

"Bad girl," Vance said. "But good work. You're doing better than me."

"How so?" she asked, stepping out of the Hummer.

"I drove into town thinking I could get the court order signed. But my new friend, Jane Pandora, apparently wasn't in the mood."

"A lot can depend on what mood we're in," she said, following him. "You met her?"

Vance pulled his boots off and tossed them on the stoop. "You could say that."

She didn't like his tone. He had nerve, acting agitated. She was the one who had the right to be angry. He'd broken his promise about not going alone. Again.

"What's she like, Jane Pandora?"

"Kinda hard to explain," he said, unlocking the door to the main house.

"Are you going to invite me in?"

"Of course." He waved her in ahead of him. "After you."

She sat in the same leather club chair as her first visit. A heavy-threaded blanket hung over the armrest. Roy's personal things. It was hard not to feel like she was trespassing. Or spying.

The picture window had a bird's-eye view of the little *casa*, the crime scene. The curtains were still drawn, the chairs on the veranda were gone and if Luther hadn't mentioned that Rosa was moving in, she would have figured the house was abandoned. Vance sat on the sofa leafing through a folder she'd lifted from Luther's office.

At first review, nothing had jumped out at her. She looked out the window admiring the scenery. Maybe a fresh set of eyes might help. The southern-facing window framed a purple orb, the sun beginning its descent behind the mountains. In a couple of hours, the stars would glitter and Venus would pop like nature's LED bulb.

She looked back at Vance, who was thumbing through the documents. "Oh my God," she said.

## INFORMATION SUPER POWERS

THERE IT WAS, handwritten in big black lettering on the backside of the same folder she'd studied.

"What?" He cocked his head and scanned the room.

"Turn it around," she said.

"Turn what around?"

"The folder. I couldn't figure out what that stood for."

Vance flipped it and saw what she'd seen: *Information Super Powers* written by hand, on the back. She knelt next to him.

"What do you think it means?"

He shook he head and shrugged. "I don't know."

Lauren sat next to him, watching as he paged through documents. On the last page, the names of the five richest Big Tech companies in the world.

"Look." Vance peeled the post-it note stuck to the inside back cover and handed it to her.

*IGGY*

"IGGY?" It was the same handwriting. "What do you suppose that means?"

Vance didn't answer. He paged through the file folders one by one, reading the tabs. He stopped when he came to one titled Isidore Global Initiative.

"I have no idea what it is," he said. "But I think I know what IGGY stands for."

She was baffled. He showed her the folder. Then the dots connected. "Isidore Global Initiative. *Iggy*."

"Bingo. It would be nice if we had Internet access."

"I'm not sure how much of this is posted online." She'd brought all her files, and showed Vance an article she'd dog-eared. Aldo Simeri had dropped his Marshal detail at the airport in Midland when he flew the last leg on a private jet owned by the DC law firm. Lauren told Vance that justices were required to travel with US Marshal detail. She'd read it half a dozen times in newspaper accounts, the pundits all asking the same question: Why did Simeri drop his security detail?

Vance agreed. "It doesn't seem prudent."

"I thought the same thing. Then again"—she brushed her hair behind one ear—"Simeri was a close personal friend of Roy's. He'd been here lots of times."

Vance rubbed the back of his neck. "It probably gets old, being followed."

A paper sailed from his lap and was about to land on the throw rug.

She caught it midair. "Look at this."

The two-page list was dated February 13 of last year. She pointed to a name. "Josh Dominguez? He's a member of the Isidore Global Initiative?" A cold sweat broke beneath her blouse.

"You did good."

She looked at him, curiously.

"Your research, the articles, the stuff about the justice. Lifting the files from Luther's office."

She sat cross-legged on the floor. Taking a deep breath, she said, "I don't know where this is going."

He stood and pointed to a window, the one with a view through the courtyard, past the pool. A shiny brown sheriff's SUV was doing a turn in the horseshoe driveway.

"Come on," he said. "I'll introduce you to Judge Pandora."

## 18

L auren hurried to her room to freshen up. She washed her face, combed her hair, and applied a little makeup. Justice Simeri must have known it was improper to accept a free ride aboard the lawyer's plane. The private jet was reportedly owned by a DC lobbying firm. Maybe that's why he dropped his Marshal detail in Midland. To keep it a secret.

She played it back. Roy's account of what happened, squared. He told the media Simeri didn't show up for breakfast. When he didn't answer the door, Roy went inside. No one from the US Marshal's office ever came to the ranch, even after the body was discovered, not even to guard it before the ME arrived. That broke protocol. Judge Pandora pronounced Simeri dead over a landline telephone. It sounded absurd: *"Judge Pandora announced that Supreme Court Justice Aldo Simeri stopped breathing."*

When the news leaked, the ranch had been besieged by the media flocking outside the gates with their satellite trucks, crews, and reporters milling about. Lauren reread Pandora's report she'd printed out.

*At four o'clock in the afternoon on the day the body was discov-*

*ered, an (sic) black Cadillac hearse arrived at Antelope Creek Ranch. The Marfidio County Deputy on duty to control traffic at the gate allowed the vehicle to enter but blocked the media from gaining access. At aproximately (sic) 4:30 pm the hearse left with almost all of the media following the vehicle.*

THE JOURNALISTS' reports were more exciting. One described the media circus as "a rabid pack, chasing the sedan all the way to a funeral home in El Paso." What they didn't know, a key detail covered in her later report, was that the hearse was empty: a decoy.

Roy Pompadour corroborated her account to a DC paper. He said that an unmarked cargo van entered the main gates "sometime later" and collected the body. Aldo Simeri was flown to Virginia, and per the family's wishes, no autopsy was performed. Roy Pompadour had thoughtfully choreographed every move from start to finish. Coolly. Effectively. Keeping the body in a room for twelve hours with a media scrum circling the property would have unnerved most people.

Roy wasn't most people. He was a retired US Army captain commanding troops on the front lines, earning six medals, including two Purple Hearts and two Bronze Stars for his service in Vietnam. Remaining calmly detached, formulating a plan to remove the body while avoiding a media sideshow fit his profile. And then another thought popped into her head: An unmarked cargo van had been used to remove Maria's body.

She spotted Vance standing under the pagoda decorated with greenery, white flowers, and streamers of red and white ribbons. He was talking to a woman she'd never seen before. His body language suggested some sort of confrontation was going on. He stood too close to the woman. Lauren slowed her step.

The buxom woman with the giant hairdo was dressed in a

uniform. He was talking to her when suddenly she turned her back on Vance. He tried to grab her by the arm but she pulled it away. What was he doing? She couldn't hear what they were saying. The woman spun and got right in his face, pointing a polished fingernail an inch from his nose. Vance backed away and when he saw Lauren, headed her direction. Except he didn't stop. He stalked past her, his jaw clenched.

"Hey," she said.

He ignored her. He was hunched over, the heels of his boots grinding the dirt.

"Wait a minute." She'd never seen him this mad. "What's wrong?" She followed him to the ranch house door.

Silence.

"Can I come in?" Still nothing.

He closed the door in her face.

She stared at the peephole, blinking. She tried the door-knob. WTF? He'd locked it. She knocked. No answer. What did she do to deserve this? She pounded on the door. After he refused to answer it, she marched over to the wedding party with a head full of steam to watch the festivities.

---

RIGHT NOW VANCE needed Lauren to stop pounding on his door and go away. Damn that Jane Pandora. Fat chance she was telling the truth that she'd *forgotten* to bring the signed court order. Vance fully expected her to ask for money. It was clear he was being jacked around. The only question was why.

While everyone was distracted, mingling ahead of the wedding ceremony, Vance headed to Rosa's office to call Jake. As he turned the corner, he saw Josh and Rosa huddled together in the cubby. He made a second approach, clearing his throat. Rosa and Josh looked guilty as shit. Josh stammered a few words and left. Rosa stayed. Vance told her he needed to use the phone, in private.

Jake answered on the first ring. "Greetings from the mosquito capitol of the world."

Vance heard slapping sounds.

"Mosquitoes might be better than what's going on around here."

"As I recall, there was strange stuff going on when I left. Come to think of it, it's the reason I left."

When it came to being a wiseass, Jake was gifted.

Vance told him about the syringe they'd found and the choral hydrate residue, and the partial fingerprint. "I need a favor. Is there a fax nearby?" Vance knew there was. The lawyers used it to send documents to Jake during the purchase.

"There's one at the clubhouse, if you could call it that." Jake put him on hold for half a minute, then gave him the number.

"Go stand by it. I'm going to send you a list of names. I want you to go through them and see if any ring a bell. Call me right back if something jumps out at you." He told Jake to hurry.

He put the document in the tray and dialed the number. The sheet was feeding when Rosa saw what he was doing.

"This is so breaking protocol," Rosa said, looking at the list he was sending.

"I'm faxing it to Jake."

"You're going to get me fired."

"You're not working for Roy Pompadour, Rosa. Luther's not your boss. But if you tell anyone about his, *I will fire you*."

She took a pair of scissors from a terra cotta pencil holder and hurried outside to the wedding party.

After she was gone, he loaded a stack of documents into the copy machine feeder. While it spat out pages, he thumbed through a rubber-banded stack of mail on Rosa's desk. A statement from a bank in Dallas caught his eye. He pulled it from the middle. It was addressed to Luther Pernod. Vance glanced around. The lobby was a ghost town. He opened it and looked at the document.

Placing it back inside the envelope, he folded it and stuck it in his back pocket. After the fax machine printed a confirmation, he tucked it inside the folder with the still-warm copies and sneaked into Luther's office. While no one was looking, he put the files—the original ones Lauren had nicked, and he'd just copied—into Luther's desk drawer.

---

JAKE JOGGED to the marina clubhouse. A moving target would make it harder for the no-see-ums and mosquitoes. It was only a few hundred feet from the slip where the *Arm* was docked but he was out of breath and his knees hurt by the time he reached the door. He yanked twice on the aluminum door to open it. It was cooler inside but the air was sticky and stale.

The front desk was unmanned and the old copy machine that doubled as the fax machine buzzed. He stood near it, scratching his legs, waiting for the document to come through.

A kid appeared on the second story landing and jaunted down the stairs. Jake recognized him. He was the one who hand-delivered mail and monthly bills to folks living at the marina. Before he could get to it, Jake took the papers from the tray. He gave the kid a twenty, hush money, and sat on the rattan sofa, scanning the two-page document.

He'd never heard of the *Isidore Global Initiative* but one name jumped off the page. Mary Katherine Diamond, Jake's first wife. She'd been a more successful investment banker than he was. The first time he'd seen her, she was on the cover of a money magazine at the newsstand on the corner near his New York co-op.

Before announcing their engagement, both had to get special dispensations from their respective corporate boards. Both firms were concerned about potential conflicts of interest. MK was in telecom while Jake worked in the energy sector. The boards agreed and months later, they married. They honeymooned in Paris. Jake booked seats on the Concorde as a surprise. Those were the good old days.

After they divorced and each remarried, their lives took divergent paths. Jake's professional and family life went to shit; MK climbed to even more rarefied air. She worked her way up to Chief Operating Officer at the world's fifth largest bank before retiring two years ago. That she socialized with Aldo Simeri didn't come as a huge surprise. Wall Street and K Street went together like Hollywood and couch casting: well known to insiders but kept under the public radar.

As corrupt as the financial world was, even Jake was surprised when Vance told him over the phone that Simeri had taken an all-expenses paid trip courtesy of a DC lobbying law firm. MK had known Roy Pompadour for thirty years and was the one who introduced them. If anyone had the inside track, she would.

---

"WELL, well, well, you remind me of an ingrown hair, the way you pop out of nowhere," Mary Katherine said when she took his call. "Heard you were back in Houston. Figured you'd call Noah to borrow an ark before you called me, with all that rain. I know you, Jake, you only call when you need something."

As usual, she was right. "Nice to hear your voice, too." He cut to the chase. He told her about the list.

Jake and MK had divorced amicably twenty years ago. They had one child, a son, before they'd split in the late '90s, after three years of marriage. The New York social scene, especially the financial one, was a tight-knit group, the same folks attending the same cocktail parties and fundraisers, ones that Jake was very much a part of before his drinking got him crossed off a lot of social calendars.

"Do you know anything about this Isidore Global Initiative? You're listed as one of the members."

"Hmmm." Which is what MK always said when she was buying time.

"Don't duck and weave."

"Ducking and weaving is what they do in Texas. Here in New York, we just 'deny all knowledge.' On a serious note, it's not something I can talk about." She changed the subject. "I heard things turned around for you. Your kids told Alex your real estate investments are doing well. I'm happy for you, Jake, I really am. Congratulations on the purchase of Antelope Creek Ranch. That's a nice piece of real estate, even if it's in the middle of nowhere."

Their son Alex and the two kids from his second marriage got along. "I heard your husband made close to seven million dollars last year with bonuses and stock options. And you're retired, busy getting your nails painted and laser treatments on your entire body."

"Geez. How do you know that?"

"About your laser treatments?"

"No. That Bill made seven million last year."

"I read it online in one of those financial rags that's gone digital. The way he invests, municipal bonds earning three percent a year. Did you hear that noise?"

"What noise?"

"Me, yawning. He's such a bore, MK. Three percent return. Yawn. Stretch. He's an expert on municipal water financials. I don't know if I could stay awake long enough to enjoy the money."

MK shot back, "From what I heard, you were broke there for a while. One of these days water will be as valuable as oil and you'll wish you hadn't missed the boat. Plus, he's a seven-million-dollar-a year bore."

"I made almost double that last year."

"Money is the root of all evil, darling."

He corrected her. "*Love* of money is the root of all evil. Either way, you qualify. Back to the topic, what do you know about this IGGY group?"

"We'll have to meet face-to-face if you want to talk about it."

"Now I'm really intrigued. How come you weren't mysterious like this when we were married?"

"I was. You were drunk."

*Touché.* "How can we meet?"

"At the ranch. Tell Luther to set it up. He'll know what to do. It's time for a group meeting. Tell Luther to call me."

"Why don't you call him direct?"

"Just do it, Jake."

"All right, keep me in suspense." He knew pressing her for more information would be a waste of his time.

"I heard you quit drinking."

"I didn't. My liver went on strike."

"You're still such a smart ass, numb nuts."

"Do you talk to Diamond Jim that way?"

"Hell, no. He treats me like royalty so I speak to him like a princess. And it's Bill Diamond, by the way. I still can't figure out what I ever saw in you."

"My charm and wit, MK."

"I suppose. I'll ask Bill if I can use the corporate jet. They let us charter it for personal use at the same rate as retail if it's avail-able. I'm warning you, once I'm there, I'm not leaving the property. And I'm not putting up with your crap if you're still hitting the bottle."

"If I fly commercial to Midland will you stop and let me hitch a ride with you? That four-lane highway out there is the *Jurassic Park* of law enforcement."

"I thought you bought the place?"

"I did but the local sheriff didn't come with the purchase. You can stop pretending, MK."

"Pretending?"

"I know it was really you who got word to me the ranch was on the auction block. You used Alex. He's the one who tipped me off." Alex, their son.

"Hmmm," MK said. "Roy used to love engaging with the tech entrepreneurs. Back when they still believed they were going to use technology to make a better world. You know, global peace, Kumbaya stuff. Roy liked them when they weren't driven by money. But greed's gotten the best of them now." She paused. "Jake, we know a lot about money, don't we, hon? Once you get a taste for it, it's hard to stop wanting more."

"You've always seen the big picture. I guess that's why you were so good at making money."

"Expect to hear from Luther. And Jake, be careful. The rattlesnakes out there in West Texas crawl on their bellies. And some of them walk upright, on two legs. And I'm not kidding about the booze. I'm not putting up with that bullshit again."

MK, still the same straight-talking girl from Arkansas. She ended the call without saying goodbye.

He smashed a mosquito on his leg, splattering blood in his palm. He wiped his hand on the frayed cushion.

MK was right. His drinking turned him into a miserable son of a bitch and an even worse investor. He blew his life savings on real estate after he retired, just before the housing market went bust.

What he'd done in Miami, taking a share of missing cartel money, wasn't worse than what the bankers on Wall Street did, skimming millions of dollars off deals.

The only real difference was that drug cash created an accounting nightmare. Buying Antelope Creek Ranch was Jake's idea and Vance agreed to go in with him. It was a great way to launder a few million. And Vance, being the Boy Scout he was, or used to be, invested an equal one-third share on Lauren's behalf. If it were up to Jake, he'd have happily taken her thirteen and a half million and split it fifty-fifty with Vance. She had walked away from it, calling it "dirty" money, as if there was any other kind. The naiveté was sweet.

On the other hand, he was glad Vance held her share. She deserved it.

MK was dead on. It wasn't hard to stop wanting more money after getting a taste for it. It was fucking impossible.

## 19

L auren sat on a bench in the courtyard with her arms around her knees, observing. The setting sun had thrown miles of pink and purple streamers across the horizon, wrapping the Chinati Mountains like a wedding gift. The nervous young couple about to get hitched stood behind a restored stagecoach. She'd seen Josh behind the wheel of the tractor earlier moving the red wagon nearer to the pagoda.

The groom pulled a silver flask from beneath the tail of his tuxedo. His nervous bride-to-be turned away and tilted her head back, gulping. The couple looked around, checking for witnesses before the groom finished it off.

Rosa hurried by, making last minute adjustments, tying more red and white bows and streamers to the latticework on the pagoda. She folded the tails of the ribbons and cut the edges into V-shapes, collecting the discarded pieces and placing them in a basket hung over her left wrist.

The wedding party itself was small but many of the guests had gathered in the courtyard, a polite distance away, to watch. Roy had hoped regular folks would see Antelope Creek Ranch as a destination right up there with Tuscany or Paris. Or was it

Rome. Either way he would have appreciated this young couple. They'd told Rosa they narrowed down their wedding venue to a choice between Antelope Creek Ranch and Prague.

If Roy really wanted people to share his vision, he should have done more to market the ranch to the public. It didn't make sense. He seemed more focused on the opposite, of keeping it under the radar. Now that he was out of the picture, Lauren was sure she could do more to promote it, once things settled down. She looked up. Vance stood over her.

"Are we on speaking terms again?" She hadn't seen him since he'd closed the door in her face and refused to answer it.

A black BMW 500 series sports car roared up the gravel path and parked shotgun in front of the lodge. A woman got out. The same woman who looked like she'd gone overboard on the butt implants. She leaned over at the waist and shook her booty, as if it needed more advertising. She plucked a manila envelope from the dash.

"Is that who I think it is?" Good grief, the woman walked right off the pages of the old Sunday funnies.

"Yep."

"What were the two of you having words about? Earlier."

"I wouldn't call it words. She was supposed to bring the signed court order. The one we need to get the results on the partials on the syringe. If she had, I would have had time to fax it to the lab before they closed for the weekend. She said she forgot."

"Jesus," Lauren said, wrinkling her nose, "I haven't seen hair or shoulder pads like that since they cancelled *Falcon Crest*." From the looks of it, Justice of the Peace Jane Pandora had changed more than just cars while she was gone.

"I'll be right back," Vance said.

"She must go to Dallas for that bleach job and hairdo."

"Meow. File those claws. Or I won't introduce you." He held

his fingers out, spreading them and bending them at the knuckles.

"I'm not being catty." She was simply stating the obvious. "How much do you think the JP of Marfidio County makes?"

"I don't know. Not much, I wouldn't think. Maybe she's married. There's a lot of oil money in West Texas."

He was defending her. Lauren watched as Vance did a rooster walk toward Jane who was leaning provocatively against the black Beemer. She handed Vance the envelope, the court order she assumed.

Then Jane tiptoed toward the awaiting nuptials, protecting the heels of her black patent leather stilettos. She strutted past Lauren, half-smiling at her. The remnants of the setting sun glinted off the one-caret diamond posts in her earlobes. Lauren kept thinking, *this is the woman who signed the esteemed Supreme Court Justice Aldo Simeri's death certificate?* It was surreal, putting it mildly.

Vance returned with the envelope tucked under his arm.

She squinted and shaded her eyes with her hand. "She's not wearing a wedding ring. What would a rich oil baron's wife be doing this job for? Calling people in the middle of the night and telling them a loved one just passed away? Spending a Saturday evening presiding over a quaint family wedding? If I were rich, this is not what I'd be doing. I wouldn't be here."

"Incorrect. You're rich and you're here." Vance looked at her. "I can't believe you."

"What?"

"You're jealous."

"I am not."

When Jane finished a short talk with the soon-to-be bride and groom, she tottered toward them. "This outta be good."

"Meow."

Lauren glared at Vance.

"So this is your business associate," Jane said to Vance. "Heard Pomps' place has a lady partner. That you?"

"Lauren Gold." She held her hand out but Jane rebuffed the gesture.

"Well, it's nice to meet you, Lauren *Gold*. Once upon a time this place was famous for silver. But never for gold. I better get this one rolling. Double-booked tonight, headed to the bingo hall for some vow renewals. Hard to keep marital infidelities a secret around here and renewals are all the rage."

When Jane was out of earshot she said, "Are you kidding me? This is movie shit."

"That might be true, but she's also part of the law around here. You need to play nice. The Justice of the Peace in a small town has a lot of clout."

"I was nice," she said defensively. "It's not me we have to worry about."

"What's that supposed to mean?"

"That woman uses everything the good Lord gave her to get what she wants from men. I give her credit."

"I have no idea what you're talking about."

Lauren harrumphed. "You're pathetic."

"I need to keep her on a string."

She laughed so loud heads turned. "Now that's funny." She worked her hands in front of her like a marionette's puppeteer. "It might be fun watching the two of you yanking each other's strings."

---

THEY'D WATCHED the ceremony from a distance and afterward Vance jogged to catch up with Jane Pandora who was leaving. He about killed himself getting to her car first, to open the door.

Lauren balled her fists and dug her nails into the skin on her palms.

Just as Vance returned from trying out for the role of Prince Valiant, the happy groom trotted up with two flutes of champagne. He gushed, thanking them both profusely for providing such a beautiful backdrop. Holding the manila envelope in one hand, Vance held up his glass to toast the couple. Rather than clinking glasses, Lauren set hers on the rock ledge.

Vance downed his glass in one gulp. "It won't stay cold for long." He reached around and grabbed hers. After the bride and groom strolled off he asked, "Why don't you drink? If you told me, I can't remember."

"Have you ever woken up in a hotel room next to a stranger wearing a turban and can't remember how you got there?"

Vance backed a half step away from her, like she had Ebola. "Seriously?"

She probably shouldn't have told him. Now she had to finish the story. "After my last husband ran off with a twenty-five year old, I went off the deep end. I went to a hotel bar in South Beach and that's what happened. I started ordering rum drinks with mango juice and the next thing you know, I woke up next to a turban. I scared the shit out of myself. I'm done with it. Now and forever."

"It doesn't explain why you slept with Jake Fleming."

*What an asshole.* "That was different. My dog died."

"Mournful dog sex?"

"Look, I'm baring my soul and you're making fun of me. I thought we weren't going to discuss that anymore. You're too insensitive to be in a relationship. You know what's scarier than waking up with a Sikh Indian in a hotel room with no memory, seeing a used condom floating in the toilet and not knowing if you put it there or he did? That I was married to my best friend for twelve years and one day he got up and walked out on me."

She flared her nostrils to take in more cool evening air.

"That's not exactly what happened. My real estate agent friend called and told me she found an apartment she thought he'd like. That's how I found out he was moving out. And after he was gone he told everyone *I kicked him out*. It's a miracle I didn't drink myself to death. Or hurt someone, driving drunk." She stared at her shoes.

When her eyes met his, he looked like he'd been gut punched.

"That sounds horrible." He rotated the envelope in his hands.

He looked sincere.

"Sorry for the download. I'm going to my room." She turned to leave. She'd wanted to see what was in the envelope but talk about her divorce from Peter sucked the life out of her. She wanted to be alone. Wisely, he let her go. She bunkered in her room for a quiet night.

## 20

Lauren awoke to a mini airshow. She'd peeked out the drapes at daybreak and had timed three private jets landing about thirty minutes apart, just long enough for the pilots to drop off their passengers, schlep bags from the cargo holds, taxi, and take off. Rosa had said the ranch was at near capacity. She dressed and went to the lodge to find out what was going on.

Josh and Luther were shuttling the arriving guests from the airstrip to the ranch where Rosa checked them in at the front desk. The pilots weren't staying. Rather Josh said they were headed to the private airport at Midland where there were enough spaces to park the planes and hotel rooms for the pilots.

Vance and Lauren rode with Josh to meet the plane bringing Jake back to the ranch. "Is this normal?" Lauren asked Josh, "all these planes? I looked at the guest manifest. Rosa told me the ranch is almost at capacity."

"MK called in a favor from Luther. She wanted to put together an impromptu gathering. She's an old friend of Roy's and we talked about it."

"MK?" Lauren asked.

"Jake's ex-wife," Josh said. "First ex-wife."

"Jake's ex-wife is putting on some sort of event? Why weren't we consulted first?" Vance asked.

Josh stuttered, "Ah . . . um. You know, I don't know why. I'm guessing we all thought someone else mentioned it to you. No one did?"

"No," Lauren said, making eye contact with Vance.

Josh said, "Her friends flying in are willing to be a little inconvenienced."

"Inconvenienced?" she asked.

"Most of them are sharing rooms. MK is bunking at the house, with Jake," Josh said.

"She is?" Vance sounded irritated.

He had the right to be annoyed. As Jake's roommate, that meant he'd be sharing the house with her. She'd have been irritated, too.

Vance got out of the Hummer and slammed the door hard enough to rock the vehicle.

"We'll be right back," Josh said.

Lauren waited in the back seat watching a Gulfstream G280 taxi and come to a stop. The door opened and a stairwell unfurled from the belly of the sleek jet. One of the pilots exited first followed by a strawberry blond in snug, bright blue jeans. Holding the railing with her right hand, she glanced down at her red cowboy boots calculating each steep step. Jake waddled down behind her, his knees jutting out sideways from under his pastel green shorts.

MK, she guessed. Jake's first ex-wife.

Josh and Vance met up with the pilot who'd opened the cargo hold. They carried luggage from the belly of the jet to the awaiting vehicle.

Both passenger doors opened simultaneously.

"Meet ex-wife number one, and I mean *number one* in every way," Jake said to her, sliding in.

Mary Katherine Fleming-Diamond climbed in from the other side.

Mary Katherine extended her palm and warmly squeezed Lauren's. "My friends call me MK."

"Nice to meet you. I'm Lauren."

"Good to see the boys thought enough to bring a woman's touch to the deal."

It wasn't like she didn't bring three million cash, too.

"Jake says you knew Roy?" Her voice went up two octaves. She hated that, knowing it sounded weak, like she was asking a question instead of making a statement.

"For thirty years. We were a bunch of banking hoodlums who elbowed our way right to the top of the heap. Well, that's not true about Roy. While we were out making jackasses of ourselves drinking and not inhaling pot, poor ol' Roy was across the Pacific making himself into a hero. How ol' Jake and I stayed friends is a mystery my current husband just can't figure."

MK jumped out of the open car door when she saw Vance and Josh wrestling her bags. She stood on tippy toes, and hugged Josh, kissing his cheek.

The rear tires of the Humvee crunched the dirt, making a dust cloud that followed the vehicle all the way to the lobby where it billowed and dissipated beneath the portico.

Luther was waiting at the door. When MK saw him, she loped over, and, embracing him in a full body hug, bent her left knee back so far she practically kicked herself in the ass with the heel of her boot.

"Thanks for putting this together last minute," MK said.

While Luther chatted with MK, Jake motioned her and

Vance over to a quiet corner of the dining hall. "Sorry I bailed on you. Those storms did a job on Texas and Florida. Davis' place in the Keys got wiped out, so he's going to stay on the *Arm* for a while." He looked at Vance. "Any news about your baby?"

"Wrecked." He laughed. "The manager at the marina took it harder than I did. And I don't have insurance."

"When did you find out?" Lauren asked. Why hadn't he mentioned it?

"I don't know." He shrugged like it was no big deal. "When I was in town and I had cell service. The guy who runs the marina, he sent me a text."

Jake looked astonished. "No insurance?"

"I was trying to stay off Uncle Sam's radar."

The fifty-foot Lagoon was a million-dollar sailing yacht purchased with illicit money, cartel cash. It was way too complicated for him to sail the thing. He'd been living on it for a few months before they'd bought the ranch.

"The guy from the marina sent me a link. I checked it out when I was in town. The carnage was unbelievable. Apparently the storm surge sent my sailboat up on the rocks, right in front of the marina restaurant." He'd looked at the wreckage just once waiting for Sue at the courthouse.

"Is it salvageable?" Jake asked looking amazed.

"Yep. As a future reef. The harbormaster said it's a total loss. He said the Coast Guard contacted him trying to find the owner. The guy who runs the marina promised to keep my identity quiet. I messaged him back and told him to sink her offshore. Sink now, pay later." He laughed a little.

Same old Florida. No shortage of people willing to deal from the bottom of the deck.

She was upset that he hadn't told her.

Jake said, "If I'd lost the *Arm*, I'd be, well . . . it didn't happen, so why be morbid, right?"

Vance minimized it. "I had some clothes and a few books. The desert and mountains suit me better, anyway. I like it here. No hurricanes, tornadoes, earthquakes or wildfires—"

"And no big snowstorms." Luther interrupted him. "Dinner is at six. Bison chops, pommes frits, brussel sprouts, and baby kale with roasted beets-salad as the first course."

The front double doors banged open and a shit storm was headed their way.

"This was in my room." MK opened the designer handbag slung over her shoulder and shoved it at Luther. He peeked inside and grimaced. Looking around to make sure no guests would see, Luther reached inside and lifted out the old-fashioned milk bottle. The scorpion inside pricked at the glass with its claws.

"Excuse my French, but *what the fuck*, Luther?" MK was practically breathing fire.

"I got one of those, too," Lauren said.

"Well, wouldn't it have been nice to know that. Last time I was here, Roy sent a lovely fruit basket and a nice bottle of Merlot to my room. Not one of these."

"Someone sent one to Jake, in Texas. Delivered by a courier," Vance said.

Jake scrunched his nose and backed away.

"Well, did you call the sheriff and report it?" MK wasn't done with Jake. "Is that true?"

Jake's face twisted into a corkscrew. "Yeah, but . . . "

"Don't get your panties bunched up, MK. A lot of strange things have been going on around here lately." Luther was saving Jake's hide. "Why don't you freshen up. I'll have room service send over a bottle of wine. We're putting a deputy at the gate."

A deputy at the gate, that was the best idea Lauren had heard so far. "That makes four scorpion deliveries," she said, testing Luther, wondering if he'd notice she'd added the fourth one, the one Vance told her about after he'd spied on Luther's conversation with Josh.

"Four?" MK gave Luther a dirty look. "Four?"

"Well," Luther said, "I didn't see the need to broadcast that I got one. It would be bad for business and create a stir with the guests if news got out."

Lauren looked around at the guests sipping wheatgrass smoothies. Since when did straight men start wearing pedal pushers and eyeliner? Luther was right. The scorpions would create quite the stir. Especially with this group. The ones wearing hiking attire were in costume. The sight of a big scorpion would have them calling out for their mothers.

---

EARLIER, before MK found the scorpion in her room, Lauren had accepted Josh's invitation to go on another ride. Thank God. Getting away from the mounting tension didn't come a minute too soon.

They'd been cantering the trail leading to the foothills when he slowed his horse to a walk. Her horse was fresh, shaking his head and swishing his tail. It took her a few strides to slow him down. She laughed. Smokey the packhorse had a new lease on life. She brought him to a walk as he flared his nostrils and snorted, then struck the hard ground with a front hoof. Cheks barked.

Josh cocked his head, grinning at the animal. "I've never seen him act like that."

When Smokey settled down they continued along the open trail to the path leading up to the first ledge. Cheks led the way through thick brush, stopping at intervals, waiting for the horses to catch up. Soon the footing turned into foot-deep piles of big jagged rocks that must have rolled down the path and gathered over time. What Lauren felt beneath her was jarring, her horse stumbling to maintain balance, hooves swiveling at the ankles.

The sounds were anything but serene with eight hooves clunking and grinding as the horses struggled, legs twisting between the boulders, forcing the rocks to grate against each other.

Nearing the apex, the footing turned soft. Josh reined his horse toward a steep uphill path rooted with brush. It was cold in the shade and she wished she'd worn more than a vest. They rode through a natural tunnel and a moment later the trail opened to a flat ledge where the sun overhead warmed her like a heat lamp. This new vantage point looked like a postcard with a 180-degree view of the ranchlands. Cheks stuck his nose in the air and sniffed, bending one knee, tail erect like the mast on a sailboat.

She breathed deeply and exhaled slowly. "It's so beautiful." She looked at him. "Why would you ever sell it?"

"Maybe I shouldn't have."

"But you did. Why are you still here?" Lauren asked. It was a good question. Why stay if he'd cashed out? Why didn't Vance and Jake do their homework? What kind or deal had they cut to keep Josh around?

"I don't know." He adjusted the rifle strapped to his back and picked up the reins. "Maybe it's just easier not to make changes when you're used to a place."

That was a lame answer. It wasn't like the ranch was some flophouse where he could park his ass indefinitely. Then again, he worked here.

The Appaloosa pricked his ears, then twitched and rotated them, tuning them like satellite dishes trying to pick up a signal.

"Let's start back." Josh gently spurred his horse and both animals half-walked, half-slid down the steep decline on their haunches, rocks grinding under their feet.

At the base, Spot broke into a trot and transitioned into an easy canter, her horse fell in behind his. They were heading for a three-foot-wide dry creek bed. The little Quarter Horse beneath her rolled his shoulders like a dolphin in the water. He opened his stride and arched his head and neck anticipating the jump. She rose from the saddle, and balancing on his neck with a handful of black mane in her hand, loosened the reins. Smokey flew over the ditch, landing on the other side with a two-foot gap to spare. The adrenaline felt good. She laughed out loud while Josh slowed Spot back to a trot. A minute later both horses walked calmly side-by-side.

"Where's Cheks?"

"Ah, he likes to go off on his own and chase jackrabbits. He'll be back."

The ride back gave her the opportunity to do a little more fishing. "My mouth is watering just thinking about dinner. What's the special occasion? If MK's friends are going to share rooms, won't that make the ranch feel overcrowded?"

"They're big boys."

Not exactly an illuminating answer. "I still can't figure out why Vance and I weren't told about it." Jake obviously knew. Jake had jetted in on MK's husband's corporate jet.

"I don't think anyone was trying to keep it a secret. Luther was under a lot of pressure, trying to organize it at the last minute."

"Why last minute?" It seemed like a stretch to plan a big gathering in the middle of nowhere on a moment's notice. On the other hand, if you fly privately and have your own pilot, last minute might not be that big of a deal. No. He was lying. These were not the kind of people who could clear their calendars at the last minute for a friendly get together. Not believable.

Josh continued to lie. "First off, you not knowing was an oversight. I guess we thought Jake would tell you." Josh reached down and patted his horse on the neck.

Yeah, right.

"MK, she seems to like you," she said.

Josh glanced at her sideways and nodded.

"She was on the guest list, the one you told me to get. The one from the thirteenth of February."

"Luther let you see it? I wasn't sure if he would. Information is power. Luther can be a power-thirsty twit."

She told him Luther didn't exactly offer it up, then pressed him again about the big rush and about MK being on the list.

"There's a group that meets annually. Since the ranch has been on the market, a lot of the members have been wondering what would happen. MK decided to fast-track it, to make sure the group doesn't start shopping for a new venue."

Now she was getting somewhere. "Your name was on the list, too." She watched his body language but he didn't seem the least bit surprised.

"We're a group of hunters." He shrugged.

"You're telling me MK *hunts*?"

"You'd be surprised. She's from Arkansas, raised in a blue-collar family."

That hardly qualified her as a hunter. Lauren did not for one second believe that Mary Katherine Diamond was a hunter.

"How long have you lived here? And how is it that you came to own the place."

"My whole life," Josh said skipping the second question.

What the hell kind of a deal did Vance get her into? Lauren felt lightheaded. From what she'd read, Roy hadn't purchased the land until the late 1990s. The dead housekeeper had confirmed it. She clicked through the timeline in her head. Maria was here before Roy, and Maria and Josh were family. More questions than answers.

"Your whole life, huh?"

"I was born here."

*Born here?* The expression on her face must have said it all.

"It's not exactly a secret, my mother—"

The sound pounded her eardrums. It was practically a sonic boom. Smokey reared into the air. She grabbed the saddle horn and stood in her stirrups, then wrapped her arms around the horse's neck to keep from falling.

"Jesus. That sounded like a cannon," she said. "What the hell was that?"

"Rifle fire," he said.

Another round pounded the air, the metal cartridge ricocheted off the rock wall making a high-pitched ping that spooked Smokey again. The shooter was either a good shot. Or a lousy one.

"Hang on." Josh dug his spurs into the flanks of his horse. "Let's go."

Spot spun a full turn like a cutting horse and lunged off his back hooves like he was sprinting from a starting gate.

Lauren dropped the reins over the saddle horn, behind the knot tied in the leather, and ducked beneath a low-hanging branch. She swatted limbs and vegetation from her face as the horses cut back and forth between the brush and boulders, their flight instinct in full force.

Gunfire, more rapid now, burst into the air and echoed like special effects. Her head pulsated, and every discharge of the rifle punched her in the brain.

When they reached the barn, streaks of dust trailed them, marking the route they'd cut like they were cartoon characters.

Lauren stroked Smokey's neck to calm him. The horse heaved. She dismounted and swept her hand over her head, plucking leaves and twigs, her heart pounding. Josh's horse huffed, exposing red velvet nostrils. Sweat lathered beneath the saddle blankets. Josh's lips were moving but she couldn't make out what he was saying. Her ears rang and when her hearing cleared, she heard a whining sound. It was Chekov. A cactus ball was pinned to his snout like a circus clown. He lifted his paw to his nose and touched it. He howled, shaking his head.

"Wait here." Josh handed her the reins to his horse and ran inside the tack room.

He returned wearing a thick glove. Holding Cheks by the collar, he ripped the ball of sharp needles from the dog's nose. The animal yelped.

"Cholla cactus, evil suckers," Josh said. "If you get too close, they jump right off the plant."

Cheks pawed his sore snout and whimpered.

Her hearing was recovering and the adrenaline receding, but her heart was still racing from their emergency escape. "Those shots, they could've hit us. Where did they come from?"

"I don't know." There was concern in his voice. The dog followed him into the tack room and lay down on the cool cement floor, his K-9 flak jacket wrapped snugly around his body. Josh hoisted his saddle onto the uppermost wooden rack.

Lauren sat on the floor next to Cheks, hands trembling. "It sounded like a cannon, like a Civil War reenactment I heard when I was a kid."

"Fifty-caliber sniper rifle."

She didn't know what that was. "A ranch rifle?"

"No. We don't have any of those here. It's a high-caliber weapon with pinpoint accuracy, the type snipers use. Mr. Pompadour would never allow them here. He thought it was unsportsmanlike to hunt with a weapon like that. It stacks the deck against the animals." He looked at her sitting next to the dog. "Why don't you go back to the ranch and clean up while I finish un-tacking the horses and putting them up. We have a big dinner tonight. You need to be fresh to meet the group."

The gallop back had been exhilarating but Josh was right, she was frazzled. She walked back to the lodge. Glancing down, she saw a rip in the knee of her jeans. The ride back was so wild she hadn't even noticed the bloody scratches on her forearms until they'd started to burn. She replayed it in her head, the earsplitting gunfire that sounded like a series of explosives. It was like a scene in the movies when the camera moves too fast, hooves pounding, branches cracking, and her eyes watering from the wind. She ran her hand over her hair. It was knotted and still full of leaf material.

Halfway back to the lodge she doubled back to the barn. It wasn't right to leave her horse tied to the railing. Plus, she was still processing what had happened. She'd rather be at the barn, going through the motions of unsaddling her horse. It would give her nerves the chance to settle. If she bumped into Vance like this, he'd lecture her about going out. She'd tried to explain it to him before, that it was her escape. But he didn't understand.

When she was within earshot of the tack room, she heard Josh talking. But, to whom? They'd been alone. She palmed both ears gently, trying to stop the buzzing. Keeping her body out of view, she peeked around the doorway, inside the tack room. Josh was kneeling next to Chekov and his lips were moving. He *was* talking to the dog. She talked to her animals all the time, but still, she didn't want to embarrass him. She backed up a couple of steps and decided she'd stomp her boots on the walkway. That, she was sure, would give him a heads up, and spare them an awkward moment.

As she stepped toward the open door, she stopped in her tracks.

*Am I losing it or did the dog answer him?*

She backed away two feet and listened from around the corner. Peering through the crack of the doorjamb she saw Josh unzip a pocket on the dog's jacket and remove a piece of paper. Cheks barked and ran toward her.

"Knock, knock," she said after the dog announced her arrival. She grabbed the saddle from the railing. "I couldn't leave you here to do all the work."

Josh was startled. He shoved something in his pant pocket. "Well, sure. I'd love the help."

Cheks sprawled on the floor and laid his head on his paws, specks of blood drying on his nose. Josh took the saddle from her and slung it on a high rack while she hung the bridle she'd used on a hook. She went outside and untied the horse from the hitching post and slipped a halter over his head. Cheks, who'd been licking his sore nose, tagged along as Lauren led the horse to the pasture and released him. Wagging his tail, the dog barked enthusiastically.

When she'd first walked in on Josh, she could have sworn she'd heard a voice coming from the dog. That was crazy. She stuck her hands in her pockets to keep Josh from seeing them shaking. That much adrenaline was taking its sweet time burning off. Josh looked up when Cheks trotted through the doorway and sat. She looked at the dog, then at Josh. What was she going to do? Ask him, about it? *Hey, is your dog related to Mr. Ed and knows how to talk?*

And then she remembered Josh was just about to tell her something right before all hell broke loose. It was something about his *mother*, something he was going to offer up directly, voluntarily. Contemplating a way to revive the conversation, she got down on one knee to pet the dog and scratched his head. Josh hung his bridle beneath Spot's nameplate on the wooden rack.

"Sorry for the scare," he said. "I'll see you at dinner."

Lauren stayed behind, sitting cross-legged on the splintered old rocker on the porch, white knuckling the chair arms. Cheks jogged to keep up with Josh's giant stride. He headed to the shed where the hunting equipment and ATVs were stored.

## 21

L auren was surprised to see Luther at her door. He had a black robe slung over his forearm and held it up.

"You're not serious. Are you?"

"It's a longstanding tradition. Everyone wears them when the group meets."

"The hunting group? They wear robes?"

"Yes."

"Why?"

"I told you, it's tradition."

"Do Jake and Vance have to wear them, too?"

"Yes. This one will fit you. There's no magic to it. It just slips on over your clothes, like a poncho."

"It seems a little ridiculous," she said, trying it on.

"Many important, powerful people have worn these. Surely you can suffer through one evening. Think of it as your duty, as one of the new owners. They want to meet you."

"Luther, let's be real. I don't know the first thing about hunting. I couldn't find the trigger on a BB gun. Plus, I love animals too much to kill anything."

"Don't worry about any of that," he said. "That's not what they talk about."

If they didn't talk about hunting, what did they talk about?

---

AFTER HE LEFT, Lauren twirled in front of the full-length mirror, first to the left, and then to the right, making the fabric whirl around her like an old-fashion hoop skirt. It looked silly. But tonight might be fun, like a secret-society party for grown-ups.

She agreed with Vance that Jake looked the most ridiculous of them all, cloaked in the black gown with bright green accents. It emphasized the bump in his arthritic back, and she laughed when Vance said Jake looked like the Hunchback of Notre Dame. The wait staff worked the room feverishly, ushering in trays of mouthwatering appetizers prepared by Chef Gordy.

He'd trained at Le Cordon Blue in Paris and had a reputation as a top chef before earning a recurring stint as a judge on a reality cooking show. Roy hired him for more than his brush with celebrity. She took a bacon-wrapped quail breast from the tray and bit into it. Her taste buds went into overdrive.

They tried mingling but she and Vance may as well have been party-crashers. After being rebuffed, they opted to stand in the corner and people-watch. The average age of the new-arrivers was much older that she'd predicted. Jake looked like he fit right in, chatting with MK and two other senior men.

"God, I hate small talk." Vance gulped beer directly from a longneck bottle.

"You're good at it."

"What's that supposed to mean?"

Josh walked like a Greek god with the black robe draping from his broad shoulders like a theater curtain. Working the crowd, he seemed to know everyone, stopping to chat with each one.

"This is weird, this secret shit. Why are they here?" she asked.

Vance lifted his robe and pulled a small notebook from the back pocket of his black jeans. "Saint Eustachius is a global organization of 'knightly hunters and wildlife conservationists.' That's according to their website."

"Where did you get that?"

"I looked it up when I was in town. The group was formed in the late sixteen-hundreds, somewhere in Europe. Austria, I think." He read from his notes.

"That just sounds weirder."

"That's what I was thinking. You know what else I think is suspicious?"

*Other than everything?* "What?"

"The mailing address for the group goes to one of those shipping stores, on M Street, in Washington DC."

She smoothed the black fabric that had bunched up a little on her left shoulder. "This is so odd." She shook her head. "I don't know what we're mixed up in but it stretches all the way to DC. Look around . . ."

"Let's work the room," he said, grabbing her by the elbow. "They're *our* paying customers, after all."

But when they tried to be social, approaching the small groups that had broken from the pack, the guests stopped talking. Even the people in earshot dropped their voices to a whisper and the topics shifted to small talk, like they were outsiders.

*How do you like West Texas?*

*Where are you two from?*

*Florida, huh.*

*Have you done much stargazing?*

*Hunting?*

*Fishing?*

"Okay, I'm officially insulted." Vance gave up on the idea of acting sociable, suggesting they go back to their corner. "We're interlopers at our own investment."

"Not all of us." She flicked her eyes toward Jake.

He'd left MK and was glad-handing, chatting for a minute or two, then moving on. Lauren scanned the room looking for Mary Katherine while Vance went to get himself another beer. Lauren felt a hand on her shoulder and turned. MK stood there with three men. One fellow split off from them.

"I'd like to introduce you to my good friends, Victor Moffett and Rick Bates."

"Hello," Lauren said nervously.

Vance returned from the bar.

"This is Lauren Gold and Vance Courage. They're partners with my ex, Jake. They're the ones who bought the ranch."

"Nice to meet you." Vance extended his hand, nudging her to do the same.

They were the business tycoons she'd recognized from the list, 'Forbes' two richest Americans. "It's nice to meet you," she said, forcing a smile, wondering if they noticed how nervous she was.

Victor Moffett was the most famous investor in America. Nicknamed the "Seeing Eye-Owan" for his uncanny stock picking ability and home state, he was also a notable tightwad, still living in the first house he'd purchased in the mid-1950s. Bates made his billions in computer software and the two were rumored to be best friends.

Both were philanthropists and when they were in the news these days, it was for donating large sums of money. She had to stop the urge to grin. What a sight, looking at them in the black robes. They looked silly and the idea that either one hunted was absurd.

"You're lucky to be the owners," Victor said.

"I agree," Rick said. "If we'd known it was for sale, Victor and I would have outbid you."

"I wonder if you'd give us a minute," MK said. She glanced at her when she said it. "I'd like to talk to Lauren alone for a moment. You boys don't run away too far."

When they had privacy MK said, "Don't be mad at ol' Jake. He didn't know what he was getting into, either." MK put her hand on her shoulder and squeezed it motherly. "These gowns do look a bit asinine." She lifted hers revealing a pair of designer jeans with plaid piping tucked into her red cowboy boots.

"Is this the group, the International Order of Saint Eustachius? I recognize a few people from a list I saw, including those two." Lauren tilted her head toward the men she'd just met.

"It is."

"Who's the third man with them?" He was the one who drifted away a moment earlier.

MK paused. "That's Kurt Berlin."

"Who's he?"

"Once upon a time he was a German auto tycoon."

"What happened?"

"Long story, a little problem with cheating on emissions tests. You have too many questions, hon."

"I wouldn't have pegged you for a hunter."

"Oh, hon, heck no, I'm no hunter. I have trouble killing flies landing on the hors d'oeuvres at the Hamptons Horse Show."

That was a relief, that her gut was right. Still it didn't make sense. "Why do you belong, then?"

"Hunting's not all they do. We'll chat more about it later. I just wanted you to know that Jake didn't hoodwink you. He knew Pomps for a long time and everyone here has a story to tell about that fella." MK excused herself to rejoin her friends.

Lauren followed her. The three men were talking with Vance, and they were laughing.

MK interrupted them. "Come on, boys, let's make the rounds."

When they were alone again, Vance asked why MK wanted to talk to her privately.

She told him what MK said, that Jake hadn't hoodwinked them.

"What do you think that's supposed to mean?"

Lauren shook her head. "Just what she said, I guess."

"Half the world's wealth is standing in this room."

"I know," she said, swallowing hard.

"You know what else is weird? Bates and Moffett are on the Isidore Global Initiative list from Luther."

She knew that. "What are you saying?" She felt her heart beating again.

"I don't think these are the members of the Order of Saint Utes-whatever. For one thing, the hunting group is men-only. There were no women in any of the photographs you printed out. I think these are the members of the Isidore Global Initiative. And I think this is *their* convention."

"I'm so confused."

"I have a theory. Maybe the hunting organization is a front."

"For what?"

"For the Isidore Global Initiative."

It was possible considering the people mixing in the dining hall. She couldn't fathom Bates and Moffett hunting. Being part of the ISP, the International Super Powers? That was much more believable. "They're hiding in plain sight."

"Yep." Vance raked his hair with his fingers. "Like the ancient

Chinese warring strategy. Don't test the weight of the emperor's cauldrons."

Lauren's eyes widened, like a game animal.

"It's just a different way of saying don't tip your hand. Don't let the enemy know you're testing their defense. They're weaker if they're unprepared. And do everything in plain sight."

"That's a leap. From a guest list to an enemies list?"

"Look around, Lauren. Do you really think all these people would get together at the last minute in the middle of nowhere if it wasn't seriously important?"

Her mouth was dry. She drank directly from the fancy glass-bottled water in her hand. "Who's the enemy?"

Vance pursed his lips. "I wish I knew."

## 22

Luther rushed around with a seating chart in his hand. When he saw Lauren and Vance, he ushered them to their places using hand gestures. He seated them across from each other at the end of one of the long tables.

Lauren hadn't had the chance to talk to Josh since their heart-pounding ride back to the stable. He'd made no effort to say hello during the cocktail hour and was seated on the same side of the table as her, but at the opposite end. She leaned forward, pretending to get the waiter's attention to spy on him. Josh looked right at home, chatting and laughing.

She'd detected a least three different languages being spoken nearby and neither she nor Vance understood much of what was being discussed. She excused herself to go to the ladies' room. She'd stopped at the desk and asked Rosa for headache meds. She cupped her hand under the bathroom faucet and swallowed them.

When she returned to her seat, the main course had been served. The bison was tender as butter and served with crispy pommes frits drizzled with truffle oil. The brussel sprouts with the syrupy balsamic dressing and caramelized-onions tasted like dessert. Her nerves were so jangled she just picked at her food.

Vance ravished the meal.

After dessert and coffee, she left the table and stepped out for some fresh air. She spread her arms, tilted her head back and gazed at the galaxy of twinkling lights overhead. A gust of wind caught the hem of her robe and as it fluttered, the feelings she'd had inside, ones of being out of place and powerless, disappeared. Vance had pointed Venus out to her on their first night at the ranch. It was easy to spot after that, the biggest and brightest star in the night sky. She hugged her ribs to block the chill.

Vance appeared with a colorful blanket. He draped it over her shoulders, from behind. The light scent of cigar smoke wafted from the patio as more guests gathered in the courtyard.

"Oh my God." She saw it first. His eyes followed hers. A shooting star streaked over the moonlit mountains, leaving a brief contrail of white light before it dropped out of sight.

Vance grabbed her by the shoulders. He cupped her chin and kissed her on the mouth.

He'd caught her off guard. "Whoa. Where did that come from?" Her heart thumped under the robe.

"I've been wanting to do that since the moment you arrived." He brushed her hair behind her ears using his fingers. He nuzzled her neck with his lips and contemplated her expression, as if searching for a response.

She froze. Using the blanket, he pulled her closer, against his body. The next kiss wasn't a surprise. Their tongues met and he paused, waiting for a signal. Her brain said stop but another part of her wanted more.

When she felt the bump in his pants against her leg, she snapped out of it.

"This is not a good idea." She pushed him back gently with her palm. "Let's go for a walk."

"Can I at least hold your hand?"

He sounded like a little boy. "No."

Her heart raced, intoxicated on hormones, or lust, or whatever they called it.

"Follow me," she said.

She led the way to a nearby trail Josh had shown her on horseback, a berm they could easily hike on foot. The climb was harder than it looked. It was night, and the scrub brush made it difficult to navigate in the dark. She lifted the bottom of the black robe to keep from tripping. He followed her. By the time they reached the flat area, they were out of breath. She sat on a big rock and brushed the dust from her robe.

He sat next to her, keeping his hands to himself.

"MK swears she couldn't kill a fly."

"I told you, they're not really a group of hunters." He fondled the black fabric on the sleeve of her robe.

Her brow creased. "You seem so sure."

"I faxed the list of names to Jake, the ones we found in the IGGY folder, when he was at the marina, to see if he could make heads or tails of it."

He told her the rest of the story, that Jake called him right away when he saw his ex-wife's name on the list. And that MK instructed Jake to tell Luther to call a meeting at her behest. And the biggest surprise: MK was the one who'd tipped Jake off that the ranch was for sale.

"And you didn't tell me?" She glared at him. "Why?"

"I didn't want you to worry. Plus, Jake doesn't know anything more than we do. Jake looked me in the eye and swore he didn't know MK had plans."

"And you believed him?" She rolled her eyes.

"I do. Jake's been pressing Luther for more information."

"And?"

"Luther told him to mind his own business."

"With all due respect, that's precisely what we're doing. *Minding our business.*"

"I agree. Jake admitted it seemed like MK was expecting his call. Sorry." Vance sounded sincere. "I should have told you."

She was quiet for a minute.

"What are you thinking?" he asked.

"That if it weren't for you, I wouldn't be involved in this mess. It's something big, Vance. We're just pawns."

He chewed on his cuticle. "Of who?"

"How am I supposed to know? You're the ex-detective."

"If I was investigating it, I'd start with MK. She's the common denominator. She's the one who fed the lead to Jake."

"Why didn't she buy it herself? Or tell Gates and Moffett? Every single person here would have paid a lot more money than we did. They'd have jumped on it. Someone wanted *us* to buy it. They offered you and Jake a killer deal and they knew you couldn't turn down."

"Getting suckered feels like shit," Vance said.

"Gee, that fills my soul with hope and optimism."

Her eyes followed his as he gazed in the direction of the dining hall where they could see the robed guests dispersing. The staff was cleaning up, busy resetting the tables. The kitchen was doing two shifts.

He looked at her, the moon catching the whites of his eyes, accenting the yellow flakes in his dark-blue eyes. "They have an agenda. I've been working on my theory some more."

"Lay it on me, Detective Courage."

"Saint Eustachius is the patron saint of hunters. Saint Isidore the Farmer is the patron saint of farmers, laborers, farmhands, and animal husbandry."

"Who knew you were so up on your saints?"

"I'm being serious. Hear me out." He stood, took the spiral notebook from his pocket and flipped to the page where he'd made notes at the courthouse. Using his cell as a flashlight, he read from it, "Here's the rub. There're *two* Saint Isidores. The other one is Saint Isidore *of Seville*. Patron saint of 'computer scientists, software engineers, computer programmers, computer technicians, computer users and students.' "

"So what you're saying is that the Internet has a patron saint?" She rolled her eyes.

"It's not as farfetched as you'd think. Astronauts have one. So do miners and carpenters, and even Special Forces. So why wouldn't the Internet, and software engineers, and computer programmers? They're the pagan gods of the modern world. What if I told you there's a patron saint for clowns?"

"I'd laugh." And she did.

"Well, it's true. Why wouldn't people in the computer industry have one?"

"You're sure about this?"

He nodded.

She wrapped the blanket tighter around the robe. "Who decides who or what is the patron saint of, well, who or what?"

"I wondered the same thing. So I looked it up. It started with the Catholic Church dating back to the Roman Empire."

"Oh God, where are you going with this?"

"You're the one who asked."

She looked up at the stars. "Educate me."

He explained that patron saints were chosen because they had a connection to the subject. Saint Joseph became the patron saint of carpenters because he was one. The church believed that humans are able act as middlemen for God. "John the Evangelist is the patron saint of authors."

He told her Saint Isidore of Seville was the first Christian writer who'd attempted to compile universal information. "He's credited as the father of the modern encyclopedia. He was revered for saving a lot of scholarly works that would otherwise have been lost."

She rubbed the back of her neck with her hand.

A rustling came from the brush.

Vance jumped to his feet, pulling her by the arm. Shielding her, he reached for his 9-millimeter and pointed it in the direction the noise was coming from.

It was Cheks. The dog was panting.

"You're carrying?"

"And you think that's a bad idea?"

No. In fact she thought it was a good idea. But he'd almost shot the dog. "Hey, boy, you scared us." When Lauren reached down to pet him, the sleeve on her robe caught on a branch, exposing part of her forearm.

"Jesus. What happened to you?" Vance took hold of her hand and pushed her sleeve higher, twisting her wrist gently, inspecting the wounds.

The scratches were still fresh.

She told him about the wild ride back to the barn after the horses were spooked by gunfire.

"You were up there? I heard it from here. That had to come from a fifty-caliber rifle."

"That's exactly what Josh said." She pulled her hand away and knelt. "Hey boy, come here." Cheks obeyed, his tail wagging so hard it snapped some twigs. The dog sat next to her and this time, let her scratch his head.

Vance holstered the gun under his left arm. "That's a pretty fancy jacket for a dog." He shined his phone light on it.

"It's a military grade K-9 flak jacket. He's, um, was, Roy's dog."

"Here, boy." Vance snapped his fingers and smooched his

lips. The dog backed away from him. "Makes sense, I guess. If you can spare no expense, why not buy the very best?"

She knelt on both knees, hoping to get a closer look at the flak jacket. Cheks spun and barked. He wanted to play. When she didn't reciprocate he sat on his haunches, just out of reach, as if waiting for her to throw a ball.

---

RED RINGS BURNED BRIGHTLY for an instant and faded, lit tips of cigars. The air was crisp. Vance could smell the aromas wafting up the canyon. From their vantage point they had a bird's-eye view of the ranch. The deputy at the gate turned the dome light on in his patrol truck. The distance was too far for him to see what he was doing in the cab. At least he wasn't sleeping.

"Do you think she forgot her hairspray," Lauren said.

Jane Pandora's black BMW pulled up to the gate. She got out and streetlights illuminating the front gates lit her beehive up like an ornamental lantern. She stood outside of the patrol vehicle, leaning forward, talking to the deputy.

"Did you two kiss and make up?"

She'd read him right. "Yeah, well, when people don't keep their promises, it pisses me off. But I was out of line. I was annoyed because when I was in town, I bumped into her at the courthouse. I already had the paperwork from Sue, the gal at the jail."

"You mean Sue the bank teller."

"That's right. I bumped into Jane just as I was leaving. She could have signed it right then and there and we could have gotten a jump on the results. But she didn't want to go out of her way." He paused. "No, come to think of it, she blamed it on Sue saying it was late on a Friday and Sue would be cranky. That's why I was pissed off when she showed up here without it. It was her idea to drop it off since she was coming out for the wedding ceremony. I chewed her out before I knew she was coming back." He kicked a rock with the toe of his boot. "I apologized."

"To who?" Something had distracted Lauren.

"Jane? Pandora?"

Lauren eyed Josh who'd joined the group of men gathered by the outdoor fire pit in the courtyard. Josh threw a log on the fire and orange embers exploded like fireworks.

"You have the hots for Josh."

"I wouldn't call it that." Her eyes tracked the men milling around the pit.

She paused, her focus turned back to the front gate where Jane was still talking to the deputy who was now standing outside his truck. "He's enigmatic. I'm curious about him." She changed the subject. "Do you trust the sheriff?"

"No."

"What about her?" Lauren pointed to the taillights of Jane's BMW disappearing in the distance.

"Nope."

"Why not?"

"Because I don't trust people I don't know."

"Did you think she smelled like booze earlier?"

"I smelled it at the courthouse. She was driving her official vehicle."

"You did?"

"Uh-huh."

"Great. That's just what we need. A real life Calamity Jane. Let's play a game."

"What kind of game?"

"A word game."

"That's not fair. Women have a higher verbal aptitude."

"This doesn't require verbal aptitude."

"Okay. Let the games begin."

"All right. Convince me you're not a sucker for those triple-F boobs."

"I tried to. A few minutes ago. But you wouldn't let me." He grinned. "Plus, I'm a leg man. That's why I'm much dumber around you than her. I need Jane to like me and I don't need you screwing it up."

"Did it occur to you I'm doing the same thing with Josh?"

Cheks moved closer to them and sat at attention, as if the desire to chase a ball had passed. His ears were pricked. Lauren scratched his head.

"Fair enough," he finally said.

"So much for my legs. They aren't going to do me much good. Unless I put on a short skirt and stand on the runway with my thumb in the air when the private planes start leaving."

Then he remembered something. He took the white envelope from his back pocket of his jeans and handed it to her.

"What's this?"

She opened it but it was too dark to read. He used his cell-phone light again.

"Where did you get this?"

"From Rosa's office."

The same thing that had caught his attention, caught hers. "Two incoming wire transfers for fifty thousand dollars? Last month?"

"Look at the balance."

Luther had over a quarter of a million dollars in his checking account.

"Two wire transfers out, the same days of the wire-ins. Ten thousand a pop."

"Yep. I doubt it's for child support. Or alimony." And they weren't coming from Luther's paycheck.

She put the statement back in the envelope and handed it to him.

"SORRY," Lauren said to Vance. "Let me get it." She'd let go of bank statement before it was in his hand.

"No, I'll get it." Vance used his cell light to search for the envelope.

"Ah, there it is." She dropped to one knee and picking it up, saw the red dot aimed at his back. There wasn't time to warn him. Vance groaned and went down as a spider web of bluish light streaked behind him and danced on his back. She heard clicking mixed with the crackling footfalls of someone coming toward them.

Cheks barked twice, then dashed into the darkness.

"Vance. Vance."

He didn't answer. He was face down in the dirt. The shadow ran through the low-lying brush near the top of the berm, hunched over.

Her heart pumped. "Vance. Get up."

Still nothing. A second later he scrambled to his feet like an angry bull.

"Run," Vance yelled.

She froze.

And then the electrical grid on his back charged back up, the maze of blue lights out of a Frankenstein movie crackled across his shoulders.

He fought to stay upright. His body convulsed. He went back down in a seizure, growling like a feral animal, cursing, "Goddamn it. Motherfucker. Cocksucker."

Vance scrabbled back up and turned blindly toward where the blue lightning had come from. Lauren backed away. Vance lit up again, the blue currents streaking, him howling in agony, his body writhing on the ground. "Fuck. Fuck. Fuck."

Panting she said, "Stop it. You're killing him."

"Give it to me," the voice said.

"What." She'd do anything to make this stop.

"That envelope, give it to me."

"I-I . . . dropped—"

The attacker fired another five seconds of voltage into Vance's back. An electrical storm sizzled on his back. He convulsed as if fiddling a Charlie Daniels tune.

"*Stop.*"

The assailant released the cartridge on the weapon and then he rushed her, pressing something against her thigh. A mini transformer lit up in a jagged arc over the black robe covering her thigh.

*STOP.*

The word was loud in her head but it wouldn't come out of her mouth. The pain. It was only a few seconds but it seemed forever. She went face first into the dirt, a few feet from Vance, who was still incapacitated. She turned her head in the soft earth and saw the man grab the white envelope on the ground between where she and Vance lay motionless.

Vance was able to scramble to his feet and stumble after the attacker. Her thigh burned like she'd been stung by a dozen bees. She rubbed it hard, massaging it, trying to make the pain stop.

A minute later she looked up and saw Vance standing over her.

"Are you okay?" he asked.

"I think so."

"That was a stun gun. It'll hurt like a bitch for an hour. Ice will help."

"I thought you were shot. I was afraid he was going to kill you."

He turned his back to her, held his cell phone over his shoulder, the flashlight still on. "I got tased."

Two wires, about a foot apart were implanted between his shoulders.

"Four times to be exact."

He shined his light on the ground and picked up the yellow cartridge. That's what she'd seen drop from the weapon. He looped the wires attached to it like a lasso and held it. It was still implanted in his flesh.

"They have barbs. I'm going to need your help."

"Oh my God." The robe was pinned to his back and it hung on an angle, like a listing shower curtain. "Who would do this?"

## 23

V ance lay face down on the comforter atop the bed in her room. Lauren straddled him, sitting on his hamstrings with one leg on either side of his. She lifted the thin black robe and the tail of his shirt underneath, and looked. The barbs had penetrated both layers and he wanted her to pull them out.

It was as if his clothing had been staple-gunned to his shoulder blades. Rings of blood wicked through the fabric.

"I told you. You're going to have to yank them out. Just grab the wires and pull."

She leaned back, biding her time, worrying how he'd react.

He tried to get up. "Fine. I'll do it myself."

She pushed him down by the back of his neck, shoved a kneecap in the small of his back, grabbed both wires at the same time and yanked the prongs out.

"Shiiiiittttt."

He rolled over, pushing her off and pounded his heels on the bed. "Cocksucker. Son of a bitch."

She scooted away from him.

"Thank you," he finally said. He pulled the robe over his

head and unbuttoned his shirt. She helped him, gently tugging one sleeve at a time. He went to the mirror and craned his neck, inspecting the holes in his back. It looked like he'd been stabbed twice with an ice pick.

"Did you get a look at him?"

She shook her head. "He was wearing a mask, like a knit cap over his face. And it was dark. He wanted that envelope you had badly enough to zap me. I woulda handed it to him but he didn't give me the chance."

"That's so fucked up, to stun gun you. Let me see your leg."

It was on her upper thigh and in order to show it to him, she'd have to take her pants off. There were burn marks on her pant leg.

"Hang on." She went into the bathroom and returned with a towel around her waist.

Vance lifted it and looked at the purple marks ripening. He pressed with his thumb.

She went slack at the knees. "Auw."

"Whoever did this has access to police-grade equipment. The weapon he used? It's a handy little dual-purpose design. Part taser, part stun gun. After the shooter releases the cartridge, it converts into a stun gun. That's what happened to you. Whoever used it is trained. He had to time it just right to make sure I was immobile long enough for him to subdue you, to get what he wanted and get away."

"I heard Cheks bark, once, maybe twice," she said. "And then the guy came up from behind, from out of nowhere. I saw a red dot."

"A laser." He slung two wet hand towels soaking in the sink, over his back. "You need to put ice on that," he touched her thigh lightly.

She threw on a pair of jeans and took the empty ice bucket from the dresser. When she opened the door to leave the room,

Luther stood under the veranda, his closed fingers facing the door like brass knuckles.

He stopped mid-knock and craned his neck, peering in through the doorway. "Goodness, am I interrupting something?"

"This isn't what it looks like," Lauren said.

Vance stood behind her, facing Luther, bare-chested but for the wet towels draped over his shoulders.

"I'm here for the robes." He didn't bother trying to be civil. "Everyone knows to return them directly to me when the meetings have concluded. Mr. Pompadour was always strict about accounting for every garment and I've been looking all over for you two." He scolded her like a headmaster.

She picked the robes up from the floor and handed them to him.

He patted the dust and dirt from the backsides and sleeves, folded them into quarters, slung them over his forearm, and left.

When he was gone, Vance said, "Wait 'til he takes a closer look. Two bloody holes drilled in the back of one and burns on the other." He laughed. "Then he'll be really annoyed."

"Stay here," Lauren said. "I'm going for ice." She stopped and faced him. "What did that feel like, being tased?" She couldn't get the primal sounds he'd made out of her head.

Vance shook his head. "I can't describe it, exactly. It's weird. I lost all my motor skills, like I was paralyzed, but my thoughts were clear. My brain wanted to go for my gun, but my command center had shut down."

"You sounded like you had Tourette's."

"Sorry about that."

---

WHEN HE FOUND out who tased him, there would be hell to pay. And he would find out. When he was still practicing law, he'd sued the Miami police department for tasing a suspect with an IQ of seventy-three. The kid shoplifted a bag of potato chips and when the storeowner called the cops, the young man tried to run. Four officers had already taken the kid down on the sidewalk but he struggled, they tased him.

He had mixed feelings about it. On the one hand, he understood the officers didn't know the suspect was a kid. Or his IQ. His mother had left him in the car.

He'd studied the surveillance video and cringed, watching one cop zap the kid twice. Vance couldn't get it out of his head for weeks, the woman's son writhing and convulsing on the sidewalk. They settled out of court. The good news, then and right now, was that he'd been convinced tasing didn't cause permanent damage.

After he found out who ambushed him tonight, he couldn't promise that person wouldn't need a walking cane. Or a wheelchair.

Lauren had left the cartridge on the bed. He held it under the light.

*That fucker lit me up me four times.*

Vance turned the darts between his fingertips, tiny metal wasp-like stingers damp with blood.

When Lauren came through the door with a full bucket of ice, he was lying face down on her bed, shirt off, boots on.

"Oh gosh," she said. "Your back, it looks like volcanoes are forming."

Good description. He'd looked at the wounds in the mirror when he'd emptied the tissue box and put the used cartridge inside it, evidence he'd deal with later. The washcloth ice packs soothed the stinging. He'd play it smart for now, chill out while letting her play nurse.

He turned his head on the pillow. "How's your leg?"

She'd changed back into the towel and sat on the edge of the bed icing her thigh.

"Cold."

He planted his face in the pillow, muffling his laughter.

"Are you going to tell anyone about what happened to us tonight?" she asked.

He was pretty sure no one heard or saw anything. The guests mingling outside were too far away. Plus, the cacophony of different conversations going on at the same time gave their assailant cover to strike. Ambushed was more like it.

"No," he finally said. "Who would we tell? And why?"

She lay down on her back, putting her head on the pillow next to him. He looked at her. He'd never seen a more beautiful creature in the world.

"I trust you," she said.

"Good. Did you hear that strange noise when Luther left?"

She sprang into a sitting position. "No."

"That squeaking sound?"

"No." She was practically breathless.

"I think it was his butt cheeks. What a tight ass."

She hit him over the head with the pillow. "You're such a jerk."

He deserved that. But he wasn't up for a pillow fight. Instead, he asked her to remind him where Luther lived. He should have known, or remembered, but for some reason he couldn't.

"He lives in the watchtower."

"No shit." He asked her how she knew that and she admitted she'd asked Luther where he'd gone when he'd sneaked into town driving the Hummer.

"The second story is reserved for special guests. Luther lives on the ground floor."

That was a surprise. The watchtower was cool.

When he'd first considered Jake's idea to invest, Jake told

him *El Fortín de Antílope* was built in the mid-1800s to protect settlers and ranchers from Indians and bandits. The land it had been built upon was a volcanic crater. Back then a wealthy rancher named Melville Saver had run 20,000 head of Longhorn cattle on the lands irrigated with water from the Marfidio spring. That same spring fed the creek that ran through the property.

He'd been intrigued by the watchtower, a crude thirty- foot high adobe cylinder with a series of observation windows cut of little squares. Vance hadn't toured it yet, but he wanted to.

It made sense that Luther's mail would be delivered to the front desk.

"How does it look?" He reached around and lifted one of the makeshift ice packs.

"Much better."

He stood over the sink, splashed cold water on his face and put his arms through the sleeves of his shirt. Fastening two buttons, he left the tails hanging out, removed the Glock from the shoulder holster and stuffed it in the back of his pants. He saw her reflection in the mirror. She looked exhausted.

"If you get scared tonight, I'll keep my side of the bed warm. And I'll see if I packed my turban."

"I'm hating you more now that I did yesterday," she said, closing the door in his face, turning the deadbolt.

He'd been pushing his luck. He counted to thirty, making sure he was alone. He headed to the main house, carrying the tissue box with the remains of the taser under his shirt. Most of the guests had turned in for the night and the only light came from the yellow bug bulbs overhead. Private jets had been landing all day and one was on the tarmac now, taxiing away.

The headlamps of the Hummer lit the dirt road. Vance ducked behind a hedge. Josh was behind the wheel shuttling someone some late arrivers from the airstrip to the lobby.

## 24

Lauren sat in one of the plush leather club chairs near the front desk, waiting for Vance. Two women standing at reception were characters right out of *Real Housewives of Silicone Valley*, if such a show existed.

The late-thirties blonde, with hair extensions and needle bruises on her upper lip, chatted with her friend. "I hate my in-laws. They used to be rich. Jason's parents lived in the Pacific Palisades when his dad was a movie producer. That's how he got into Stanford. Then my father-in-law lost all his money and he's like seventy-five years old now. They want us to visit them because they don't have money to travel."

They were waiting on Rosa to finish a call on the landline.

The blonde's friend, an Asian millennial with long, shiny black hair, recoiled. "Oh my God, yours sounds almost as bad as mine. My mother-in-law's nuts. She gardens, and you won't believe what she sent us. A bulb of garlic she grew herself. It still had nasty dirt hanging on the roots." She scrunched her nose. "I told my husband to throw that shit out but I know he hid it somewhere in the house."

The blonde glared at Rosa. "I watched a *Ted Talk* about

resentments, about how it's so much healthier to forgive and move on. I just wish Jason would just cut ties with his parents. They're so depressing. They live on Social Security and expect us to drive to Bakersfield. Give me your garlic and I'll send it to them."

They laughed at their joke.

"Jason's company is on the brink of becoming a unicorn."

The woman with the garlic-sending mother-in-law palmed the bell on the desk. She banged it so hard it clanged off-key. "What is taking this chick so long?"

Patrons eating a late breakfast in the dining room turned to see who'd made the noise.

Long-suffering Rosa hurried to the desk with her ever-present, easy smile. She asked them how she could help.

"How long is the airstrip going to be closed?" the blonde asked, obviously put out. "And why weren't we told in advance?"

"I'm not sure," Rosa said. "They're doing repairs, I think. I can get the manager if you'd like."

The brunette held her hand in Rosa's face like, 'Shut up.'

Rosa said, "I hope you enjoy your stay. And let us know if you need anything."

They ignored her as if she were invisible. "God, her hair color is horrible," the brunette said loud enough for Rosa to hear.

"And those piercings, jeez. She looks like the minions that ride the company bus."

The two women grabbed coffees and joined their nannies and children who'd been waiting in the courtyard.

Lauren walked up to the desk.

"How women find men who will put up with that is beyond me," Rosa's voice cracked.

"Heartlessness might beget heartlessness," Lauren said.

"Men are so dumb."

"I know. What's a unicorn?"

Vance sidled up. "It's an imaginary horse with a horn sticking out of its forehead."

Jake had joined them and leaned on his elbows, his curved back facing Rosa. "It's a privately held company with a market cap of a billion dollars or more."

"A billion?" *A billion dollars?*

Rosa leafed through a file, blinking, and swiped at the welling tears. When she looked up her mood changed on a dime. MK was heading for the front desk.

"Did you know these hoodie-wearing robber barons send their kids to private schools where there's no Internet." MK said. "They know what screen time does to children and they don't want their kids brain-damaged."

Lauren twisted the ends of her hair with her fingers.

"What's your point?" Vance sounded impatient.

"They spend *billions* to keep the government off their backs. And they're powerful," MK said. "Twenty years ago, the five biggest companies in the world were not invented yet. Pissants are running four of five of 'em. Roy found them repugnant. 'Elite shits' are the exact words, I believe. Sucking up resources while pretending to care about the world. Meanwhile, no one is trying to rein them in."

"I didn't know about the group therapy session," Vance said.

"Don't be such a cynic, especially since I was just starting to like you. Every one of 'em carries multiple passports for themselves and their families." She tossed her head in the direction of the dining room full of men who looked like they were dressed for Swiss mountain climbing, some pushing thousand-dollar strollers, others carrying babies on their chests in slings.

"Why do they need passports to other countries?" The idea of leaving the country had never crossed Lauren's mind.

"Why do you think?" she asked.

MK paused to let a group of yoga-pant-clad wives and girl-friends pass by.

"Because after they're done exploiting the free markets and our society turns to shit, and the revolution begins, they can hop on their private jets with their crypto currency on thumb drives and spend their golden years in New Zealand or the British Virgin Islands."

Surely MK was exaggerating. What if she wasn't? What if that was exactly what was happening? This new generation of billionaires was plundering the country and planning to leave? Like arsonists running from a burning building?

"One of those phony-Kumbayers said in a TV interview that the mission of his company is to 'bring the world together.' "

"Coke tried that," Jake said. "They wanted to teach the world to sing, remember?"

MK sneered at him.

Jake slid his thumb and forefinger across his mouth, promising to zip it.

MK said, "One of those shits even floated the idea of giving everyone a living wage, for doing nothing. As if their fellow Americans are basically a bunch of feudal serfs with no good ideas."

"They tried it. It's called welfare," Jake said.

"I thought you were zipping it." MK clenched her jaw and shot him a look that promised a third time would not be tolerated. "There has to be a hierarchy. It's human nature. This crop of sanctimonious shits has consolidated too much power. They believe they're superior. Give people money with no purpose and the next thing you know they're gobbling opioids and sticking needles in their arms."

"That's already happening," Lauren said.

"Or taking up arms against you," Vance said.

"That's exactly right," MK said, nodding.

"Happiness comes from love, too." Lauren cringed inside and her face felt like it was on fire.

MK surprised her by hugging her tightly. "That's exactly the point, hon. So many of them have lost their humanity. They think they've written the final chapter of mankind. They dress like skateboarders, thinking we won't know who they really are." She gazed out the picture window. "They believe life is a chess game and they've captured the king."

"Is that why the Isidore Global Initiative is here?" Lauren asked.

MK didn't look at all surprised by the question. "Yes. 'Cause we're going to conduct the biggest intervention in the history of mankind." She licked her lips. "Someone has to stop them. We can't stop them, but we can at least try to tap the brakes."

Vance hung on every word. "Who's going to stop who, from doing what, exactly?"

"We don't have time," MK said. "Right now, I have a zillion details to attend to and I have to go see Gordy and Luther. Meanwhile I need you three to play the part of the new owners. After that, we'll talk."

Lauren had a zillion questions but not a single one she could articulate.

Before Jake left with MK, he likened their situation to bad weather. "It's a hurricane. We're going to have to shelter in and see what happens."

When they were alone, Vance said, "I didn't know about any of this." He crossed his heart. "I hope you believe me."

---

FRANK CONN AWOKE with an internal rage clawing his guts. His fists and hands were bruised from yesterday's outburst. After pounding on the metal bars for five minutes straight, his fingers had swollen so big he was agonizing over the idea of unzipping his orange jumpsuit to take a piss.

As he sat up and swung his feet down on the cold cement floor, he knocked something over: The noise startled him. It appeared to be a glass container of some sort. He reached for it, his fat fingers recoiling when the thing inside the milk bottle moved. His eyes hadn't adjusted to the morning light, and without his readers, he was having trouble making out the emperor scorpion pecking at the glass with the stinger atop its curved tail.

Frank sat on the metal toilet in the middle of the cell with his jail overalls bunched around his ankles, middle-age paunch covering his flaccid pecker like blooming dough. He was mid-fart when the sheriff strolled in and leaned against the metal bars.

"Hey. Can I get a little privacy here?" His stomach ached. He doubled over in pain at every cramp. No sense in trying to hold it any longer. God knows he'd tried.

"Privacy? Most prisoners are glad to use their anatomy the way you're using it now. That dinosaur eye can turn into a two-way street, if you know what I mean." The sheriff held a blue paisley scarf over his nose and mouth. "Woowee. I've smelled some bad stuff before but this might be the winner," he said, turning to leave.

"Wait." Frank wiped, pulled his underwear up, then waddled over with his jumpsuit around his ankles. He picked up the bottle. "I have something to show you."

"A used shit rag?"

"No, this. Look."

The sheriff held his breath to come closer to look. He squinted. "Where'd this damn thing come from?"

"I thought you might know." Frank's stomach cramped again and he doubled over. "It was here when I woke up." His voice croaked like a frog. "Where I come from . . . ah . . . people respect the rule of law. We don't . . . ah . . . frame folks for murder."

"Respect the rule of law? Now that's a good one. You're confusing the rule of law with justice," the sheriff said.

Frank groaned. "When do I get out of here?"

"It's up to the judge. After bail is set. Or you bond out. You know how it goes. You're a dang lawyer."

"When do I see the judge?"

"Far as I know you're not on any docket to see any judge. See, we have us a problem, Frank-O. Since you're representing yourself, it makes it hard for the system to work. Every time the court tries to serve you notice, the poor dummy of a process server thinks he's screwing up. We give him the notice. He drives off, gets to the four-way stop and scratches his head. Thinks Sue made a mistake 'cause the document is going to the same address he just left. So, he does a U-turn, brings it back and says he'll come back tomorrow. Groundhog Day. You following me?"

Frank stood and pulled up the prison jumper.

"The 'Frank Conn, Esq.' thing is a double whammy for the dummy," Manny said. "He never heard of a lawyer that can't get hisself out of jail so it don't occur to him to deliver it to *you*. He gets as far as the corner, palms himself on the forehead, and comes back. Sue tried explaining it to him. Now she just calls him Boomerang."

"Well, shit." Frank's swollen knuckles made it hard to pull his underpants down in a hurry.

"Sue tells him it's not a typo but that just don't make sense to him. You see, people around here like to keep things simple, 'cause that's how things have always been."

His intestines had to be empty. He stood and pulled the jumper back up over his shoulders, zipping it to the waist. The air in the windowless cell was rotten.

"Be glad it's just your shit you have to smell. Border Patrol is bringing you more playmates. We're holding 'em 'til ICE comes to get them. Enjoy your privacy, Counselor. And remember, things can always get worse."

"If I change my mind and want to hire a local attorney, can you recommend someone?" Frank bent over in pain. He yanked the zipper down and sat on the metal toilet seat.

Manny grimaced and pulled the bandana tighter over his nose. "You know I can't do that. Conflict of interest. We go by the law around here, the good old-fashioned Ten Commandments kind of law. Your DNA was on the body of a homicide victim. You shoulda lawyered up when we arrested you."

"Look," Frank begged, "I'm not a criminal defense lawyer and I don't know anything about criminal law. I practice corporate law. We make deals happen." He paused to grunt, wincing. "We don't handle physical evidence like DNA and fingerprints. That's tantamount to a brain surgeon doing a root canal."

"Big words ain't gonna help. Your kind hides behind the small print that no one ever reads." The sheriff lifted his arm and put his scarf-covered nose in the crook of his elbow.

Frank's vision went blurry. He didn't care if he rolled off the steel toilet and died. The sloughed snakeskin may as well have been a candy wrapper for all he cared. This must be the first stage of death, when your body rebels so completely that the thinking mind bargains with the subconscious with no deal about how it will end, just the promise it will *end*. "I don't know what I did to deserve this."

"You remember Juanita White?" Manny asked.

"Juanita who?" In no way did the name ring any kind of bell.

The sheriff lifted the bottom triangle of the paisley scarf resting against his chin. "That's what I thought. Well, you got your little pet in the bottle to keep you company 'til Border Patrol brings you some *amigos*."

Turning to leave, Manny gagged. He placed the five-gallon

Stetson he'd been pressing over his heart back on top of his head. Holding the door leading to the office ajar with the toe of his boot, he let the odor permeate the office. He picked up the milk bottle and put it under his arm.

———

SURLY SUE WAS at her desk touching up her eyebrows with a makeup pencil. She checked her handiwork in the mirror, just before the odor reached her nose. "God almighty, what the hell, Sheriff? Smells like something done gone off and died back there."

"Deputy Torres check in with you yet? I been trying to get him on the radio, before I stopped in to visit our prisoner."

"No. But I doubt he's gone AWOL. Probably just outta range is all. For chrissake, will you please close that damn door before one of us dies of air pollution? I'm going out back to smoke. I need to clear my nose."

Manny laughed, taking his foot off the threshold, letting it close with a bang.

———

FRANK CONN'S thinking was fuzzy. Why did the sheriff want to know about a woman, Juanita something or another? *Juanita. Juanita. Juanita.* His stomach ached. The name meant nothing to him. He didn't know any *Juanitas.* What did Manny say her last name was? *Last name, last name, last name.* White. Manny said her last name was White. He mopped the sweat on his brow with the loose sleeve of his jumpsuit. Juanita White.

She sounded like a Mexican married to a *gringo.* He'd never heard of her. Maybe the sheriff was confused. *God help me.* Through the fog of whatever was ailing him, he was certain of one thing: He had nothing to do with the death of the house-keeper at Antelope Creek Ranch. Someone was framing him and he had no idea who or why.

His dying wish was that he'd never set foot in Marfidio County. He shouldn't have let the younger lawyers talk him into it. Hell, the place had no golf course. If he'd known that he would never have agreed to go.

He put his head in his hands. The sheriff said Border Patrol agents were bringing more prisoners. Maybe they'd kill a middle-aged *gringo* with a nasty case of the shits. And that'd put him out of his misery. Yesterday, Sheriff Manny warned the gangbangers. "*No matas a mi prisionero*": "Don't kill my prisoner." Frank was sure he was on his own, that the sheriff was done protecting him.

And Frank couldn't give a shit.

## 25

They had gathered in the foyer: Lauren, MK, Jake, and Vance. Lauren was impressed that MK made good on her word, promising a powwow before things got underway. Vance insisted it be somewhere that would double as a lookout point. One of the outposts would have been perfect but the ranch was over capacity and every space, including all the forts, was occupied. They settled on the foyer near the front door, adjacent to the front desk. Vance had moved the leather chairs closer together, for privacy. When she asked about Luther, MK said he had his hands full prepping for the summit. She'd promised a full briefing and cut right to the chase.

"Too bad Roy's not here right now," MK wished aloud. "IGGY's mission is his brainchild. He meant for it to unite as many powerful forces as we could to rein in the Big Five, before it's too late. We're starting with Numeral II."

*The Big Five? The names she'd seen on the back of the folder?*

"The Big Five what?" Vance asked.

Lauren glanced sideways, at Rosa. "Should we be talking in front of her?" She whispered, to be polite.

Rosa spoke up. "I already know all this. Plus, I can read lips.

Remember?" It was a rare moment of peace and quiet at the desk. Rosa stepped out and addressed them. "Roy talked a lot about the evils of technology. He really hated social media. He thought it brought out the worst in people. He called it a high-tech stoning because he said it was like ancient Rome 'cause people could throw rocks anonymously trying to stone someone to death. He told me human nature hasn't changed one bit. Kids are bullied until they end it all. Terrorists and school shooters plan attacks and live-stream them. He thought it was ruining the country."

"She's right," MK said. "Roy just couldn't see the upside. Not one worth all the chaos, anyway. One of the best friends he had in DC was Justice Simeri. Roy believed the *Big Shits* would never self-regulate. They're just too greedy. As much as Roy hated big government, he thought Uncle Sam needed to step in. Aldo was trying to learn as much as he could about them. The Big Five have amassed a ton of power and money. They have lawyers on top of lawyers. Roy started out admiring them. He believed they'd gotten way ahead of themselves."

Vance repeated his question. "Big Five?"

MK said, "You know them, one's cornered the retail market, another controls search information, one makes the best smartphones and tablets—in *China*. Then there's the video platform and Roy's personal favorite, the social media giant. Roy started out wanting to make this place the Sun Valley of the Southwest. He was impressed with the innovations and wanted to get to know the next generation of entrepreneurs. Boy was he disappointed. Their lack of social conscience really bothered him, especially since they try really hard to *look* like they care.

"They dress cool because they know most young people are idealistic and impressionable. Roy didn't think it's going to end well. It's why Roy formed the Isidore Global Initiative."

Rosa left the group to answer the telephone ringing at the desk.

*Wow.* Did it get any bigger than this? Roy Pompadour was cultivating a Supreme Court Justice as some sort of backstop to slow the tech giants? MK had more to say.

"Pomps made most of his money on an early investment in a startup that's now the biggest cell phone and computer maker on the planet. He'd gotten rich watching it morph into something hideous. Hiding cash reserves offshore, abusing state and federal tax laws, manufacturing products in China. Do you know the facility in China installed circus nets to keep workers from jumping off rooftops? The conditions are so awful they're trying to kill themselves. Roy thought it was disgraceful and a human rights violation. But stock price is everything."

She said Roy knew the minute the billionaires started wearing hoodies and sneakers, they'd gone undercover. He said it was a survival instinct, that deep down they knew one day the mob would come for them. Once decent folks figured the greatest and most prosperous society in the history of man had been wrecked, they'd need an escape. "'Death by shiny shit, made in China.' To quote Roy."

MK didn't mince words.

*That's why they carry multiple passports.*

*They planned to take on the world's Big Five companies, here? Tonight? At the ranch she owned one-third of?*

"MK was a telecom investment banker," Jake said. "She had a hand in all the biggest deals back in the 'nineties."

"Yeah, and all of them have been killed off, or swallowed like minnows." MK shook her head. "Messages pop up on our phones because some stupid story is Trending. It's Trending because some millennial made it Trend. Did you know two new-media companies took in ninety-percent of all advertising dollars last year? Who knows? Maybe it's too late."

*Don't say that.*

"What was Roy's prediction, exactly?" Was Lauren stupid for not knowing, for asking for clarification, especially after MK's quasi-diatribe?

"I'll just use one of Pomps' favorite expressions: 'People aren't born knowing the Ten Commandments.' He could see power, money, and influence concentrating more and more in the hands of fewer and fewer. He admired success, not wealth. Some of them suspected what Pomps was up to."

"Which was?" Lauren asked.

"Let's just say there are forces out there that knew Roy wanted to pull on the reins," MK said.

The ranch seemed ghostly quiet, considering the mission underway. MK told them she'd asked the kitchen to prepare an early lunch for them.

"It's the calm before the storm," Vance whispered in her ear, like a clairvoyant.

They'd disbanded and were following MK the short distance to the dining hall when Josh passed heading the opposite direction, and stopped at the desk.

Babies gazed innocently from designer strollers pushed by nannies, followed by rich dads and pampered moms who had no clue this was not going to be the usual restorative getaway. Lauren smiled. She knew something they didn't. She made eye contact with Vance. He nodded. This round of visitors had checked into a trap.

The group of powerful, older scions, the ones who'd run the world for a generation, was already bunkered in. The picture was getting clearer. The clock was ticking. Antelope Creek Ranch was preparing for an epic showdown.

## 26

"You got my word," Barry Landeros said. "All systems are a go. Operation Antelope is on standby, The Secondmen willing and able."

Operation Antelope was Roy Pompadour's brainchild and Luther had been Barry's point man since Roy's untimely departure.

Barry had joined The Secondmen because like the rest of the volunteer members, he was a frustrated Texan sick of the federal government's refusal to enforce border security. At least half the men were veterans of the Iraq, Afghanistan, and Vietnam wars. Some were retired police officers and deputies, and three were former Texas Rangers.

The landowners along the southern border were the second largest group, and the most active members. Illegal immigrants regularly set fires in order to distract border enforcement. Ranchers returned to find their livestock killed for food, property stolen, and homes ransacked by illegals who'd squatted for days and even weeks. All had discovered corpses of migrants who'd been ditched by the cartels with no food or water.

Barry was an oddball, a petroleum geologist with a master's degree from the Colorado School of Mines. When the group discovered that he had deep resentments toward academia, they promptly elected him president of The Secondmen during his first year as a full-time member. Operation Antelope had become his baby.

He ran a zero-tolerance organization. One volunteer created a website stating the rules. *The Secondmen Manifesto* was published on the home page. Total transparency is what Barry demanded.

Racists, haters, xenophobes, white supremacists, and anarchists were not welcome to join. All who signed up had to agree to uphold the highest standards set forth by the group. That meant respecting the land, the laws, and not engaging in any aggressive behavior. No brandishing weapons. No aggressive posturing. No snarky remarks.

"I want you to think of the guards at Buckingham Palace." It was a visual he used often, hoping the men would understand the demeanor he wanted them to depict. "Grind your teeth if you feel like someone is trying to provoke you. If you see illegal activity, do not engage. Call it in."

"I had this made," one member yelled out from the crowd. He removed his mouth guard and waved it in the air. "I bite down on it when I need help to keep my pie hole shut."

The dental device got a resounding mix of applause and laughter.

Barry stood on the tailgate of his pickup. "You have the right to carry weapons. You have all been subjected to intensive background checks. You have been found to be mentally stable. You are peaceable, law-abiding patriots with licenses to carry concealed handguns. By a show of hands, whose CHL is current?"

Hands were raised as far as he could see. Not a soul in their right mind would come to this part of the world unarmed, or without a valid license-to-carry.

"What is our mission statement?" he called out.

They chanted in unison. "We are a peaceable volunteer border watch group."

"I CAN'T HEAR YOU."

"WE ARE A PEACEABLE VOLUNTEER BORDER WATCH GROUP."

The Secondmen held one thing sacred above the common cause for border security: a special affinity for Roy Pompadour. Roy had hosted annual fundraisers at the ranch, inviting disabled veterans and injured officers and their families on all-expense-paid trips to Antelope Creek Ranch. Wealthy guests were expected to donate generously. Roy personally oversaw the proceeds, making sure they went to a handful of organizations he scrutinized for transparency.

Barry found Roy to be a paradox: a billionaire who'd made his fortune on Wall Street who gave back to folks who'd spent their lives in service. While he didn't pretend to understand it, he deeply admired Roy's commitment. Roy also made it known that he thought the geologists and engineers who'd developed the energy industry had done more to advance humankind than the *Five Shits* ever would. Shut down social media tomorrow, and the world would be a better place.

While he and others in the petroleum industry were busy developing ingenious, cheaper ways to keep Silicon Valley's energy-sucking, society-wrecking cloud computing services running, the Silicon Valley elites bashed them in the public square. They wanted to develop alternative energy so they could amass even more power. They could give a rat's ass if the oceans rose. They'd move inland, or to Mars.

*It's easy to mold perceptions when you control the flow of information.*

Barry had met plenty of local folks who'd admitted they'd doubted Roy's original promise to revive the land. They'd also admitted they were wrong. Roy told a reporter at the *Antelope Weekly Standard* the minute he set eyes on the ruins of the pre-Civil War forts on the overgrazed, drought-hardened land, something inside "lit up" and he knew he had to rebuild and revitalize it.

Barry looked out over the flotilla of Harleys, late-model pickup trucks—some costing as much as a hundred grand, others on their last legs—and recreational vehicles outfitted for camping, and toy-haulers that had converged earlier. They'd come on their own nickel, and convened on privately owned ranch land southwest of the airstrip. Barry had been leading The Secondmen recon missions for over a year.

The one set for tonight was the real deal.

At first, the Border Patrol welcomed the added eyes and ears monitoring and reporting activity. Then the shit storm hit. The group took a big PR hit a couple years back when a video went viral showing one of them shooting and killing an unarmed Mexican man. The media condemned them. Even border agents who'd become friends, distanced themselves. They had to raise funds for their legal defense.

After the story died down, two old guys with no connection to The Secondmen admitted they'd made the fake videos out of "patriotic frustration" over illegal immigration. The dead migrant was actually their alive-and-well landscaper, a native born Mexican-American with aspirations of making it in Hollywood. They'd apologized, but the damage was done. The haters on social media had a field day. When it was proved to be fake news, the mob did nothing to retract it. He learned later it was Roy who'd anonymously paid their legal fees.

There is nothing quite like being vilified as a nut job. Barry harnessed their collective anger, convincing them Operation Antelope would be the perfect payback.

He joined a breakaway group of dozen or so of the men sitting on folding chairs and coolers. He stuck a fork into a plastic bag of reconstituted beef. "Did you know cloud computing produces two percent of global greenhouse gas emissions? They're the second biggest fossil fuel burners in the world, right behind the airlines."

That elicited a lot of grumbling and headshaking.

His buddy, Mike, chimed in. "I trade carbon credits for a living. I make a freaking shit pile of cash. It's like selling bad mortgages during the housing crisis, except we're selling canned air without cans. At least there were actual houses during the mortgage meltdown. For all the money we suck from businesses, it's not like we're doing anything to reduce carbon." Mike laughed, perched on the bottom stair of his million-dollar Prevost Motor Coach.

An old geezer said, "Two percent? How many John Q citizens know that? The tech A-holes could give a flip about saving the planet."

Mike said, "I wish I wasn't such a hypocrite. Guilt is what brings me here today. I want to be like Roy Pompadour. Make my money, then find ways to give back. Starting today."

"At least you're honest. That's refreshing." Barry loaded his fork with more goo and shoved it in his mouth.

A retired Texas Ranger spoke up. "Remember when the hole in the ozone layer was going to burn all of us to a crisp?" He lifted one butt cheek and farted.

"We have a better chance of getting scorched by one of those," Mike, the carbon trader said, scratching the stubble on his chin.

The old Ranger said, "Those pipsqueaks penned up at

Pomps' place with their spiky hair and tattoos think they're the center of the dadgum universe. What a bunch of pricks."

Barry hopped up on the tailgate and spoke loudly. "Let the record show, we will work with local and federal law enforcement to secure the ranch tonight. Our sole purpose is to keep any guests from leaving. No escapees. That's it. *Do you understand*?"

"*YES, SIR.*"

He laid a three-by-three-foot US Geological survey map on the dirt. The men knelt, squatted, and stood three deep to get a good last look at it. The updated Antelope Creek Ranch borders had been redrawn with a yellow highlighter. Red X's marked the lookout points where The Secondmen would be posted. Their two-way radios had open channels to local and federal law enforcement.

After they cleaned camp, the fifty-man volunteer group was instructed to rest. At nightfall they'd take their positions, securing the perimeter around Antelope Creek Ranch, keeping watch.

The radio on Barry's belt squelched. "Barry. Do you copy?" It was Luther Pernod.

"Copy."

"I'm with the sheriff. The lockdown has officially begun."

"Ten-four," Barry said. "No guests are armed. Is that correct?"

"Affirmative," Luther said.

He reattached the radio to his belt and checked his watch. The show was about to begin.

The top bed sheet flew back and human head popped up from under the covers, panting. Justice of the Peace Jane Pandora screamed so loud during her third orgasm Deputy John Torres was afraid someone might have made a 911 call. He monitored his cackling police radio hoping no one mistook her wailing for a crime in progress. He swiped his mouth with the back of his hand and went into the bathroom to rinse and spit.

Jane lay across the fraying bedspread like she'd been crucified. Arms stuck out at right angles, her delicate feet crossed at the ankles. Her huge breasts as round as party balloons and as solid as the Chinati Mountains. John was surprised she'd fallen asleep so fast. He lifted one edge of the whitish sheet to cover her boobs.

A big rig downshifted on the highway. Jane sat upright, spooking him, as if rising from the dead. The hiss coming from the airbrakes whooshed. He peeked out the drapes and saw the truck pulling into the motel parking lot.

"Come here, big boy," Jane said.

Deputy Torres wasn't feeling like a big boy. Jane had put a lot of effort into it, but his Johnson wasn't cooperating. Jane even sprang for an X-rated lesbian porn movie on the closed-circuit television, but it didn't help. Lesbian porn used to be a big turn on except now all he could think about was how women were trying to take over the world. The idea made his dick limp.

When Torres' tongue had cramped up the first time and he'd come up for fresh air, Jane used two hands to push his head back down between her legs. Her eyes were glued to the lesbo porn show. Three orgasms, that was impressive. Torres knew it was the TV, not him, that deserved the credit.

"There's always next time," Jane said, rustling the hair on the top of his head.

He recoiled. The last thing he needed was a post-mortem on his erectile dysfunction. Maybe Jane was the problem. This was the third time in a row it had happened, the dick problem.

"You can get yourself some little blue pills. You don't have to go to a doctor, neither," she said. "I keep a few in my purse. Next time you need a little help, I got your back."

Deputy Torres didn't need a blue pill. He needed to go home and take his wife out to a nice meal at the chain Mexican restaurant that opened last month. She'd be impressed with the fancy tortilla machine next to the front door. He'd heard you could watch dough balls drop behind a glass window where they were machine-flattened and cooked in a matter of seconds. Then John Torres thought of his own balls.

"Oh, babe, your problem is you're just too Catholic sometimes, I swear it," Jane said.

She was pushing her luck. Deputy John Torres got dressed in a hurry. He stepped into his cowboy boots, pulled his jeans down over the leather tops and walked over to give Jane a peck on the forehead.

She tried to stop him from leaving.

"I gotta go." He brushed her hand away firmly, keeping his

thoughts to himself. "I really do have to go." He had the good sense to be civil enough to keep his options open for the future.

"You're kinda hurting my feelings." Jane sat up, pouting.

All Torres could see was the thousand truckers who'd slept in the same motel bed.

She pulled her knees under her bare breasts and wrapped her arms around her calves. A wave of regret came over him. She pushed her beehive up straight where it had tilted off to one side, her eyeliner smudged beneath her eyes. Her massive tits rested on her kneecaps. There was a time he'd have bargained with the devil just to touch them.

"What's wrong with you?" Jane asked.

He held his fingers to his lips. "Shush." He turned his ear toward the door, heard the sound of a metal key being inserted into the motel room lock. He watched from the inside as the dead bolt turned to the unlocked position. Jane jumped, pulling the sheet from the bed, running into the bathroom. Deputy Torres drew his weapon. The door cracked open. The chain stopped it.

"This room is occupied," Torres said.

"Ah, shit. That dumb bitch at the front desk told me this was my room." The trucker sounded like he was from Alabama or Kentucky or some other down-South state. "Sorry, man," he said. "Good thing the dang chain is on. Happened last time, too."

It was a good thing for the trucker. That's how people got themselves killed. Torres' radio crackled. He holstered his weapon.

"Thirty-eight, do you copy?" It was Surly Sue.

"Copy."

"What's your twenty?"

Deputy Torres had parked his patrol truck across the street at the waffle place. He told Sue he was at the restaurant.

"You're needed back at the station. *Pronto*."

He pressed the talk button. "En route."

Torres ducked out of the motel room, hung the Do Not Disturb sign on the door, looked both ways and jogged across four lanes of deserted highway. Jane had parked her Beemer behind the no-tell motel. He appreciated that at least Jane was discreet. While his tongue went numb working on her pussy, she'd been swigging gin from a pint bottle, and was drunk as a skunk before noon. When he left, her speech was slurred. He hoped she'd sleep it off. The last thing he needed was a state trooper pulling the local JP over for a DUI.

He pulled onto Highway 90 and headed west to the courthouse. Jane's vanity would be his saving grace. Even impaired, she'd never leave the motel with a hair out of place. In a speck of a town like Marfidio, she couldn't drive a mile without running into someone she knew.

Sure, he was a cheating dog with a fragile ego, but Jane was power hungry. She was a big fish in an itty-bitty pond. The farther he got from the motel, the more sure he was that things between him and Jane Pandora were over. The only question now was how he could put an end to it without things getting too messy.

## 28

W hile Lauren and the others finished lunch, Luther went table-to-table in the dining hall with the news that the ranch was on lockdown. The Big Shits looked concerned, but were measured in their reactions.

She, Vance, MK, and Jake had an unobstructed view of the guestrooms through the west-facing windows overlooking the courtyard and pool. While Luther went room-to-room knocking on doors, it was clear he was getting a raft of crap about the security threat.

She and Vance had seen the document for the first time over lunch. At first Lauren thought it was real, the notice printed on Homeland Security letterhead. MK said it was "real" insofar it had been prepared as a "favor" by an unidentified "friend" at the agency, and that the stationery was authentic. MK told them not to worry, that the plan had been hatched long before they'd bought the ranch, and the time had come to deploy it.

MK looked as amused as she was watching Luther, whose step had slowed considerably, bearing the bad news. MK held her hand over her mouth as one angry guest grabbed the paper from Luther, read it, then charged at him landing a shoulder bump that twirled the weasel a half revolution.

"That guy looks pissed," Vance said.

The next guest shook his finger in Luther's face. MK smiled, licking her lips. The one after that slammed the door in Luther's face.

MK was right. They were a bunch of ill-mannered pissants who appeared to believe the rarefied air they breathed was even beyond Homeland Security.

The phony document was a notice that Antelope Creek Ranch was on lockdown. A terrorist plot had been "detected" and the federal government was in the process of "searching for suspects." Whoever authored it didn't stop there, claiming the ranch was the "target."

Vance was obviously enjoying the show. "It's not a bad plan. I like watching them squirm."

It was as good as anything Lauren could have come up with. Given a choice, she'd have taken the next flight out of Midland.

"They think their planes were diverted to do repairs on the airstrip," MK said to Vance. "You can thank Pomps for that idea."

Josh had parked the ranch tractor on the tarmac and dropped a load of sand right in the middle. There was no way any more planes were coming or going.

MK had the inside track. "A veteran who'd served with Roy in 'Nam is a high-ranking official at Homeland. Those little shits thought they'd get helicopters. But without communication to the outside world, they're shit out of luck. Plus, I instructed Luther to tell them Homeland closed the airspace."

"Can you imagine how they're feeling?" Jake asked. "They're not used to this."

"I like the idea," MK said, rubbing her hands together, "a little dose of reality will do them good."

"You really don't like them, do you," Lauren said.

"Nope." MK smacked her lips. "Most of their pilots are ex-military and they're more loyal to the memory of Roy Pompadour than their girly-man bosses. Can you imagine? Answering to man-boys who've highlighted their hair." She smiled at the thought. "Now they're stuck here, and beholden to *us*."

Luther had finished canvassing the rooms and was heading their way.

Lauren felt like a pawn. She should have stayed in Miami and let the boys test drive Antelope Creek Ranch. But she'd wanted to see Vance.

"They could care less about the security of the public," MK said. "This day shall serve as a reminder to them, what it feels like to be vulnerable."

Luther took a seat. "I rather like using their own tactics against them, controlling the flow of information."

MK said, "We have old-fart billionaires sleeping on the floor to make room for these snits. How many of them would be willing to make a sacrifice like that? Roy thought they'd have to be divided to be conquered."

Luther stroked his black goatee, eyes glinting.

A stranger's voice butted in. "Did I hear someone say 'divide and conquer?'"

They all looked up blankly at a millennial standing over them.

"It's a computer expression. Um . . . a binary term applied to algorithms? When the search engines are trying to break down information, they use tail recursion? Syntactic analysis? They call it 'divide and conquer?'" The young man noticed the glazed looks. "Oh, sorry," he said. "I'm Spike. I'm with Numeral II Corp, the Internet search company?"

They stared at him without speaking.

"All-righty, then," he said, dismissing himself. He headed

toward the guest refrigerator in the dining hall and took an armload of bottled waters.

"He seemed pleasant enough," Lauren said. She watched him walk out carrying so many bottles he had to use his butt to push the door open.

"Spike," MK purred. "A nickname for his hair products, perhaps?"

Another one about the same age with a perfect five o'clock shadow rushed in from the back entrance, making a beeline to the front desk. He was so loud everyone could hear him. He demanded Rosa call his pilot from the landline and that his plane brought back to the ranch immediately. He yelled at Rosa, somehow blaming her for his being in the shower while Luther had gone door-to-door.

Rosa assured him she felt his frustration but that it was an impossible request.

"You're welcome to look at the airstrip, if you'd like. I can call and have someone drive you to see it. It's really a moot point, anyway," she said, "since we're on a security lockdown."

"I want a vehicle," he said. "Not a fucking scenic tour of the airstrip. I need to leave *immediately*. I can go by car," he roared. "I have important business to attend to."

Rosa held firm. "I have no control over Homeland Security."

He took his phone out of his pocket and looked at it. "My plane has a cell tower. This is bullshit. No cell service without my corporate plane here? I need to make a call. I need to use your phone." He stared at Rosa's landline.

"Our phones are down."

He pushed his way around the desk, past Rosa. He picked up the receiver and held it to his ear. The line was dead. He smashed the receiver on top of the front desk. The mouthpiece cracked in half and shrapnel flew into the air, clattering on the tile floor. Rosa cowered.

The line wasn't really dead. Luther had unplugged it from the wall earlier, in the event something like this happened. Now the desktop phone really was broken. Vance got up and jogged over to the desk to defend her.

The young man cursed at Rosa and when he saw Vance coming, backed away.

Rosa shrugged. Lauren wasn't sure if she could roll with the punches the way Rosa did. Watching the man smash the phone had unnerved her.

The prick slunk out the back door. He was a dick. And a chicken.

"They're all like that," Rosa said, picking up the pieces of another broken phone. "The deaf ones, the rich ones, the wives, the kids. It used to bother me but I guess now I just expect it." She smiled at Vance. "Thanks for coming to my defense. Usually they just threaten to get me fired, sue the ranch, or ruin our reputation on the Web."

When he returned to the table, Vance said, "That guy is scared. He wanted to intimidate her but he's an animal backed into a corner. He doesn't like being exposed, cut off from the outside world. Can you imagine? A guy like that feeling unprotected and isolated, a guy used to 'round-the-clock armed security?"

"All I saw was an asshole," Jake said.

Luther weighed in. "When they figure out what we have in store for them, they won't like it. Then you'll see what real fear looks like. They'll be baffled when they find out their bodyguards and pilots aren't as beholden to them as they think they are."

"What do you mean?" Lauren asked.

MK weighed in. "Most of the pilots and bodyguards are veterans. They had a lot more respect for Roy than the pricks they work for. Roy introduced half of them. This was all Roy's idea, Homeland lockdown, shutting the airstrip down for phony repairs. He knew those cowards would try to run and he knew without communication and transportation they'd be . . . well . . . um, I hate to sound crude . . . but in Roy's words, they're fucked."

"You're saying their pilots and their security detail are part of whatever is going on here?" Lauren asked.

"Enough of them to get the others to go along with it." Luther pushed his glasses up on his nose. "The members of the Isidore Global Initiative all agreed with Roy. It's not like this wasn't discussed ad nauseam." He stood. "I hate to be rude but I have work to do."

When Luther was out of earshot, MK warned them: "Watch your backs. The most dangerous enemies are usually within."

*What did that mean?*

Lauren saw the sheriff coming through the front door.

*What is he doing here?*

He was making a beeline for Luther. He was carrying something.

---

VANCE SPRUNG to his feet to stop the sheriff. "You shouldn't be here right now."

Manny glared at him. "Any idea how this woulda gotten in Frank Conn's cell?"

Vance looked at the bottle. "No."

"I need to speak to Luther."

"I can't let you do that."

"I'm the sheriff. I do as I like."

"No, you don't."

Manny threw dagger eyes at him. "Who died and made you the law around here?"

"Come on, Sheriff. You can't run roughshod over this place whenever it suits you."

"I'd say murder constitutes a damned good reason to sharp-elbow my way around here."

Vance squared his jaw. "Frank is innocent until proven guilty." They stood toe-to-toe. "You need a warrant to take another step on my property."

Manny held the bottle with the scorpion inside under his arm and used both hands to put his wraparounds on, hooking an end behind each ear.

He was hot under the collar. Vance was dealing with something far bigger than a small town sheriff. He was dealing with an ego the size of Texas.

"Well, maybe one of them illegals left it behind. We hold Border Patrol collars until ICE picks them up. Found a lot of strange contraband over the years," Sheriff Manny said.

*Jesus, Frank was in the same cell as ICE collars?* Vance wanted to read him the riot act. He kept his mouth shut and followed Manny past the front desk, to the exit. The sheriff stopped in his tracks and Vance almost ran into his back.

"If my memory serves me"—Manny lowered his shades and narrowed his eyes—"Frank was in that cell all by his lonesome when he woke up with that damn thing." He paused. "It's West Texas. Stranger things have happened. Rest assured you can depend on the Marfidio Sheriff's Office for anything you need." He pushed his glasses up and tipped his hat.

Lauren had caught up with them.

Manny's patrol truck was tucked away on the south side of the gravel driveway, behind Rosa's windowless office.

A horde of guests had spotted the vehicle and formed a mob, chasing the sheriff to his truck. Manny jumped in and spun the pickup, pointing it toward the gates. Stomping the pedal, the V-8 howled and the back end fishtailed as rear tires spit gravel like shotgun pellets. The throng chased him on foot. The blast of small pebbles and dirt sprayed them. A giant dust cloud erupted and visibility went to zero.

---

WHEN THE BALL of dirt settled, Lauren saw Spike rubbing his eyes. He was standing in the middle of the driveway twenty feet from the lobby doors. She ran to help him.

"That sort of thing is absolutely uncalled for," Spike said. "I could have lost an eye." He massaged an area an inch from his eyelid.

A red spot marked the place where a gravel pellet barely missed his eyeball.

"That's no way for law enforcement to behave. Even if we are in a high security situation," Spike said.

Vance joined her and warned him. "You can't chase the local sheriff. He's just trying to do his job. Remind me of your name?"

"Jason Spike. My friends call me Spike for short."

"You raided the fridge, for water," Vance said. "And you work for Numeral II Corp, right? Software engineer?"

Spike nodded. "Computer programmer."

Vance coughed as they walked back to the portico attached to the main entrance. The dust cloud was still settling. "The sheriff doesn't like technology types, especially ones who chase him like pack animals."

Manny had had no choice but to bolt before they swarmed his truck and tried to glom on like bees to a hive. Lauren could see Spike's point of view, too. Everyone was on edge.

"It's not that he doesn't like *you*," Lauren said. "He just needed to go."

"Who are you?" Spike asked.

"Oh. Sorry. Lauren Gold. I'm one of the owners."

"Nice to meet you," Spike said, "It's not as if I don't respect law enforcement. I'm a US Marine Corp veteran."

Vance studied him. "Is that so."

"Did two tours in Afghanistan and one in Iraq before I was honorably discharged."

"It's a pity you didn't have the chance to meet the previous owner," Vance said. "Roy Pompadour, he'd have liked you."

"It's the reason I signed up for this trip last year," Spike said. "I could care less about fancy food and hiking. I've shot enough rounds of ammo, climbed enough mountains, and swallowed enough dust to last me a lifetime. I wanted to meet the man. Mr. Pompadour was a living legend. I read a lot about him. He's done a lot for veterans. I was one of the lucky ones. I came home in one piece and got a good job with Numeral II Corp. I guess he and I weren't destined to meet."

"Perhaps not," Vance said.

"Destiny is a curious thing," Lauren said. "Sorry about your eye. I'd put some ice on it. Rosa at the front desk can give you something for the pain. If there's anything else we can do for you, please don't hesitate to ask."

## 29

MK took the lead at their final meeting before dinner. She'd chosen the outdoor alcove behind the main building. They huddled on the hardwood benches built into the U-shaped adobe pavilion. MK was sitting next to Josh.

"We don't have much time," MK said. "As you know, Roy thought they could be influenced by mentoring them. He'd come to believe they had passed that point."

Luther plucked a handkerchief from his pant pocket and huffed on the blue lenses of his glasses. He held them up at different angles, polishing the glass.

"When Roy and the others concluded they had to take a different course of action, he planned something dubbed Operation Antelope." MK opened her makeup compact and looked in the mirror. She blotted her forehead with powder then stretched her mouth wide open, rubbing melted lipstick from the creases around her lips.

MK caught Jake about to speak and held her hand up, snapping the compact shut.

"Operation Antelope?" This was the first time Lauren had

heard anything about an operation. The ranch was supposed to be a refuge, not some hostile outpost.

Josh asked, "Did any of you three watch the hearings on Capitol Hill, when they grilled Zack Wisenberg?"

Lauren, Jake, and Vance looked at each other blankly. She hadn't watched it and apparently neither had they.

"I did," Josh said.

"What's Zack Wisenberg got to do with it?" Jake leaned forward with his chin in his hands, elbows on his bare knees.

"There were a couple of things that stood out," Josh said. "When the Senator from Texas asked what constitutes hate speech, Zack testified that their platform was 'too big to police,' and that in ten years they'd use 'artificial intelligence' to decide."

MK took over. "The tech companies are a threat to free speech and not one of those schmucks seem the least bit concerned. They could care less about the rights of everyday Americans. They've already been caught shadow-banning folks who have opinions they don't agree with."

Lauren felt a pit open in her stomach. She tugged on the cuffs of her sweater.

"Here's what was even more astonishing," Josh said. "Wisenberg testified that his company plans to hire more foreign workers to monitor every language on the planet. He tried to make it sound like a good thing. But it's not. They'll have the power to dominate global speech."

MK said, "That social media prick testified that there are two-hundred-million users in the US. That's two-thirds of America. His platform has more than two billion users. He told Congress if the US shuts him down, which of course they won't, they'd still have almost a couple billion users. Members of Congress looked amazed, like they didn't know any of this. During their time to grill him, one of them asked Zack why there isn't more diversity in their hiring practices. It won't matter very much what their employees look like if the First Amendment dies."

Vance cracked his knuckles. "How did he answer that?"

"The same as all the others." MK mocked Wisenberg. " 'I don't know the answer, Senator, but I'll have my team get back to you.' The little shit testified they should all be proud that his company was started in America."

"And then he argued he shouldn't be over-regulated because it would hurt startups," Josh said. "He said his company had enough lawyers to fight the Feds but companies being incubated in dorm rooms and garages across the county would never be born."

That got Jake's attention. "Are you serious? He actually made that argument?"

MK nodded.

"Is Congress really that stupid?" Jake's eyes were wide.

"Some of 'em." MK shrugged. "Not all of them. Mostly they're corrupt and power hungry."

"Can you imagine if we'd said some bullshit like that in our heyday?" Jake was genuinely surprised. "We'd have been laughed off Capitol Hill and then fired back at the office."

Josh said, "Who's going to fire the chairman, founder, and CEO? Not one senator challenged him."

Lauren's jaw hurt from clenching her teeth.

"Well," MK said, "you can see the pickle we're in. It's not just Wisenberg's company. We're targeting four others, too."

"So that's why you've corralled them here." A picture was forming in Lauren's head. "How do you plan to stop them?"

"We can't stop them. All we can do is knock some sense into them," MK said, "with a little help from our friends."

Lauren was confused. "The government is behind this?"

Josh laughed. "Not exactly. Roy had suspicions about Justice Simeri's death but he wasn't able to prove anything. It's no secret that the Big Data companies have been focusing on the courts. They've had armies of lawyers preparing. They were on to Roy."

Lauren's stomach roiled. "What are you saying?"

Josh said, "Roy was convinced the Big Five were violating every antitrust law ever written and their legions of Ivy League lawyers had been stonewalling, starting with the district courts. Roy's plan was to help move it up to the Supreme Court."

"This is big," Vance said.

"As big as it gets. During Zack's kabuki theater in front of Congress, they had to add chairs in the chamber." MK smirked. "You know why?"

"Enlighten us," Jake said.

"So the lobbyists would have somewhere to sit." MK put her big sunglasses over her eyes. The lenses mirrored the brilliant sky and clouds.

"After Justice Simeri died, Roy decided to take them on," Josh said.

Jake cocked his head. He'd been studying Josh. "How do you know all this?"

Josh looked to MK for guidance. "Go ahead, tell him."

Josh paused for what seemed like a long time. "My great-great uncle, Melville Saver, built this place."

Wow. Lauren had read the history.

"When Roy bought it, back in nineteen ninety-nine, it was practically rubble. It had been passed down to my aunt, Melville's widow's grandniece. I know, it sounds complicated. But it's not. Melville never had kids of his own and eventually my aunt became his next of kin."

Lauren's head spun. If Josh had family ties pre-dating Roy's purchase of the ranch, the blind trust made sense. Maybe Josh held a stake in the place all along. And it reverted back to him upon Roy's passing. She had so many new questions. She felt her nostrils flare like the horses' did when they were on high alert. Her heart thrummed under her shirt. She wasn't cut out for this. Maybe if she held her breath long enough, she'd pass out.

Vance snapped his fingers in front of her face.

"Luther," MK said, "go fetch some water for Lauren."

He glared at MK, then jumped to his feet and trotted toward the lodge.

"You'll be fine, hon." MK put her hand over her sunglasses to block a spear of vertical sunlight that found its way through the slats overhead. "We have a plan." She smacked her lips together.

Lauren had had one, too: to get out of debt and lead a normal life. This investment was supposed to be part of that plan. Launder a big chunk of money and lead a comfortable life.

Vance looked at MK, and asked, "What *is* the plan, Mary Katherine?"

"Well, now that we have those little pricks corralled, we'll loosen them up tonight with a few cocktails and then they can meet our friends." MK's eyes sparkled.

A light bulb popped in Lauren's head. "This is why the ranch is off the grid."

"That's right, hon," MK said. "Pomps knew the only way to capture them was to go dark. Of course, after they started bringing their own portable cell towers, he had to tweak things. He planned on shutting down the airstrip, anyway. Bye-bye airplanes and *adios* communications. We all know enough about the plan to carry it out, with or without Roy.

"You know what finally sent Roy over the edge? When terrorists starting using social media to plan attacks. And live-streaming. He couldn't believe it. Silicon Valley is run by such a bunch of fakes, Roy had taken to calling it *Silicone* Valley."

Lauren headed for the courtyard.

"Where are you going?" Vance tried to stop her.

Lauren shook her head. "I don't know."

Suddenly Luther was running toward them, waving his hands and yelling.

*What the hell?*

Luther pointed to something in the distance. It was too far away to be certain, but it looked like a vehicle, speeding from the south, across the desert toward the ranch.

Vance jumped to his feet and ran from the alcove to get a better look.

Lauren felt a painful grip on her collarbone. Josh had dug his fingers into her flesh. She dropped halfway to her knees, wincing. Josh pulled her upright. His eyes looked wild.

"What's happening?" she asked, bewildered.

"GO, GO, GO," Josh shouted, turning her out of the alcove and toward the driveway. "Run. To the lobby." He pushed her so hard she almost fell.

The guests mingling outside watched as she sprinted through the courtyard and past the pool. Inside the lobby, she warned Rosa that something was going down. She ran toward the southern-facing window but turned and sprinted away. Whatever it was, it was heading for the dining hall. One guest, a young man, jumped to his feet and stood on one of the long benches. He sounded the alarm and soon guests were panicking, dropping their belongings, wrangling baby strollers, grabbing kids, and stampeding.

Lauren snaked her way through the mob. She stood on tiptoes. What was hurtling toward the dining hall? It looked like a low-altitude missile inside a massive dirt cloud, a contrail of dust chasing it like a rooster tail. She scanned the empty tables. Jake was struggling to get through the crowd.

She waved her hands over her head. Jake saw her and lumbered toward her, bumping and pushing his way through the pack of people standing five-deep at the opposite side, near the front desk, away from the window.

"It's some kind of vehicle," Jake said, squinting and craning his neck.

It was closing in fast. There were no roads out there, just flatlands and sparse prairie grasses leading to the foothills. The sun glinted off something.

"Holy shit. It's the Humvee." Jake said.

The sun overhead gleamed off the front grill as it barreled toward them, the front bumper bouncing.

"Oh my God." The panic attack she'd staved off a couple of minutes ago sent her into full flight mode.

Jake grabbed her arm.

She froze.

"Come on, Lauren." He yanked on her arm.

"He's right." It was MK's voice. "We gotta get away from the window."

They ran.

This was not what she'd signed up for. None of what was happening was part of the plan. Not remotely. She pushed her way through the pack of looky-loos jammed near the reception desk. She needed to get outside.

---

THE HUMMER CLOSED in on the building, the murky air billowing up, obscuring it. The front grill smashed into the low adobe wall and shook the ground beneath Vance's feet. It struggled like an angry bull, raging against the foot-thick mud wall surrounding the south side of the dining hall like a moat. The vehicle's back tires dug in, it fishtailed, the wide tires traversing the ground like a grotesque slow-motion metronome.

Torque from the rear wheels drove the back end down, forcing the nose up, until the angle was steep enough to give it the chance to slingshot over the wall. Gravel shot from the cloud mushrooming behind the vehicle. The H-1 climbed the barrier and teetered, its twisted metal grill vibrating. Then the heavy vehicle jumped the wall and smashed into the huge pane of glass framing the mountains.

---

LAUREN STOOD on tiptoe looking for Jake. She'd gotten stuck in the gawking crowd. He must have lost track of her, too. The guests screamed when the big window exploded. She lunged backward, away from the noise and fell against a hutch to keep from being trampled.

Shattering glass followed. She stuck her head face down on a shelf and covered her eyes with her hands. The biggest shards clattered down, hitting the tile and breaking into a thousand pieces.

She lifted her head and saw she had a line of sight. Squinting, she covered her eyes and looked through her fingers. The Hummer screamed like a trapped bear, its body stuck atop the wall, its wide front grill mangled from the initial impact. Still, it struggled to break free, the dust cloud ballooning.

Lauren jerked her sweater over her face, shivering, waiting for the suicide bomb to go off. More shards and fragments hailed down. She lowered the fabric and peeked again between her fingers. The smell of burnt rubber and diesel stung her nostrils. Her eyes welled. Tears streamed down her cheeks. Tire smoke tinted the air, and then the brownish dust cloud rolled in behind it, through the gaping hole where the window used to be.

No bomb blast, just the ferocious sounds of the V-8's back tires clawing at the earth, the front double pair spinning freely, like roulette wheels on steroids.

Vance went into action. He hurdled over the wall, using one hand.

She funneled her hands over her mouth. "Stop." she yelled to him. "Don't go near it."

There was no way in hell he could hear her over the noise. She flapped her hands over her head like a maniacal bird, trying to get his attention. But he kept on going, disappearing into the abyss of smoke and dust. She stayed back. And watched. The driver's-side door was tilted up on an angle, and swinging wildly.

"Be careful." she yelled.

The outline of Vance's body danced alongside it, like a boxer looking for a place to land a jab, trying to grab the door handle. When he made his move, he miscalculated and the door hit him in the back, the force knocking him to his knees.

She cupped her hands over her mouth. "Look out." The door was going to kill him. "Get down."

The guests moved closer to watch, keeping a safe distance from the action. She followed. The fortified wall was holding, but for how much longer?

The Hummer fell back on its haunches, the nose pointing up on a steeper angle, the rear wheels rooting deeper into the earth, creating its own launch pad. The back end seesawed violently. Using his open hands, Vance's torso swayed, mimicking the action of the Hummer, like he was sizing up his opening in a game of skip rope. He dogged the driver's-side door, back and forth, his shoulders and neck mirroring the movements.

No one was coming to his aid. The spectators were in a trance, their heads turning left and right, watching his movements like a tennis match.

*Why isn't anyone helping him?*

He ducked and weaved and then made his move, diving in through a gap, disappearing into the cockpit. A second later, the scene went quiet. The back wheels stopped abruptly, but the fronts continued to spin, making a soft thumping sound.

Lauren ran to him and jumped the wall. The Hummer rested on a steep angle. Vance was slumped over the steering wheel, groaning and holding his rib cage. She saw the red metal bar locked on the wheel. Vance leaned toward the center console and groped the steering column. She watched him fumble for the ignition, she on tiptoes, standing a couple of feet back. Coughing and cursing, he pulled the key fob from the ignition and tossed it to her. He hadn't done anything: the vehicle was out of gas.

"A-ah-ah-ah." The sounds came out in short breaths. "Damn thing, ah-a," he stuttered, holding the bar attached to the steering wheel. "I think I bruised, my, a-ah, rib."

The bristled end of a broomstick was mounted to the anti-theft bar on the steering wheel held with heavy-duty zip ties. The other end, the wooden handle, was affixed to a flat metal plate and duct-taped to the gas pedal, pushing it to the floor-board. How Vance had threaded the needle and landed in the driver seat without killing himself was a miracle.

Jake moseyed over. He saw Vance doubled over with his head on the steering column. "Are you okay?"

Vance patted his rib cage. "Yeah. Bruised a rib, I think."

"Been there," Jake said. "It's painful. Let me help you."

"You better let me help him." It was Josh. He stared at the hooked end of the red metal bar, the length of a baseball bat, locked onto the steering wheel.

"Ouch." Josh grimaced, offering his forearm to Vance who held onto it, twisting on one hip to get out. His legs hung down on the running board, the vehicle on a steep angle. Balancing on Josh's arm, Vance hopped down.

Vance staggered the first few steps. "Who'd do this?"

The wreckage was even worse up close. What if Vance hadn't

rushed into action? What if it had enough fuel to keep going, it could have rocketed over the wall and plowed through the dining hall.

"I don't know," Josh said, gazing over the flats, shaking his head.

"Now we have a lovely outdoor patio," Jake said, looking at an area about as wide as a sidewalk, where the dining hall, now missing a window, opened up to the great outdoors.

"I'm going to go help Luther. We need to calm the folks. I'll get this cleaned up later," Josh said.

When they were alone, Vance said, "I could make . . . a ah-ah . . . turban out of what's left of my shirt."

"I ought to slap you," Lauren said.

"Then I'll tell you what I like." He started to laugh but clutched his abdomen and doubled over.

"Maybe you should go to the hospital."

"They can't do, ah-h, anything about a bruised, ah-h, rib. Besides we're, ah-h, on lockdown. Remember?"

"How do you know it's not broken?"

"If it was, I'd be crying." Vance laughed. Then he gasped, pressing his hand on his abdomen. His eyes got big.

"What?" Lauren asked.

"Ah . . . ah . . . a-choo." Vance sneezed, then fell to the ground in pain.

Her face turned white.

"Definitely bruised," he said, looking up at her. "Otherwise, I'd have passed out."

He was tougher than her. That was for sure.

———

VANCE LEFT and Lauren watched Luther and Josh talking to the worried guests. The terror on their faces eased after each encounter. Cheks had arrived and was glued to Josh's heels.

MK startled her. "That worked just the way we wanted it to," she whispered. "Maybe a thimble too much of gasoline."

"What are you talking about?" Lauren said.

"You didn't think for a minute that was random. Did you?"

Lauren crinkled her brow. Now she was getting pissed off.

"We have boots on the ground, hon, out there." She tilted her chin toward the flatlands leading to the foothills. "I call them FOPs, Friends of Pomps'. They're actually a volunteer group that helps Border Patrol. They call themselves The Secondmen."

Lauren rubbed her temples with her thumbs, lowering them to massage her jawbones. Peter's voice was in her head again. *You're so blind you can't see what's right under your nose.*

"It was risky, but it's paying dividends. They're feeling vulnerable. Sorry about Vance. He wasn't supposed to get hurt, but overall it was a successful operation." MK looked pleased.

*Are you kidding?* "A successful operation? Are you serious?" She'd been terrorized and Vance injured.

"Those pipsqueaks are scared shitless. They'll be all ears tonight," MK said.

A small group of guests approached cautiously.

"Can we take pictures?" one asked. "Of the wreckage?"

"Knock yourself out," MK said. She turned to Lauren and whispered, "By the time they share these pictures on social media, they won't know what hit them."

Her brain went foggy.

"Earth to Lauren. Hello?" MK grabbed her by her shoulders and shook her. "You're a million miles away."

"I wish," she said.

"You need to start wearing your big girl britches," MK said. "The show has only just begun."

## 30

S heriff Manny Rodriguez had one cowboy boot on the desktop and the other on the floor. He scrolled through his phone, looking at the photos he'd taken about an hour ago.

*Incontrovertible evidence.*

Sue barged in. She'd finally raised Deputy Torres on the radio. He'd stopped for a bite on the east side of town.

That was bullshit. The sheriff knew exactly where his deputy was. Manny also knew who'd he been with.

After narrowly escaping the mob at the ranch, he was pulling into the lot at the courthouse when he saw John Torres slip out the side door. Manny waited until Torres was at the intersection, then hung a U-turn. He'd tailed him to the truck stop/waffle joint on the edge of town and saw his deputy jog across the four-lane to the no-tell-motel across the street.

*Stopped for a bite, my ass.*

Lust was a damned drug and caused the afflicted, generally of the male variety, to act with the same poor judgment as the drunks. Case in point, John was clueless he was being followed. The sheriff got a kick out of listening to Sue trying to raise John on the radio. When he finally surfaced, Manny awarded Torres extra credit for incorporating a kernel of truth into the lie he told Sue: that he'd been eating his lunch.

Manny had been nursing a coffee across the street when Jane Pandora pulled into the motel and parked around back.

He clicked photos and recorded video of John letting Jane in. Then, he headed back to the station. The drive gave him time to think. John reinforced something Manny already knew to be true: A man's tallywacker sure could make him stupid.

The photos and video were insurance.

"Would you quit already?" It wasn't a secret his toe-tapping drove Sue crazy. She'd told him once she'd dreamt she was amputating his foot.

"When's he due back?" Manny asked.

"Any minute. Coming from the pancake place out on Route 90."

He could have corrected her. The waffle joint didn't serve *fricking* pancakes. Old Sue was set in her ways. Mighta been her best quality.

He got up from the rolling chair and pushed it back with the heel of his boot. The plastic back bounced off the metal desk. He walked out the door, toward the waiting room.

He faced the one-way glass with the peeling, tinted film. Deputy Torres turned onto Main Street. He drove past the building and pulled into the single parking spot in the alley. John was planning to sneak in through the side door, the same way he slipped out. Manny heard the key go in the lock.

Torres did a double take, startled to see him standing there. "Howdy," he said, trying to conceal his surprise, turning his back to the sheriff, relocking the door from the inside.

"Where have you been?"

"I was out, east of town. Checking for speeders." Torres turned sideways to slide by him.

"Catch any?"

"No, sir."

"No speeders for three hours? That's gotta be a record." Manny followed him to his cubicle. "Sue was trying to get you on the radio. Geez, John, what's that smell?"

"It's the smell of Eve," Sue said. "As in how Adam smelled after getting to know Eve."

Sue, she just couldn't help herself.

"I'm hoping it was a little afternoon delight. With the missus," Manny said, watching Torres' reaction.

"What are you implying?" John glared at Sue, who looked like she could care less.

"He smells just like the JP, if you ask me," Sue said.

Torres' dark eyes smoldered. "No one asked you."

"Don't need to ask me. I know the exact smell of all the perfumes I can't afford to buy. It's like that woman won the dang lottery." The phone rang at Sue's desk. "She's not doing a good job of keeping it a secret or sharing in the spoils." She tapped her shellacked hairdo and picked up the phone. "Marfidio. How can I be of help?"

What a pity. Sue would make a right good detective if Marfidio County ever got its foot into the twenty-first century and hired women deputies. Good call, sniffing Pandora's scent. Since he didn't have smell-a-vision, the photos would be a lot more useful. He motioned to John to follow him outside to the parking lot out front where they would have more privacy.

"You got something going on with ol' Calamity Jane?"

John stared down at his own boots.

"Jesus Christ, John. You look guilty as all get out."

"It's over." Torres tipped his chin and talked to the buttons on his shirt. "It was wrong, I know."

"It'd better be over. All we need around here is crap like this to complicate things, some story about my deputy carrying on with the JP."

Part of Manny wanted to congratulate him. He didn't have it in him to bed Jane Pandora but oh, how he'd like to know details. Instead, he stayed on track, reaching into the top pocket of his shirt and showing him the pictures he'd taken from across the street.

"You had me followed?" Torres seethed.

"Followed you myself. Best way to keep this between us."

"Sue knows?"

"Aah, she's just guessing. She likes to torture you. If it ain't over, then cut it off now. If not, it'll cost you your standing in the community and likely, your marriage and family. This part I promise you, it will cost you your job. Do you understand me?"

John nodded and followed him back inside, passing between the recycled school desks.

"It's over. I swear it on my mama's grave, I am done with that woman."

Swearing on his mama's grave carried weight. John was not the sharpest cactus in the desert. It would not have occurred to him that Jane Pandora might have her own agenda. Men with half a brain knew that woman had a reputation for playing men, plenty of ones smarter, richer, and better-looking than John Torres.

"Go home, John. Pick up some flowers for the missus on the way and get your head out of your boxers."

Surly Sue came out the door that separated the cubicles from the front lobby. She stuck an unlit cigarette in her mouth. "Maybe the horse people got it right. They geld 'em, almost all of 'em. The ones that are worth a darn, they freeze their semen. Less than one in a hundred get to keep their testicles. I think that's about right. About one in a hundred of you ought to be walking around with your balls intact. I look forward to the day. But first, I'm going out to enjoy my smoke break."

Sue had taken to going out the front door to avoid passing Frank Conn's cell.

"That woman's harsh," Torres said.

"Maybe so. But she might be right."

Manny joined Sue out back. She drew deeply on her cigarette and blew a thin streamer of smoke out the side of her mouth, tapping her ashes into a five-gallon bucket filled with sand and butts.

"I don't much like Frank Conn," she said. "And I don't much care for his whining or stomach problems. But it's the smell of fear coming off him. And that look in his eyes. Can't go back there until you let him go, Sheriff. Why you really holding him? That BS story about his DNA being at the crime scene is as good as Torres' story about being at the pancake place." She dragged on her cigarette and blew two smoke rings. "You know, an innocent man knows he ain't done nothing wrong."

A Border Patrol van pulled up and two uniforms got out. They slid the side door open. A pair of fearsome dudes, cuffed and belly-chained, stepped onto the running boards.

"Jesus Christ, Sheriff. You're not putting them maniacs in with that lawyer, are you?" She stubbed her half-smoked cigarette in the bucket and shook her head. "Well, I want no part of this. You and I both know he ain't got nothing to do with any murder."

She glared at him.

He had nothing to say.

"You know who else knows he done nothing wrong?" Sue kept at it. "God knows. That's who. This is some crazy shit you're doing, boss. If you wasn't paying me overtime on a Saturday cuz of some kinda problem out at Pomps' place, I wouldn't be dealing with this horse pucky."

She turned on her heel and waddled around the corner, toward the front of the building.

Approximately nothing got by 'ol Sue. That was a well-known fact. Her invoking the name God without adding *damn* during a lecture about a prisoner, well, that might have been a first.

Manny had taken precautions, though. He needed a dead lawyer in his jail like he needed his face on a Ten Most Wanted poster.

## 31

Barry and the boys had watched the staged wreck play out through binoculars. They were perched in thirteen-foot-high deer hunting stands. Rigged with a broomstick and steering wheel lock, the unmanned Hummer drag-raced toward the main lodge and when it smashed into the low adobe wall, it reared into the air like stadium monster truck.

They belly-laughed so hard it hurt, rocking the unstable stands. It was a miracle the cheap pieces of crap didn't tip over, sending a man to the hospital. They didn't laugh because it was funny, rather they howled like Eskimos who'd narrowly escaped being mauled by a mama grizzly. The wall had stopped the vehicle exactly the way the volunteer engineer on their team promised it would.

Barry, a man with a deeply held belief in Murphy's Law, was relieved. It was a sight to behold, especially watching the rich girly boys running for cover. Courageous men like Barry and The Secondmen didn't run from danger. They laughed fear in the face.

Phase One was successfully complete but for one small miscalculation. The runaway vehicle was supposed to run out of fuel before it jumped the wall and took out the dining room window.

Barry's radio hissed.

"Nice work." Luther's voice cackled. "We got their attention."

Barry pressed the talk button. "Ten-four. We copy that. We're on standby. All systems are a go. Is the hero okay?" Barry covered his mouth with his hand to muffle the laughter building in his belly.

"He'll live. He's got a bruise or two from the steering wheel lock."

"Yeah, when we saw him dive in we thought that might happen. Sorry about that. But it could have been a lot worse."

"He's one of the new owners, an ex-police officer," Luther said. "Turned lawyer."

Barry felt bad for an instant. Up until the part when Luther said "turned lawyer." "We're good to go. We're moving on to Phase Two."

"Ten-four."

Barry turned off the radio and clipped the microphone to his belt. Up in the deer stands the men cackled like grackles roosting on a telephone line.

---

LAUREN AWOKE DISORIENTED. She'd meant to close her eyes for a few minutes, to calm down. Instead, she woke up in the middle of a dream she couldn't remember. It was still daylight out. She peered through the drapes. Josh was behind the wheel of an idling front-end loader on the opposite side of the courtyard. That's what had awakened her, the noises of the rumbling tractor engine and the scraping sounds of rocks being scooped up. The pop, pop, pop of a nail gun.

Josh supervised from the catbird seat. Ranch laborers

unloaded bowling-ball-sized boulders from the tractor scoop. They were fortifying the wall where the Hummer had rammed it. Others were up on ladders fitting and nailing a black screen over the missing window, using a nail gun. Pop. Pop. Pop.

She looked at the clock on the nightstand. It was two-thirty in the afternoon. The one-hour nap refreshed her but she was still edgy.

The Secondmen.

*A volunteer Border Watch group. Friends of Pomps'.*

Vance could have been killed. She looked at her dead cell phone on the dresser and sighed.

Waiting for the shower to heat up, she disrobed, then stepped in and stood beneath the hot water. Brownish water swirled the drain on the white tile floor. She coughed and spit dust she'd inhaled.

*This is bullshit.*

She stamped her foot, took a deep breath, closed her eyes and faced the jets. The droplets hitting her face couldn't drown out the new reality, that being the owner of the ranch wasn't giving her the fresh start Vance had promised.

If MK knew the accident was staged, that meant others were in on it, too. Which ones knew? Did Jake know? Jake had become a wild card. MK said Jake didn't know, but why should Lauren take MK at her word? Plus, Jake had lied to her before. The others, they'd all misjudged Vance. What if they'd been wrong, and rather than rearing up and getting stuck on it, what if the Hummer had torn down the wall? She dried off and dressed quickly to go find out.

---

STAFF MEMBERS SCURRIED, sweeping up broken glass, mopping

the floors and dusting the furniture while the repairs continued outside.

"That was something," Rosa said. "Talk about drama." She'd left her post at the desk when she saw Lauren come in.

"I know. I don't understand how you do it." Poor Rosa. "Have you seen MK?"

"She's out by the pool. Reading, I think."

---

MK WAS SPRAWLED out on a chaise lounge dressed in navy capris and a blue-and-white-striped shirt, her face hidden behind big sunglasses. Lauren sat on the edge of the lounge with no cushions, across from her. MK was using them both: one pad folded in half to support her back, the other to prop up her knees to balance her book. She looked maddeningly relaxed.

MK closed the book and lowered her sunglasses to the tip of her nose. "You look better."

Lauren had come to confront her about the car crash. "What would have happened if Vance hadn't been there?"

At first MK looked confused. "Oh, dear, *that*. I told you how badly I feel he got injured. It would have run out of gas any second. I really am sorry. He wasn't supposed to go all hero on us like that."

"I was afraid. I thought it was a terrorist attack."

"Oh, goody." MK clapped her hands like a trained seal. "That's what it was supposed to look like."

That took the wind out of her sails.

"Don't take it so personally. It was meant to scare them, not you." MK sat up and leaned forward, her fine skin shimmering pink under the red umbrella. "Good God, I'm hogging all the pillows."

"No, no. It's okay."

"Most gals woulda cut and run by now." She pulled the cushion from under her knees and tossed it to her.

If cutting and running were an option, Lauren would have been long gone. "Thanks for the vote of confidence."

"We girls need to stick together." MK squeezed sunblock from a metal tube. "Things are going to get a lot messier before they settle down." She set her sunglasses down, raised the brim of her hat on her forehead and dotted the cream in a dozen places. "That's how it happened with me. One day I'd had enough of being pushed around so I started pushing back. Once I got a taste for it, there was no looking back."

She looked into her compact mirror and stretched her upper lip over her teeth, rubbing her face gently with her fingers until the white dots were invisible.

"Jake says you had your own business in Florida."

"I did. I had a small video production business."

"He said you turned down thirteen million dollars. Is that true?"

Was anything sacred? "Thirteen and a half."

"Why? Could you afford to?"

"Gosh, no." Who could?

"Why did you?"

"It was dirty money."

"It's all dirty money, hon. Heck, I don't know if I should hug you or slap you. I've never heard of anyone walking away from that much cash, especially someone who could use it. It's a good thing you didn't trust ol' Jake to hold it for you. He's a shark."

"I didn't want it because I didn't earn it. There were days I regretted not taking it."

"How do you think investment bankers make millions of dollars?" MK let out a hearty laugh. "They sure don't earn it."

"They don't have to hide it."

MK sighed. "That does complicate things." She sat up,

reached over and grasped her hand. "Do you think I earned my money by working any harder than you? Or Jake? Or Vance? Kids at fast food joints and car washes, they're the ones who're working hard."

"I don't know," Lauren said.

MK sipped from a bottle of water, then leaned forward and raised her knees. The book she was reading tipped forward, the spine bending the wrong way, resting between her breasts. "People can work very hard and not make much money. It can be the other way around, too."

"Did Jake tell you how we made the money?"

"He said it was a salvage operation, like a treasure hunt."

Typical. The King of Omission left the part out about it being cocaine cartel money. "Jake said that you were a very successful investment banker."

"If by success you mean I made a lot of money, that's true. Got out the first chance I could."

If MK could enjoy her money by not thinking too much about it, why couldn't she do the same thing?

"You're going to have to up your game if you want to hang onto it," MK said. "Having money puts a target on your back. You can play offense or defense."

The target thing rang true.

"Jake says you don't have children. If you don't want them, I certainly won't judge you. Or even if you don't like kids, I'd understand that, too."

A new voice joined their talk. "MK loves to ask personal questions." It was Jake. "She likes to know what makes people tick."

"How long have you been eavesdropping, you old dog?" MK asked.

He was annoying, butting in with a wiseass remark, showing

up unannounced. At least she was off the hook for the kid question, for which she had no good answer.

Jake took the spare cushion and sat next to Lauren. She slid away from him.

MK laughed.

"I only heard the part about you interrogating her about motherhood."

"We were talking about other things, too," MK said. "Like how the guests are probably feeling nervous right now. You all need to keep your heads screwed on straight because they're likely to react like cornered animals. Josh was supposed to take care of the crash scene. Not your partner."

"Were you in on it?" Lauren asked Jake.

"No."

"He's telling the truth," MK said. "He's on a need-to-know basis."

"The new owners didn't need to know?" It was fair to ask.

MK dodged the question. "I told you. This was all planned long before you bought the place and I don't have time to do a dissertation."

Rosa interrupted from a polite distance. "Excuse me. Mr. Moffett and friends would like to know what time they should join you for dinner."

"Seven o'clock," MK said.

Rosa stepped closer. "Attire? Mr. Bates wants to know."

"Casual," MK said. She sighed aloud. "God knows what the kids will wear. They all dress like they're about to climb Mount Kilimanjaro."

Rosa turned to leave.

"Wait." MK held her hand up.

Rosa stopped.

"Tell Mr. Moffett how grateful I am, we all are, that they're here, bunking three and four to a room like frat boys. What a game bunch of old farts. Considering they're used to five-star resorts."

"I'll let him know. The younger guests are getting restless. They want to know when—"

"Tell them it's not up to us," MK said. "You have my permission to tell them to stick it."

"Of course," Rosa said, looking more anxious now than when she'd arrived.

"I don't envy her," Lauren said. "Being on the front lines and having to deal with them. I couldn't do it. I'm going to the barn. I'm going out for a ride."

"With who?" Jake asked.

"I'm going alone."

"Are you sure that's a good idea?" MK's eyebrows went to full staff.

"I need to clear my head."

"I should probably try to stop you," MK said. "Except I rather like this version of you. Just don't go too far, and don't go anywhere you haven't been before. Promise me that."

"I promise," Lauren said.

---

Lauren backtracked through the lobby to grab an apple for Smokey, stealing two from a basket in the dining hall. A line of guests six wide and three deep had gathered around the front desk. Lauren went around them and behind the desk to fetch a backpack she'd stowed in Rosa's office. Josh was there, sitting at Rosa's desk. She startled him. He got up from the chair and stammered. She apologized for disturbing him, grabbed her bag and walked around the throng.

Rosa was holding her own, speaking over the buzzing and popping of power tools, telling them she had no idea how long the ranch would be on lockdown. It wasn't up to her, she explained, suggesting they try to remain calm.

The walk to the barn was a welcome respite, away from the chaos. Smokey trotted to the gate when he saw her, swishing his tail.

"Just another day for you." Lauren massaged his muzzle and fed him an apple from her hand. She saved the second apple as a treat for later.

He turned it into mush, slurping every drop from her palm.

"We're going for a ride, boy."

Looping the rope around the wooden railing, she turned toward the tack room. Cheks sat near the doorway, his tongue hanging from his mouth, tail sweeping the floor. Lauren scratched his head and passed him, setting her bag on the tack room floor. Slinging the bridle over her shoulder, she picked the saddle up with both hands, and slung it over Smokey's back.

Cheks barked as she mounted the horse, the same way he had the last time she'd left the barn with Josh leading the way. Cheks dashed ahead of her, toward the foothills. Smokey trotted behind him. The route the dog was on was different from the trails Josh had taken her on. She stood in the stirrups and held onto the saddle horn, taking in the afternoon sunlight and clatter of hooves.

She loosened the reins to let the horse stretch and run. Tears welled from the wind. She checked on the reins at the ledge at the top of the first incline.

"Cheks."

Lauren stuck two fingers in her mouth and let out a sharp whistle. Smokey shook his head and pricked his ears. "Cheks. Here, boy."

Lauren dismounted. She knelt and followed the fresh paw prints leading to a narrow cavern between two tall rock walls barely wide enough for the horse. She walked ahead on foot, leading the horse by the reins. The leather stirrups brushed the sides.

It opened to a vista facing northeast with a view of the airstrip. She walked forward toward a vertical drop, to look. The horse stopped, snorted, and backed up.

"Come on." She clucked her tongue. "Easy." She pulled on the reins but the horse refused.

She led him away from the edge of the ledge and when he dropped his head, she got back on. Squeezing his flanks with her calves, she urged him forward. But he'd planted his hooves.

"Cheks. Here, boy."

Smokey snorted, this time loudly, taking in the scent of something that ignited his flight instinct. He spun a hundred eighty on his back hooves and dropped on his hocks. She grabbed the saddle horn to keep from falling. Her stomach pitched, like a sudden drop on an airplane.

The horse pinned his ears and bolted one powerful stride. She had a few hundred feet to stop the horse before they reached the rock-walled tunnel. There was too much slack in the reins. She spun the leather in her hands.

"Whoa." The gap was closing fast.

She shoved her feet forward, up against his shoulders. She needed leverage. When the reins were taut in her hands, she leaned forward, then heaved her body back, and pulled with all her might. The pain in his mouth.

*Oh my God.*

He slid to a stop on his heels, sparks coming from his metal horseshoes. He reared in the air, less than a foot from the entrance. She lurched forward, wrapping her arms around his neck.

She had to stop him like that.

She'd have been dismembered.

When he landed on his front feet she jumped to the ground.

He backed away from her, red velvet nostrils flaring, saliva foaming in his mouth. Eyes flashing, he threw his head in the air.

She moved with him, following his lead like a dancer while he snorted and pawed the ground. A drop of pink saliva formed in the corner of his mouth. She'd cut him with the bit, a mortal sin committed on horse by rider.

*Oh my God. I'm sorry.*

"Hey, now," she said, slowly holding her hand out. He arched his neck and snapped his head in the air. The reins cracked like a bullwhip.

"Whoa, now," she said softly. "Whoa." She let some slack in the reins and moved closer. He stepped back. She held her hand out until he lowered his head a little, as if recalling the apple she'd fed him earlier.

"I'm so sorry," she said, massaging his muzzle.

He flung his head away from her.

She stopped fighting with him. He needed time to settle down. When he did, she separated the corner of his lip to inspect the wound. He raised his head and shook it in protest. If only she had a treat in her pocket, something to make the apology understood. She thought of the apple she'd left behind, and sighed.

"We have to go home," she said.

The sun was just beginning to drop in the west.

Reading her mind, he nuzzled her shoulder and bumped her arm playfully with his head.

Apology accepted.

She patted his neck. Cueing him as if to put the bit in his mouth, she used her thumb and forefinger to spread his lips. He opened his mouth. She'd cut his tongue, too.

She left the reins around his neck like a leash, removed the bit from the bridle and reconfigured it, attaching the reins to the noseband, creating a makeshift hackamore. He followed her on foot to the entry to the tunnel. She'd walk him through it and mount from the other side. If he bolted now, with no bit in his mouth, he'd get away from her.

Instead, he turned into a damned mule. She clucked softly and tugged the reins, leading him toward the gap. He balked and backed up. She clicked and clucked and smooched to encourage him. He dug his back hooves in and leaned on his haunches as if he might sit. She turned him around. Sometimes a new angle worked with a reluctant horse. Not today.

"Come on, boy."

The harder she pulled the reins, the more he resisted.

"Okay, time out." She sat on a rock. A minute later he lifted his head and craned it over her, letting her scratch his chin.

"I don't blame you," she said.

Cheks appeared, nose first, standing on the narrow ledge near the vertical drop. He barked at her.

"There you are, you little devil."

If it weren't for the dog, she wouldn't have come this way. She reached for his collar but he teased her instead, spinning just outside her grasp, barking playfully.

Smokey pricked his ears forward and sniffed the dog, then snorted and backed away toward home, toward the tunnel he'd just refused to go through. Then he began nibbling on vegetation growing in the crevices of the nearby rocks. She looped the reins around a low-hanging tree branch and tied the horse to it. She followed the dog on foot.

The ledge leading to the other side of the cliff was just a couple of feet wide. The drop down was vertical, a hundred feet, maybe more. She peered around but the arc in the rock blocked the view to the other side. She'd only have to go ten feet or so to cross over. Cheks taunted her, running back and forth, barking.

Pressing her shoulders against the vertical rock, she took one baby step onto the ledge. Planting her feet, she craned her neck, hoping to see what was on the other side. One step wasn't enough to see anything. She glanced down. The visual effects were dizzying. She retreated to solid ground. Smokey was busy rubbing his front teeth on a dead tree trunk.

Facing the cliff wall this time, she dug her fingernails into the rock and took a step onto the ledge. Sucking air through her nose, she exhaled and moved another step onto the natural catwalk. Hugging the wall and using both arms, she took small steps. Right foot. Left foot. Right foot. Left foot. When she reached the other side, she fell forward on her knees, to safety.

It was beautiful. She tilted her eyes up. The large plateau led to a series of overhanging cliffs with natural caves cut into the rock. Josh had shown her primitive drawings, remnants of the indigenous people, but he'd not brought her here. This must have been where the ancients lived. The cliff was massive, the base surrounded by fallen boulders and natural vegetation.

Cheks galloped in a small circle, barking joyfully, avoiding the low-lying cacti dotting the landscape. What was the dog trying to tell her? She scanned the perimeter, squinting into the sun, tilting her head up.

The small caves led to a big black hole. It had to be the main cave, but she couldn't see inside. The sun glinted off something shiny. What was it? She stepped forward a few paces; the dog barked. As she got closer, the dog flipped from playful to defensive. The spaniel lowered his neck and growled, showing his canines.

She froze. The reflection was coming off a rifle muzzle poking out from the opening, the barrel resting on an inverted V-shaped stand. The type snipers use. She backed away quietly but the dog had already announced her presence. Maybe it was abandoned. Her gut told her to flee. The dog disappeared inside the cavity. She turned to run, tripping over a branch. Using her hands to break the fall, she caught the edge of a cactus plant. Several spikes stuck in her open palm.

"Damn it."

"Hey, there. Are you okay?" A man's voice boomed from the cave.

She grabbed the tree branches poking up through the rocks with her good hand and balancing on the biggest one like a ski pole, pulled herself up and started to run.

"Hey, slow down." the man yelled. "Be careful, young lady."

Lauren didn't look back. She needed to get the hell out of there. She scrambled to the walkway and crawled to the other side.

If it weren't for the dog, she would never have crossed the ledge and she'd have missed the high-tech rifle in the stand. It blended in with the natural terrain. Maybe the man was a hunter. She slowed as she approached the horse, walking softly. Smokey smelled fear on her, the whites of his eyes flashed.

She pulled the cactus pins from her hand, dots of blood welling, and untied the horse, focusing on the cadence of her movements, keeping them steady.

Tugging on the reins with her back to the horse, he walked forward. She picked up the pace and he trotted behind her through the narrow tunnel. On the other side she stuck her foot in the stirrup and grabbed the saddle horn with her right hand, the wrong one, trying to pull herself up. The horse broke into a gallop. She clung to the side of the saddle like a trick rider. Hanging on as if with on foot on a ladder, she counted to three, and then dropped her right foot down to the hard ground.

*Ouch.*

She pogoed up with enough force to hook her ankle over the saddle but she was hanging upside down. She did an abdominal crunch and grabbed the mane with her free hand, but didn't have enough strength to pull her leg over the horse's withers.

*Just let go.*

The terrain was rugged. Disoriented and hanging like a bat, she had to try again to get vertical. She closed her eyes and let her body relax, clinging to the side of the horse feeling for the rhythm of the action.

Hooves pounding the hard ground, she counted a two-beat.

One, two.

One, two.

Adrenaline surged up her spine, through her neck, into super-human strength, as if being pulled like a marionette. A split second later she was in the saddle, one foot in a stirrup, hugging Smokey's neck as the horse galloped flat out for home.

A single shot exploded from the canyon. A flock of turkey vultures sprang up from behind the cottonwoods. It was the same sound of a fifty-caliber rifle she'd heard when she'd ridden with Josh. The sound came from the direction of the cave, drowning out the pounding of hooves.

Two jackrabbits dashed across her path. Her heart pumped. The single gunshot reverberated off the cliffs and echoed down the canyon walls. Smokey sped to a dead run. She lay flat on his neck, breaking the wind.

They were halfway home before Lauren gathered the reins. Pulling on the noseband, the horse slowed from a dead gallop, to a lope, to a bouncy trot, and finally to a prancing walk. He was scared. And tired.

Lauren rubbed his neck.

"It's okay, boy. I don't blame you for taking off."

She brushed dirt from her pants and wiggled her fingers and toes. The prick wounds on her left palm itched, pins of blood had dried to a dark brown. She rubbed her kneecaps and elbows with the back of her hands. Her clothes were torn and her right ankle ached. Twisted, not broken. Smokey leapt sideways. It was Chekov, hiding in the sagebrush. He was running in circles, chasing his tail. She heard a strange sound coming from the same direction, a hissing noise, like static interference.

She dismounted and hobbled toward the dog, twigs and branches crackling beneath her boots. This time the dog didn't run. He let her scratch his head. The weird audio was coming from the dog's flak jacket. A red light flashed on his collar. It looked like some sort of transmitter. Cheks stuck his nose in the air and barked, long ears flailing, but when she reached for his collar, he took off again.

Lauren remounted. From atop the horse, Cheks was a black-and-white dot, racing back up the same trail.

She dug her heels into Smokey's ribs.

"Yah." The horse galloped for home.

## 32

C orporate security let the two men in the building. Special Agent Tyrone Smith wondered what it would look like inside. It didn't disappoint. He and Special Agent Felix Martinez stood in front of the chest-high reception desk. The young woman sitting behind it didn't take them seriously.

"You swear you're not from the singing telegram place?" Peyton Marsh asked.

"No, ma'am," Tyrone said.

"Oh, you guys are good." She twisted the ends of her long red hair around her fingertips in little arcs.

She had a primo job. When the company went public, the initial offering made the social media's founder the youngest billionaire in history and it was common knowledge Zack Wisenberg made his employees rich, too, handing out stock options. Now that it was the second most valuable company on the planet, security at the building was tighter than most international airports.

It was clear she wasn't buying it, that Tyrone and his partner's royal blue jackets with big yellow FBI lettering weren't part of a gag. She giggled when he flashed his shiny badge pinned to a leather holder.

"Let me see whose birthday it is." She tapped her keyboard and looked at the screen. "Give me a second." She gazed at her monitor, then looked at Tyrone, perplexed. Holding her phone up she clicked a picture of him. "This one's going to be a winner. We get points for the most shares of the day."

She was about to post the picture to her social media account.

"DO NOT, I repeat, do not push the SEND button," he warned.

She cocked her head and laughed. "You're good."

He shouldered the reception desk and struck like a cobra, clamping his hand on her wrist.

"Hey," she protested as he peeled her fingers off the device one at a time. "You can't do this."

He was going easy on her. She was clueless about his power. He removed the memory card and battery and handed them to his partner. Agent Martinez placed them in clear plastic bag and shoved it into the front pocket of his black pants. Tyrone handed the phone back to her.

"What do you think you're doing?" She was furious. "Even if this isn't a joke, you can't do this. I'm calling security."

"How do you think we got in?" He paused to read her nametag. "Ms. Marsh, we have a warrant. Who is your supervisor?"

His partner, ten years older than him, stubbed the sole of his wingtip on the floor like he was putting out a lit cigarette, a nervous habit that drove Tyrone nuts.

"Let me see it." She put her hand out.

She wanted to see the warrant, like she'd know the difference between it and that takeout menu to the vegan place down the road. He repeated his request to call her supervisor.

"The warrant," she said. "I'd like to see it first."

Tyrone held it up, out of her reach. For all the training she'd had, she appeared unable to recall what to do in the event the FBI's Cyber Action Team showed up. She was on the frontlines of one of the richest, most powerful companies in the history of the planet, and she was childlike.

"How do I know this is real?"

"Please contact your supervisor," Tyrone's partner, Felix, said, agitated.

Her hands trembled as she picked up the landline receiver, rested it on her shoulder and thumbed through the company directory on her desk. She dialed the extension to Human Resources and told the person on the other end that two men claiming to be from the FBI were at the front desk. She said didn't know who else to call.

"I don't know. Security let them in." Peyton paused, listening. "Because they took the memory card out of my phone." Her tone was one of uncertainty. Another pause. "Uh-huh . . . uh-huh . . . Um . . . I'll find out . . . Hang on." She looked at Tyrone. "My supervisor wants to know who sent you and what you want."

"I am not at liberty to share that information, Miss," he said.

Peyton repeated what Tyrone said to the person on the other end of the line.

"Uh-huh. Uh-huh . . . Yes, I did, I asked them for ID . . . Yes. They showed me their badges . . . Yes. I'll ask . . . My supervisor wants to know if you're carrying *firearms*."

"Yes," Tyrone said, almost laughing, "Federal law requires FBI agents to be armed at all times."

"We need to speak to your supervisor," Felix said, "ASAP."

She tilted her head on her shoulder, cradling the mouthpiece and looked up at them with wide eyes. Her voice cracked. "Uh-huh . . . they said yes. I told you, they said they're from the

FBI . . . Uh-huh . . . Uh-huh, yes." She hung up the phone. "My supervisor said to wait here. She's coming down."

"Thank you, Miss," Agent Martinez said matter-of-factly.

"You could chill out a little you know," Peyton said nervously, picking at the gray polish on her nails. "When do I get my memory card and battery back?" She sat on her hands.

"I don't know," Tyrone said.

Martinez rubbed something invisible under his shoe while Tyrone instinctively scanned the building.

The epicenter of the most influential social media company in the world was an architectural façade meant to look like a rehabbed industrial building. It was supposed to look hip, like it was located in the warehouse district in New York City, but it lacked the authenticity, like a fourteen-year-old girl trying to look thirty. The location was less New York. More Alcatraz.

A luxury shuttle bus pulled up at the entrance and an army of workers bounded down the stairs and streamed through the front doors like ants. Carrying laptops under their arms and staring at smaller screens in their hands, inside they split off in different directions. None seemed to notice him in his bright blue FBI jacket hovering at the front desk. Not a single one of them did so much as a double take.

"It wouldn't kill you to be a little friendlier." Peyton looked like she'd calmed down a little. "And I'd really appreciate it if you gave me my SIM card back. I can't imagine why you're here or why you took it from me. This is a wonderful place to work, a dream really, a super safe space."

She could have saved the sales pitch. Instead, she kept at it.

"They do our laundry for free. We have massage therapists, free ice cream, and snacks. The bus that just drove up, that's the company shuttle. We get free transportation to and from work, and there's complimentary high-speed Wi-Fi, too." She made a pouty face jutting her lower lip out and resumed twirling the ends of her auburn hair.

A fleet of luxury buses built on the drivel people posted on social media? All of it was hard to imagine.

"Can you believe this place?" Tyrone whispered.

"No joke. We are surrounded by the world's brightest, most cooperative inmates."

"You know what's strange?"

"Other than guys with blue hair?" Felix was on guard, his eyes casing the building.

"Seriously, these kids are math and science whizzes and they are willing to live in third world housing in order to work here. I heard a bunch of them live in a trailer park. It's lousy economics."

Tyrone saw her first.

A smartly dressed fortyish woman in a navy-blue suit and dark-blue pumps trotted down the concrete slab stairs, her heels clattering like hooves. Her hand slid along the wrought-iron railing, added he figured, to make it look like the company was somewhere other than suburban San Francisco.

The stuffed skirt from Human Resources stopped on the bottom stair and gestured to them.

They met her at the base of the staircase.

"What can I do for you?" she asked.

They introduced themselves as Special Agents Felix Martinez and Tyrone Smith, showing IDs and handing her the warrant. "We're in charge of this field operation."

She took the paper from Tyrone without making eye contact. Unlike the cute redhead at the desk, this one seemed to know what to do. She put the glasses hanging on her shirt on her nose and looked at the paper.

"A search warrant from the FBI Cyber Action Team?"

Her poise caught Tyrone off guard, but he'd been trained to

hide his feelings, too. Scanning each paragraph, her expression did not change. She handed the paper back to him and stepped away to make a phone call on her mobile. A minute later she was back. "Follow me."

Tyrone and his partner followed her up the stairs, past a dozen rooms filled with teams of young people making notes on yellow pads. Sloppily dressed employees collaborated in workspaces behind glass-partitioned rooms outfitted with furniture that looked liked it belonged in a low-income public housing project, not at a company that was breaking market caps on Wall Street.

Tyrone reached under his jacket and tapped his chest, just above his heart. It was the spot where he'd had the tattoo artist ink a cross over his heart, right after he'd graduated the academy. Most kids from the housing projects of West Oakland didn't make it to Special Agent. The magnitude of what he was about to do was setting in.

When they reached the end of a long corridor, their escort, the Human Resources woman who'd not given her name, knocked on the door. "Wait here."

She went inside the office with a copy of the warrant and a minute later, motioned them into the corner office. A pudgy, bespectacled man invited them in. A diploma hung on the wall: Doctor of Jurisprudence, Stanford University.

The lawyer had an unusual tic that made his neck twitch to the left while his right eye blinked simultaneously. His attire was disheveled, and his office minimalist, a black metal desk with a low-backed rolling chair.

"I'm Henry Wiggins," he said. "Have a seat."

Wiggins was famous for being Zack Wisenberg's college roommate. The in-house, go-to lawyer was revered more for his unwavering loyalty to Zack Wisenberg than for any legal prowess.

Wiggins read the warrant, crinkling his nose, showing rat teeth, his expression changing as the levity sank in. Wiggins' tic appeared to activate Felix's shoe twisting. Tyrone looked away, out the window overlooking the manicured landscaping, tuning them out.

When Wiggins was done reading, he raised his bushy eyebrows. "This is a warrant? To search our computers? That's a big ask. Do you have any idea how much data is stored here? We host more than two billion social accounts."

"You know better," Tyrone said. "If you read the warrant correctly, you'd see the scope of our search is limited. Plus, your servers aren't here."

Wiggins stood wringing his hands. "Is-is-is," he stammered, "is the request for specific data?" He put the document on his desk and rubbed his bare head with two open palms. "With all the recent bad PR we've gotten over privacy, this will unduly harm our business."

The warrant didn't ask for customer data.

Tyrone said, "If you need more time to read it, please take it. The scope is narrow."

The search was limited to specific internal corporate communications. It wasn't that Wiggins didn't understand the warrant. He was buying time, considering his options. The element of surprise had worked the way Tyrone had hoped.

"Why do you want the information? Is the company being investigated for criminal activity?" Wiggins asked.

"I'm sure you know I'm not at liberty to discuss an ongoing investigation," Tyrone said.

Wiggins picked up the document. "It says here that the search and seizure is a matter of national security. The Foreign Intelligence Surveillance Court issued this warrant and we've been being monitored? Us? The company? For what?" the lawyer asked. "A FISA warrant? Come on."

Felix backed him up. "Sir, we are not at liberty to discuss the specifics of the operation."

"Operation?" The lawyer looked shaky. "I-I-I," he stuttered, "can't authorize this. Mr. Wisenberg is not on the premises. Something of this magnitude would have to go through him, and through outside counsel. We have several firms representing us." His tic was getting worse.

"Apparently you missed this course at Stanford," Tyrone said. "An FBI search warrant has no legal remedy."

Wiggins stood and walked toward the window. "Jesus. What the fuck?"

A convoy of unmarked vehicles had surrounded the building. An infantry of agents lined the perimeter. An FBI chopper approached, the chuffing of blades coming closer.

"No, no, no, no," Henry Wiggins said, spotting the helicopter. "No, no, no. I need to clear this with Mr. Wisenberg." He paced, rubbing his head. "Mr. Wisenberg can't be reached."

Tyrone was enjoying the show.

"He's off the grid, and we've lost contact with him," the lawyer said. "And Mr. Wisenberg is *never* off the grid."

"Have you been able to reach him the last twenty-four hours?" Tyrone knew the answer was no.

"Would someone please tell me what's going on here?" Henry took his phone from the pocket of his wrinkled shirt and fumbled it, dropping it on the hard floor.

"I'll take that." Felix knelt and picked it up.

"That's mine," Wiggins said. "You-you-you can't have it."

Felix removed the memory card. "They'll fight over this at the field office to see who gets to look at this treasure trove first." He handed the phone to Tyrone.

"You'll never get past the encryption." Wiggins's tone had turned hostile.

"You might be surprised." Tyrone put the memory card in a

plastic evidence bag before handing it to a young man standing in the doorway to the lawyer's office.

"Hey, there, Try-One-On. It's the criminalist who loves the minimalist. Digging these digs, brother."

Rayvon loved to play the bro card.

"It's *Agent* Smith," Tyrone said.

Rayvon was the best forensic tech in the FBI's Cyber Action Team, a gifted mathematician with the perfect personality disorder for the Cyber team. The Bureau chief handpicked him to lead computer forensics on the FBI's first raid in Silicon Valley history.

"I was just having a little fun, bro." The young black man took pictures while he talked. Felix handed Rayvon the memory cards from the receptionist. "I dig the architecture. The temple of social media is a sick, badass place."

Henry Wiggins wobbled to the desk. He planted his palm on the top to steady himself and doubled over like he'd been gut punched. His face was as white as the walls.

"Cooperate with us, sir. That will assure you that you get the best possible outcome." Special Agent Tyrone Smith pulled the rolling chair out from behind the lawyer's desk and helped a stricken Henry Wiggins into it.

## 33

L auren waited until there was a break at the front desk, then approached Rosa.

"Where have you been? Everyone's been worried. MK said you went out for a ride. Are you limping?"

She slipped into Rosa's office. "Can you get me some food? Something light."

"That's asking a lot. Gordy is on the verge of a full-scale melt-down. They've been working 'round the clock in the kitchen. This lockdown has everyone on pins and needles." Rosa's eyes swept over her. Shaking her head, she said. "Don't worry, I won't ask what happened. Hold down the fort while I see what I can do."

It was five-thirty in the evening and Lauren expected the common areas to be filled with guests. Instead, there was a smat-tering of people, young and old, segregated by age gathered in small groups at opposite ends of the long tables. The cooling air wafted all the way from the repaired window to the front desk. The screen kept the wildlife out, but not the dust. Rosa returned with a plate of food covered with tinfoil, utensils wrapped in a colorful cloth napkin.

"It's a madhouse in there." She handed her the plate, barely smiling.

"Thank you." She peeked under the foil; it smelled heavenly. "Where is everyone?"

"I think they've accepted they're stuck here and they're making the most of it. Look." Rosa pointed to the bookshelves in the lobby.

They were half empty.

"There was a bit of a squabble over them, if you can believe it. It's been kind of nice since then. We're way beyond capacity. Guests have been wandering into the kitchen, trying to get room service. Gordy threatened to butcher one and serve his head on a plate. It's been quiet since then.

"I'll be glad when things get back to normal. Who would ever have guessed that Mr. Pompadour's book collection would one day be my saving grace. I was about to lose it with all the moaning and complaining when it occurred to them they could entertain themselves reading books and watching DVDs. Two families are in the media room with their kids." Rosa tossed her head that direction. "Did you hear someone left one of those awful bugs in Gordy's locker? He was so mad I thought he might burn down the lodge."

Her stomach turned. "Seriously? Someone messed with the chef?"

"Josh had to calm him down. He threatened to walk off the job. Or release that creature in the dining room." Rosa eyed the plate of food. "You owe me."

"Who would do that? That would have been a disaster." She lost her appetite. "Oh my God. Is that who I think it is?"

Rosa nodded.

Lauren had seen his picture in dozens of magazines and on websites. The social media tycoon wore his signature hoodie and was making a beeline for the reception desk. The front of his sweatshirt bulged, his hands stuffed in the pass-through front pocket.

He stopped abruptly, half-smiled, and asked, "What should I do with this?" He removed the milk bottle from inside his shirt and set it on the counter.

Rosa recoiled and covered her mouth with her hand. Lauren took two steps back.

Zack Wisenberg was composed. "My wife found this in our room."

Rosa swallowed hard. "I am soooo sorry. How awful for her, and for you. I'll take care of it." Rosa reached for it.

He stopped her, putting his hand over hers. "I thought this place was secure." His demeanor was calm and his tone soft but his knuckles were turning white from gripping the bottle. "My wife and I, we have a toddler with us, in our room."

"I'm aware of that." Rosa spoke a little louder, over his shoulder. She looked at Lauren. "Would you please get Luther?"

Lauren ran out the side door, through the courtyard. She spotted MK's red boots under the veranda outside the main ranch house Jake shared with Vance. Lauren tapped on the door. Jake answered.

"Is Luther here?" She panted.

"Where have you been?" Vance's voice was filled with worry.

Luther pushed past Vance and Jake. "Indeed, I am. Come in, dear. What seems to be the emergency this time? Such drama."

Lauren told him about the scorpion in the bottle and who'd brought it to the front desk.

Luther was pissed. "Where is he now?"

"He's at the desk, talking with Rosa. With one of those things." Lauren shivered and grimaced.

Luther brushed past her and sprinted toward the lobby. Vance and Jake looked at each other and shrugged their shoulders, partially closing the door.

MK had overheard. "Come on," she said sliding out, grabbing Lauren's arm, following Luther. "This oughta be good."

"Luther, there you are." The voice came from the pool area.

Luther stopped in his tracks, looking around.

Lauren recognized it. "That's him," she whispered to MK. The two women moved to a spot behind the hedge close enough where they could watch and listen.

"What the fuck is this, Luther?" He held the milk bottle up. "It's fascinating, no doubt, but how did it get in my room? Who would put it there? Are you pranking me or shooting a reality show?"

"Of course not." Luther took umbrage.

"I heard a rumor that one of the new owners is in the video business. If you're in on this, I'll sue you into the Stone Age, I swear to God, Luther. You tell them that, the new owners."

Lauren's face burned red. She looked at MK wide-eyed.

"Don't worry," MK whispered. "He's fishing. Of course, it doesn't help that he got one of those horrible creatures. I don't blame him for being angry."

Luther fingered his black goatee. He reached for the bottle. Zack pulled it away from him like a child unwilling to share.

"No, we're not making a reality television show, or any kind of show. We would never do that."

MK and Lauren craned their necks in unison, cupping their ears, turning their heads to get a better angle to listen.

The billionaire reached into the front pocket of his hoodie. "It came with a note."

"A note?" Luther folded his arms across his chest. "What kind of a *note*?"

"I was hoping you could help me out with that." Zack unfolded it and read aloud. " 'Remember what Holmes said?' That's what the note says, Luther. I want an explanation."

Luther was on guard. "I don't know what to say."

Lauren looked at MK, blinking.

MK answered with a shrug.

"You don't know anything about this?" Zack picked up the glass bottle and rolled it in his hands. He watched the scorpion slide on the revolving glass like a hamster on an icy wheel. "The message doesn't mean anything to you."

"It does not. I admit I am somewhat embarrassed to say that I have no clue. Maybe it's a joke, like a Dr. Watson-Sherlock Holmes thing."

"Are you kidding? A joke? This place is getting weirder by the hour. We should have stopped coming after Roy passed away. Now I'm stuck here. My plane is gone. I have no communication to the outside world. Yet someone can come in my room? I need to get out of here, Luther. I run a company with a market cap of over three hundred billion dollars. You know what that means? Not you or anyone can hold me prisoner. Do you understand? You need to make it happen. I'll make it worth your while."

Luther considered it. "I can't."

MK whispered, "I'm going back to my room. This is going to get ugly."

Lauren nodded for her to go, and when MK was out of sight, Lauren pressed her heel into the gravel and marched out from behind the hedge.

Luther lurched sideways, startled.

"Oh, I'm so sorry. Am I interrupting something?" she asked.

"Goodness," Luther said. "What happened to you? What happened to your foot?"

"I went for a ride and the horse spooked. I think I sprained it." She extended her hand. "You must be Zack Wisenberg. I am truly sorry for that." She gestured to the milk bottle.

"And you are?"

"Lauren Gold. I'm one of the new owners."

"A scorpion. In a bottle." Zack's tone was caustic.

"Did Luther tell you he got one, too?"

Zack glared at him. "Is that true, Luther?"

"Well . . . "

"Who else got one?" Zack asked.

"I did," MK said.

She must have changed her mind about going back to her room.

"I didn't know you were here," Luther said.

Jake walked up with Vance. "I got one, too. Special delivery to my yacht."

"You are?" Zack asked.

"We're Lauren's partners. I'm Jake Fleming and this is Vance Courage."

Zack set the milk bottle down. "How many total?"

"Partners?" Jake asked.

"No." Zack held the milk bottle up. "How many of *these*?"

Lauren was counting in her head. She was about to say six.

Vance beat her to it. "Eight."

She played it back in her head and counted six: *Me, Luther, Jake, Gordy, MK, and Zack. Six.*

"Eight?" Zack asked, shoving the bottle into Luther's chest. "Add this one to your collection."

After Luther and Zack stormed off, Lauren confronted Vance in front of MK and Jake.

"Eight? I only counted six. Me. Luther, MK, Jake, Gordy, and Zack. Six."

Vance said. "Frank Conn got one."

"Frank Conn?" Lauren repeated. Then she remembered the sheriff had stopped by earlier. He'd had words with Vance.

"The lawyer? From Pinch & Elders?" MK looked surprised.

"It's a long story," Jake said.

"Where's Frank?" MK asked. "I haven't seen him."

"In jail."

"For what?" MK shook her head, perplexed.

"For murder," Vance said. "And someone deposited one of those things in his cell."

"Murder? How do you know that?" MK was stumped.

"The sheriff," Vance said.

"Who is he supposed to have murdered?" MK asked.

"Maria. The housekeeper," Lauren said.

"Jesus. Effing. Christ. He's in jail for murdering the house-keeper?" MK rubbed her palms together.

Lauren was about to explode.

MK sensed it and took things down a notch. "We're on the same team here. Let's step back. Seven of those things have been delivered. What do we all have in common?"

"Antelope Creek Ranch," Vance said.

"That's right. Cinderella is going to go get ready for the ball." MK turned to leave, then stopped. "I can't believe you guys left Frank Conn in jail."

"I tried bailing him out. He's being held without bond," Vance said.

Jake followed MK away.

Lauren said, "Someone is sending us a message." She stared hard at Vance. "Eight? You meant seven, didn't you?"

He looked sheepish. "I got one, too. I just hadn't told you yet. I was hoping we'd figure out who's doing it first."

MK yelled. "It's how men try to help, hon. He's trying to protect you."

That was the last thing she needed, protection from the truth. She heard his voice in her head again, her ex, Peter, telling her how she ignored the things that were right under her nose. Like the affair he'd been having with the intern at his office.

"I don't want to be protected," Lauren said. "Especially from reality."

"Are you okay? You look, um, banged up."

"I'm fine. I'd like to be alone. Do you mind?"

"Next time you decide to go off and ride by yourself, let me know, will you? I'll see you at dinner." He kissed her on the cheek and left for his room.

She limped toward the *acequia*. Sitting on the edge of the wooden walkover bridge, she dropped her sore ankle into the cold water. Luther had left the milk bottle next to the chaise, upright. He came back to get it and saw her sitting alone.

"Thank you for sticking up for me," Lauren said.

"Sticking up for you?"

"I heard Zack ask you if I had anything to do with it. The reality show thing."

"You spied on me? While I spoke to Zack?" He took exception.

"Really? You need to get over it, Luther." A light breeze came out of nowhere. Lauren brushed a lock of hair from her face.

"You cannot speak to me that way."

"Is that right? I am an equal owner of this ranch. As such, I'm your boss. We all recognize the valuable service you perform here. You really *are* good at what you do. But why did you lie, pretending he was the only one who got a surprise bottle, when you knew several had been delivered? You told him it was probably a *joke*. There are so many lies circling this place, I personally can't keep up with them all. Not to mention all the errors of omission."

"May I have it back?" It was Zack. He stood over her, gesturing to the milk bottle in Luther's hands. "Will you excuse us, please?"

Lauren grabbed the hand railing, and pulled herself up to leave.

"Not you, him," Zack said.

Luther's head jerked. "Me? You want me to leave?"

"Yes. I'd like to talk to her. In private."

Luther's mouth fell open but no words came out. He blinked like a toddler.

"Ground Control to Luther," Zack said. "May we please have some privacy? I'd like to talk to Lauren. Alone."

"Well, fine," Luther huffed.

Zack gripped the bottle with both hands. His eyes glinted. He shielded them with his hands, his pupils dilated into black holes with outer rings of electric blue.

She wrapped her arms around herself, shivering. The sun was most of the way down and the temperature plummeting. He set the bottle down, unzipped the hoodie and took it off. He held it out to her.

What was she supposed to do with it? When she didn't take it, he squatted behind her and gently draped it over her shoulders. It was still warm.

"Are you sure? You'll get cold in a tee-shirt."

"I'm sure. I won't get cold. I'm used to it. Where are you from?"

"Miami."

"That explains it. The temperature doesn't change much from day to night." He paused. "Are you Jewish by any chance? Gold. The name."

"Oh." Her face flushed. "No. My ex, he's Jewish."

"My wife is Korean and she complains that I keep the house at sixty degrees. She teases me that the Jews are still trying to cool down from wandering the desert for forty years."

Lauren smiled. She was sucker for a sense of humor. "I am so sorry about that thing you found in your room. Please accept my deepest apology."

"Why should you be sorry?"

"I guess I feel responsible."

"When I heard the ranch was sold, I was disappointed, I won't lie. I would have liked the chance to buy it. I would have paid any price. I had no idea it was for sale. Lucky you."

"Yeah. Lucky me . . . lucky us, I mean."

"Any update on this Homeland Security thing? What's it about anyway." Zack picked up the bottle and traced his finger around the bottom. The scorpion used one pincher to balance itself and the other to follow his finger playfully, like a cat.

"I . . . we . . . don't know."

He nodded, teasing the scorpion.

"You seem to have a way with insects." She'd been watching the creature following Zack's finger.

"It's not an insect. It a predatory arachnid."

Vance had corrected her the same way.

"You could get me out of here. You could fire Luther."

While part two was an attractive idea, she pushed back. "I wish I could. But I can't. If I could leave, I would. Firing Luther won't change anything. We'll just be stuck here with a guy with a grudge."

Twirling her ankle in the cold water, she pulled the sweatshirt tighter around her torso. A breeze kicked up. A lock of hair swished in her face. She pulled the hood over her head.

Zack stood. "You can keep it."

Lauren looked up him, cocking her head.

He tapped his finger on the top of his head. "The hoodie. You can keep it. I have more. Oh, and I hope your ankle feels better."

"I'll see you at dinner," she said.

Her ankle did feel better. She took her foot out of the water and looked at it. The pain was gone and the cold water was probably going to keep the swelling down. Tomorrow, that's when it would really start to hurt.

"You could sell that and make serious money."

It was that asshole, Luther, again.

"The sweatshirt, you could sell it online and make a fortune."

"I could sell my share of the ranch to him and make my money ten times over, or more. The sky's the limit."

"No, I don't believe you could," Luther said.

There was a loud whistling in the distance. She pushed the hood back and cupped her ear in the direction it was coming. "Did you hear that?"

"It sounds like Josh calling Cheks. Mr. Pompadour would whistle like that and that dog would pop up from right out of nowhere. Scared the daylights out of me a time or two."

She laughed and changed the subject back to the sale of the ranch. "If Jake and Vance agree, we could sell it for a lot more than what we paid. Zack said it himself. He said he'd love to buy it and we could name our price."

"Think what you wish. However, you may wish to double-check the sales agreement first. There's a first right of refusal written into the contract. Maybe you're getting a little ahead of yourself, Ms. Gold. If you'd read the fine print, you might have known that Mr. Pompadour's executors were careful not to let the ranch fall into the wrong hands."

Wrong hands? "You mean Josh Dominguez was being careful not to let the ranch fall into the wrong hands."

He ignored her. "The people who live in rarefied air, they use the law in dubious ways. They hire the best lawyers to get an edge on the competition. I could go on and on about that. About half of the annual revenues here come from DC lobbyists. The deaf group that was here, they're lobbying Congress mandating all law enforcement learn sign language. Roy thought it was high time to push back on them, the special interest groups. Not that I have anything against the deaf."

"As sorry as I am for them, can we please get back to the sale?"

"Don't you wonder how it is that you and your two friends are the new owners when a fellow like Zack Wisenberg has told you he'd meet any offer? There are dozens of others with unlimited resources who'd pay a king's ransom for this place. You got a killer deal when you bought it."

"Maybe you're not aware it was on the market for six months and there were no offers."

"Apparently you did not conduct your due diligence. Mr. Pompadour has not been dead for six months. Did you bother to confirm that?"

Her face flushed. "What are you saying?"

"You may be the new owner of Antelope Creek Ranch, but let's not forget the lead lawyer who closed on your deal is sitting in the Marfidio County jail, charged with murder."

"What's that supposed to mean?" Lauren rubbed her temple. A dull throb thumped in her head.

"Nothing. Except he should have pointed out the first right of refusal clause," Luther said.

"Who has first right of refusal? If we put the ranch up for sale?"

"Ask your boyfriend. He's a lawyer."

"Vance?" She scowled at him. "He's not my boyfriend."

"We'll play it your way. Ask your lawyer *friend* if knows who has first right of refusal. He should have a copy of the agreement." Luther tilted his head back and looked up through his tinted lenses at the last remnants of the setting sun.

"You probably overlooked my employment agreement, too. It would be very, very, *very* expensive for you or your partners to fire me, for any reason."

How did they miss this? Especially Vance and Jake?

"Your naiveté is rather sweet, my dear. In fact, I find it

refreshing. We need to get ready. Tonight is the big night." Luther walked a few steps toward the lodge, stopped and turned back toward the bridge. He hovered over her. "I saw you kissing him."

"What?"

"Your *not* boyfriend-lawyer. I saw you kissing him last night."

## 34

Peyton collapsed in her thousand-dollar ergonomic chair behind the reception desk. She'd seen the army of FBI agents on the ground through the window overlooking the front of the campus.

Tyrone's boss at the San Francisco field office had made it clear he didn't want any screw-ups, nothing Zack Wisenberg's legions of lawyers could use in court.

They'd been focused on Henry Wiggins, who was the target. It was no longer a stealth operation. They'd generated excitement securing the thirty-acre site, especially when the FBI chopper landed on the building's rooftop helipad, usually reserved for the CEO and big shareholders.

The receptionist picked up her dead smartphone and tapped the keys like a child playing make believe. She twirled the ends of her hair obsessively.

"Um . . . Miss," Tyrone said, unable to remember her name.

Peyton looked up from her chair, wide-eyed. "Yes?"

He held his hand out. "Here you go. Sorry for the inconvenience."

She took the SIM card and battery from him carefully, as if

they were precious things. "Did you find what you're looking for?"

"I can't discuss it," he said.

He was sure they'd gotten everything they could within the parameters of the warrant: Wiggins' laptop, cell phone, and tablet. He'd have loved to copy the contents of the lawyer's hard drive but according to the criminalist, the drive wasn't partitioned and they'd breach the scope of the warrant if they did. *Don't fuck this up.*

Tyrone looked out over the manicured visitors' parking area. The media already smelled blood. Scruffy men in jeans and T-shirts scurried around a flotilla of trucks, opening compartments and pulling out rings of cable like stacks of garden hoses from the bellies of the trucks. More were lined up, jockeying for position. Two drivers argued on the street. One pushed the other, shoving him hard enough to knock his opponent off balance. The smaller, less hostile one held his hand up, surrendering, letting the more aggressive driver move ahead of him, taking prime space to set up his satellite truck.

Tyrone smiled at the engraved placard on Peyton's desk: COMMITTED TO MAKING THE WORLD BETTER, ONE PERSON AT A TIME

The Stanford punk heading this company was either the biggest bullshitter in the history of mankind or he actually believed he could change human nature.

*You're done playing God, you punk.*

The scrum of reporters outside jostled for position, pushing and shoving. Passenger cars arrived and hogged all the handicapped parking spots. He shook his head, and chuckled when he saw local TV news reporters scrambling out of cars.

Peyton cautioned him. "I don't find any of this funny." She snapped her phone back together. When the screen lit up, dozens of text messages pinged like a Vegas slot machine. Her thumbs went to work.

He could only guess how the social media giant was going to handle another blow to its image, especially since Zack Wisenberg had been off the grid for almost forty-eight hours.

He'd agreed to man the lobby while Felix and the cyber forensics team finished up in Wiggins' office. They wanted to exercise caution and follow protocol.

*Don't fuck it up.*

Peyton riffled through a drawer full of visitor badges. Her fingers trembled on the TV remote, scrolling through the menu. She changed from the in-house propaganda channel to a local San Francisco affiliate. She ducked when she saw a camera with a long lens pointed at the window where she was sitting. She spun through the channels. Every news outlet was covering the raid.

Shows in progress were interrupted with breaking news. Two other big technology firms were going through the same thing. Numeral II Corporation, the largest search engine company, was on lockdown, too. So was the behemoth online retailer up in Oregon.

Tyrone told her to turn up the volume.

Early reports were sketchy. Reporters blamed the "fascists" running the White House. Others predicted the end of Western civilization. Some opined the FBI was being manipulated, retaliation for the never-ending investigations into the White House.

One outlier, an analyst at one of the big cable financial shows, said it was about time Uncle Sam reined in the tech companies, that these monopolies were "disrupting everything from banking and shopping to news." He was promptly branded a nut job by the news anchors and the producers cut away from him.

The legal pundits were weighing in now. It was obvious the

FBI's San Francisco field office was leaking information. Tyrone's breakfast almost came up when a talking head reported that an unnamed source told him that the FBI Cyber Crimes Division was investigating the possible *assassination* of a high-profile Washington DC judge.

Tyrone held his breath.

When asked if it had anything to do with the two other contemporaneous raids, the analyst said, "Yes. My sources have confirmed it."

The television screen went to a quad-split showing scenes of the three raids with a live field reporter in the fourth box. When pressed by the anchors at the news desk about the identity of the judge, she seemed to be in the dark.

It would morph into a shit show when it broke that the FBI was investigating the murder of a Supreme Court Justice.

That could hurt the investigation.

*Don't fuck it up, Tyrone.*

## 35

Manny stopped in to see how Frank Conn was doing. Sue told him Immigration & Customs Enforcement agents had picked up their prisoners. Sue told him even the ICE agents were concerned at Frank Conn's mental and physical condition.

"I think he's about to take a dirt nap."

Sue had seen a lot of things in her twenty years working the Marfidio County jail, and when she told him the lawyer looked like he might die, Manny felt panicky. The sheriff kicked himself; a dead lawyer was not part of the plan.

When he went to see him, Frank refused to speak. His eyes were glassy and saliva dripped from the corner of his mouth. The sheriff went into the cell and knelt next to him, shaking him by the shoulders. Frank's body rippled like a rag doll. He used one knee to keep the lawyer from toppling over.

"Come on, Frank. Talk to me."

"Wish me . . . a speedy death. Tell my family I wish I'd been . . . a better husband and father," Frank mumbled. He sat on the concrete jail floor, listing against the cinder block wall, head hanging down.

"You're still alive. Don't think about dying on us."

"Then lucky you, I guess. Unlucky me. Dear God . . . remove me from my misery.

"If you weren't stubborn as a mule, you might be out on bond. You'd have gotten a lawyer."

Sue arrived and entered the cell, handing Manny an energy drink, then headed back to her office.

"Drink this, Frank."

He pushed Manny's hand away. "I don't know why you're framing me. I never set foot in that maid's room . . . where you say you found my DNA."

"I never said it came from the room. Matter of fact, I never told you where they found it. Come on, Frank. You need to drink this." Manny held the water under Frank's nose like a mother coaxing a baby with a warm bottle.

Frank stuck his tongue out and took in a few drops, then grabbed the plastic bottle from the sheriff and tilted it back in his mouth, taking deep breaths between gulps.

Frank staggered to his feet. He was gaunt, like he'd lost ten pounds in two days.

"That phony DUI you charged Jake Fleming with? I saw what you did with my own eyes." He tightened the sleeves tied at the waist of the jumpsuit. "I told you, I never, ever saw that woman."

Surly Sue returned and stuck her head in the cell, "Sorry to interrupt." She studied Frank. "At least he's looking better. Thank Jesus for that. Sheriff, there's someone up front to see you. Good-looking fellow, so feel free to take your time."

"Well, don't go dying on me here. I don't need the trouble and your family needs a breadwinner. You hear me, Frank?"

"Then let me go. You'll have one less thing to worry about. You could give me my wallet and phone and I promise never to set foot in sorry ass town again. We could just put this whole thing behind us."

"I'll think about it," Manny said, locking Frank in. He would consider it, but right now he had bigger things to worry about, like figuring out who the mystery man was waiting for him in the lobby. It wasn't like Sue not to know the name, rank, and serial number of everyone within a fifty-mile radius. It was even less likely that she couldn't find out.

Manny didn't recognize the man pacing back and forth, either. The stranger was mid-forties, tall and athletic, with icy turquoise eyes and thinning blond hair. His jacket sleeves were pushed up to his elbows and he wore a dark-blue ball cap with a hand-stitched American flag on the brim.

Kinda fruity-looking.

The muscle on his forearm flexed when he held his hand out to shake Manny's.

One of them gym rats.

"I'm an old friend of Roy's," he said, fixing his eyes on the sheriff.

"Is that so?" *You're all friends of Roy's. Especially now that he's gone.*

"Barry Landeros. I'm running The Secondmen operation, out at the ranch." He twirled his sunglasses in his fingers.

"Heck. Good to meet you. Heard a lot of good things about you. Everything hunky dory?" *Tonight was the big night and Manny wasn't in any mood for bad news.*

Barry told him about the accident they'd staged. "Did a little more damage to the building than we planned. Plus, we had an injury."

"What kinda injury?"

"One guy tried to be a hero, but otherwise the operation was a success."

He didn't have to ask to know it was Vance Courage. Other

than Josh, who was in on the plan, the only one with any balls was the ex-cop. "What brings ya here?" He'd been monitoring his Motorola twenty-four/seven and didn't think he'd missed any radio transmissions.

"Do you have a minute?"

"Sure."

"Somewhere where we can talk privately?" Barry asked.

"Sure. Follow me out back."

Barry climbed into the passenger seat of the sheriff's patrol truck. Manny started the engine and turned on the A/C. The midday sun had heated up the interior of the truck like a magnifying glass on a bug.

"One of my guys saw a black Beemer come on the property last night. It was late, around eleven o'clock. It was a woman, a blonde, I can't be sure, but she looked like she'd been drinking, staggering a bit."

Manny was alarmed. "Was there security at the gate?"

"Yeah, one your guys. But here's the weird thing. He let her in and she spent the night at the ranch."

"Are you sure?" Manny twisted the string tie around his neck. He'd assigned Torres to the gate. A dumb move.

"Yeah. I saw her car leave early this morning."

"You're sure it was a BMW?"

"Positive. Multiple eyewitness accounts. I've got fifty guys out there, all over the perimeter."

"You're sure it was a blond-haired woman?"

"Well, that was the thing. When the first guy spotted her, the rest of them went bat-shit crazy. A sort of nineteen-fifties pinup gal, you know, with curves in all the right places. They spotted her first with a night vision scope and then when she stood under the light, the radio went crazy with reports of *wildlife*. The guys were scrapping over the binoculars. Stakeouts are mind-numbing. A bombshell, you know, with big blond hair, showing up out of the blue, it lit the crew up." Barry gazed out the passenger window. "Like I said, she looked drunk, or like she was on something."

"Anything else?"

"Yeah, they saw something strange when headlights first hit the gate. It looked like she was having a dustup, words you know, with your deputy posted out front. It looked like your man was trying to stop her but then he let her in. It's a ways from our vantage point and we were using night vision, so I can't be a hundred-percent sure."

Manny was anxious, bordering on angry. All he needed was that woman screwing things up. "Do you know who she was with or where she went?" Fucking Torres.

"She was alone. We were all sort of shocked, her pulling up the driveway fishtailing with her high beams on. I can't swear to it, but I think it was Luther, the manager, who met her out front, at the top of the driveway. If it wasn't Luther, then someone else motioned her in, showing her where to park.

"Then they walked to one of the rooms. She looked unstable and whoever was escorting her was trying to keep her from falling. She spent the night. Kept the night patrol busy, you know, waiting to see if she came out or her car moved. But she didn't leave until dawn."

"Well, thanks for telling me."

Barry shrugged. "I thought you should know."

"You did the right thing."

"Do you know who she is?"

The sheriff rolled his shoulders. "Only one woman fits the description. Jane Pandora."

"Is that a joke?"

"No. It's her real name. She's the local Justice of the Peace."

A look of amazement crossed Barry's face. "You're serious."

"Yup, she takes some getting used to. Her family's been here for over a hundred years. Out-of-towners, they're always intrigued."

Barry opened the passenger door to get out. "Well, I need to get back to the guys. I didn't want to put this out on the radio. I thought it would be best to report it in person."

"Good call."

"It's gonna be a long rest of the day."

Manny walked him to the front of the building where he'd parked his old red Dodge Ram 2500. He reached in through the window and opened the door from the inside. Manny smiled. Barry was low maintenance. The guy would have to be downright rustic to spend his weekends volunteering to do one of the shittiest jobs in America: unpaid border patrol.

Barry gunned the diesel, producing a cloud of black exhaust as he turned onto Main Street.

That was enlightening. That stupid woman could have blown up their plan. Maybe she already had. She had no business with Luther Pernod, that arrogant prick. And what part of "Don't let anyone inside the gates" did that moron John Torres not understand? How could a man's pecker listen to its owner when it didn't have ears.

Speaking of the devil. Deputy Torres' patrol unit had pulled in the space next to the one out front Barry had vacated. John must have arrived during his impromptu meeting with Barry. He was about to have a word with him. Starting with: *What the fuck was Jane doing at the ranch last night and why did you let her in?*

The department ran on a shoestring, three deputies total. He'd put Torres on night watch to keep him busy, away from her. Torres had told him the day before he was done with ol' Jane. Manny didn't believe it, mostly because he'd put money on Jane being the one who'd decide when things between her and Torres were over. Manny's blood was simmering when he went inside to confront John Torres.

Sue stood behind the open frosted glass window. "Everything okay, boss?"

"Yeah. A friend of Roy's."

Sue's bullshit detector went off. She raised one carefully drawn eyebrow. "Aren't they all? Torres is back."

"Yep, saw his truck out front. Seems ol' Jane's been on another one of her benders. Went out to the ranch drunk last night. That fella, the friend of Roy's, that's what he come to tell me."

"One of these days you boys are gonna have to stop bailing that woman out. Or one of the wives is gonna catch her and you're gonna have to charge some hardworking housewife with homicide."

"I know. She shoulda stayed married and stayed put in Dallas. Woulda made all our lives simpler."

Sue put a cigarette behind her ear. "We both know they'll keep voting for her until she's dead. Maybe they'll cast votes at her grave."

He couldn't have put it better himself. Her family legacy was revered such that it would take at least another generation for the townsfolk to forget they owed Jane Pandora nothing. Sue was right. Even in death, her tombstone might show up on the ballot.

"You been watching the news, Sheriff?"

"Haven't had time."

"FBI's conducting raids up there in San Fran Sucko and Organ. It's a pretty big deal. That social media outfit and a couple of other biggie tech companies."

"What for?"

"Don't know. Some sort of investigation, but the FBI ain't saying. Reporters on TV are yammering about the president, Russians, and such. Searched 'FBI raid' and 'San Francisco' on Google. There's so much crap, I wouldn't know where to start or what to believe. Miss the old days, ya know?"

"Yep. Before everyone started goggling everything."

"Goggling. Good one, Boss." Sue shrugged and closed her creaky window. Her phone was ringing.

Not only did he remember those days, he missed the hell out of them. Long distance haulers drinking coffee at the truck stop were a more reliable news source if he had any interest in knowing what was really going on in the world. The techie pricks had taken over the planet and distorted everything like a funhouse mirror.

---

WHEN BARRY HAD LEFT to pay the sheriff a visit, The Secondmen were finishing a late breakfast of dry cereal and coffee. He'd driven for miles on a single lane dirt road carved mostly by ATV tire tracks. It was the only route that connected their encampment to the four-lane highway.

Barry parked the old Dodge at base camp and walked to where most of the men were assembled. He told them he'd gone to town to see the sheriff, to report the breach, the woman who'd shown up last night. They were dumbfounded when he told them she was the local Justice of the Peace.

"That woman is built for comfort, not justice," one of the guys said eliciting a round of laughter and more comments.

"A big, beautiful BarcaLounger."

"Did you see the *headlights*?"

The double entendre could not be topped.

That she was the JP with certain judicial powers was not lost on any of them. Jane the drunken bombshell, not Jane the JP, was an image that could not be un-stuck from their brains. After sleeping outside for two nights, in Barry's case in the bed of his pickup, the odds of a woman like that showing up during the stakeout ranked up there with a UFO sighting.

Other than the Jane sighting, the nightly surveillance had been a mind-numbing affair. The hardest part for the night watch was staying awake. Barry finished his cereal and tossed the paper bowl into a black plastic garbage bag. He went back to the truck to get the backpack he'd stashed under the passenger seat. He did a double take. Something rolled out from under the seat and reflected a beam of sunshine.

He picked up the thick glass bottle from the rubber floor mat.

*WTF?*

How did an emperor scorpion with beady black eyes, all eight eyeballs, get inside his truck? He held it up under the sunlight and studied it like a gemologist looking through a loop.

*Pandinus imperator.* Female, about four inches, not full grown, native to West Africa, life expectancy 6-8 years. Popular in the pet trade and recently added to the endangered species list.

*If you're trying to fuck with my head, you just struck out.*

"What am I going to name you?" Barry stroked the milk bottle.

When Roy had asked Barry to trust him, he'd pledged his word. While his better judgment would have rejected running Operation Antelope on blind faith, Roy's word was worth more than a hundred thousand signed contracts. Not that Barry was being paid, because he wasn't. Like Roy, he was driven by something different, something bigger, and he'd be damned before he did anything that compromised his deeply held convictions.

Roy had been upfront about his acquired distaste for Big Tech and his worry about the growing imbalance of power between Silicon Valley and the rest of the world, an imbalance Roy attributed to their concentration of wealth. When Barry first brought up the idea of screwing with the rich punks by debunking the myth that money could guarantee them the security of rarefied air, Roy's eyes twinkled.

Roy beamed when Barry took it a step further, floating the idea of the fake Homeland Security lockdown.

Barry laughed out loud.

*Rarefied air.*

Without their private jets and bodyguards, those elitists would be stuck at sea level. Where they belonged.

The Secondmen had refined their plan, conducting recon runs for months. They'd cracked plenty of jokes about hair gel and man buns while sharing shots of tequila over campfires. Their shirt buttons popped thanks to Budweiser and McDonald's. Not because they'd dropped a thousand dollars on a shrunken Italian suit that looked like it was stolen from the costume department at *Pee-wee's Playhouse*.

The Secondmen would rather eat termites and drink from a pond than nibble tofu and suck wheatgrass from a straw.

*No siree bob.*

Not here in Marfidio County, not in a five thousand-mile radius of the place. He put his hands on his hips and stared at the Chinatis.

*The higher you are on the mountain, the harder the wind blows.*

Real men like Barry knew about certain immutable facts.

"I bet you're hungry, girl."

"Who you talking to, Chief?" Mike the carbon-credit-trader stood behind him.

Barry showed him the emperor scorpion in the bottle.

"A scorpion? In a bottle? That's fucked up." Mike shook his head and jogged back his luxury motor coach.

## 36

L auren walked toward the courtyard, hugging the hoodie, wondering if the shivering was from cold or fear. The pain had subsided. She'd be able to wear the high heels and little black dress she'd brought along, just in case. The powder-blue sky had turned gray-blue and the mountain air had dropped another ten degrees. A ring of red rose behind the Chinati Mountains and tonight's light show featured purples and pinks. She gasped. An adult Pronghorn stood less than fifty feet from her, erect, still as stone and on high alert.

A long shadow cast over her, cutting the last rays of sun. She turned, shivering.

Josh stood behind her admiring the animal. "Roy would have taken this as a sign."

"A sign?"

"Yes. A good sign."

"Of what?"

"I don't think he would have tried to figure that part out."

"Won't they be hunted and killed?"

"Of course."

"I don't understand. Bringing them back, to kill them?"

"Roy believed that hunting connects man to the earth. The same way a woman giving birth connects a woman to the universe." He hesitated. "I hope I haven't offended you."

"How so?"

"You're not a mother."

"Oh, there's no need to apologize. I *had* a mother."

"City folks forget about nature. It changes them. Roy spent almost thirty years on Wall Street. But whenever he could, he came here. He always found it restorative."

"A lot of city people have pets. But I know what you mean. It's not the same thing as seeing an animal in its natural habitat."

"You know how to ride a horse. There aren't many things in the world that can connect us to the natural world more than being able to communicate with a horse beneath you. It was one of Roy's greatest regrets, that he never learned to ride."

"I went out for a ride, earlier."

"Alone, I heard."

"Word travels fast."

"Vance was worried. So was I. Where did you go?"

"I don't know exactly. Your dog led the way."

"You followed Cheks?"

"I didn't plan it that way. It just happened."

Josh was agitated. "What direction did you ride?"

"I don't know."

"You don't know?"

She shook her head.

"The airstrip is a good landmark. You can see it from almost every vantage point."

"I wasn't really paying attention. I saw a narrow tunnel between two rock walls. It was barely wide enough to ride through."

"You went that way?"

"Someone is up there. I saw a rifle poking out of a cave. It was on a tripod or a stand or something. It looked high tech, like the kind you see in the movies."

"Did you see anyone?"

"N-No," she stuttered. "I heard a voice and got scared . . . and . . . ran on foot. Whoever's in the cave up there fired a warning round. It spooked my horse. I had to mount at a gallop. I twisted my ankle." She showed it to him, and her hands, where she'd pulled the cactus spikes from her palms.

"You're all right. That's the main thing. You shouldn't have gone alone. There're mountain lions in the caves."

*Mountain lions?* If she'd known that, she would never, ever have gone. Her heart pounded at the thought. What if that's what Smokey picked up, the scent of a mountain lion?

A throng of guests passed by en route to the dining hall. They all looked glum.

"I wish I'd met him."

Josh looked at her curiously. "Who?"

"Roy Pompadour. I wish I'd met him."

"I'll see you tonight."

"I have a question." She paused to reconsider. *This is going to sound nuts.* "Is it possible that there's some sort of transmitter on Cheks's jacket?"

He looked at her like she was crazy, squinting until his eyes were slivers.

"I thought I heard something, and maybe I saw a light, flashing, on his collar?"

"The vest's high tech. I told you that. It has built-in GPS and runs on a battery. I just changed the nine-volt. Maybe that's what you saw, or heard." He shrugged.

That was a reasonable explanation. The battery was low.

"See you at dinner. It'll be the biggest event we've ever hosted here. It's going to be epic."

## 37

B arry placed the milk bottle in his backpack and gently slung it over his shoulder. He scavenged the campsite for food, collecting power bars, bags of chips, a blackened banana, a vitamin water, cookies, and even the last few ripe blueberries in a small cardboard crate. He took the milk bottle from the top of his backpack and loaded the goodies beneath it.

He tapped a couple droplets of water into the bottle with his fingertip. *Pandinus imperator* drank enthusiastically. That meant she was hungry, too. He placed her glass house on top of the foodstuffs he'd foraged and loaded her back into his pack.

He hiked a quarter mile south to a path leading to the foothills and climbed a steepening slope. The first flat ledge was fifty feet up and had a wide view of the ranch. He stopped to catch his breath, and fished his binoculars from a side pocket of his backpack.

Antelope Creek Ranch was busy, like an anthill, with people crisscrossing the manicured courtyard. Two dozen guests had broken into smaller groups and were seated around the turquoise pool. The courtyard decking, composed of inlaid rocks surrounded by manicured hedges, looked like an architect's model. He panned his binoculars to the east. The delivery area behind the kitchen bustled with kitchen staff scurrying in and out.

His mouth watered. He'd been a guest before and recalled the stick-to-your ribs meals Roy's chef prepared. No sense in thinking about food now.

He climbed higher, using his hands to steady himself, selecting the rocks and boulders he could use as steps. The natural vegetation was sparse and prickly, the cacti blooming purple flowers. His foot slipped. He tried to recover but fell, banging his knee and scraping his hands.

Motherfucker. Hopping on one foot, the pack on his back bouncing, he sat on the edge of a boulder. He was less than a foot from where the ancient volcanic rock pile stopped, where the incline ahead turned into dirt as smooth as a freshly paved highway.

He lifted his pant leg. The swelling had already started. He stood, rotating his ankle to test his leg, and bent over to rub his kneecap. Seeing multiple sets of horse hooves mixed in with paw prints was a surprise. One set was headed up the mountain, the other back down. They had to be new, hours old. The brisk evening breezes would have erased them.

He hobbled onward toward the twin rock walls forming a natural tunnel. A ray of sunlight revealed a set of human footprints mixed in with the hooves. The shoe tracks were too small to be a man's, too big to be a child's. Adrenaline flowed. Someone had been up to the cave on horseback. He pulled the 9-millimeter from his belt and, holding it in front, entered the tunnel. Streaks of light coming from the opening at the exit blinded him like lasers.

He scanned the mountain, his eyes recovering from the sunlight enough to inspect the mesa floor. Had there been a scuffle between the horse and rider? Only one set of prints led in, but the ground was covered with hoof and shoe marks. He followed the human prints to the narrow ledge leading to the other side of the cliff. Half the shoe prints pointed toe-first facing the vertical drop, others were reversed, suggesting the explorer had been tentative, trying different approaches to cross the treacherous walkway.

He sidestepped the ledge six inches at a time, using his back and shoulders as a guide. He kept his eyes up, away from the vertical drop. Once safely to the other side of the precipice, he pointed the Glock at a big black hole, the mouth of the main cave. He swiveled his head left and right, preparing for an ambush. A sniper rifle poked out of the cave, the scope in plain view. The barrel rested on a metal tripod.

"Hello."

No answer.

He cupped his hands over his mouth. "HELLO. Is anyone there?"

"Barry," a voice called out from the cave, "is that you?"

"Yeah. I brought supplies. Are you alone?"

"Indeed, I am," the man said, stepping out into the sunlight.

He was tall and stood as erect as a two-by-four. His appearance had changed dramatically since he'd been living in the hollow. Beneath the mountain man, there was still the aura of grace and elegance. He wore desert camouflage and lace-up boots with a matching square-brimmed cap. He looked more like Fidel Castro than a Wall Street billionaire. His skin had browned, but his attentive eyes, still clear and piercing, glistened like polished jade.

"What did you bring me?" Roy Pompadour asked, watching Barry hobble to a nearby boulder and set the backpack down. "And what did you do to your leg? Come here, and let me take a have a look."

Barry entered the cave. Roy turned on the battery-powered

lantern. A neatly rolled sleeping bag atop a canvas-laced metal platform serving as a bed was pushed up against the natural wall. Beneath the bed were boxes of GI Meals Ready to Eat, cases of bottled water, a bucket, and other supplies. The cot served as a makeshift command station with radios, a satellite phone, solar-powered chargers, and a transmitter that blinked green.

"Believe it or not, the place has grown on me." Roy chuckled and grabbed his high-powered binoculars, walked outside, squatted with one foot on either side of the rifle and peered down at the ranch.

For a man in his mid-seventies, he was agile as a cat.

Barry said, "I tracked human and horse prints up here. And dog."

"You can blame Chekov. Someone was up here earlier, followed the dog up, I think. She knows there's someone here but I scared her off with a 50-caliber round."

*She?* What was the deal with these women appearing in the middle of Operation Antelope? "Do you know who she is?"

"One of the new owners."

Barry arched one eyebrow. "Did she see you?"

"No, but she heard me." Roy lit up. "Do I smell bananas? What I would do for something fresh."

Barry handed him the half-full box of ripe blueberries.

Roy grabbed them like a starving man, slowly dropping them into his mouth, savoring each one. Roy's eyes rolled back in their sockets.

"When in doubt, blame the dog," Barry said.

Roy laughed. "He likes to spend most of his time down at the ranch. The food's better."

Barry rolled his pant leg up over his injured knee. He rubbed the spot where his kneecap had smashed into the boulder when he'd fallen *up* the mountain. He'd torn the skin and the surface wound stung. The joint pulsated.

"That doesn't look good," Roy said, savoring the last blueberry. He noticed Barry looking at the electronics on the fold-up bed.

Roy gestured to the emergency radio. "Don't believe the advertising. I can't even tune in the local AM radio station."

That must have been tough for a guy like Roy Pompadour, to be cut off from outside events. Barry wasn't surprised when Roy asked him what was going on in the world.

"Numeral II's CEO was set to testify in front of Congress."

Roy lit up. "And?"

"He pulled a no-show."

Roy shook his head, disgusted. "What's been the fallout?"

Barry shrugged.

"You mean they didn't do *anything?*"

"Nope."

"That's not acceptable. At least when Zack Wisenberg was asked, he had the decency to show up." Roy smiled. "And then that kid ran rings around those elected politicians."

"True," Barry said. "He's added a new feature to his social media platform. Readers can tag something as 'hateful.' "

Roy looked disgusted, shaking his head.

"Zack's company sent out a press release admitting Silicon Valley has a political bent."

Roy belly-laughed. "Spoiler alert." He laughed some more. He sobered up when Barry told him there had been another school shooting, almost twenty kids killed.

"This time it's different. The kids have organized marches and sit-ins. One young man had a few days of fame ranting on the twenty-four-hour cable news shows about how guns are killing people. The White House hosted a listening session." He hated telling Roy any of it.

Roy rubbed his eyes with his thumbs. His Adam's apple twitched. He composed himself. "I don't blame those kids. We might have acted the same way. To think the politicians and the media exploit them."

Barry told him about all the missteps the FBI and local law enforcement made, the killer's social media posts about wanting to be a school shooter, the cowardly deputy on the scene who ran, and the school's incompetence.

Roy cast his eyes down.

"The kids are demanding that something be done."

"Can you blame them?"

"Of course not," Barry said.

"How's the knee pain?"

"I might have broken something."

"Do you mind?"

Barry nodded.

Roy closed his eyes, and putting a thumb and forefinger on Barry's knee, pressed down on the bone. "Nah. If you broke it, you'd be on your back howling like a stuck pig."

Roy shined his flashlight under the makeshift bed. He found the military grade STOMP disaster backpack. He unzipped it and laid it open: forceps, scissors, ammonia inhalants, a stethoscope, and needle probes.

"Put your foot up."

When he was finished wrapping his knee, Roy asked him if he had any questions.

Barry had lots of them, but none Roy could answer without a crystal ball. Shaking his head, he stood, testing the wrap.

"Tell the guys I really appreciate their hard work and dedication," Roy said.

Barry reminded him that the men believed Roy was dead.

"I forgot. Solitary confinement, it'll disorient a man quickly. Battling the silence is harder than fighting the Viet Cong."

"I know." He pulled his pant leg over the bandage. "Isolation is a bitch."

Roy stood and squinted. Seeing something, he stepped outside the cave and peered through the binoculars hanging around his neck. "Take a look."

Barry limped to the opening.

Roy handed him the field glasses.

"I don't need them. I can see them from here. Wow." It was a Pronghorn.

"It's an omen." He put the binoculars back over his eyes, crunching his face into a Popeye expression, and panned his head slowly, like a motion picture camera.

A good omen, he hoped. "Oh, I almost forgot. I wanted to show you something." He reached into the bag and held the milk bottle for Roy to see.

"Knowing you, you've already named him."

"Her."

"Only you would know that."

"She's a gift."

"From who?"

"I don't know. I've been backtracking it in my head and I'm pretty sure someone put it in my truck when I stopped to see the sheriff." Barry told him why he'd gone to see Sheriff Manny.

Deep lines formed on Roy's forehead. "Jane Pandora was at the ranch last night? Are you sure?"

Barry told him the story, about the men spotting her with night vision scopes and goggles.

When Barry left the cave, Roy looked worried.

## 38

L auren entered the dining room at just after seven o'clock. The transformation was breathtaking. The long wooden tables with benches had been replaced with a dozen round tops with seating for ten. White linens draped from the edges, and in the center of each a rich bouquet of dark red roses and burgundy flowers tied with gold ribbons fire-worked out of low crystal bowls filled with pebbles. A least a hundred white candles of all sizes and shapes had been staged around the room, flickering in concert. Classical violin music piped in at the perfect level, creating an ambience that invited conversation.

"Wow," Vance whispered in her ear. He walked around her, doing an inspection. "You look gorgeous."

She'd worn the only appropriate attire she'd brought, a black crepe sleeveless cocktail dress lined with a silk fabric that felt smooth against her thighs.

She smiled at him. The cold water had done wonders to keep the swelling down and she'd been able to wear the high heel sling-backs she'd brought.

He grabbed her by the elbow. He wanted them to look like *a couple*.

Jake did a double take when he saw her, too. "You look stunning. Absolutely stunning."

"Stop ogling." MK glared at Jake.

They bickered like a married couple.

"You're sitting up front with us." MK gestured to a table on the front row, to the far left of a lectern.

That was weird. A podium? It clashed with the atmosphere. It was standing room only. A server pushed past, taking drink orders, and then another with a tray of hors d'oeuvres. Lauren bit into a warm mushroom cap filled with soft cheese.

Vance sipped red wine from a long-stemmed glass. "You're turning heads. It's amazing," Vance whispered in her ear. "That this could be arranged on short notice."

"The room, it's so beautiful."

"You're so beautiful."

Vance puffed up when Josh appeared. He was dressed in a suit and tie and looked like he'd just walked off the cover of a magazine featuring high fashion for bodybuilders.

"You look gorgeous," Josh said, scanning her from head to toe.

"Thanks," she said, feeling the blood stinging her cheeks.

Josh went back to mingling.

When they were alone again, Vance said, "I feel like a bum. I didn't pack for the occasion."

Yep. Chinos, a light black jacket over a button-down shirt and newish cowboy boots equaled underdressed. "You look very handsome. Look around. You're black tie compared to some of them."

MK had predicted the younger guests would be underdressed and they did not disappoint. Shiny basketball shorts down to their knees, T-shirts, hiking pants, down vests, and fluorescent mesh sneakers.

Lauren grinned at him. "At least you don't have a nose ring."

"Well, there's that. Let's take our seats."

She followed him, squeezing through the crowd. Each place setting had name cards drawn in calligraphy. Vance did a sneaky switcheroo to be seated next to her.

Josh stood at the podium and using a fork, pinged the edge of a water glass to get the crowd's attention. After three tries, increasing the volume each time, the guests piped down enough for him to speak.

"Good evening, ladies and gentlemen, may I have your attention. Please take a moment to look around for your assigned seat."

The guests milled between tables, looking for their names, signaling to those they knew when they found a match.

Josh joined their table and sat next to Luther.

MK sat to the right of Jake. Rick Bates and his king-of-investments buddy, Victor Moffett, sat on MK's right.

The table was situated a few feet from the where the Hummer had crashed through the glass earlier. Earlier. It seemed like weeks.

A row of tall butane heaters lined the patio between the temporary window repair and the damaged wall. Still it was chilly inside.

She turned to Vance. "How's the rib?"

"Funny. If you hadn't asked, I would have forgotten." He reached under the table, surprising her when he felt for her hand.

Whoever had arranged the seating chart had mixed the younger guests at other tables with their older counterparts. Kurt Berlin, the German automobile magnate who'd been ousted after his company was discovered to have installed cheater emissions software, was a late arrival. He took the seat to the right of Vance, leaning over, introducing himself. Three other chairs were filled with people she'd never seen before.

The meal began with a poached pear topped with Gorgonzola cheese and candied pecans nestled in a bed of peppery arugula. Their service staff finished the salad courses with a tableside drizzle of balsamic reduction.

She'd reviewed the guest list in her head. Was the culprit who'd delivered the scorpions sitting among them? She picked at the soft pear with her fork.

"Are you okay?" Vance asked. "You look a little pale."

She leaned over and whispered, "I wish we'd gotten the results from the lab." The partial print might have been a piece that solved the puzzle. But the court order Vance got finally from Jane Pandora was currently useless since the lab had closed for the weekend.

Their waiter hovered with pen to paper. "Apple wood-smoked back strap of venison, or our house-made fettuccini Carbonara with white truffle oil?"

Vance ordered Bambi.

Her stomach was doing flips but she ordered the pasta anyway.

"Look at their faces." Vance tilted his head toward the table behind them.

She swiveled hers to look. The millennials seated behind them didn't seem to like the choices and argued with the servers. She nudged Vance's knee under the table. "Be cool, but look to your right, at about three o'clock."

He leaned down, pretending to pick something up and craned his head. "Jason Spike doesn't look like he's having a very good time."

That's what she was thinking, too. Spike was bundled in a

sleeveless down vest over a denim shirt. And he was watching their table intently.

---

BARRY LOOKED AT HIS WATCH. He'd shut down the assigned two-way radio channel at 7:33 PM and switched to a back frequency. He'd gone over communication protocol with the men during reconnaissance runs. They understood once Operation Antelope got underway radio transmissions would be limited to emergencies only.

He stood in the bed of his truck and saw dots of blue flames flickering where the large window had been before they'd staged the crash. The butane heaters lining the south side of the building reminded him of vintage street lamps. Inside the dining hall, pinpoints of light shone from dozens of candles twinkling like night stars. He tilted his head back and stared at the starlit sky. The men would begin their move on foot in ten minutes, first surrounding the perimeter and securing it, then making sure there were no escapees.

Roy had insisted on coming down from the mountain alone. He'd told Barry he'd use dusk for cover. The men would be shocked when they found out Roy Pompadour was alive. He was sure Roy would personally apologize to the ones who felt slighted, the ones who hadn't been invited to his mock memorial service.

There was one thing The Secondmen unanimously agreed upon: Roy's world had seemed to spiral out of control after the death of his good friend, Aldo Simeri. Barry could have done more to tamp down the wild conspiracy theories about the justice's death. But suspicions about foul play forged a bond that kept The Secondmen focused on the mission.

Suited up in desert camo, Barry climbed behind the wheel of

the Dodge. Catching a glimpse of his reflection in the side view mirror, he looked like an alien-being wearing the helmet-mounted night vision goggles, a skinny binocular jutting front from each eye. His sight adjusted to the shades of fluorescent greens separating the ranch buildings from the vegetation. The chartreuse coming from the butane lamps was blinding.

He turned his head. The dozen men hunched down in the bed of his truck glowed like Martians. The back end of the Dodge was overweight; the rear shocks coughed and groaned, back tires chewing the gravel as the truck crawled toward the lodge.

They'd conducted practice runs a dozen times before. It would take his men ten minutes to secure the north perimeter, the most vulnerable escape route facing the highway where the sheriff posted the deputy on duty, his patrol truck now blocking the exit.

Hand signaling, he instructed the men to drop quietly from the truck bed and fan out. Without night vision the tri-color desert garb made The Secondmen practically invisible.

Three breakout groups were doing the same, covering the south and west boundaries, where guests might try to escape.

Barry abandoned the Dodge a hundred yards west of the service exit behind the kitchen and hobbled toward the portico covering the main entrance. First, he had to get by the kitchen staff. Some scurried to dump garbage, others to take a breather. Two women stepped out back to drag on a shared cigarette.

Crouching, he crabbed behind the low east-facing wall. Making his way north to the front side, he leaned against the building and peered into the lobby window. A young woman stood behind the front desk. A few guests headed down the hallway where the bathrooms were located.

Kneeling on his good leg, he placed the night vision goggles over his eyes and scoped the gates at the bottom of the gravel driveway. He squinted through the goggles. The deputy behind the wheel flicked his dome light on. It blinded Barry like a million-watt orb. He tipped the brim to his ball cap over his nose to cut the light. With a little luck, his eyes would recover quickly.

He'd memorized the schedule. He glanced at his watch: 7:45. So far, so good. Tilting the brim of his cap up, he scanned the area under the awning.

He scooted past the big wooden doors leading to the lobby and glanced through a vertical pane of glass. He had to hurry. A man was detouring past the front desk, and appeared to be headed out front.

Barry moved into the shadows and squatted against the hedges growing alongside the building. The stranger wearing a down vest continued straight, and walked out the door. His nose filled with the aromas he'd been trying to ignore, the delicious scents of roasted meats and garlic and herbs.

The young man wearing the vest raised his chin and swiveled his head, listening. Sniffing. Looking.

Barry held his breath. A contest of ancient instincts had begun.

*Who was he?*

Barry focused on his breath, keeping it shallow. He glanced at his forearm. A bead of blood welled. He must have scratched it taking cover in the bushes. The wetness tickled as it pooled on his forearm and dripped.

The young man standing beneath the awning in front of the lobby raised the collar on his vest, snapping the top button. Barry checked his breathing.

Headlights approached from the east, the machine-gunning of a big rig downshifting, the driver slowing as he approached the now-flashing yellow light bar atop the deputy's patrol truck. The semi rolled past, the driver upshifting through the gears. A minute later the engine sounds faded. He watched the stranger walk back inside.

Barry wiped the blood on his pants.

He glanced back at the gate with his naked eyes. The flickering bar atop the patrol truck had gone dark. He didn't know if it was before or after the semi passed. Did the stranger under the awning see the patrol truck go dark?

*Was it a sign?*

He gazed through the night goggles. The deputy opened the driver's-side door. The interior dome light went on again like a flashbulb.

*Ouch.*

He blinked. When his sight recovered the deputy was out of the vehicle. He stood in front of the keypad. An instant later, the ornamental gates began to open.

This was not part of the plan. Barry went to the back channel on his radio and pressed the talk button.

"Sheriff, do you copy?"

"Ten-four."

"The deputy at the gate is heading up the driveway. Please advise."

"Shadow him."

"Copy that."

Like a ship on a dark sea, Deputy Torres steered the patrol truck toward the building with headlights out, cockpit dark. Barry looked again through the night vision. Torres' body was craned forward, his chin practically on the dash, his cowboy hat tipped back. He seemed to be relying on the dim landscape lighting to guide the truck.

Barry let the vehicle pass and ran a zigzag pattern, until he was behind it. Crouched and hobbling, he grabbed the tailgate, hoisted himself onto the rear bumper, and climbed over into the bed where he curled on his side.

The deputy behind the wheel stared straight ahead.

Barry rolled onto his good knee and crawled closer to the rear window. He pointed his 9-millimeter at the driver's skull. A kill shot would be a piece of cake. But killing a cop would not. An AR-15 rifle leaned against the back window, on the passenger's-side.

## 39

M K returned to the table with a fresh layer of crimson lipstick.

She stood over Lauren. "Are you all right, dear?"

That was the second time in thirty minutes someone had asked her if she was okay. Earlier she was "beautiful," "stunning," and "gorgeous." Now something was wrong.

MK noticed Josh had taken her seat while she was freshening up, and she was miffed. Josh was deep into a discussion with the pair who traded places as the worlds' richest men, Victor Moffett and Rick Bates. MK took the empty seat where Kurt Berlin, the deposed German automaker had been sitting.

MK leaned back in her chair and addressed Lauren from behind. "You haven't touched your food. You should have ordered the venison. It was out of this world."

There was no way she'd order Bambi even if her nerves weren't raw.

*No, thank you.*

The servers and busboys hustled, collecting dinner plates, returning with dishes of strawberries and fresh whipped cream, presented in crispy caramel waffle cones. She was about to dip her spoon into the dessert when Josh got up from the table and walked to the podium.

He removed a folded paper from the inside pocket of his coat, then cleared his throat.

"Thank you," he said, "for attending tonight's dinner." The crowd buzzed with small talk.

Lauren adjusted her chair to getter a better view from the side angle where she'd been seated.

"Thank you." Josh spoke louder. "Thank you."

The people quieted.

"We've asked you to gather tonight because we have some important business to discuss."

"I hope it's good news about getting out of here," someone yelled from the back of the room.

There was collective grumbling and people twisted in their seats to see where the wisecrack came from. Josh paused, waiting for the guests to quiet.

"We have gathered this evening to introduce you to our group, the Isidore Global Initiative. Will the members please stand."

The younger folks looked around at each other, confused.

The distinguished men at each table slowly rose, the sole female member, Mary Katherine Diamond, stood with them. Other than Rick Bates and Victor Moffett, the rest were not familiar faces.

"Now, I would like to turn the podium over to a special guest who will explain more about why we are here this evening."

On cue, a man wearing military fatigues emerged from the dark corner behind Josh. He strode to the lectern. His beard and cap disguised him, even to his closest friends. Lauren had no idea who he was. He could have been Fidel Castro's twin brother for all she knew. More mumbling and grumbling sounds passed through the room.

The man patted Josh on the back. Beneath a single overhead light, he stood as erect as the steel heat lamps in the background, squared shoulders, chin up, head swiveling back and forth across the room like a searchlight.

Lauren nudged Vance. He looked at her and shrugged.

"Good evening," he said. "My name is Roy Pompadour and contrary to common belief, I am alive and well."

The room gasped. The guests twisted in their chairs, shuffled, and whispered to one another. Then the room went so quiet Lauren could hear the soft hiss coming from the butane lamps.

Lauren's heart hammered. She looked at Vance who was mesmerized. She leaned closer to him, adrenaline surging and mouthed, "Where's Luther?"

He shook his head and whispered, "Something's off. There's no way he's missing this part."

Josh returned to their table and sat. Lauren, Vance, and Jake exchanged looks. MK smiled knowingly. Rick and Victor folded their arms across their chests.

*Where was Kurt Berlin?*

She hadn't noticed him leave his seat, either. Vance was right: Luther wouldn't miss this.

"As you all know," Roy said with great authority, "Supreme Court Justice Aldo Simeri was a good friend of mine as well as an active member of our initiative. And he was concerned about the pace of new technologies and what effects it was having on society, and," he paused for emphasis, "especially on our children.

"Never in the history of America has there been a greater threat to our civil liberties and national security than the borderless Internet. The elder statesmen joining you tonight, along with our one female member"—he glanced at MK—"are giants in industries around the globe. We had the good fortune of being more mature with a better sense of the world than many of you when we made our fortunes.

"While your genius is as significant, if not more than ours, many sitting here today paved the way for your successes. I am here to ask you an important question. Now that you are the wealthiest, most powerful generation in the history of the world, are you capable of responsibly stewarding a future that's moving at warp speed?"

Roy paused. The only sounds came from bodies shuffling in chairs.

"I was fifty years old when I made my first million. Henry Ford cared about the greater good when he revolutionized manufacturing. Rick Bates did not become Forbes' richest man ten minutes after his software company went public. And Victor Moffett, well, let's just say he still counts out exact change for the same breakfast every morning behind the wheel of his 'ninety-nine Toyota, going to the same fast food drive-thru in that boring Midwestern state he calls home."

The crowd erupted in laughter. Bates and Moffett grinned.

"And let's be honest, a lot of you are smarter than two-thirds of Congress."

That elicited roaring laughter.

"There are no enforceable, relevant laws to regulate social media platforms or Internet search engines. I'm not here to lecture you. I'm here to warn you. It will not end well. Your companies are more powerful than world governments. You simply can't hide behind Section 230 of the Communications Decency Act forever."

Lauren looked at Vance. "The what?" she mouthed.

Vance shrugged, and said, "I got a bad feeling. I'm going to look for Luther. You stay here. I'll be back."

He headed toward the men's room picking up the pace passing the reception desk, and hurried out the front door.

"The laws need to be changed now. If you think I'm an alarmist, consider this: Supreme Court Justice Aldo Simeri was murdered. Right here, on my land, on my watch. Each and every one of you played a role in it."

The people rocked back in their chairs in a wave pattern, gasping, and looking around to see who might have known this.

Zack Wisenberg raised his hand.

"Hello, Zack," Roy said. "Do you have a question?"

Zack stood. "I do. How do you know Justice Simeri was *murdered?*"

"Is it fair to assume the name Henry Wiggins rings a bell?"

"It does. He's our in-house lawyer. What does that have to do with this?"

"Are you aware the FBI raided your headquarters yesterday? And that your man Wiggins is in custody? He's been charged with conspiracy to commit murder. A murder-for-hire plot."

A murmur passed through the room, then the crowd fell deadly silent.

"There were three raids yesterday, one at your company, at Zingger, and Numeral II. Others dodged a bullet. This time," he warned. "FBI Cyber Action Teams seized computers and cell phones. I'm no computer genius, but there are people working for you doing a lot more than writing code or stealing personal data."

People stared at Wisenberg.

"I'm not saying what you've developed hasn't revolutionized the world in many wonderful ways, but trying to thwart government oversight by—"

Vehicle high beams switched on behind Roy, turning him into a silhouette. Then flashing yellow lights and the whoop of a siren.

*Why were the cops here?*

Frenzied shouts came from the crowd.

GET DOWN.

LOOK OUT.

WHAT THE *FUCK*?

Josh rushed the podium knocking Roy down, dropping on him like a human shield.

The spinning yellow light veered suddenly away from the building and headed toward the airstrip.

## 40

Deputy John Torres stomped the gas, cutting a short diagonal beeline toward the watchtower at the edge of the property.

Barry gripped the inside frame of the truck with his fingernails, grimacing, shifting his weight onto his good leg. The sudden acceleration turned the truck bed into a poker table and he was the dice. His hand slipped and he bumped his head on the edge of the metal bed.

The driver slowed, windows rolled-up, headlights out, as a skinny silhouette, a rat of a human, emerged from the watchtower cradling something in his arms.

Torres put the truck in park, giving Barry the time to balance and retrieve his goggles. He glanced up into the cab, head low, and holding the night vision over his eyes with his left hand, watched the skinny man creeping toward the passenger door. Disguised by the lit taillight, he tested the laser on his gun, covering the red dot glowing against the truck bed with his hand. He wriggled on his belly toward the tailgate. The passenger door of the truck opened. The skinny man got in, carrying a cylinder.

Barry spotted the green outline of another human through his night vision—invisible to the naked eye—crouched in the shadows near the watchtower. The deputy put the truck in drive. The silhouette remained covered, moving parallel at the same speed as the truck.

He lowered the night vision from his eyes and got to his knees, high enough to get a clearer view into the cab, watching the two men from the space between the headrests.

Deputy Torres shined his flashlight on a dull green cylinder shaped like a telescope, the metal thick as a fire hydrant, half the diameter, and at least twice as long.

His heart jumped into his throat. A MATADOR shoulder-fired rocket launcher. Torres picked it up and rotated it in his hands, admiring it. That sucker had enough firepower to bust open a concrete bunker.

Torres tapped the brakes. Barry turned away from the cockpit and crouched lower. What was on the edge of the tailgate?

The red glow from the tail lamps lit up eight curled fingers. He pulled the 9-mil from the front of his waistband, and kneeling, supporting his torso with his elbows, wrapped both hands on the gun and pointed it.

The top of a head appeared between the hands. He was about to take a shot when Torres tapped the brakes again, lighting the face. The truck bounced once. He recognized the man riding on the back bumper.

---

VANCE COURAGE HAD SEEN it play out from his stealth position. When Deputy Torres broke orders, breaching the perimeter, lights out, Vance gambled, taking cover near the watchtower.

He'd seen the figure of a man mount the back bumper and disappear into the bed of the truck.

The patrol vehicle stopped adjacent the watchtower and Luther emerged from the darkness, jogging, and got in, activating the dome light. For two seconds it lit John Torres' face and Luther, who was carrying something in his arms. A cylinder. He wished he knew what the hell was going on. He reached around and tapped the Glock in the back waistband on his pants.

He fell in on foot behind the rear bumper of Torres' pickup. Moving slowly. Deliberately. Staying low. Assessing the situation.

He planted one hand on the edge of the truck gate, then the other. Swung one boot up on the bumper while he pogoed two steps with the other, following the slow rolling vehicle. Using both hands he hopped onto the bumper as the truck inched forward, headlights out, diesel fumes wafting.

Gripping the tailgate with both hands, he pressed his knees against it, squatting, balancing as he arose slowly, like a periscope, enough to peer into the bed. The man he'd tracked on the ground, now hiding inside the back of the open truck, pointed the business end of a pistol at the tailgate, *at him. Shit.*

Vance ducked.

Thinking.

His heart pumped. The darkness and the brim of a ball cap blocked the man's face.

He could easily have taken a shot at Vance. But he didn't. It would've blown his cover, too. Their cover. The enemies, their enemies, were in the cab. He processed the situation quickly. The guy wasn't careless. Not a hothead. Vance rose, this time with one finger to his lips. The stranger in the bed of the truck expected him. He hand signaled back okay.

He dropped down, crouching on the bumper. Their best bet

would be on foot. He rose again, and cupping his right hand, rotated it rapidly in a small circle, signaling the man jump. They'd be better positioned on the ground.

The man climbed over the tailgate slowly, carefully, as if dismounting a horse, and dropped onto the dirt next to him. They crouched behind the patrol truck, using the tail for cover, shadowing the rear bumper in lockstep.

"They've got an RPG," the man whispered. He recognized him now as the man he'd seen wearing the ball cap with the American flag stitched into the brim, the one from the coroner's office, the same guy who'd driven the van with dead body hidden in the canvas laundry cart. Vance tilted his head left then right, signaling they spread apart.

Vance palmed his Glock, tapped the barrel with his index finger, and cocked his head toward the passenger seat, signaling the man go for Luther. He'd take Deputy Torres and let the man next to him take on that sorry ass, poor excuse for a manager-prick, Luther. They fanned out, each taking a place behind a back tire, hunched over, following the pickup.

---

Deputy John Torres feathered the pedal and inched the truck south, past the lodge, toward the watchtower, headlights out, using the low voltage landscape lights as landmarks. Head craned over the dash, he gazed into the blackness in the direction of the airstrip, the perfect staging area to launch the shoulder rocket. With a firing range of 1600 feet and a muzzle velocity of over 800 feet per second he could fire it from the ground and hit the target.

One shot was all he had. And all he needed. With the help of night vision optics and a laser rangefinder, he could hit the side of the barn. Blindfolded. Those fucking elitists would never know what hit them.

Luther had been right about Kurt Berlin. He'd proved to be a man of his word. He'd promised to smuggle the anti-tank MATADOR in on his private jet. At just over three feet long and weighing under twenty pounds, Kurt had delivered it to Luther himself, stowed in a golf bag.

Torres needed only to get close. He'd helped load the 90-millimeter projectile into the metal tube earlier, before they'd hidden it in Luther's quarters at the tower.

Sure, Luther was as big a prick as the rest of them. He'd made John Torres richer in six months than if he'd kept every penny from every paycheck he'd earn for the next twenty years. Fuck those rich assholes living it up in the dining hall. Luther bragged he'd corralled half the world's wealth in West Fucking Texas on a two-day notice. If they were dumb enough to trust Luther, they had it coming.

Fuck that ex-cop Vance Courage, too. What was about to happen was on him for sticking his nose where it didn't belong. Deputy Torres white knuckled the wheel of the truck. Luther, that dumbass sitting next to him hugging that rocket launcher, told him Jane signed the court order the ex-cop wanted. That slut. The washed up detective wouldn't live to see the lab reports.

FUCK Jane Pandora.

FUCK the corpse of Roy Pompadour, too.

Last but not least FUCK Luther Pernod. He felt for his service weapon. He'd take care of that weasel last. John Torres would be hailed as a hero for putting Luther down, *almost* foiling the ranch manager's plot to blow up the ranch.

He'd relish planting a bullet between his beady eyes. It would be his pleasure. If he had time, he'd waste a second shot blasting that fucking goatee off his face. Maybe he'd plug him with a third round, payback for convincing him Jane's stupid idea about sending scorpions around would spook people. The scorpions didn't scare anyone like he'd promised. They'd just managed to piss people off.

Soon he'd be driving the Audi R-8 stored in his garage—with the tinted windows down—for all to see. He'd take that 600-horsepower leg-spreader to the Big D and troll for pussy.

He clenched the wheel, inching toward the spot he'd scouted a dozen times before. He'd stage the truck a thousand feet from the back of the building with a clear view to the dining hall where those fucking rich pricks would be stuffing themselves with fancy desserts.

That would be a good way for them to go. Blown to kingdom come, sipping hundred-dollar brandy from dainty little snifters while nibbling strawberries with their dental implants and Colgate smiles.

---

A CLEAN SHOT would be almost impossible. Vance released the triple safeties on the Glock. In a perfect world, he'd test the laser on his 9-mil, but the red dot might alert the targets in the cab. He and his comrade kept pace behind the slow-moving truck. They'd have to take their chances.

Mano a mano. Face-to-face. Hand-to-hand.

An ambush was the best bet to gain the advantage.

He wanted to warn the guests. Firing a couple of rounds toward the dining hall would do the trick. The noise would scatter the guests. It would also reveal them and their position. He could shoot accurately to fifty yards but they were at least a hundred-fifty from the building.

They separated, each crabbing in the shadows near the pickup moving like a ghost ship across the desert.

Vance moved around a back tire and looked alongside the wheel well. The driver sped up, heading toward the airstrip. He picked up the pace to a steady run and the man with the ball cap kept up.

He jogged laterally and when he got next to him, spoke into Barry's ear. "Let's get their attention. Count of three."

He pointed his Glock at the driver's-side window and cracked his neck toward the passenger's-side. Barry nodded. Cowering to maintain cover, he held up three fingers. Barry nodded. A three count.

Both drew their weapons.

*Three . . . two . . . one.*

They squeezed the triggers in concert. Glass shattered. They'd shot out the side windows of the truck, the slugs passing through the windshield like exit wounds.

Torres opened the door, stomped the gas pedal, then dropped and rolled onto the desert floor, hugging the MATADOR like a newborn. The driverless truck lurched forward. Luther dove for the AR-15.

Barry circled the back of the runaway truck, toward the driver's side where Torres had dropped.

Deputy John Torres scrambled to his feet carrying the MATADOR and ran.

Vance's eyes hurt from the lights, and from clouds of dust and diesel smoke. Pellets of gravel stung his face and arms. The sudden acceleration dirtied the air, blurring his visual reference.

He leapt in the direction Torres had run. He felt for him, for anything he could grab. He caught the cuff of Torres' pant leg, pulling him down. He went down, too, landing on his sore rib. He recoiled in agony. The Glock slipped from his hand. He felt for it, sifting handfuls of dirt.

Torres clambered to his feet.

Vance needed backup.

He looked for Barry and spotted him running in a squatting position, ducking and weaving, looking for an opening as the driver's-side truck door swung like a screen door on a gusty day, the driverless truck bouncing along the desert dirt.

Vance got to his feet, and clenching his teeth, chased after Torres who'd gotten a head start. The deputy stopped, hoisted the rocket launcher on his shoulder and steadied it, pointing it at the lodge. He was too far away. He couldn't get to Torres fast enough. The truck's high beams threw light on it, a fucking sewer pipe from hell.

The launcher capacity was a single rocket. A time bomb ticked in his head. Torres had precious seconds to balance it on his collarbone. Torres had to plant his feet to fire it. And unleashing hell on Antelope Creek Ranch boiled down to one simple action: All the deputy had to do was to squeeze the trigger on the pistol grip.

Fast calculation. The time Torres needed to set the shot was the same he needed to stop him. The dust had settled. His night vision improved. He scanned the dirt, looking for the Glock. Torres' eye was pressed against the rubber eyepiece of the scope. There was no time to search for his weapon. He sprinted toward the madman, lowering his shoulder and running full speed, T-boning John Torres in the kidney.

---

BARRY FOUND an opening and dove up and into the cockpit, smashing his head into Luther's ribs, the long gun twirling over-head like a majorette's baton. Luther gained control, pointing the AR-15 at Barry's chest.

He batted the muzzle and used his heels to lunge back-ward toward the open door, glass fragments tearing his clothes. Off balance, he gripped the inside door panel, the desert floor whizzing by, his head bobbing upside down, a foot off the dirt.

Bending his good knee and twisting his body to the left, spring loading it, he released like a cobra doing a sit-up, jamming the heel of his shoe into Luther's skinny shoulder. Luther grunted and fell back. He sprang forward again, like a bear trap, head-butting Luther who slumped in the seat, dazed, grunting.

He planted the rifle between his left thigh and elbow, and ran his hand over the dash, reading the maze of electronics like braille, searching for the headlights. He twisted knobs and turned the ends of plastic sticks sprouting from the steering column. The radio blared, windshield wipers flapped. He leaned forward, balancing the rifle muzzle in the crook of his elbow, looking.

Luther sprang to life, lunging at him, clubbing him on the ear with palms clasped. Instant vertigo. Barry tossed his head in waves, trying to shake it. He pawed the dash on his left, felt a knob, and turned it. Bright lights flooded the foreground.

Luther grabbed hold and cranked the wheel hard left, pointing the truck at the dining hall, shoving his scrawny leg through an opening on the driver's side. Fishing for the gas pedal with his toe, he jammed his shoe on top of Barry's. The truck sped up.

Barry yanked his shoe from under Luther's and heeled him in the ankle, grasping for his wiry hands, grappling, trying to pry them off the wheel, the AR-15 now an afterthought, the truck seesawing over the desert terrain.

Bright headlights hit the building and the people inside began to scramble. Luther reached down and whooped the siren, flicking on the yellow light bar atop the patrol truck.

Barry cursed himself. He should have taken the shot when he'd had the chance. He shouldn't have let it get this far. He'd had the perfect kill shot to the back of Torres' head from the bed of the truck. The killing a cop thing stopped him from taking it.

Where was his gun?

The distance was closing fast. What were the options? He rolled into a ball, and using the passenger door for leverage, booted Luther in the throat. Luther fell back. Barry lifted his body from the seat and ran his hand the long crease until he felt the metal. The gun.

Luther used two hands and sawed the wheel hard right, knocking Barry off balance. He rolled left shoulder-first into the steering column, grabbing the door handle for balance.

It should have been an easy shot, close range, like hitting a duck in a barrel. Except the barrel he was in was a roller-coaster ride. His hands flailed. He steadied his aim with one hand but the truck hit a boulder, then vaulted, knocking him into the air.

*Fuck it. I'll empty the chamber into his brain.*

Barry closed his eyes and pulled the trigger, discharging three bullets. The third round hit Luther Pernod. He screamed and slumped forward against the steering column. The vehicle slowed, horn blaring. Barry grabbed the wheel and cut hard right. By then, the truck had hit the first butane lamp and they went down like dominoes.

———————————

TWO BRIGHT LIGHTS raced toward the building.

Headlights.

Oh my God.

Where was Vance?

A woman screamed.

Chairs went down.

Lauren did a quick scan of the room, looking for Vance but didn't see him.

A hand grabbed her from behind, pulling her by the shoulder. She toppled, breaking the fall with her hands, scrambling beneath the table on all fours.

Guests fell from their chairs, diving for cover, crawling like scared animals. The set of knees in front of her belonged to Victor Moffett. She lifted the tablecloth and peeked up. He sat in his chair, alone, cowering with his head on the tabletop.

She scooted back, counted one, two, three, dove out, and pulled the old man by his arm, tipping his chair, knocking him to the floor. Rick Bates grabbed one ankle and together they dragged the old man under the table.

Lauren peered out from under the tablecloth. Oh my God. A pair of white halos bounced inside a jaundiced cloud of billowing dust, emergency lights flickering.

Yes. An emergency vehicle.

Three flashes of orange, three shots—BAM, BAM, BAM—in rapid succession. Coming from the cab.

Panicky voices from all around.

"Get down."

"Stay down."

"Active shooter."

THEN THE PATROL TRUCK SLOWED, and the horn blared, and the stationary headlamps lit the dining hall like a concert stage, blinding her.

She wanted to run, but froze. The smell of burning brush and diesel fuel rolled inside. She covered her nose with the edge of the tablecloth. An army of shadows emerged from the darkness and headed for the brushfire. The front bumper of the vehicle had hit a butane lamp, knocking the rest down, setting fire to the dry scrub vegetation.

Several men stamped the blaze with their feet, others

removed their shirts and snuffed the flames by hand. Shadows rushed to the courtyard, dipping ceramic pots into the pool, hand-carrying water to fight the fire. More struggled to kill the flow of butane from the red-hot lanterns. The vehicle's high beams went dark. The horn blared and the bright yellow light bar flickered.

It was a circus.

DEPUTY TORRES STOOD, slung the launcher on his shoulder and gyrated away from Vance. Wrong move. The twenty-pound weapon unbalanced him. He staggered like a top running out of spin. Taking a few steps forward and back, he widened his stance, trying to root his feet on the ground.

The bunker buster had the power to take down a fortified structure. The ranch would be leveled. All Torres had to do was point and pull the damn trigger. Boom. A ball of fire.

The lodge was filled with people.

Lauren was inside.

*No can do.*

Vance got a running start and kneed Torres in the hamstrings. Deputy Fuckwad plunged to his knees, hugging the MATADOR, landing chest-first on the metal. He scrambled to his feet bear-hugging the rocket. Vance came at him from behind, clamping arms around his neck, tightening the choke-hold, but couldn't hold it. His ribs. He let out small breaths. Torres elbowed him in the gut, hitting a rib.

Vance went insane, the pain. He screamed you dead mother-fucker and kicked the weapon from the deputy's hand with the toe of his shoe.

Torres leapt for it, the whites of his eyes flashing. If the weapon went off now, Vance might as well be wearing a suicide vest. His last memory would be of his own eyeballs looking at the confetti made of his own flesh and bones.

---

HER HEART THRUMMED under her little black dress. Her high heels had come off in the chaos.

MK reached for her hand under the table, yelling over the blaring car horn. "You okay?"

Lauren nodded.

"This was not part of the plan," MK shouted. "I hope Roy's all right."

*Not part of the plan?*

MK didn't mention Roy would rise from the dead.

Jake was on his knees, head down, hands covering his ears. Fear had them huddling. Where was Vance?

She stuck a finger in each ear to deaden the shrieking horn and using her elbow, lifted the tablecloth, scanning the nearby tables. Josh hovered over Roy, who'd gone down first, next to the podium. Not one guest had gone to aid them. The males had stampeded to shelter, toppling drinks into half-eaten desserts, grabbing onto whatever they could as they rushed to safety beneath tables, outside, out front, every direction but the direction of danger.

The horn went silent. People who'd taken cover under the tables stayed put. A dog barked. Cheks appeared and galloped toward Roy.

Josh's voice boomed. "Stay where you are until we do a damage assessment."

Heads peeked out. Lauren reached for a missing shoe. MK saw the other black heel and kicked it toward her.

Vance's jacket was on the floor, near his chair. He must have dropped it in his rush to wherever. She pulled it under the table and hugged it tight to her chest, burying her nose in the fabric, breathing deeply.

The blaring horn was soon replaced with the soft chuffing of a helicopter. Seconds later a searchlight beamed down in a white cone, sweeping the desert landscape in the distance. The thumping got louder until it rattled the dinnerware above her.

———

TORRES SCUTTLED on the desert floor and clawed for the weapon. Vance slammed the heel of his boot on his bare knuckles. He heard them crack. Torres rolled onto his back, knees bent, yowling. John reached again for the MATADOR. Vance stomped the fingers on his good hand. Torres rolled into a ball and writhed, then popped back to life and crawled toward the rocket launcher.

Vance heard the chopper before the pilot activated the searchlight. A bright cone lit the desert like a theater stage. Deputy Torres reached for the launcher, his filthy fingers dangling from his bloody hands. He pawed at the shoulder cannon with the heels of his palms. The anti-tank weapon could rip the chopper from the sky.

He kicked the rocket from his reach. It skidded ten feet. Torres squirmed on the ground, and using his elbows, crawled on top of it.

Vance was enjoying the show. Torres rolled onto his back with the dull green tube resting on his chest, hands too mangled to pull the trigger.

A perfect ending.

Suddenly Torres raised the dull green tube over his chest with his palms. He screamed pulling the trigger with his one good finger, unleashing a contrail of fire, and the short-range missile.

The chopper pilot turned and sped north toward the highway. Torres' aim was random. A trail of light, shaped like a crescent moon, arched toward the airstrip.

Vance fell to his knees and covered his ears. The projectile crashed to earth. The first explosion deafened him. The second shocked the desert floor. An orange inferno rose from the airstrip. Chunks of earth and asphalt blew overhead and rained down.

He jumped to his feet and straddled the dirty deputy. He planted his foot on Torres' chest, knelt, unfastened Torres' tooled leather belt, removed the service weapon, and aimed it at the deputy's head.

The helicopter circled, then descended, lighting up the battlefield. An army of reinforcements arrived and surrounded Deputy John Torres. It was like being in Afghanistan, in the midst of a sandstorm.

No.

More like a shit storm.

## 41

This must be what war was like. A deafening boom shook the ground as an orange rooster tail flared from an unidentified object flying toward the airstrip. Lauren recoiled, covering her head with her hands. When it landed, it flashed and detonated. The sonic boom from the second explosion was mightier, lighting up the desert like a sunburst. She squinted at the inferno rising four stories. The giant torch burned out quickly.

After a minute, the world began to grind back to life. Heads popped like gophers, the guests gawked. The chopper landed and a blanket of dust drifted in through the temporary screens covering the windows.

Lauren scooted into the huddle of bodies beneath the table. Tears welled. Jake felt for her trembling hand. The five of them had clumped together, waiting for the world to end.

A long minute later, the edge of the tablecloth lifted. Lauren retreated tighter into the pack.

"It's me," Vance said, panting. He squatted, reaching for her.

She clasped his palm and let him pull her out gently, helping her to her feet, his face contorting in pain. He was filthy and gory, his face darkened, splattered with dirt and blood.

"Come here," he said, wrapping his arms lightly around her, holding her. She clung to him tighter. He grunted and groaned, gently pushing her away, putting his hands over his ribs. She leaned toward him and turned her head, burying it in his chest. She didn't want him to let go. Tears streamed down her face.

———

SHERIFF MANNY RODRIGUEZ led the way, pushing through the crowd standing around the tables. Six or so FBI agents in blue windbreakers followed. Jane Pandora was on their heels, carrying something under her arm.

"I'll be right back. Wait here," Vance said to Lauren.

"I'm going with you." Barefoot, carrying her shoes by the heels, she used her free arm to grab his.

He whirled around. "Damn it." He placed his palm against his ribcage, bending at the waist.

She winced. "Sorry, sorry, sorry." She trotted next to him. "I think I figured it out."

"Figured what out?"

"The milk bottles. The scorpions."

He paused and looked at her, confused.

"I think I know what they mean."

The room was still coming back to life with the normal sounds of people.

"What they mean?" He sounded irritated.

"They're a message."

Vance studied her expression. "I know that. *We all know that.*" He cocked his head toward the aftermath. "This isn't the time."

She followed him out. "Zack Wisenberg said his note was signed Holmes."

He furrowed his brow. "Let's talk about this later."

She couldn't wait. "I was thinking it was a riddle, like Sherlock Holmes. But that's the wrong Holmes." She used her hand to balance on his shoulder and felt it tighten. She hopped on one foot, putting her left shoe on, switched feet, and put the other on. "Holmes is Oliver Wendell Holmes, the former Chief Justice."

"A history lesson. That's nice. Your theory, it's going to have to wait."

She ran it in her head again. She, Vance, Jake, MK, Luther, Zack, Frank, and Gordy all got one. "Eight were delivered," she said, trotting in her heels, clinging onto him, the pain in her ankle beginning to throb. "One's missing."

"Come on," he said.

She navigated the footing in the darkness on tiptoe, stumbling once and almost falling. He caught her by her elbow, grunting.

The vehicle that had knocked over the butane lamp and started the brushfire was a Marfidio County Sheriff's Office patrol pickup truck. Thirty, maybe forty men dressed in desert camouflage surrounded it.

Vance pushed his way through. "I'm one of the new owners," he said.

The man standing closest to the driver's-side window said, "Let him through."

She elbowed her own way past, staying close to Vance as he approached the cockpit of the truck.

"Jesus," he said.

Lauren leaned on Vance's back and tried to look over his shoulder.

"Move back." He held his hand up, covering her eyes. "You don't need to see this. God, what a mess."

Barry limped over to shake his hand. "We didn't expect any heroes. Especially not twice in one day."

"Heroes?" Vance sounded confused. "Twice in one day?"

"The Hummer crash, at lunch. My idea to stage it. Sorry about that. We didn't expect you to try to save the day." Barry thumped him on the back. Directly on the holes from the taser.

Vance tipped at the waist and groaned.

Jane Pandora about knocked Lauren over pushing her way toward the pickup. She wore a sheriff-issue button-down shirt and matching A-line skirt. And she reeked of alcohol. Pulling a milk bottle from under her arm, she tossed it into the cab of the truck.

"Nice shot," Vance said.

The bottle had landed on Luther's zipper.

Luther said, "Fuck you, Jane."

"Open it up. Maybe you can pinch yourself a vasectomy, you prick."

Vance opened the truck driver's-side door.

"He's not dead?" Lauren couldn't believe it. Broken glass sparkled rosy with blood spatter.

"Yeah, he's still alive. He'll make it," Vance said.

Luther gripped his bloody shoulder. "I need an ambulance."

"Come on," Vance said. "Let's get out of here."

Jane Pandora's scorpion totaled nine. Lauren was sure her theory was right.

---

BARRY STOOD near the pickup as a flotilla of unmarked sedans raced to the scene. Some slid to a stop, others continued on to the airstrip, high beams lighting both scenes like Vegas.

Sheriff Manny plucked the hat from his head and fished a zip tie from inside the brim. He leaned inside Deputy Torres' damaged pickup truck. Luther groaned, begging for medical help.

"Put your hands out front," Manny ordered.

Tears streamed down Luther's face as Manny cinched his wrists with a police-issue Flexi-Cuff.

"He wasn't supposed to get this far," Barry said to Manny.

"Well, you know what they say about the best laid plans." The sheriff tipped the brim of his hat.

FBI agents walked John Torres past the truck, his brown shirt blackened with shiny blood. An EMT truck arrived, red-and-blue lights turning. Agents dispersed the gawkers.

Luther Pernod was helped onto a gurney and loaded into the back of the response vehicle.

Barry hung around, waiting for the adrenaline rush to subside. Manny motioned the criminalist to collect the AR-15 rifle on the passenger seat. The FBI had already seized the shoulder rocket. The sheriff reached inside the cab and tossed the glass bottle to Barry. "A souvenir."

Barry caught it. "Thanks," he said. "Now I have two."

The sheriff thanked Barry Landeros for his bravery and followed the FBI agents escorting John Torres away. He saw Lauren and Vance heading toward the lodge and jogged to catch up with them.

---

"That was a close call," Vance said to Barry.

Lauren's eyes narrowed. Barry rolled the milk bottle between his palms.

"A gift," Barry said. "To Jane, from Luther, then re-gifted to me. Now I have two."

"What?" she said.

"Someone left one in my truck. Pretty sure it happened when I was at the courthouse."

That made ten. It punched a hole in her theory.

"Luther and Torres were the only ones that coulda delivered 'em," Barry said.

Vance agreed.

Luther used a master key to access Maria's place. Then she remembered John Torres picking up that delivery. The one with the English-Spanish LIVE ANIMALS label. The he told her Luther said he could have shipped to the ranch. For his kid's school project.

Luther would have had Jake's address. He could have hired a courier, put the rest of them in the rooms. If rumors were true, John had access to Jane's place. And Barry's truck at the courthouse.

"That makes a total of ten," she said.

Barry cocked his head. "Ten what?"

"Scorpions in bottles. Ten blows my theory but at least we know who did it."

Barry chuckled. "I don't know anything about a theory. I don't feel special, now. I thought I was the only one who got one."

"You are the only one who got two. Thanks for your help, man," Vance said. "I couldn't have done it without you."

Barry put the milk bottle under his left arm, shook Vance's hand, then limped toward the awaiting truck loaded with men. He climbed into the passenger's-side of the cab.

"What's this hypothesis of yours?" Vance asked.

"Ten ruins it."

"Maybe not. Lay it on me."

"Okay. Chief Justice Oliver Wendell Holmes described the Supreme Court Justices as 'nine scorpions in a bottle.' "

"I never heard of it. How do you know that?"

"High school history class. It's a famous quote."

"I'm sort of impressed."

"Don't be. I counted ten so it's a moot point."

"No, it's not."

"What do you mean?"

"There weren't ten."

She thought about it. She ran the list back through her head. Her premise had been perfect until Barry said he'd gotten one, now two. She, Vance, Jake, MK, Jane, Luther, Zack, Frank and Gordy. Barry made ten.

She said it out loud. "Me, Jake, MK, Luther, Zack, Frank, Jane and Gordy all got one. Then Barry. And you. That makes ten."

"Gordy?"

"Yeah. In his locker."

"Didn't know about Gordy," he said. "I lied."

"Lied?"

"I didn't get one."

Anger ignited. "Why did you do that?"

"I thought you would be less scared if I told you I got one, too."

She stamped her heel. A lie?

"Sorry."

She paused to collect her thoughts. "Why do you think you didn't get one?"

"I wondered about that. My best guess is Luther didn't want to take the chance of me shooting him. Maybe he figured leaving one in your room was a two-fer."

It was hardly a secret that Vance packed the Glock. "A two-fer?"

"Yeah. A two-for-one. Why waste two when one would have the desired effect."

She paused to consider it but didn't weigh in.

He put his hand on her shoulder. "Good job. You might be

right about the Oliver Wendell Holmes thing. On another note, why do you suppose Luther sent one to himself?"

Good question.

---

A SEA of men dressed for an Operation Desert Storm reunion gathered around Roy Pompadour. They broke into whistles and loud applause.

Roy funneled his hands over his mouth. "Thank you, gentlemen. Operation Antelope is one for the books."

"Hear, hear," they called in unison.

Jake stepped through the debris field. He congratulated Sheriff Manny who'd joined the men. "Good job, asshole," he said, thumping him on the back.

That reminded Lauren that poor Frank Conn was still being held in the county jail on suspicion of murder.

"You okay?" Jake asked.

MK answered for her. "She's fine. You remember Jason Spike."

He was standing with MK, still wearing his puffy down vest.

"*Special Agent* Jason Spike," he corrected.

Lauren felt her brow tighten. Shivering, she pulled Vance's jacket tighter. "FBI?"

Vance felt for her hand.

"Yup. Been embedded at Numeral II since Roy tipped the Bureau off that Justice Simeri might've been murdered. The FBI's San Francisco office has been working the case. If convicted, Deputy Torres and Luther Pernod will never spend another day outside a prison. You two helped with the case."

He told them Associate Supreme Court Justice Aldo Simeri was diabetic and a partial print of his was found on the syringe with traces of chloral hydrate, the one Vance had sent to the lab.

He told them the FBI seized the evidence from the laboratory in El Paso. Torres' wife couldn't wait to hand over his credit card and cash receipts.

Torres blamed Luther and Luther accused Torres of planting the insulin in Aldo Simeri's room. But Rosa saw Luther go in the room that night. She saw him plant the scorpion in Lauren's room, too.

"Torres bought the scorpions from a seller in Monterrey, Mexico. That dummy left the bottle of chloral hydrate in the glove box of a two-hundred-thousand-dollar sports car parked in his garage."

"Let me guess," Vance said. "Used his credit card."

"Uh-huh. Had them shipped here." Spike tsk-tsked.

"To the ranch?" Vance looked incredulous.

She'd guessed right. Torres and Luther were behind the strange deliveries. "Why'd they do it? Poison him?"

"I'm thinking of a five-letter word," Spike said.

Roy interrupted, putting his arm across Lauren's shoulder. "Sorry to spook your horse like that. With all the law enforcement and security crawling around, you're the one who came closest to finding me up there in that cave. I would have hated to take you hostage." Roy smiled at the thought.

She placed her hand over her thrumming heart and shuddered. Her hands trembled, her brain fast-forwarding through the rifle fire, the frightened horse galloping from the scene, Lauren barely clinging on.

Roy shook Special Agent Spike's hand. "Thanks again."

Crime scene tape hung from stakes wrapped around the mud walls of the watchtower where Luther had been living. FBI agents guarded the perimeter.

"Is Victor okay?" Lauren remembered pulling him from his chair.

"He's fine, just tore his jacket, is all. Maybe he'll finally buy a new one. Ol' Victor, he has such a hard time parting with a dollar," MK purred. "We finally got ol' Kurt Berlin."

"What?" Kurt Berlin, what part did he play?

MK promised to explain it to her later.

Lauren took a deep breath, closed her eyes, and exhaled slowly. Roy Pompadour really was a hero.

"Let's go," Vance said. He walked her to her room. "See you in the morning," he said before turning to leave.

She was too spent to expect more from him. It had been enough for one night, enough for a lifetime, actually.

"*I'm thinking of a five-letter word.*"

That could only be one thing.

## 42

## THE DAY AFTER

I t really was God's country. Lauren stuck her head out the door to her room, taking in a lungful of cool morning air. A tiny pocket mouse with big shiny eyes sniffed and scurried across the courtyard, stopping for an instant, head twitching, then disappeared. A magenta halo rose coloring the sky pink behind the Chinati Mountains.

She heard laughter. A young mother trotted behind her two small children, the father jogging to catch up with them. It was dawn and the lights were already burning brightly, and the common areas coming to life. She dressed quickly.

Taking the long way past last night's aftermath, she stopped to watch the activity. The morning sun backlit the tow truck hooking Deputy Torres' patrol truck. A silhouette climbed into the cab, steel rope creaking as it winched the pickup onto the flatbed. The unmarked cruisers hadn't moved overnight, surrounding the area cordoned off with yellow tape. The remains smelled like a cold campsite.

She sidestepped charred patches of earth where the patio heaters had turned over, lighting the scrub brush on fire. They'd been up-righted and reignited. Frisbees of blue flames flickered, radiating enough heat to warm her. She rubbed her hands together. A young man she assumed was the criminalist, looked through the lens, shooting pictures of the pickup truck and tire tracks. An official approached and asked her to leave. She obliged.

There was no trace of last night's elegance inside the dining hall, the long rustic tables back in their places.

Vance sat on a bench with his back against the table, arms folded, watching the investigators work the crime scene.

"Morning," she said.

"How are you feeling?"

"Better." She sat next to him. "Now what?"

He shrugged. "Some people are going to jail."

"What about us?"

"You mean you and me?"

"Yeah. Have we done anything, um, illegal?"

"Not lately." He grinned. "They have bigger fish to fry."

"Did you know? About any of it?" She studied his face.

He stared ahead at Torres' pickup truck on the flatbed as the driver started the tow truck engine. "About this?"

She nodded.

"Of course not."

"Why us?"

He shrugged. "I have no idea."

Why *did* Roy target them from a pond of potential buyers? The story that the ranch was on the market for six months with no offers was a ruse. Roy was in the background the entire time, running the show.

"You're a lawyer. Why didn't you read the fine print?"

"Yeah, lawyers are like doctors, they're specialized. I've never done transactional work. That would be like asking your dentist to replace your grandmother's hip. Plus, I'm not licensed in Texas."

That made sense.

MK had told Vance about Kurt Berlin over coffee and he shared it with Lauren. The deposed head of the German car company had been supporting his old lifestyle as an arms dealer. It was Roy's idea to trick Luther into buying the shoulder-fired rocket system from him. "A two-fer, that's what MK called it. Soon as things settle down, Roy wants to talk to us," Vance said.

Another two-fer.

The dining hall began to fill with guests. Children laughed and people shook hands the ways folks are supposed to, friends introducing friends to new friends. The guests looked different. Human.

---

LATER THAT AFTERNOON she and Vance saw Roy cloistered in a back corner of the media room deep in conversation with Zack Wisenberg, Rick Bates, and Victor Moffett. The foursome huddled sitting on deerskin chairs behind a felt-covered table. Roy hadn't shaved, he was dressed in a starched white shirt and worn jeans with a vertical white stripe from pressing.

Roy called them over. "Join us, please."

Lauren pulled two side chairs and moved them enough for them to sit and listen. He pointed to his ribs. Roy nodded.

"I heard you got pretty banged up," Roy said to Vance.

"Yeah, well, it's not quite as impressive as living in a cave for months."

"Compared to Vietnam and the sandbox, it was luxury living." Roy reached down and petted the spaniel at his feet. "I couldn't have done it without this guy." He meant the dog. "And you." Roy looked at Lauren. "Josh was worried when you asked about his fancy jacket."

Roy told them the dog's flak jacket was outfitted with a two-way radio. It's how he stayed in contact.

"That was a close call, when you heard Josh talking to me from the tack room. I heard all of it."

It wasn't her imagination.

Roy smiled. "If it wasn't for you, young lady, I'm not sure any of us would be sitting here right now."

"Me? What could I possibly have to do with it?" She was baffled.

"First, let me start by saying I'm buying my ranch back from you. There is a first right of refusal clause in the sales agreement."

Roy explained the deal. They were both surprised that Jake had known that if the estate wanted to buy it back within six months of purchase, it could be repurchased with a million-dollar profit for each partner.

"I've known Jake for over thirty years, and excuse my French, but the man is a whore for money. Which brings me to you," he looked at Lauren with his piercing eyes. "When I heard you'd turned down thirteen million dollars because . . . let's see . . . what would be the best way to put this? Because you didn't come by it the old-fashioned way. That's when I began to consider MK's idea to sell to the three of you. When I learned Vance was a retired cop, let's just say that sealed the deal."

Roy told them MK had talked to Jake after Roy asked her to look for a short-term buyer. "I would never have sold to Jake as the sole owner. I don't trust him, and he knows it.

"I felt you would be the best custodians. I was stuck with

Jake. Every deal has its compromise." Roy looked around the table. "Zack here is talking with Victor about building a corporate campus in Iowa."

"Wow." Lauren said.

"There goes affordable housing in Cedar Rapids," Victor said.

Zack said, "And we're going to open trade schools to train the next generation to write code, teach them skills they'll need in the new economy."

"And I'm going to focus more of my money here at home," Rick Bates said. "If America is to remain a beacon for the rest of the world, we need to keep our side of the pond clean. It's easy to get caught up in solving the problems of the world. My mother used say, 'Charity starts at home.' "

Barry arrived, still wearing desert fatigues and the same ball cap with the American flag stitched onto the brim. He stood a few feet from them. "I'd like to say something before I head out."

"Go ahead," Roy said.

"Well, it's for Zack."

Roy nodded, giving Barry permission.

"Every question Congress asked you, you said, 'I'll have my team look into it.' "

Zack sat quietly with his hands folded on the green felt card table.

Roy cocked his head at Zack. "Why *did* you dodge like that? Your team doesn't tell you what to do. You tell them."

Zack stared off into space.

Roy looked annoyed. "You should quit being a pawn for all those lawyers you're paying and start acting like a human."

Zack straightened in the chair, and said, "All good thoughts."

Roy put his hands behind his neck, crossed his left ankle over his right knee and leaned back. "You could walk away, Zack.

Cash out while the stock price is high. Do something more important with your life."

"That's a bit extreme," Zack said. "It's not like I knew Henry Wiggins was a co-conspirator."

Lauren was amazed. "How could you not know?"

Roy raised his voice. "Wiggins didn't want the government overturning CDA 230. That would be a game changer—"

This was the second time she'd heard that. "The what?"

"Section 230 of the Communications Decency Act. Internet companies are immune from liability for republishing content. The lobbyists spend half their time defending it. Talk about one-upping City Hall."

"Wait a second." Lauren had to think for a minute. "You mean they *can't be sued*?"

"That's right," Roy said.

"We are very responsible stewards." Zack smirked.

Seriously? "School shooters and terrorists plan horrible things on his platforms and the public has *no legal recourse*?" Lauren fish-eyed Zack waiting for someone to clarify. No one denied it.

Roy said, "Wiggins knew the argument was destined for the Supreme Court and he knew how Justice Simeri would rule."

"Or to Congress," Vance added.

Roy guffawed. "*Congress?*" That sent him into a diatribe. "While technology moves at the speed of light, human nature is at a standstill. The Romans built the Coliseum and filled them with peasants giddy to see a lion tear a human to pieces. Social media is a virtual amphitheater. There's no binary code that can change human nature."

"That's not true," Zack said.

Roy changed the subject. Looking at Barry, he said, "We'll have our annual event in the spring. Help me get the word out. Let the guys know I'm going to host the biggest one yet." Roy

Pompadour stood and marched up to Barry. He hugged him, and slapped him on the back.

"I'd like to add one more thing," Barry said, addressing Zack. "You looked good in a suit, on TV. Nice to meet you all." He limped toward the foyer, waved to Rosa and got into his red Dodge parked under the portico.

After he was gone, Roy said to Zack, "That man is a petroleum geologist. Popular culture glorifies you and vilifies him. Go figure."

"About your fundraisers," Zack said. "I could use my platform to raise awareness."

"That would be great," Lauren said. "Think what you could do."

"You have to believe me," Zack said. "I had no idea. I'm going to make changes. Regardless of what the lawyers or Board of Directors have to say."

"It took that lawyer of yours, Wiggins, about ten seconds to turn on Luther," Roy said. "Spilled his guts. He paid Luther to poison the justice and Luther paid Torres to be his accomplice and cover their tracks. They left a money trail a mile long. You know what they say about stuff running down hill." Roy paused and looked at Zack. "I'm proud, son, that you're thinking about how to change things. I was afraid you'd try to cover it up. Make your decisions principled. You'll never have to second-guess yourself."

"If my company survives," Zack said.

"Why don't you pioneer another world-changing idea, be the first to implement an ethics department. Expand your snack bar. Start feeding the soul," Roy's eyes glinted. "It's what Justice Simeri believed, that a return to reasoned thinking and civility is sorely needed. And proper government oversight. You have the platform and influence. You'll have to fight tooth and nail since ethics has no dollar value and the lawyers and investors will fight you."

The legend of Roy Pompadour was no myth. The decorated war hero, wildly successful Wall Street investor who'd spent a fortune restoring the 1800s fort really was motivated by something greater than money. And, in the process, he'd become a target. Now, he'd avenged his good friend's murder.

Zack left without saying anything.

Roy said to Lauren and Vance, "Join me for dinner this evening."

He wasn't asking, he was telling them. It was also their cue to leave.

"We'd be honored," Vance said.

"Dress up, we're having a little impromptu party afterward. It's a bit of a surprise."

Old Victor Moffett struggled up from his chair. Wobbling a bit, he said, "Whatever you have in life, you kids should cherish it. Listen to your elders. There's not much to learn from the youngsters. We've been your age already. You've not been ours. Keep your ears cleaned out, and listen."

His friend Rick Gates nodded.

Vance whispered, "I wish he'd given us some investment advice."

"I'm old, but I'm not deaf," Victor barked, and then he grinned. "But I am cranky. Here's some good advice. Buy my funds, the Class-A shares. From what I gather, you can afford to."

A five-letter word: money, money, money, money . . . money. Money.

———

SHE STEPPED OUTSIDE with Vance to watch the setting sun finish its arc over the mountains. Two dump trucks had begun work on the cratered airstrip. They were done for the day and the runway remained closed. The bunker-busting rocket had obliterated it. Had it reached the ranch, it would have leveled it.

Lauren spotted MK at the reception desk. They detoured inside. Josh had been driving the guests to Midland using Jane's official SUV. He'd returned from a run and was carrying MK's bags to the open hatchback. Jake stood next to her at the front desk.

"Well, I guess this is goodbye," MK said to Lauren.

"I'm hitching a ride as far as Midland," Jake said. "I went to town earlier, to check my phone. I had at least fifty messages from Davis. He wants to go see what's left of his place in the Florida Keys. Where will you two go?"

"I don't know. My boat's a total loss," Vance said.

"You two are welcome to visit me," Jake said.

Mary Katherine Diamond held her hand out. Lauren's eyes welled. "Now, now," MK said.

Lauren hugged her, a tear dripped on MK's linen jacket.

"Come on," MK said, pushing her back and holding her by the shoulders.

Lauren dabbed her eyes with her thumbs. "I'm going to miss you."

"Come visit me, anytime, in New York."

"You can meet her exciting husband." Jake grinned. "He can tell you about the future of municipal water."

MK punched him softly in the arm. "Such a smart aleck."

Vance hugged MK. He shook Jake's hand. "Call us when you get to Freeport and give us an update."

He wanted to know that their money, thirty million cash, was still safe and sound in the belly of Jake's yacht.

"Will do," Jake said. "I'll see you kids soon. We have ranch business to finish."

It was time to return Antelope Creek Ranch to its rightful owner, and there would be papers to sign. Rosa came out from behind the desk with a box of Kleenex. Lauren dabbed her eyes and told Vance she was going to her room to rest and freshen up. She had a lot of questions for Roy. First she needed time to herself, to regroup.

## 43

L auren didn't expect to see Zack, Victor, and Rick with Roy at dinner, figuring they'd have jetted out of Midland by now. She took a seat next to Vance, at one end.

A few guests had stayed and were scattered in small groups at the long tables.

As the waiter filled their water glasses, Roy's eyes shifted over her shoulder. Lauren turned to see what caught his attention. Sheriff Manny Rodriguez was escorting Frank Conn into the building. The lawyer was pale and gaunt. Dark half-moons hung beneath his eyes, and his posture sagged.

Roy stood. "Excuse us." He gestured to Lauren and Vance to follow him. "I need to finish a little business," he said to the others seated at the table.

THE FIVE SAT in the same anteroom off the main lobby, at the green felt-covered table.

"Frank has agreed to draft the paperwork to sell the ranch

back to me," Roy said. "I want to make sure we're all on the same page."

Lauren looked at Vance, then Roy and Frank.

She nodded along with the others. "Okay."

Frank spoke with the excitement of a man given weeks to live. "Roy has already gotten you up to speed on the sale back to him." He cleared his throat. "The associates are working on it. Mr. Pompadour has asked me to increase Ms. Gold's bonus."

"You don't have to do that," Lauren said.

"Excuse me," Frank said.

"I don't need a bonus. If I break even, I'll be happy. It's extraordinary, what Roy's done here. It's been an honor to be part of it."

Roy smiled at her warmly. "That's why in increasing your bonus to five million."

Vance snorted. "How do you think Jake will take the news?"

Frank looked shocked at the amount. "Now, Roy—"

Lauren interrupted. "I don't need it. Your offer is already beyond generous."

"I'm afraid you can't convince me to change my mind," Roy said. "Frank will contact you when the paperwork is ready. Do something good with it, the money."

"My friend, Davis, he lost everything in Hurricane Irma. I could start by helping him out."

"What does your friend do?"

"He's a videographer. He's good, too."

"Don't give a man charity," he said. "Let him work. I'm hiring you to produce a video for Antelope Creek Ranch. That's what you do, right?"

She nodded.

"Then you hire him. He'll be earning his money. It's the better way to help a man."

She could see it already. Drone footage of the desert at dusk,

4K interior shots of the beautifully restored fort with its attention to detail. She remembered the online reviews by guests who marveled at the museum-quality artifacts. "I can write and produce it. For free, of course."

"We can work it out later," Roy said.

A luxury bus pulled up outside and a parade of incoming guests bounded down the steps and through the front door.

Lauren didn't recognize the fellow working the desk, checking in the new arrivals. "Where's Rosa?"

"We can talk about that later, too." Roy crossed one cowboy boot over his knee. "I want you to both to stay for the next part of the conversation because I think you should hear it firsthand. And I'll be adding a confidentiality agreement to the sales contract, just to be sure." He looked at the sheriff. "I'll let Manny pick it up from here."

Manny started out by apologizing that he had no idea Jake was a recovering alcoholic, adding that he doubted such a thing existed, but if it did, "I wouldn't have done what I did, making him drink on the roadside. Frank Conn was the target."

The circles under Frank's eyes looked like grease beneath a quarterback's on a sunny day.

"We all got agendas," the sheriff said, removing his hat and balancing it on his thigh. "Roy here knew about my wife's sister. She lost all her life savings and died a pauper, all because of this guy." He snapped his head toward Frank.

Frank Conn looked baffled.

Manny glared at the lawyer. "'Member when I asked you if you knew a Juanita White?"

"I told you, I've never heard of her."

"Of course you haven't," Manny said. "'Cause she's just collateral damage."

"Collateral damage?" Frank furrowed his sallow brow.

"My sister-in-law worked at that big pipeline company for

twenty-five years. She put her life savings into company stock because that's what you and the other lawyers repping the company told her to do."

Frank's face drooped.

The biggest bankruptcy in US history had happened in Houston. What did that have to do with Frank and the ranch?

"You were lead counsel, your John Hancock was on the memo telling employees to put company stock in their 401Ks. When it went down in a ball of flames, they lost a hell of a lot more than just their jobs. Lost their life savings and retirement, too. My wife's sister was one of them folks. Her husband run off with a younger gal. After that, Juanita come home and drank herself into an early grave. The missus and I paid for the funeral. Had to borrow the money for it. Wife's never been the same." Manny shook his head.

"I got a story, too," Roy said. "One of my college classmates was the grandson of the founder of the widely–respected accounting firm that went down with the ship. Do you know what happened to him?"

Frank shook his head slowly.

"He committed suicide," Roy said. "First he lost everything. The hundred-year-old company his grandfather built, bankrupt. The case went to the Supreme Court. They ruled nine-to-zero the accounting firm had done nothing wrong. Justice Aldo Simeri heard the case. And what price did Pinch and Elders, LLP pay?"

"You got off scot free," Manny said. He was angry. "There was a time I'd have killed you with my bare hands and happily spent my life in prison. Instead, I restrained myself and waited for the day I could catch you. I put you in jail for a few days, put a laxative in your food and watched you suffer. Watching you worry you'd get the death penalty, well, it don't really compare to what you done to others. But it was something."

Roy said, "Look at the bright side, Frank. The deal brought new business into the firm. I'm sure you won't let your conscience get in the way of future deals. That would require having one. You can go now. And do me a favor. Stay out of my town."

"You're admitting you conspired to frame me? For a murder?" Frank wailed. "I could have been killed sitting in that jail cell with those animals. The indignity—"

Roy was disgusted. "Get him out of here, Manny."

The sheriff rested his wrist on his butt of his gun latched to his belt. "Part of me hoped them gangbangers would kill you. They didn't. It's good. I guess. Less of a mess to clean up." He grabbed Frank's arm. "Let's go. And don't make a scene."

Frank stood. He was unsteady, his gait uneven. He wobbled toward the lobby where the sheriff's truck was parked outside, beneath the awning.

Roy remained sitting with his long arms sprawled on the chair rests. "One last piece of advice, Frank." Roy's voice boomed. "When you think you're the smartest guy in the room, it's usually a sign you're not."

The beaten-down lawyer nodded, but he did not turn back to face Roy. He shuffled past the desk where the new clerk, a young man who'd heard the tail end of the conversation, looked perplexed.

It all made perfect sense. Frank Conn had gotten his come-uppance.

She followed Vance back to the dining hall.

Sheriff Manny didn't believe in alcoholism even though his sister-in-law 'drank herself to death.'

## 44

P lates of neatly arranged red-and-yellow heirloom tomatoes and buffalo mozzarella topped with fresh basil were set at the table, along with beakers of golden olive oil and syrupy balsamic vinegar.

Jane Pandora joined them halfway through the salad course. She looked rough, like she'd spent the day in bed, wearing yesterday's rumpled sheriff-issue skirt and blouse. Reaching across the table, she grabbed a goblet filled with red wine.

"Cheers," she said, tipping it in her mouth. "To the hair of the dog. And to John Torres, that bastard." She leaned over and whispered in Lauren's ear. "May I borrow your makeup, hon? I have an event tonight and I didn't pack for the occasion."

"Sure."

Jane poured another glass of wine and took it with her.

"She's an institution," Roy said when Jane was gone. "A flawed, but good egg. She's the one who tipped me off that Deputy Torres and Luther were in cahoots. What some folks will do for money." He shook his head and told a story.

*Money.*

Six months after he'd gotten violently ill for the third time in two weeks, he went to see his physician in Houston who'd insisted on blood work.

"I'd noticed a pattern."

Roy said that Luther had taken a sudden interest in delivering Roy his afternoon beer.

"One day I took it to my room and instead of drinking it, I saved it. I gave it to Jane. She sent it to the crime lab and it tested positive for cyanide. I told my doc and they reran my labs and I'll be damned if my blood didn't test positive for cyanide."

Roy told them he poured the beer down the drain the next few times and then one day he took a bottle with him on a ride on his ATV.

"Josh went with me and we staged the accident."

"Why would Luther want to kill you?" Lauren asked.

Vance answered. "He knew Roy had proof the justice had been murdered."

"Very good, Detective Courage," Roy said. "And he needed to cover his tracks. When he got wind that you had your suspicions, he must have decided to blow the whole place up."

Jane had returned and was listening. "That's exactly what they decided. Henry Wiggins paid Luther to kill the justice. Then John Torres got greedy and was blackmailing Luther. It don't go on like that for long," she said, tapping the back of her beehive. "With everyone stabbin' each other in the back."

Roy took a bite of trout and savored it for a minute. "I contacted the FBI. They traced payments, lots of them, from Henry Wiggins to Luther. And Luther was paying John Torres. And old Kurt Berlin was laundering money through an offshore account. Justice Simeri was poisoned. His insulin tainted. Maria planted the used syringe in the safe in Lauren's room. It was our insurance policy, in case my plan failed."

Lauren watched Zack's expression. He looked shocked.

Did you know?" Roy looked at Zack.

"I did not," the young billionaire said.

Jane looked refreshed. She'd restyled her hair into a fresh cone of cotton candy. Lauren couldn't tell if it was the makeup or the hair of the dog. Either way, she looked better.

"The groom looks ready," Jane said.

Josh Dominguez smiled.

*What?*

## 45

Potted plants surrounded the trellis erected near the pool. Red, white, and blue ribbons tied to the latticework sailed in the breeze.

Lauren looked at Vance, who shrugged. The strolling guitarist wearing a bedazzled black jacket and sombrero plucked the strings as he passed them, stomping his feet to the beat.

Vance gazed at her.

Victor, Zack, and Rick gathered in front of Jane, who stood beneath the archway.

The guitarist changed tempo, to that of a bullfighter, fingers flying. The onlookers whistled and wolf called to the music.

The silhouette of a woman emerged from the side entrance to the lodge. She wore a simple, floor-length white dress, her hair flowing over her shoulders.

Josh met her, and holding his bride by the wrist, walked her toward the archway. A petite woman, whose face was shrouded under a small veil, led the way, lining the path with rose petals from a basket.

Lauren swallowed hard. "Rosa is marrying Josh?" she whispered to Vance, her eyes big.

A minute later Jane Pandora began the ceremony. "Do you, Josh Dominguez, take this woman, Rosa Teresa Montoya, to be your lawful wedded wife—?"

"Roy, look." Josh interrupted his own vows, gesturing toward the mountains. A Pronghorn doe and her fawn stood frozen, the mother holding her head erect, sniffing the air.

Roy raised his hand, signaling Jane to pause the service. The woman with the basket of roses lifted the veil to see the animals.

Oh my God. The housekeeper, Maria. "I just can't believe it." Lauren dabbed her eyes.

They all stood in silence until the Pronghorn and her fawn moved on.

After the ceremony, Lauren caught up with Rosa to congratulate her. Rosa tapped her belly, smiling.

"You're pregnant," Lauren said.

Rosa beamed.

The two women walked to the dining hall. Gordy and the staff had transformed it again. It smelled like lavender, apple wood, and romance.

Rosa reminded Lauren that she'd been an aspiring makeup artist in L.A.

A light went on in her brain. "You faked the suicide, or homicide, or whatever? The strangulation marks, all of it?"

"And I did the wardrobe, too, and the awful smell? I burnt some of my hair. Sorry."

"You suckered me," Vance said, forcing a laugh.

Lauren ran the events through her head.

"The van showing up, all of it was a ruse?" she asked Rosa.

The soon-to-be bride nodded. "That was Barry, he's a friend of Roy's. It *was* laundry in the laundry cart." Rosa glanced at

Vance and contorted her face. "You weren't supposed to get hurt."

---

JOSH TOASTED THE SMALL GATHERING. "To my family." He held his champagne glass up. "To my bride, Rosa, my Aunt Maria, and the man who has been like a father to me, Roy Pompadour."

Josh sat with them for a while, telling the story. It turned out to be true that his Great-great Uncle Melville Saver had built Antelope Creek Ranch in 1857 and when he died, the ranch passed down to his only heir, his young Mexican-born wife. Two generations later, Josh's mother and his aunt, Maria, inherited the fort. By then it was in ruins.

Maria sat next to Josh, listening, looking at him admiringly.

"After Roy bought the ranch," Josh said, "my aunt accepted his offer to us to stay." Josh's mother, he explained, had left him at the ranch with her sister, Maria. She'd followed her lover to Mexico, never to return for the young son she'd left behind.

"I was a little kid," Josh said, "And Roy Pompadour treated me like I was his own."

---

SHE AND VANCE had moved to the courtyard. Darkness had fallen and the galaxy of night stars winked overhead.

Jane Pandora came to say goodbye. "Y'all did the right thing, sending the syringe to the lab over in El Paso. Seriously. Thank you." She held a flute filled with champagne. Placing her hand over her heart, she said, "I'll see you two around."

"Wait," Lauren said. "I have a question."

Jane pressed the flute to her lips and sipped. "Yes?"

"Did Deputy Torres and Luther deliver those scorpions?"

"Yeah. The deliveries wasn't all Deputy Torres's doing. Luther hand-delivered the ones here. He shipped the one to Jake on his boat. He had information on everyone, including ya'll's addresses from the sales docs. Torres left the one in Barry's truck. It was kinda a spare and when Barry went to see the sheriff, Torres put it in his truck. Oh, and he planted the one in Frank's cell at the jail, too.

"I needed John and Luther to believe I was in on their scheme so I come up with the idea." She chugged the rest of the champagne. "Manny thought it was genius, 'cause John kept putting stuff on his credit cards, including those critters. Manny said it would help with a circumstantial case if we struck out on the prints on the syringe. And then that creep went and put one in my house."

"Why?" That didn't make sense.

"Because he suspected I wasn't into him anymore. I just couldn't stomach it, sleeping with him undercover. I promised the sheriff I'd do my best keeping an eye on him." She said it started out like affairs do, with a mutual attraction. "Once I got to know John Torres, he made me sick. Had me hitting the bottle pretty hard to keep up the act."

"One more question," Lauren said. "Why on earth did Luther send himself a scorpion? And how would he even do that?"

"Oh," Jane chuckled. "Luther didn't do that, John did. He thought it would be kinda funny."

"Kinda funny?"

"Well, yeah. See, comin' up with the idea of delivering nine scorpions in bottles woulda made my daddy proud 'a me 'cause he was a big admirer of Chief Justice Oliver Wendell Holmes. Daddy disagreed with Justice Simeri to the point 'a his blood boiling.'" Jane smoothed her skirt. "Symbolic, ya know. *Nine scorpions in a bottle*. Conjures up a picture in the minds 'a men. John thought sending it was like stabbing Luther in the back with an imaginary stinger."

Symbolic. Lauren had been right about the Oliver Wendell Holmes angle. It never occurred to her it was Jane's idea.

Jane left to say goodbye to the newlyweds.

Lauren closed her eyes and took a deep breath. Vance draped his jacket over her shoulders.

"What a weird fucking place," Vance said. "A beautiful, strange fucking place."

## 46

The Uber driver had asked Lauren and Vance three times if they understood how much it was going to cost to drive them to Midland before he unlocked the back passenger doors of his crew cab truck.

The trip would be a nice way to unwind. Vance promised not to turn his phone on until they landed.

"We're homeless, you know," Lauren said.

The driver looked at them wide-eyed, from the rear view.

"She's kidding."

The kid looked relieved. "Where are ya'll heading?"

"Houston," he said.

---

THE AIRLINE GOUGED them at the counter and the TSA agent assigned to Lauren molested her. Red-faced with a head full of steam, Vance tried to calm her down. He used two fingers, miming to keep her mouth zipped.

She was pissed. "My doctor can't do what that woman just did to me without asking first."

The agent summoned her boss. He read from the manual. " 'A pat down may include inspection of the head, neck, arms, torso, legs, and feet. This includes head coverings and sensitive areas such as breasts, groin, and the buttocks.' "

"That agent karate chopped me, between my legs."

He continued. ". . . our agents may run their hand up the back of each leg until it meets resistance—"

"Resistance?" She couldn't believe what she was hearing. "Do you know what the backstop is, anatomically speaking?"

"Um, we're not allowed to say *that*. You paid cash," the man said. "What did you expect?"

Lauren was on fire. "I was assaulted."

The agent and her boss shrugged.

*Pat down.*

That didn't quite catch the spirit of it. If Vance hadn't been there, things would have escalated.

"Come on," he said. "We can't win this."

Her hands shook. How humiliating. "That woman can karate chop me in the privates and I have to roll with it?"

"Let it go, Lauren."

She marched back up to the man in charge. "Next time, I'd like that guy to *pat me up*." She pointed to a handsome African American fellow working security two lanes over.

Vance's mouth was half-open. He pulled her gently by the arm. "Come on."

"I can't believe you. I thought you were on my side."

"I am. But this is a no-win."

Lauren took out her phone and held it up.

"Ma'am." A third agent approached. "No pictures or video recordings allowed in this area."

Roy Pompadour was right. Something had to change. It was at that very moment that she'd made a decision. She would donate one million dollars to the job-training program Zack

Wisenberg promised to seed in Iowa. If he didn't keep his word, she'd use the next the next million to hire a badass PR firm, one in DC.

———

IT WAS nightfall when they reached the end of Highway 288 in Freeport, Texas. The scene was eerie, the night air thick with mist. They drove the rental past dozens of refineries, some with orange flares burning in the distance. The monster candles illuminated gray clouds spewing from smokestacks.

Vance took a lefthand turn under a massive concrete overpass arching over the Intracoastal Waterway. He stopped at the guardhouse, a rundown shack surrounded by weeds. It was boarded up.

Lauren called Jake from her cell. He told them to drive straight ahead.

Lights burned from the *Arm & A Leg*, by far the largest boat at the marina. The yacht was docked stern-first, taking up two slips at the south end of the canal near deep water. Jake leaned against the stainless railing, misting bug killer from a can. Davis Frost stood on the bulkhead chatting with two men. One looked familiar. Davis went inside.

The taller of the two walked with a limp.

"Barry?" Vance asked. He wasn't wearing his ball cap with the needlepoint flag.

"Meet my brother, Karl," Barry said.

"What are you doing here?"

"We're renting a house across the canal." Barry pointed across the water to a row of houses built on pilings. "Roy wanted to make sure Davis was safe. There's a rumor you're stowing some valuable cargo. Karl here, he's a Lake Jackson police officer. Well, we'd best be going. Oh, and I hope Zack keeps his word."

"Me, too," Lauren said.

Barry hobbled toward the parking lot but stopped and limped back. "Sorry about tasing you," he said to Vance. "And geez, I hated stun-gunning you," he said to Lauren. "Scout's honor, I wish I didn't have to do it." He crossed his heart. "Rosa told me Luther's bank statement was missing from her desk. Vance had been in there and Rosa was sure he took it. I needed it, for Roy."

He gave them an anemic smile and caught up with Karl. He climbed behind the wheel of his red Dodge pickup.

Another version of Vance would have liked to bury his fist in Barry's face. God knows the geologist earned it zapping them. Instead, he yelled, "Be careful."

---

A WET BREEZE flowed from the south. Lauren felt the sting of a mosquito and waved her hands in front of her face as she and Vance jogged in lockstep, him holding his bad rib.

They boarded the *Arm*.

Davis came up from below.

Lauren hugged him. "I'm so sorry to hear about your place. I heard you lost everything."

"A lot of people did. But not everyone made the news," Davis said.

Jake stood in the galley. He handed her the newspaper. There was a picture of Zack Wisenberg on the cover, beneath it a headline:

FBI RAIDS SOCIAL MEDIA GIANT, WISENBERG DENIES
TIES TO JUSTICE SIMERI MURDER

"He's lying," Lauren said.

"What did you think he'd say?" Jake handed her the paper. "The story is probably Trending."

She read the first paragraph. Zack's company planned to hire twenty thousand foreign language speakers to expand the social media company's global footprint. They were opening new offices in Moscow and Beijing. Her stomach did a cartwheel.

"Did you read the whole story?" she asked.

Jake nodded.

She read aloud. " 'The sellers of Antelope Creek Ranch have ties to a drug cartel, a representative from Wisenberg's company said. The company alleges that the previous owners were involved in a murder-for-hire conspiracy and that Associate Justice Aldo Simeri was the target.' " *WTF?* "He's blaming us?"

Her phone pinged. It was a new post on her social media account. She opened it. It was a link to a picture of her and Vance, taken at the ranch. A symbol was watermarked over their faces, a group claiming to be anti-fascists. She clicked it. It linked to another page with her cell number and home address in Miami. Her phone blew up with dozens of texts and posts threatening her and Vance.

Jake's phone blew up with the same links and threats.

Vance's buzzed. He took it out of his pocket and turned it off. "Gimme those," he said.

Jake and Lauren handed him their phones. He opened the cabin door. She knew what he was going to do. Jake tried to stop him, pleading for the pictures of his kids. It was too late. She heard the splashes.

"They're not worth keeping," Vance said. He looked at Lauren. "How did you think he'd react? By hiring Mother Teresa to teach the writings of Aristotle and Plato?" Vance shook his head. "Get real, Lauren. He doesn't think he's God. He *knows* he is."

## 47

J ake had invited them to spend the night on his yacht. He'd warned them the sleeping quarters would be tight and far from private. Davis performed a magic trick converting the U-shaped dining table into a queen-sized couchette. Jake brought a set of linens, blankets, and pillows, and left them on the corner of the foldout.

Vance took off his jacket and un-holstered the 9-millimeter he'd checked as baggage, placing it on the counter. He riffled through his carry-on and handed her a clean T-shirt, insisting he'd make the bed, giving her time to get ready for sleep.

She climbed under the covers and looked out the window.

Neatly spaced lights atop giant pylons lit the Intracoastal. Two tugboat pilots guided a barge through a double-bend in the waterway, buzzing back and forth across the bowlines like sheepdogs, herding them a little left, a little right. She got out of bed and knelt, looking through the misty windows. There were no stars in the sky.

She closed her eyes and listened to the low hum of the air conditioning. A pair of hands gently rested on her shoulders, from behind. She leaned into his chest. He grunted.

"Oh, sorry," she said, grimacing, turning to face him.

"It's okay. Will you miss them?" he asked. "The night stars," as if reading her mind.

"No. I would miss you, though."

"I'm a rookie, you said it yourself. Not experienced relationship material."

"And I lack all clarity when it comes to men."

"Come on," he said, pulling her gently by the arm. "Time for you to go to bed."

The sounds of the working waterway quieted. Her mind slowed until all she heard was the cadence of his breath.

"How does it feel to sleep on top of thirty million bucks?" he whispered.

Rolling onto her right elbow and cupping her chin, she gazed at him. "Is that where it is? Here?"

"Yeah. Your portion, too."

"It feels strange." She curled and backed gently against his abdomen.

He ran his fingers through her hair.

"What are you thinking?" she asked.

"I'm thinking I'm happy right now."

Her heart pounded. "Me, too."

"You need to rest. I'll watch over you."

In one breath, she was asleep.

# ABOUT THE AUTHOR

Karen S. Gordon is an emerging author of action/adventure thrillers. If you enjoyed *Killer Deal,* or have comments you'd like to share, she would appreciate you leaving a review at the portal of your choice. *Killer Deal* is the second installment of the Gold & Courage Series.

The adventures of Vance Courage and Lauren Gold will continue . . .

Please sign up for Karen's newsletter at karensgordon.com.

Thank you. Without you, the reader, none of this would be possible.

# ALSO BY KAREN S. GORDON

The Mutiny Girl

"An outstanding debut thriller that has it all: misdirection, intrigue, murder, and family. Captivating and engrossing." — *The BookLife Prize*

"A taut, thrilling drama told exceptionally well." — *Steve Berry, NYT Bestselling Author*

"An engagingly written series starter with a bounty of plot twists and Miami vices." — *Kirkus Reviews*